PLANTED IN
CHRISTMAS

Planted in Christmas is published under Reverie, a sectionalized division under Di Angelo Publications, Inc.

REVERIE

Reverie is an imprint of Di Angelo Publications.
Copyright 2023.
All rights reserved.
Printed in the United States of America.

Di Angelo Publications
Los Angeles, California

Library of Congress
Planted in Christmas
ISBN: 978-1-955690-55-3
Paperback

Words: Willa Frederic
Cover Design: Savina Mayeur
Interior Design: Kimberly James
Editors: Willy Rowberry, Jessica Caramanica

Downloadable via www.dapbooks.shop and other e-book retailers

For educational, business, and bulk orders, contact distribution@diangelopublications.com.

1. Fiction --- Romance --- Holiday

PLANTED IN CHRISTMAS

WILLA FREDERIC

ONE

"Come on already," Brynn Callaway muttered, snatching an overgrown basil plant from beneath the row of grow lights behind the counter. Between the inconsistent flow of that morning's customers and an obnoxiously chipper stream of Christmas songs, she'd been willing her cell to ring. Nothing. Not even a spam call.

Brynn watched a rusty pickup glide past the shop window as her fingers expertly pinched off the basil's outer leaves. She sighed, inhaling the peppery scent that was released with every snip.

Don't look at your phone. Think of something else.

She popped the cuttings into a water-filled mason jar to save for her mom. Sometimes Greta cooked with them like normal people did, sometimes they became an ingredient in whatever salve or potion she was into that week. You never knew with Greta.

Brynn carried the freshly trimmed plant back to its shelf, carefully nestling it between Thai basil, cinnamon basil, and ten or so other varieties. Basil was notoriously tricky to grow indoors, especially in winter, but Brynn had a way with just about any indoor plant. It was probably the main reason her shop Planted in Twin had just survived its first year. *Well, one of the reasons.*

She heard a ping and dove for her phone, nearly knocking over the jar. Her eyes darkened as she saw a YouTube notification: *Green Goddess posted a new video!*

Ugh.

Brynn pressed her lips together and set the phone face down on the counter. The last thing she needed to see at that moment was that smug model's perfectly Botoxed face.

Brynn folded her arms across her chest, allowing the muggy glow of the room to calm her nerves. Her shop Planted in Twin had slowly grown from a pipe dream to a fragile reality, and it had been her happy place ever since she'd first seen the cashew hardwood and exposed brick. Sunlight only entered the narrow building through the century-old windows along Addison Street, but Brynn had spent the past several months filling every corner with grow lights and thrifted antique lamps. Now, between the cozy luminosity, whirring humidifiers and hundreds of houseplants, she had created an urban jungle.

She glanced at the clock over the door: 12:57. Close enough.

Brynn threw on her peacoat, grabbed her purse from under the counter, and snatched a sturdy maidenhead fern from a window display. As she hurried out the front door, she flipped the *Closed for Lunch!* sign into place against the glass.

A biting gust whipped against her bare legs as she hurried down the empty sidewalk to the public parking lot. The air was bone dry with no sign of snow, but Brynn knew you could never guess the weather in Twin Falls. Still, always a lover of fashion, Brynn wouldn't switch to pants until the temps dropped close to zero.

Tights. Tomorrow, I'll wear tights.

A blast of welcomed heat greeted Brynn as she stumbled into the entryway of the tidy one-story house, balancing the fern as she tossed her coat on the shoe bench. When both of her children had moved out, Brynn's mother Greta had sold her four-bedroom transitional style and downsized to a cute newer build close to the canyon, which also happened to be close to the independent living community where Brynn's grandparents lived.

Brynn slid her phone from her purse as she heard the muffled murmur of familiar voices. Still nothing. As she tapped the screen, her finger hovered over her Favorites list, and she chewed her lip. Caleb Whitaker was still listed as number two? That proverbial ship had sailed. She blinked away an image of her ex's lean, bare chest, and silently resolved to delete his contact altogether when she was in less of a hurry. She took a breath and tapped Katie's name.

"Hey, you," Katie said from the other end.

"Hi, it's me," Brynn whispered.

"Obviously," Katie snorted.

Katie Dilworth had been Brynn's best friend since college, and one of the best days of Brynn's life had been when Katie had moved from Chicago to Twin Falls.

"Still nothing?" Brynn asked, tucking a loose strand of hair behind her ears.

"Still nothing," Katie confirmed.

"Same," Brynn said, pressing her palm to her forehead. "Even though I know they'd call you first, I couldn't help but stare at my phone every five seconds."

"Brynn? That you, baby?" Greta's voice echoed from the living room.

"I better go," Brynn said. "I'm on lunch and I'm at my mom's house."

"The assistant said they'd be calling soon," Katie said. "And I'm pulling your latest demo stats to bring with me later. Did you know nearly thirty percent of your subscribers are in the UK?"

"Sounds like we need a business trip to London," Brynn said with a laugh.

"Been there, done that," Katie said. "All my trips from here on out are vacations."

"I guess that's one of the plus sides of going fully remote," Brynn said.

"Well, I'd say another was escaping Chicago winters, but of course you *had* to live in Twin Falls," Katie teased.

Brynn smiled. She loved having her best friend a stone's throw away.

After they hung up, Brynn headed toward the living room, where her grandparents were huddled with total seriousness over a half-assembled puzzle. Sometimes, she thought they looked like cartoon characters—tiny Grandma Connie, better known as Gram, her legs swinging back and forth as her frizzy bottle-red bangs fell in her focused eyes, and Grandpa Jeff, who Brynn's older brother had lovingly named Paps, loomed over what looked like a child-size table beside his six-foot-four frame. They both looked up and grinned as Brynn crossed over to inspect their progress.

"We got all the edges put together," Paps said, rubbing a hand over his bald head. "You want in?"

"I wish I could," Brynn said. "I can only stay a few minutes."

"Oh, how precious!" Gram said, her eyes widening at the tiny plant under Brynn's arm. "Is that for me, dear?" Gram rubbed the little leaves and clucked approvingly. "They always look their best before I get my hands on them."

Brynn laughed, feeling the same pride she always did when one of her plant babies found a new home. Propagating ferns wasn't easy—it involved plucking spores from the fronds and planting them in sealed glass containers—but Brynn finally had the hang of it.

"I could have come in and gotten it myself," Gram said.

"Nah," Brynn replied. "You know how busy I can get at work. This way we can actually talk."

"Business been good, then?" Paps asked, and both grandparents blinked hopefully at Brynn.

"It's getting better, yeah," Brynn said breezily. Between running a new business and creating content for her YouTube channel, she was always overwhelmed, but she could only hope that the holiday season meant more actual shoppers at Planted in Twin.

"Glad to hear it," Gram said, squeezing Brynn's shoulder with a wrinkled hand.

"I used fresh mint," Greta said, appearing from the kitchen and thrusting a mimosa in her direction. Brynn's mother was just as likely to be grinding dried herbs for her arthritis or an upset stomach as she was to mix it in a drink for happy hour.

Brynn clinked her glass against her mother's before taking a sip.

"Mom, I have to be back in a half hour," Brynn sputtered as a bubbly warmth spread through her insides. "Are you sure there's any juice in here?"

"Close up for the day!" her mom said, her wide-eyed glee making her look decades younger. "Katie told me how slow the store has been; I'm sure no one will complain."

Dang it, Katie. The last thing Brynn needed was for her mom to know the store was still struggling. She shot a quick glance at her grandparents, but they didn't seem to be listening.

Brynn had been raised by a single mother, though with Gram and Paps always nearby, she'd never felt like she was short on loving grownups. And though her dad had moved to Puerto Rico when she was too young to remember, her older brother Tyler said he didn't remember him being around much when he had lived with them. Brynn learned early on from her schoolmate's reactions that her relationship with her dad was highly unusual. People tended to assume she must be traumatized, or they didn't understand why she didn't have her dad's last name of Arroyo. Still, Brynn didn't know anything different, and her mother didn't strike her as particularly lonely. But then again, Greta had always marched to the beat of her own drum.

"Sure you don't want to jump in here, Brynnie?" Gram asked, setting the spiky little fern next to her coffee mug. "This one is called 'Holly on the Mountaintop.' Our first thousand-piecer!"

"You know how it is, Mom," Greta said. "No time for us thanks to work, work, work."

"Mom, don't be dramatic," Brynn said.

"I'm just saying, life is about so much more than money." Greta raised her hands defensively.

"Yes, Mom, I know!" Brynn snapped before she could stop herself. "Can we please not do this today?"

Greta blinked and sighed, twisting up one side of her mouth as she began to sort through a cluster of dark blue pieces.

"It's just a puzzle," Paps said, giving his daughter's shoulders a squeeze. "We'll have plenty of time to spend together as things slow down for Christmas."

"Speaking of Christmas," Brynn said, slipping her grandfather a grateful smile for the change of subject. "Are we still on for hanging lights this Friday?"

"Of course," Greta replied softly as she pressed the last piece of a chapel bell into place. Mostly, Brynn found her mom's sensitivity admirable. Endearing, even. Greta had raised Brynn to imagine what a zoo cat might be feeling as it paces in its cage, to really *feel* complex music of any genre, to notice kindness in a stranger's words at the supermarket. But other times, it felt like walking on eggshells around a kid who might burst into tears at any moment. These "other times" seemed even more frequent lately. Ever since Brynn had opened the store and thrown herself into her YouTube channel.

"I saw those little wooden reindeers on sale," Brynn said, leaning over Greta to hand her a snow-covered piece. "I was thinking of getting you a couple."

"Like the Chapmans had?" Gram asked without looking up from the puzzle.

Brynn nodded.

"That would be lovely down by the fence," Greta admitted, her grimace softening.

The ceasefire might prove to be short-lived, but Brynn would take it.

"Oh, Tyler called this morning," Greta said before downing the last of her mimosa. "He's on the road."

"Already?" Paps asked.

"Actually, he has three weeks off," Greta said. "He might even get to extend through New Year's."

"Three weeks?" Brynn asked. "He barely got three days off last year."

"One of the perks of the new job," Greta said brightly. At least one of her kids was changing their ways.

"Oh, that's wonderful," Gram said, clapping her hands together. "That's more family time than we've had since the kids graduated."

Greta said nothing, but she shot Brynn a look that said it all as she carried her empty glass from the table to the kitchen: *don't be the one to ruin it.*

Brynn opened her mouth and then closed it again, unwilling to take the bait. She had accepted long ago that for any new business to have a chance it would take long hours and major hustle. But she also knew that when Greta made up her mind, there was no convincing her otherwise. Maybe Tyler would try to talk some sense into their mother while he was staying there.

Brynn's twin and only sibling had started working for the National Park Service right out of college and had accepted a transfer to Glacier National Park in Montana that past spring. While neither of them had inherited their mother's love of all things New Age, they both shared her love of plants.

"Well, I better get moving," Brynn said, swallowing the last of her mimosa as she knelt next to Gram's chair and fingered the fern's delicate fronds. "Be careful not to overwater this one, Gram."

"I know, I know," Gram said with a chuckle before dutifully reciting: "*Moist, not wet. And bright, indirect light.* I'll get it right this time."

"Oh, I told the choir I'd grab a few poinsettias for the open house," Greta said, her champagne glass now replaced by a coffee mug. "I'll come by later."

"I'm out of stock," Brynn said. "But I'm placing a big order today and could have more by Wednesday. Why don't you come scroll through the website and pick some to add? I'll be there late tonight."

"Of course you will," Greta said, but most of the edge had left her voice. Brynn stood and smoothed her wool skirt, giving her mother an automatic hug goodbye as she ignored the comment.

"Just text me if you're stopping by," Brynn said. She kissed her grandparents on the cheek. "See you Friday."

As she navigated the front steps in her skinny heels, she couldn't resist another glace at her phone. Still nothing.

TWO

Jordan Damon propped the Douglas fir against one hip with ease. "You got a blanket you want under the tree?" he called into the open driver's side window.

"You can't hurt anything on this old girl," the woman said, chuckling as she strapped her wiggly toddler into his car seat. "Just toss it on there!"

Jordan grunted as he swiftly hoisted the seven-footer onto the Nissan's roof, sweat beading on his forehead despite the cold brittle wind. He grabbed a wad of twine from the back pocket of his Wranglers and looped it through each of the car's windows before tying the ends into a quick release knot.

"All set!" he said, hopping off the sideboard and waving as the SUV crunched across the gravel drive. "Merry Christmas, Mrs. Diaz!"

Suddenly, the brake lights flashed as a cloud of dust kicked up behind them.

"Move it, Toby!" Jordan shouted just as a blondish shaggy blur emerged from the cloud and loped over to him.

"Good boy," Jordan said, scratching Toby's head as he gave the allclear salute to Mrs. Diaz.

"Just as I thought, a little WD-40 and good as new," a gravelly voice called from the shop.

Jordan winced as he watched his dad sidestep slowly down the wooden stairs. Though Charlie had gotten the all clear from his hip replacement more than a year ago, Jordan couldn't help worrying about him.

"Three trees before noon ain't too shabby, kiddo," Charlie said, clapping Jordan on the shoulder. He handed the pruning shears to Jordan who opened and closed them a few times for good measure.

"Better than yesterday," Jordan agreed. "But you know it's nowhere near what we need."

"I'm still holding out for a Christmas miracle," Charlie said, his crinkly eyes still smiling.

Jordan sighed. A miracle is what it would take at this point, though if one of the Damon men needed to worry about the future of the farm, he'd rather spare his father's heart and hip the stress. Charlie may have declared himself semi-retired when he moved from the farmhouse to his condo in town, but Jordan knew he loved Evergreen Acres as much as his son. Charlie was always able to find the bright side. His mother's favorite saying echoed through his mind as it did so often these days: *no reason to live through the worst case scenario until it happens —and it usually doesn't.*

Suddenly, he heard the shriek of tires on pavement. Jordan watched as a sleek sports car squealed into the long driveway and sped to the parking lot, kicking a swarm of rocks in its wake. He couldn't believe the driver was bringing a car like that all the way to the South Hills. If there even *was* a driver; the windows were tinted so dark, he couldn't even see anyone through the windshield.

"Can't imagine they'll want a tree thrown on that roof," Jordan muttered.

"Maybe they've heard about your gentle touch," Charlie said, giving the car a friendly wave.

The car screeched to a stop a foot in front of them and Jordan cursed as Charlie hobbled out of the way. Whoever it was, they must be in too big of a hurry to bother with the clearly marked parking spaces.

"Welcome to Evergreen Acres!" Charlie called as the driver's doors flew open. As the tall man in a tailored suit unfolded himself from tiny car, Charlie's smile froze. "Oh. Hello, Russell."

The man pulled his mouth tightly in what must have been an attempt at smile. Russell Sutkamp had to be in his late 50s, but it was hard to tell with all the obvious plastic surgery.

Toby let out a muffled growl.

"Mr. Sutkamp," Jordan said, forcing his face into an even smile. "What can we do for you?"

"Just thought I'd have a browse," Sutkamp said with a smirk. "Don't you have other customers to assist?"

"We have most of our pre-cut trees in the front lot if you're looking for something specific," Jordan said, letting the question slide by.

Sutkamp gave Jordan a vague nod before charging toward a tree-dotted field with narrowed eyes.

Jordan shot Charlie a look, but his dad looked equally perplexed.

Moments later, Sutkamp returned, looking impossibly smugger than when he'd arrived. What the heck did this scumbag want?

"I heard Evergreen Acres will be ripe for the picking very soon," Sutkamp said, his voice toneless. "The location is quite good, but

I need to see if it's more than just a dried-out patch of scrawny trees."

Jordan's lips formed words, but none came out. He forced himself to return Sutkamp's aggressive gaze, refusing to show how flustered he was.

"I have no idea what you're talking about," Charlie said. "We aren't going anywhere."

"This place will definitely require some scaling and leveling," Sutkamp continued, ignoring him. "But it may hold potential."

"For what?" Jordan asked, unable to resist the bait any longer.

"For the future location of my first planned living community," Sutkamp replied, his eyes lighting up as he watched for Jordan's reaction.

Though Jordan had begun to suspect that the notorious Twin Falls developer was there on business, hearing the words come out of that smarmy mouth made Jordan want to throw up.

"You heard my dad," Jordan said coolly.

"Cute with the cowboy act," Sutkamp said with a hollow laugh. "The corpse may still be warm, but I have friends at the bank. Friends who talk. January first is a big day for you, isn't it?"

"New Year's is a big day for everyone, Russell," Charlie said flatly.

"At least your legacy will carry on," Sutkamp quipped, ignoring Charlie. "I'm even generous enough to name the project after you—Evergreen Meadows."

"I'm not sure who these 'friends' of yours are, but they're wrong," Jordan said tightly, reminding himself that a fist fight wouldn't be good for business no matter who the recipient was. "Now, I'm going to kindly ask you to leave."

Sutkamp chuckled. "Fair enough. Time will tell, won't it?" He flashed his pearly teeth at them, then turned back just once, giving them a little salute before disappearing back inside his car, flipping around, and speeding down the driveway.

"Even when he was just a cocky kid, Russell was already a sad, lonely old man," Charlie said, shaking his head as Sutkamp sped toward the road, finally disappearing onto the tree-lined road.

"How the Hell could he know all that?" Jordan asked.

"It doesn't matter, and it doesn't change a thing," Charlie said, though Jordan didn't buy his indifference.

"Do you know how much the folks out here would hate some kind of fancy subdivision?" Jordan asked. People at the base of the South Hills were usually there for a reason—they liked privacy and space, and they wanted nothing do with city folk.

"We're running out of time, Dad," Jordan said, running a calloused hand through his thick black hair.

Charlie squeezed him into a side hug. "Whatever happens, time marches on and so do we." Clearly finished speaking in motivational metaphors, he grabbed a rake and began sweeping the pine needles from the walkway.

Jordan's pulse throbbed in his temples as he climbed the fence, winding the giant spool of twine and tucking the loose end into the center. He swung his boot-clad foot over the top, perching on the fence post, his mind whirling. He watched the road and listened, but he didn't have much hope for an afternoon rush of customers.

"Those tree-in-a-box websites are what I don't get," Charlie called, wheezing a bit as he propped himself against the rake. "Between free shipping and the increase in sapling costs? How they can sell quality for fifty bucks is beyond me."

"That's just it, Dad, they can't," Jordan said. "But somehow, they're still winning."

Sure, the busiest people would never find time to buy a tree if it couldn't be ordered with a click. Jordan sighed. They must be missing something. What about holiday tradition? There weren't any tree farms in the area big enough to compete with Evergreen, but Jordan made a mental note to check in with a few and see how their seasons were faring in comparison.

Jordan hopped off the fence and took the rake from Charlie, peeling off his sherpa-lined gloves as they climbed the steps to the store. Jordan knew his dad cared more about the future of the business than he let on. Charlie may have married into the business, but he'd been doing it his entire adult life, immediately catching his wife's passion for the daily ins and outs of tree farming. There was nowhere Jordan felt her presence more than when he trudged through the fields in the crisp morning air, and he suspected his dad felt her presence there too.

Any family-owned business that lasted more than a generation was something to be proud of, but Jordan had always thought theirs had something extra special. From the way his grandparents had been happiest at the farm, preferring to spend vacation time in the rockers on the porch rather than on any tropical beach, to the expressions of pure glee on the faces of the kids who scampered through the even mazes of pines each winter.

Not that Evergreen Acres didn't have bumps along the last century. The gates had opened only a few years before the Great Depression. Then there were the tales of destructive pests, devastating tree viruses, world wars, and even a fire. Jordan could remember his mom's stories about how worried her dad had been when artificial trees came on the market. It had turned out there was enough room for both. Evergreen Acres had always made it through. But why did this time feel different?

"Maybe we should try that social media," Charlie said as they crossed the wooden porch. "Some online advertising? A, uh... whatcha call it? Croupon?"

"Not you too," Jordan groaned, though he couldn't suppress an amused smile. "Did Gina brainwash you? Are you a millennial now?"

"Gina has a point!"

"Dad," Jordan said, shaking his head. "We developed more than one disease-resistant species of tree. We were among the first in the state—probably the country—to sell trees with a root ball that could be replanted. Don't you think if we were doing something wrong, we would have gone bankrupt long before now?"

"Maybe," Charlie said quietly. Jordan hadn't meant to sound harsh, but he was tired of talking in circles.

"I don't know anything about this stuff," Jordan said by way of apology. "But I'll do some research. See if I can make heads or tails of it."

Before Jordan could grab the knob, the door swung open.

"My word, it's frigid!" Gina bellowed as she turned sideways to squeeze through the door frame. She shuffled and stretched out two thermoses. "Hot coffee, splash of cocoa, just the way my Gram made it."

"Thanks, Gina," Jordan said as he twisted open the lid and let the warm steam envelop his frozen face.

"Did I see that snake Sutkamp poking around?" she asked, glancing down the driveway.

"Unfortunately," Charlie said.

Gina made a clucking sound and raised a disapproving eyebrow.

"I'll let you fill Gina in," Jordan said with a sigh as he screwed the lid back on. "I'm going to walk the west field."

Charlie tasted his own coffee and nodded approvingly to Gina. "You have no idea how much I needed this." He turned to Jordan. "Still up for the village tonight?"

"Wouldn't miss it," Jordan said. "I'll load up the boxes after close and bring them over."

A stony wind stung Jordan's cheeks as he rounded the corner of the little wooden store, his dad's muffled voice slowly fading into silence. His gaze wandered absent-mindedly over the east field, its hundreds of saplings still too short for him to see over the fence line.

As he trudged up the gently sloping hillside, he pictured his great-grandfather, a tobacco pipe between his lips as he stepped out of the old two-room wooden house. Though the house had long ago become a tool shed, and Jordan had only ever seen one tiny black and white portrait of his ancestor, it wasn't hard to visualize Ezekial Arroyo loading Idaho's native spruces onto horse-drawn carriages as Christmas trees were first becoming commonplace. He could almost hear his mom's high-pitched giggle as a round-faced child, selling peppermint sticks to customers who knew her all by name. Once, the Arroyo family had been no different than the thousands of other poor desperate European immigrants who'd boarded the ships alongside them. A century later, Jordan wondered what Twin Falls would have been like without them.

He paused to catch his breath, gazing over the scattered buildings below. If Sutkamp got his hands on Evergreen Acres, he would destroy the heart of this place. Jordan shivered and zipped his coat up to his Adam's apple. It wasn't going to happen. It couldn't. Not for Sutkamp, not for a paved subdivision in the middle of nowhere. This land was theirs. He just had to find a way to keep it in the family for another hundred years.

THREE

"I tried to get a reservation at the library, did I tell you that?" Henry asked as Brynn scraped a few crumbs from the counter onto her napkin.

"No, I don't think you did," Brynn said politely, though many past lunches told her where this conversation was headed.

"Yep. Couldn't get in. Turns out it was booked," Henry said, shooting her a sideways glance before grinning. Brynn groaned and shook her head, but couldn't help but laugh.

After stopping by her mom's, Brynn had grabbed her usual blueberry crumble coffee cake and oat milk latte from the Earlybird Espresso next to Planted. The ten minutes she had left in her lunch break had been all she'd needed to warm her numb nose and allow the caffeine to hit her veins. Or maybe it was the steady stream of dad jokes from Henry Lee that refreshed her. Henry had owned a chain of coffee shops back in Chicago, shops that he told her were clones of Earlybird Espresso with its black matte paint, dark leather armchairs, and daily newspapers on every surface. It seemed new faces were flocking to Twin Falls by the minute these days, city people who craved lower housing prices and a "big small town" feel. But in Brynn's opinion, Henry was the best of them. When Brynn had opened Planted in Twin,

Henry had shown up on the first day with a basket of bear claws in hand and plenty of business advice. Brynn had gratefully accepted both, but quickly learned they came with an endless stream of corny jokes.

"Thanks, Henry," Brynn called as she held open the door for a bundled-up trio of police officers.

"Leaving already?" Henry asked. "I was hoping you'd finally meet my son, he's on his way over."

"Sorry, I'm already late," Brynn said. "I'll stay longer next time."

"Well, you know what all my Yelp reviews say," Henry said. "Come for the java—"

"Stay for the jokes," Brynn finished on cue, eliciting a comically proud smile from Henry.

Brynn felt lighter as she hurried the ten feet to the brick storefront of Planted in Twin. She unlocked the door and flipped the sign back to *Open!* as a gust of icy wind lapped at her bare neck. After tossing her belongings onto the couch in the back room, she started her afternoon rounds. Some plants needed extra spritzing despite the humidifiers in every corner, others needed lights or stakes adjusted.

She stopped at a metal shelf full of Alocasia Polly plants, fingering the leathery leaves that looked like dragon wings from a fairy tale.

She slid behind the counter, clicking the mouse to wake the computer, then reset the timer on the row of grow lights behind her. Tiny, white roots had sprouted from at least four of the philodendron cuttings, and Brynn expected the rest of the cups would bear a tiny heart shaped leaf in the next day or so. She bent close to the tiny plants, lifting leaves and checking for any signs of pests.

"Hi, my little friends," she cooed. "How was your lunch break?"

"Great, thanks!" a voice called as she heard the back door slam shut. "I had a panini with that press you got me."

Katie threw aside the curtain with a grin before grabbing a peppermint candy from the basket on the counter.

"So..." Brynn began.

Katie shook her head. "No news. But you know I would have called the second I had anything to report."

"I know," Brynn said, forcing a smile and tried to swallow the lump that had been there all morning. For a few minutes, she'd managed to forget to check her phone every ten seconds. Henry was good for that.

"Hey, it's still early," Katie said, tenderly squeezing Brynn's shoulder. "Don't give up hope. I can't imagine why Homestead TV would turn down the chance to work with you."

Homestead TV. Even just hearing the network's name said aloud caused a nervous heat to rush to Brynn's face. The number one home and garden channel in the entire country—scratch that, the entire *world*—knew about Brynn and her YouTube channel. After one Zoom meeting and multiple phone calls expressing interest, was it really such a stretch to think they might offer her a houseplant television show? Brynn swallowed. *Yes. Yes, it was.* Still, nothing to do but wait for the phone to ring.

"I think I'm more concerned that they're sold on the idea of a houseplant show at all, let alone having me host it," Brynn muttered.

"Well, there's already talk of a new garden show on the Homestead subreddit!" Katie countered. "And you know the network is responsible for most of the best rumors on there."

Brynn considered this. That was a good sign.

"Was it busy this morning?" Katie asked, hopping onto the tall swivel stool behind the counter and crisscrossing her petite overall-clad legs.

"The usual," Brynn said, sighing as she sipped the last of her oat milk latte. "Not busy enough."

Katie worked her PR job in the morning most days and usually came to Planted in the afternoon to help with all things social media, ad partnerships, and any other tasks that her work experience made her uniquely qualified to handle. Originally, she had also offered to help work the store when it got too busy, but, so far, they'd never been busy enough to need her. Brynn had pictured herself slowly spending more time in the store and less online, but she couldn't afford to do that. Thank goodness she had Katie.

Brynn had been dreaming of her own plant shop since college, but she thought she'd never save enough to make it happen. After graduation, her now ex-boyfriend Caleb suggested she make some YouTube videos to share her green thumb. A videographer, he offered to film them and teach her the basics of editing. Though most of this suggestion was coming from a loving place, Brynn also knew Caleb was tired of listening to her to drone on about Latin names, moisture levels, and the other plant facts that never seemed to excite anyone as much as her. As it turned out, Brynn was far from alone. What started as a few short videos passed obligingly among family and friends quickly grew to a hundred subscribers. A year later, a hundred thousand—and it never stopped growing. As of that morning, *Planted*, Brynn's channel which later inspired her shop name, had over 920,000 subscribers.

Paid sponsorships and ad revenue had quickly started pouring in, and a shocked Brynn suddenly was making three times what she made at the catering company where she worked part time. Though she could do without the online trolls and the negotiations with advertisers, she loved writing new content and connecting with plant lovers from all over the world. Caleb refused her offer to share these earnings and, as the demand for more videos grew, Brynn could feel his frustration growing. She couldn't blame him; he'd signed up to help her with a small hobby, not an entire career.

So, she quit her catering job, bought her own filming equipment, and started growing the channel full time. She saved every dollar she could, and before she knew it, she had enough money to rent an old bakery on Addison and soon opened her own houseplant shop. She named it Planted in Twin in homage to her YouTube channel that had made it all possible.

Before, Brynn hadn't minded all the sleepless nights spent learning how to go viral on TikTok or editing out street sounds from her newly recorded videos. But once Planted in Twin opened, her head began to spin. She cancelled more than one date night with Caleb, forgot her Paps' birthday, and slowly drifted apart from her circle of childhood friends. One day, she even fell asleep behind the store counter while multiple customers were shopping.

That was about the time her mom started begging her to find more balance. It was also about the time Caleb had given her an ultimatum—the channel or him. When she'd hesitated, he'd dumped her. Fortunately, that was also about the time Katie Dilworth had moved to Twin Falls and saved Brynn from an utterly heartbreaking and lonely chapter.

Randomly assigned as roommates sophomore year at Boise State, Katie and Brynn had become immediately inseparable. After graduation, Brynn had moved back to Twin Falls to figure out her next move, while Katie headed to Chicago for an internship with a top PR firm. They hadn't seen each other once since Boise, both swamped by student debt and busy lives, but they never went a single day without texting.

Then, Covid hit, and offices around the world moved online. Until that point, Katie had been a patient participant in countless tearful, wine-drenched phone marathons as Brynn struggled to get over Caleb while keeping her two businesses single-handedly afloat. Without a word, Katie accepted a fully remote position with the firm that had quickly promoted her through the ranks from intern to PR supervisor. When she'd burst through the door at Planted in Twin and told Brynn she was there to stay, Brynn had cried ugly tears as she squeezed her old friend.

Katie promptly declared herself Brynn's publicist and manager and assigned herself a minimum wage hourly rate. As much as Brynn felt she should protest her friend's generosity, she was too mentally drained to put up a fight. Slowly, Katie began to teach Brynn everything she knew about online marketing and tracked all her social media accounts. She negotiated with sponsors, interacted with followers, and made sure Brynn's content was frequent and consistent. Finally, Brynn was able to focus more on the store and writing new videos, two of the things that brought her the most joy. Katie liked to say that Brynn was the talent, and she was the muscle. In truth, Brynn would have drowned without Katie.

Brynn managed a smile before taking in Katie's close-cropped pixie cut. "Is it just me, or is it greener?"

Katie shrugged. "It was starting to fade and I'm really going for that vibrant Christmas emerald green. I think I'm getting closer, don't you?"

Brynn laughed. Between the nose piercings and the mood ring hair, she loved that the corporate world hadn't changed her bestie's funky college style.

Brynn pulled the remote from under the computer and turned on the wall-mounted flat screen TV as a commercial for laundry detergent faded into a repeat of *Urban Farm*. She always had Homestead on in the background these days. She watched as Georgina and Paul, the network's golden couple, elbowed each other and tossed light conversation back and forth. Georgina trimmed the stems of a colorful flower arrangement, while Paul stirred a massive pot on the restaurant-worthy stove. Brynn had wondered if the magazine-ready, perfectly lit kitchen was a soundstage, but she had stalked them enough online to learn it was actually their home. A graphic banner on the bottom of the screen read "Farm to Table Entertaining on a Budget!"

"Look at that," Brynn said, narrowing her eyes. "Not a houseplant in sight."

"That's why the network needs you!" Katie said, plugging her laptop into the charging cord.

"To be a set decorator for Urban Farm?" Brynn teased.

"To be the first ever queen of houseplants!" Katie said, rolling her eyes theatrically.

"I really, really want it," Brynn said, as she watched the perfectly groomed couple taste Paul's concoction.

"It would be pretty epic," Katie said, following Brynn's gaze back to the TV. Georgina was coughing and waving a hand at her mouth as Paul doubled over in laughter.

"The only downside would be wearing makeup every day," Brynn said.

Katie snorted. "Wow, what a dilemma! You should tell them that instead of having a makeup artist, you want someone whose job is to take it all off for you."

Brynn laughed and glanced back to the screen. "See, that's how

I would do my show. Approachable and real, but also touching on some deeper stuff. Like, did you know that in a study, two-thirds of adults reported an improvement in their mental well-being when surrounded by houseplants?"

"I think you've mentioned that one or a million times," Katie quipped.

"Well, it's that important!" Brynn protested. "Maybe then I could stop trying to keep up with the rarest, trendiest plants and just talk about some regular old snake plants."

"What's keeping you from doing that now?" Katie asked.

"You know my views skyrocket when I add a black ZZ plant or something else hard to find," Brynn groaned. "You're the one who taught me about those 'sum keywords' or whatever."

"SEM keywords," Katie replied with her usual patience. "It stands for Search Engine Marketing."

"Whatever," Brynn said, blowing a loose wave out of her eyes. "That."

"That was before you really knew what you wanted to say," Katie said. "Now you have your own voice. I bet your subscribers would love the raw mess of plants I see here in the shop."

Brynn looked around. Did it really look that messy?

"Listen, I'm learning too," Katie said, placing a gentle hand on Brynn's arm. "I might know publicity, but I don't know plants. Nine months ago, all we could do was mirror what was working for other channels."

"By other channels, you mean *The Green Goddess*?"

Now it was Katie's turn to groan. "Gross," she said. "I like Green Gag Me much better."

"Well, at this point, it's not going to matter anyway," Brynn said. "Homestead has the pitch, which is what it is. Besides being amazing and inspirational, of course. I mean, you are the one who wrote it."

Katie shrugged, but her eyes glowed with pride. Brynn had read an interview with Homestead's CEO where he mentioned they were considering expanding the channel's decorating, real estate, and cooking content to include a wider scope. Brynn had called Katie, giddy at the idea of submitting a proposal to them—though having no clue how to begin—and Katie had immediately gotten to work.

"Well, it can't hurt that last week's video went viral," Katie said, maximizing her browser as a *Planted* video filled the screen. 'How to Pick a Plant on Black Friday' was superimposed above a muted Brynn. She watched herself gesturing wildly with her hands, a tiny rubber plant in front of her, as her red, lipsticked mouth silently taught them how to find a good deal.

"Look!" Katie tapped the screen under the video. "Over three million views! That's at least a couple hundred thousand more than last night."

"I hope Homestead sees that," Brynn said, grabbing her apron from its hook on the wall and tying it snugly around her waist.

"I bet they're watching everything you do," Katie said. "But it's out of our hands. You've done everything you can do."

"I guess," Brynn said.

"*Three million views*, Brynnie!"

"Some are probably repeats by you and my grandparents."

"Speaking of grandparents, my mom wants to know where your Gram got her stockings," Katie said, scrolling through the video's analytics. "She must have posted a pic on Facebook or something."

"I'll ask her," Brynn said, staring through the window at the two bare trees that lined the sidewalk. "The holidays are really sneaking up on me this year."

"You have tunnel vision," Katie teased. "Have you looked outside?"

Brynn laughed. It was true, Twin Falls had already begun to transform for Christmas, especially in the historic downtown district where Planted in Twin shared a block with Earlybird Espresso, and the old Orpheum Theatre. Even though Thanksgiving had just passed, there were already giant ribbons and snowflakes on nearly every pole. Just like always, Kurt's pharmacy looked more like a holiday boutique, and though the tree in the square wouldn't be illuminated for another week or so, she had seen plenty of ice-skaters on the rink when she'd driven by.

"What happened to my roomie who hung paper ornaments on her plants in the dorm?" Katie asked, playfully nudging Brynn with her elbow.

"It just seems like I can barely keep up these days," Brynn said, letting out a hollow breath. "I feel like no one knows our store is here yet. But with the channel growing, I need to make more content. Then there's all the comments to respond to—"

"You know I can do that stuff," Katie said. "That's my job."

"One tiny part of one of your many jobs," Brynn said.

"Once you get the show, maybe you can back off of the social media stuff a little," Katie suggested.

"And if I don't get it?" Brynn asked, flicking the TV off as she smiled at two women in suits who entered and began browsing.

"Well, then, you'll still have your shop," Katie said. "You'll continue to make a difference every day, face-to-face. You could just make videos when you want, and I'll post stuff on Instagram once a week."

Brynn groaned and spoke quietly. "Only if business picks up here."

"You're barely into year two of a new business," Katie said. "Give it time."

Brynn grumbled, but nodded. "Are you still free to help me tonight?"

"As long as you don't force me to be on camera again," Katie said.

"I remembered to bring makeup this time," Brynn said, laughing. "Besides, the viewers loved you."

"Uh huh," Katie said flatly, cocking an eyebrow.

"Fine, I promise." Brynn grabbed her bucket of tools. "Some of the philodendrons sprouted roots. Want to help me pot them?"

"Nah, I'll stick to what I'm good at," Katie said, clicking her laptop's trackpad. "Plus, I need to catch up on emails. Here's one from, quote, 'an avid fan'. He has a line of homemade self-tanning lotion and wants to know if you'd be interested in some free product in exchange for sharing it on your channel."

"That's not even remotely plant related," Brynn groaned.

"So, I take it that's a hard pass," Katie said, as the two shoppers flashed them an apologetic wave and stepped back out onto the sidewalk.

Just as Brynn grabbed her potting mat, a familiar trill of classical music blasted from the laptop's tiny speakers.

"Really?" Brynn asked.

"Hey, you just said you wanted to keep tabs on the competition," Katie said, smirking. "The Green Gag Me just uploaded a new video."

Brynn wiped her hands on her apron and stepped closer to the computer with a sigh.

"The Green Goddess" title card faded from view, revealing a perfectly made-up face amidst a sterile white filming set. There was no denying the raven-haired woman's irritatingly sculpted face, but something about her appearance made Brynn think of a viper about to swallow a rat.

"Hello, GG fans, and welcome back," the woman said, a syrupy lilt filling every word. "Let's start today by calling it how I see it— Brynn Callaway is just as basic as her plants."

Brynn's throat tightened as fury pulsed in her temples. Jessica Southgate, a.k.a. the Green Goddess, had certainly hinted at her feelings toward Brynn before, but never directly by name, and never right at the beginning of a video. Why was Jessica attacking her so blatantly now? Suddenly, an icy cold suspicion slithered through Brynn's mind.

"Ew, she's the worst," Katie said as a montage of every plant Brynn had shared in the past month filled the screen. Of course, Jessica left out any clips showing Brynn's segments on her Silvery Ann pothos or her Fucata prayer plant. No collector would ever refer to such hard-to-find specimen as "basic."

"I can't listen to her dumb, fake voice," Katie said, clicking mute just as Jessica blew the camera a kiss and held up a giant bottle of fertilizer she must be getting paid to promote. "My panini is going to reappear."

"I bet she's never even tried that product," Brynn snorted. "How does she have so many followers?"

"Probably from modeling," Katie said, her eyes quickly scanning the comments. "She sent fans over from Instagram and they followed like little Botoxed, spray-tanned minions."

"Modeling," Brynn said. "No wonder she always looks so perfect." She watched as Jessica pulled a vibrant pink and green plant from off-screen. "Wait!" Brynn exclaimed. "Where did she get a PPP?!"

"A what now?" Katie asked.

"A pink princess philodendron!" Brynn squeaked.

Katie's face was blank.

"I've been looking for one for years!" Brynn, touching the screen as if she could feel the leaves. "It's impossible to find unless you have thousands to drop on a single plant or know someone who will give you a cutting. Even those go for hundreds of dollars with no guarantee it will actually root."

"Oh, for crying out loud," Katie said, slapping her palm on the counter. "Look at that view count. It's only been up for two hours!

"How can I possibly compete with that?!" Brynn said, pressing her face into her hands.

Katie wrinkled her nose and slammed the laptop shut just as a loud buzzing sound drew both of their eyes to Katie's corduroy messenger bag.

"The business cell!" Katie exclaimed, rifling through the pockets.

"Put it on speaker!" Brynn said.

"Hello, Katie Dilworth speaking," she said, tapping the speakerphone icon, instantly switching to a smooth professional tone that was basically a superpower to Brynn.

"Hi Katie, John at Homestead," said a bored voice. "I have Sofia Camp for you?"

"Put her through," Katie said with a wink. Brynn couldn't breathe. The VP of Homestead TV wanted to talk to *them*? It was either a really great sign or a really terrible sign.

What felt like infinite seconds passed in dead silence before Brynn finally heard a click.

"Katie, Sofia Camp. How's it going?"

"Couldn't be better," Katie said. Brynn pressed her lips together so hard she thought they might bleed. "Great to finally speak with you."

"Listen," Sofia said. "I was hoping to speak with both you and your client."

"Of course," Katie said. "Can you hold for a second? Let me see if she's available."

Katie tapped the mute icon and started to wiggle her shoulders in a happy dance, grinning as Brynn clasped one hand to her forehead. Katie met Brynn's gaze and gave her a pointed look: *you ready?* Brynn didn't know if she'd ever be ready. The only thing more intimidating than talking to the Homestead VP would be talking to the Homestead CEO himself. Brynn swallowed and nodded as Katie unmuted the call.

"OK, I have Brynn on the line," Katie said.

"Hi, Ms. Camp," Brynn said, more than a little surprised her voice sounded somewhat normal.

"Brynn, glad we could catch you," Sofia said as Katie squeezed Brynn's hand. "Your content is really on brand with this huge urban gardening trend we've been tracking." Brynn held her breath. "At Homestead, our success depends on keeping up with our viewers' interests."

Katie widened her eyes at Brynn, but Brynn just held up a finger. *Wait.*

"The fans have spoken," Sofia continued. "Homestead TV will

debut its first ever houseplant lifestyle show, filmed right here on the lot in Los Angeles."

Brynn's heart pounded against her ribcage as Katie tightened her grip on her hand. They shared a look that said it all. It was happening. It was really happening.

As Katie offered Sofia her congratulations on the project, the last part of Sofia's words finally caught up to Brynn. *Los Angeles.* Of course. Brynn felt like such a rookie. As if they'd let her film in Twin Falls when the studio had an entire filming lot in California? Brynn swallowed, shoving this information to a place for later review as platitudes like "move the needle" and "data never lies" floated past her ears. A slight hitch in Sofia's tone brought Brynn's attention back to the conversation.

"I want you to know that we are still making a decision concerning casting," Sofia said quickly as Brynn felt her lungs deflate. She had pitched the show to Homestead TV. It had never occurred to her they might hire someone else to host it. Her cheeks burned.

"It's down to you and one other potential host," Sofia continued. "Another influencer, one who also has a houseplant channel. I should mention this person does have quite a few more subscribers than you."

"I see," Brynn managed. She silently mouthed *Jessica* as Katie flared her nostrils and frowned. Brynn couldn't be sure, but her gut told her she was right.

"The team is torn," Sofia continued, a slight apology in her tone. "So, our CEO Mark Barnes has asked us to take another couple weeks to review all your content and chart your followers' demographics. Who can bring the most eyeballs to our programming? Which host most aligns with our brand's values?"

"I understand," Brynn said steadily, but her mind was spinning.

Mark Barnes actually knew who Brynn was?

"Everyone is looking for the next Georgina or Paul," Sofia said. "A host with personality and passion...a host that could end up with a book deal and a merchandise line in our stores, as was the case with *Urban Farm*."

Book Deal?! Merchandise line?!

"So when will we know?" Katie asked, stifling a laugh as Brynn opened and closed her mouth like a gaping fish.

"We'll announce the new host live during the airing of the Homestead Christmas Day Parade," Sofia said. "So, we'll have to sign paperwork before then."

"I see," Katie said evenly.

"Between us," Sofia said, before hesitating a beat. "If it were my decision alone, I would have already hired you. Brynn, could I offer you one piece of advice?"

"Absolutely," Brynn said, wiping the back of her hand against her clammy forehead.

"I'm not supposed to tell you a name, but can you guess why you're up against?" Sofia asked, her voice suddenly quieter.

"Is it Jessica Southgate?" Brynn asked, feeling queasy. "*The Green Goddess*?"

"I knew you were smart," Sofia said. "Our CEO has a hard time looking past viewership numbers. Maybe see if you can borrow any ideas from her that might earn you a few more eyeballs this month."

"I will," Brynn said confidently, though her stomach twisted. What else could she do that she wasn't already doing? "Thank you for telling me."

"Just keep your show's authentic heart," Sofia said. "Your approachability and obvious skills are really special."

"I appreciate that," Brynn said.

"Great," Sofia said, her voice once again brisk and neutral. "Katie, we'll be in touch."

"Thanks, Sofia," Katie said before ending the call and turning to Brynn. "So, good stuff, right?"

"I guess," Brynn said, twisting a hair tie around her thick waves. "But who knows if they'll pick me?"

"There's no world in which they won't see through Jessica if they're serious about watching more content," Katie said, leaning against the counter. "She's such mean girl. I doubt anyone finds the Green Goddess relatable."

"Well, it's show business," Brynn said. "And she has big numbers."

"And Los Angeles?!" Katie said, her voice nearly cracking. "How exciting is that?"

"Yeah," Brynn said vaguely.

"Sunshine all year long, palm trees, famous people," Katie said, seemingly oblivious to the growing conflict in Brynn's mind. "We could eat dinner from any country in the whole world if we lived in LA."

"That's true," Brynn said slowly. "But what about my store?"

"Someone could manage it for you," Katie said, her eyes glowing. "And I bet you'd get plenty more business from the show. Look at all the people who travel to Utah just to visit the real Urban Farm? They built a store to meet the demand of all the tourists. You already have one!"

"I guess you're right," Brynn said, wiping a smudge of dirt off the counter with her fingernail, as a couple hurried in rubbing their hands together from the cold. "Welcome to Planted in

Twin!" Brynn called. "Let me know if you need any help."

They threw her a grateful smile and began to browse.

"I'll gather some intel on Jessica and do an Instagram deep dive," Katie said, heading to the back.

As Brynn showed the two customers her newest stock, she played back the conversation in her mind. Her goal was always to run her own plant shop, but what if she couldn't keep it going on her own? Though an hour earlier she would have sworn she'd give it all up for her own TV show. Reality was sinking in. Was she really willing to leave all this behind to make it happen?

After she'd rung up a tray of seedlings and seen the couple out, the store was once again quiet. She headed to the back, throwing open the curtain so she had a view of the door in case anyone came in. She plopped onto the worn, tweed loveseat, gazing over her makeshift set. She'd done pretty well with the hundred-dollar lighting kit she'd ordered online and the used DLSR camera. The exposed brick with translucent block windows served as the backdrop, and Brynn had painted the adjacent wall a bright white to reflect as much light as possible. A long, wooden counter-height table served as her workspace and brightly colored macramé hangings adorned the open wall.

She grabbed a steno pad from the battered coffee table and wrote "You know that plant you got for Christmas? Here's how to make it happy!" She doodled a little cactus before staring blankly at the page, wondering if Sofia Camp had called her or Jessica Southgate first. Brynn knew she needed to be in this fight with all guns blazing, but as she opened TikTok, all she could do was scroll *The Green Goddess*'s feed, searching for any signs of what her opponent was doing to beat her.

FOUR

"I'm thinking one more should get us through the outskirts of the village," Jordan said, snatching the empty whiskey glasses as Charlie changed a bulb on a miniature ceramic firehouse. "You want another round?"

"You know it," Charlie said without looking up.

Toby blinked at the men a few times, circled, then plopped back down under the sideboard and closed his eyes.

Once in the kitchen, Jordan splashed bitters over the sugar, the liquor warming his chest. Work might be stressful, but their annual tradition of assembling the Christmas village came as a welcome distraction.

Marissa, Jordan's mother, had given Charlie a little brown porcelain general store on their first Christmas as a married couple. Every year, she had gifted another piece, and once Jordan was old enough, he helped her choose Charlie's gifts. One year it was an old-fashioned schoolhouse, the next a livery stable. Jordan's favorites had always been the tiny ice-skating rink and the chapel with the little nativity in the yard. The little cityscape had felt magical when he was a kid. Now, each one stood as a memory of their beloved Marissa.

Jordan and Charlie kept the tradition going, though they no longer added new pieces. The mugs of hot cocoa had been replaced by cocktails, but otherwise, not much had changed. And every year, they followed Marissa's creased hand-drawn map to the letter.

Jordan reentered the living room, maneuvering around the overstuffed recliners. It was hard to believe it had been nearly five years since Charlie had moved to the tidy ranch; five years since he convinced Jordan to take over the farmhouse. Charlie handed his dad the old-fashioned.

"Thanks," Charlie said, clinking his glass against Jordan's before taking a sip. He set the tumbler aside and plugged a tiny hand-painted toy store into a power strip. "Bulb's still good."

Jordan picked up an old-fashioned trolley car, flipping it over out of habit and rubbing his thumb along his mother's neat handwriting: *Love, M.D.* He carefully lifted the thin paper map from the side table.

"I'm glad we still do this," Jordan said, sneaking a glance at Charlie's crinkly face as he placed the trolley car in front of the miniature town square. "But I still miss the way it used to be."

"It all hits harder at the holidays," Charlie said, clearing his throat as he swirled his ice cubes around his glass. "Then with the anniversary of the accident in January...well, I don't have to tell you. It's a loaded season."

"I don't know how Megan does it," Jordan said. "First Mom, then Eric?"

"Your sister is a strong woman," Charlie said, pinching a little red bulb between his fingers, giving it a little shake before tossing it in the trash bag on the floor. "Always has been."

"I wonder if she regrets it," Jordan said, pulling a Styrofoam-wrapped treehouse from its box. "You know, getting married in the first place knowing what she does now."

"I doubt Megan would change a thing," Charlie said, smiling as he set his empty glass next to Jordan's. "Neither would I." The first row of Marissa's tiny buildings burst into a warm yellow glow as he plugged the master cord into the power strip.

"I'd have regrets if I was in Megan's shoes," Jordan said. "At least you had a more than forty years with mom."

"Forever wouldn't have been long enough with your mother," Charlie said, a soft smile curling his lips as he surveyed the village below, looking like a giant from one of the old fairy tales Jordan remembered. Charlie's once black hair was now almost entirely silver and the skin on his neck looked as thin as tissue paper. When had his dad turned into an old man?

"Looks good, Dad," Jordan said softly, looping his arm around Charlie's shoulders.

"Sure does," Charlie agreed. "Only halfway there, but I love seeing it come together."

They stood there a moment longer, each remembering.

"Speaking of your sister," Charlie said, clearing his throat and wiping his sleeve across his eyes. "Talked to her lately?"

Jordan shook his head. "She called me last weekend, but I haven't had a chance to call her back yet. Everything okay?"

"It's more than okay," Charlie said with a throaty chuckle. "She's moving back."

"Back to Twin?!" Jordan asked. "What about her job?"

Megan had gone to college in Ohio and then settled there after graduation. Jordan barely saw his older sister outside of major holidays when she'd fly in bearing handknitted gifts she'd worked on throughout the year. He missed her, but they mostly just exchanged a few texts these days. Twin had always felt too quiet without her, especially after their mom had died.

"She's taking a third-grade teacher position," Charlie said. "I guess Lottie Townsend is finally retiring."

"That's great," Jordan said. He made a mental note to call her back that evening. "I figured if she didn't come home after the accident, she never would."

"Take it from me," Charlie said, cocking his head to one side, his eyes bright with amusement. "Women always have their reasons. Whether or not they share them with us is another story."

"Ah, the self-proclaimed expert strikes again," Jordan said, laughing.

"Speaking of women," Charlie said, his eyes narrowing. "You haven't mentioned Stephanie in a while."

"You mean Taylor?" Jordan asked, crossing his arms over his chest. "Stephanie was ages ago."

"Ok, then what's up with Taylor?" his dad asked, his innocent tone not fooling Jordan for a second.

"I don't know, Dad," Jordan said with a sigh. "We've been so busy, I think she gave up on me."

He left out mentioning the torrent of curse words that Taylor had hurled at him when they'd last met for coffee. She was gorgeous, petite, and bubbly with a great smile, and the conversation had been easy when they'd first met. They'd seen each other nearly every weekend for a few months, but neither had discussed making it official. He hadn't meant to forget her sister's wedding, nor the rehearsal dinner he had agreed to attend the day before. But Taylor hardly heard him. When he pointed out that inviting him to a family wedding so early in a relationship was weird anyway, Taylor's tear-stained threats had increased to a downpour.

"We better get moving if we're going to finish this before midnight," Jordan said, lifting the lid of a bulging container and peering inside. "What do you say to one more round?"

"I say make it half-strength and you got yourself a deal," Charlie said.

Jordan wandered into the kitchen, his chest tight with nostalgia as he pulled the top from the decanter. If he'd learned one thing from his mom, it was to never take the little moments for granted. As long as the drinks kept flowing, he didn't care if the village took all night.

FIVE

"Your tips were a lifesaver!" the man said, his round face beaming as Brynn slid the rubber plant into a paper sleeve and passed it across the counter. "My arrowhead is doing great. Maybe I can keep more than one plant alive!" He pushed his glasses up on his nose before taking the receipt from her hand, his eyes shining with excitement.

"All you needed was some confidence," Brynn said, but her face warmed with pride. "Oh, and that little water meter. But even I use one!"

The man tucked the little plant inside his jacket before swinging open the door and ducking his head into the frosty morning air. Just as the shop fell silent once more, Katie came stomping in from the back, an annoyed grimace on her elfin face.

"That good, huh?" Brynn asked, popping a mint in her mouth before tossing one to Katie.

"Your follower count *has* gone up, but Jessica is still over a million ahead," Katie said, crossing her arms over her oversized tunic.

Brynn groaned as she studied Katie's pensive face. "Why do I feel like there's more?"

"Because there *is* more," Katie said, never one to sugarcoat.

"Spill," Brynn said, swallowing to clear the bitter taste in her mouth.

"Her new video attacks you again," Katie said. "And it's tracking to be her most viewed to date."

"Well, at least she lacks originality," Brynn said darkly. "Should we consider it free advertising?"

"She gets all specific about why you should be cancelled," Katie continued. "Reason number one was that you didn't train in Paris."

"Barf," Brynn replied. "Who cares? They're plants."

"She also said you went big game hunting in Africa," Katie said, biting her lip.

"What?!" Brynn exclaimed, and they both giggled. "I've never even *been* to Africa. Is this, like, a real problem?"

"Some people love fake news," Katie said with a shrug. "I say good riddance." She hopped on the swivel stool and spun herself around. "We don't want followers dumb enough to believe her anyway."

"Well, I made a list of my own," Brynn said, pulling a folded paper from her back pocket and passing it to Katie. "A list of ideas I can borrow. Remember, like Sofia at Homestead suggested? Jessica Southgate might be the worst, but she's clearly doing some things right."

"Number one: oversharing," Katie read. She arched an eyebrow at Brynn.

"I know everything about Jessica," Brynn said. "What she worked through in therapy, what age she had her first kiss, the fact that she doesn't like her stepmother." Brynn tucked a frizzy wave behind her ear. "I never talk about my personal life in my videos. Maybe I should."

Katie narrowed her eyes at Brynn, but continued reading: "Number two: selfies."

Katie stuck out her tongue and mimed sticking a finger down her throat.

"What?!" Brynn asked. "I read that selfies get more than three times the engagement of a regular photo. Most of my Instagram is just clips from my channel. I need more selfies!"

"If you say so," Katie said, scanning the list once more. "Number three: super rare plants?"

"Three words: pink princess philodendron," Brynn said. "Some people follow her just to glimpse plants they could never find in their own towns. If I can follow some leads, track down something super rare, maybe I can catch up."

"I thought she already had one of those things," Katie said.

"That was barely more than a cutting," Brynn said. "I'll find a full size one and then we can propagate it and see them in the store too!" She opened her hands wide and wiggled her fingers. "Ta da! Two birds, one stone."

"Yeah, but how?" Katie asked. "You already drive to the nurseries twice a week."

Brynn could feel the skepticism practically dripping off her best friend.

"I'll find out who unloads the trucks and see if they'll tip me off to anything good," Brynn said. "I'll slip them some cash if I have to."

"I'm having Beanie Babies flashbacks," Katie said with a snort.

"But with much less competition," Brynn said, her voice rising with conviction. "Rare houseplants are popular, but the community isn't huge. Besides, I can have them shipped too! It's not like I used the internet to track down Beanie Babies."

"How are you gonna have time for all of that?" Katie asked. "You hardly have time for videos as it is."

"I'll find the time," Brynn said, trying to keep the frustration from her voice. It's not like Katie had come up with *any* plan other than to stay the course and see what happened.

"You know I'm in your corner," Katie said, albeit a bit reluctantly. "I've followed you this far, haven't I?"

"Great," Brynn said, grinning. She would take what she could get. "So, Operation Mega Plant Influencer starts right now."

"Catchy," Katie said. "Say that five times fast."

"Feel free to come up with a better title," Brynn said, ignoring the sarcasm as she shook the mouse to wake the store computer. "But I got a tip that the garden center on Eastland is restocking Hoya carnosa Compacta at noon. And I can buy online and pick it up."

"I'm guessing that's a good thing?" Katie quipped as she pulled a stack of brightly printed paper from her bag.

"It's a super rare plant, so, yes, it's a very good thing," Brynn said, scrolling the website. "The page is loaded, ten minutes and counting."

"I'm sure if anyone can make it happen, it's you," Katie said, her tone softening as she pulled down some old flyers from the bulletin board and tossed them into the recycling can. "But do you think your viewers really care?"

"I'm not doing it for *my* viewers," Brynn said. "I'm doing it for *more* viewers."

"Gotcha," Katie said, but Brynn could tell she wasn't fully

convinced. "I better finish the upload so we can release it before your noon peak."

Brynn nodded as she glanced at the clock—six minutes to go. She reloaded the page for good measure.

"Um, hi?"

"Oh!" Brynn said, jumping a little as she glanced over the computer toward a gangly teenage boy. She'd been so focused she hadn't heard the door. The boy had his hands shoved in his pockets as he surveyed the store. His eyes were so wide, he looked as if he thought the plants might bite him.

"Sorry," Brynn said, forcing a smile as she eyed her watch. "How can I help you?"

The boy chewed his lip, not answering right away as he eyed the door.

"Would you like help finding a plant?" Brynn prodded.

"I guess," he said as he mustered a shaky smile. "Thanks. I wanted to buy a plant—like, a special plant. But everything is just so...green. And I don't know anything."

There was something so endearing about this pale-faced boy, almost like a nervous baby deer. She wanted to help him. She snuck a peek at the clock—three minutes.

Dang it.

"Well, would you like something easy or a little more challenging?" she asked, forcing her attention back to the boy.

"I guess easy?" he said with a shrug. "It would be bad if it died."

"I can help you make sure that doesn't happen," Brynn said gently. She headed to the round table near the windows as the boy trailed closely behind. "Plants are intimidating to everyone at first, but you're in the right place."

"This is a golden pothos," she said, handing him a small vining plant with green and yellow marbled leaves. "It's fine in most light, it doesn't need much care, and it grows really fast. Plus, it's notoriously hard to kill."

"It's pretty," the boy said, gently fingering a smooth leaf. "Can I buy one, please?"

"Of course!" she said, leading him back to the register, smiling as she noticed some of the color had returned to his face.

She clicked the mouse, and the nursery website filled the screen. She glanced at the computer clock. 12:00. *Crap!*

She kept her face even as she clicked the add-to-cart button. Suddenly, red text appeared below. *We're sorry, that item is no longer available.* Brynn blinked and pressed her lips together as her stomach clenched.

"Are you OK?" the boy asked.

"Sorry, yes, just fine," Brynn said, taking a deep breath and entering the plant name into the store database. She processed the sale and handed him his change. "I'm adding a few care tips and the name of a good fertilizer," she said as she scribbled on a blank sales slip before stapling it to the receipt.

"Thank you," the boy said, looking much lighter. When he smiled, he was actually a pretty cute kid. "Happy holidays."

"You too," she said, feeling the familiar warmth that she always felt when she helped someone buy their first plant. But as the door jangled closed behind the boy, she ran back to the computer and to add the Hoya to her cart once more. No dice.

Katie pushed aside the curtain and rejoined Brynn, a steaming mug of coffee in each hand.

"The video's up," she said as Brynn took a sip. "Figured you needed this as much as I do."

"Yep," Brynn said, sighing as she placed the mug on the counter.

"No rare plant?" Katie said.

Brynn simply shook her head.

"Oh, well," Katie said. "There are always other plants in the forest."

"Thanks, Kate," Brynn said, resting her head on her friend's shoulder. "I don't know what I'd do without you."

"You'd fall apart," Katie said with a grin. "Which is why I'll have to move to California with you. I can't imagine putting up with year-round sunshine and movie stars all over the place, but I'd do it for you."

Brynn laughed. Although it had been less than a year, she could barely remember Twin Falls without Katie. She certainly couldn't picture Los Angeles without her, though at this point she could hardly picture Los Angeles at all.

"Thanks again for letting me hang a flyer," Jordan said, shaking hands with the owner of Sam's Café.

"Always great to see your face," Sam said, following him onto the parkway. "I swear, you look more and more like your mother every time I see you."

"That's what I hear," Jordan said, swallowing a little smile. He secretly loved when people compared him to Marissa. It was hard for him to see when he looked in the mirror, but he had definitely inherited her thick black lashes and chiseled cheekbones.

"Be sure to tell your dad I said hello," Sam said. "Just waiting until Landen gets home on Friday to come get our tree."

"Will do," Jordan said, giving him a little salute as he started down the sidewalk. When he'd first started hanging new flyers for Evergreen Acres early that morning, his nose had quickly gone numb, and his eyes had stung in the brittle dry air. Though the temperature couldn't have risen more than five or so degrees, the winter sun felt delicious as it warmed his face. He laughed as tiny white specs swirled around him, disappearing before they reached the pavement. There was something about snowflakes in the sunlight that felt like pure magic, just like rainbows on a clear day.

As he rounded the corner onto Addison, he saw a crimson red bundle on the sidewalk. As he drew closer, he realized the bundle was moving. It was a woman, kneeling on the sidewalk, leaning on one elbow as she squinted at the bright, snowy sky. As he drew closer to the shop behind her, his breath caught in his throat. She was beautiful, her hair a messy shawl of yellow waves, her pale skin the color of cream. Her cherubic round face was screwed up into a look of fierce determination as she held a wrapped gift under one arm and a phone in the other. Just then a gust of wind surged past, and the woman yelped as her long hair swept across her face. He began to walk around her, resisting the urge to stare at this woman who looked as if she'd stepped out of a painting. He resisted a wild urge to brush away a tiny snowflake he could see melting atop her eyelashes. She lowered her phone, her face reddening as it twisted into a sheepish grimace.

"You need help?" Jordan asked, shoving the stack of flyers under his arm.

"No, I got it!" the woman exclaimed, dusting off her butt as she scrambled to her feet. He kept his eyes on hers, forcing himself not to inspect it for himself. "We just decorated the shop for Christmas, and—" She crinkled her nose as her eyes lifted to his. "I'm sorry, do I know you?"

I think I'd remember you, he thought.

"You don't look familiar to me," he said, managing a non-committal shrug.

"Same," she said, but she continued to study him, her light eyes sparkling in the morning light. He broke their gaze, shoving his hands into his pocket as something electric rushed through his chest.

"Sorry, what was I saying?" she asked, her nose crinkling once more. Man, she was cute.

"Something about Christmas?" Jordan offered.

"Right," she said, glancing from the gift box to her phone. "I was going to post a selfie on Instagram—" She grimaced. "I know how that sounds, but, like, for my store? I guess you saw how well that's going."

Was she nervous?

"Want me to take it for you?" Jordan asked, surprising himself by the offer. What did he know about photography?

"Sure, thanks," she said, smiling with her whole face. "Selfies are seriously overrated."

She passed him her phone and leaned against the storefront window, frantically smoothing her hair before tucking it behind one ear. She grinned, flipping a pointed toe behind her as she playfully dangled the shiny wrapped gift by its ribbon.

Jordan snapped a couple shots, checking them before taking more. Not bad. Though when the subject looked like that and knew how to do that thing with her foot... He swallowed and snapped a few more.

"Whatcha got in there?" Jordan asked as she shifted the gift to the other hand.

"Oh, it's empty," she said, laughing as she shook it. "See? Just decoration."

"Well, that's anti-climactic," he said playfully. "Check those out and see if they look okay." He passed the phone back to her, stiffening as her smooth, icy fingers brushed against his.

As she scrolled through his shots, favoriting a few and nodding in approval at most, he peered in the shop window. Lush, marbled vines twisted around a silver aluminum tree, and in place of a star, a spindly cactus crowned the top. He read the blue sign above the door: Planted in Twin. Jordan had never noticed what had taken the old bakery's place and he wondered how many times he'd walked by without noticing it. Without noticing *her*.

"These will be perfect! Thank you," the woman said, her eyes crinkling ever so slightly at the corners as she stuck out her hand. "I'm Brynn, by the way."

"Jordan," he said, suddenly aware of his calloused hand as her tiny fingers disappeared into his grip. He didn't let go and neither did she.

"Hey, Bee!" a voice called from inside. The door swung open as a green-haired woman popped her head out, and Brynn stepped away just as Jordan crossed his arms tightly across his chest. "Customer on the line with a repotting question and it sounds like Mandarin to me." She glanced up at Jordan with curiosity and a tiny hint of a smile. "Hi there," she said, and Jordan nodded in return.

"I'll be right in," Brynn said, looking everywhere but at Jordan's face as the door closed once more.

"Are you from here?" Jordan asked.

"Born and raised," she said. "You?"

"Yep," he said.

"Did you go to Twin Falls High?"

He shook his head. "Hansen. I live out near the South Hills."

"That's way out there," she said with a small smile. She pointed to the papers under his arm. "What's that?"

"Oh!" Jordan said, remembering the flyers. "I have a local business and I've been hanging some new flyers around Twin."

"You should come inside," Brynn said as she held open the door. "We've got a bulletin board."

Jordan followed, doing his best to pretend he wasn't thrilled for even a few more minutes in her presence.

Brynn felt the store's familiar muggy air graze her cheeks as she snuck a glance over her shoulder. Was Jordan from Twin Falls? He looked around the same age as her, but she definitely would have remembered any guy who looked like that. It might be a cliché, but this man gave new meaning to tall, dark, and handsome. Not to mention, even his sherpa-lined trucker jacket couldn't hide the sharp lines of his muscular body. She blinked as he caught her eye and let out a low whistle.

"I hardly recognize this place," Jordan said, nodding in obvious approval as he rubbed a heart-shaped leaf between two fingers.

"Thanks," Brynn said, a shiver running down her spine as she remembered the feel of that coarse hand. "We're coming up on our first anniversary."

"Just beautiful," he said, meeting her eyes.

OK, wow.

He obviously meant the store, but her body didn't get the memo as her heartbeat quickened. It was impossible to look away from those dark, intense eyes.

"Are you a plant person?" she asked, rearranging her expression into something she hoped came off neutral.

He chuckled. "You could say that."

"You can hang your flyer over there," she said, pointing to the corkboard. "If you can't find a pin, let me know. I'm gonna take that call really quick."

"Thanks, Brynn," he said, heading for the bulletin board.

She liked the way her name sounded coming from his mouth, almost breathy. She gave him a crisp nod as she headed into the back room, passing a furiously typing Katie on the couch. She wondered if he would wait and couldn't help hoping he would. She sat on top of the desk, shoving his stubbled jaw from her mind as she pressed the handset to her ear.

Brynn raised her voice after Lorena, an elderly regular who was more than a little hard of hearing, told her the roots of her prayer plant had creeped through the pot's drainage holes. As quickly as she could, Brynn suggested she move the Maranta to a bigger pot and had Lorena write down her favorite homemade potting mix. Once she wrapped up the call, she rushed toward the front, slowing her breath and her steps as she pushed past the curtain.

A surge of disappointment flooded her body as she quickly scanned the empty shop. Did she expect him to hang around? She saw movement out of the corner of her eye and suddenly, there he was, kneeling beside a table, frantically scraping the floor into something black. What was he doing? As she drew closer, one hand flew to her mouth as she saw him shove an African mask plant into a half-filled nursery pot, its bare roots sticking precariously over the top.

"What are you doing!?" she gasped as he turned to face her, his eyes wide against his crimson face. "That's the plant for my next video!"

"I'm sorry!" he said, two lines appearing between his eyebrows as he shook a fistful of dirt onto the roots. "I'll fix it."

Oh, no, this was bad. This was really, really bad. It had taken Brynn weeks to track down an affordable African mask, and when she finally had, she'd found it leggy and covered in fungus gnats. Slowly and slightly impatiently, she'd quarantined it and cultivated it into a perfect specimen. She'd been teasing the final reveal for months on her channel, eager to show off her success. She clutched her chest, feeling nauseous as she realized she had exactly zero footage of the plant's final result.

"I'm sure it will bounce back," Jordan said, his hand shaky as he patted the soil around the base of the plant.

"Bounce back?" Brynn repeated, almost laughing. "Do you know what it says when you Google how to keep an African mask alive?" Her voice started to shake as he shook his head and set the pot on the table beside them. "It says—and I'm not making this up—you can't. Unless you live in an actual jungle, it is *not possible*. And yet I did!" She swiped at her face, too upset to be embarrassed as her eyes stung with tears.

"I'll buy it, I'm so sorry," Jordan said, sweat beading his furrowed brow. "I watered it, and I accidentally bumped it when I turned to water that little tree beside it."

"You *what*?" Brynn said, suddenly noticing Jordan had her small watering can clutched defensively against his chest. "Why would you that?!"

"Because it's dry," Jordan said, his eyes darting around the store as if to look for help. Long gone was his lingering gaze from minutes before.

"Where did you get the water?" she demanded, afraid of the answer.

"From the sink," he said with a shrug. Brynn was almost too upset to notice the way he chewed on his full lips as he watched her with confusion. Almost.

"The sink?!" she repeated, defeat in her voice. "Do you have any idea—that's an *Alocasia polly*, you can't just use *sink* water!"

"I'm, I—it's fine," Jordan sputtered, taking a step away from her. "I know a thing or two about plants."

"Oh yeah?" Brynn said, no longer bothering to dampen the hysteria in her voice. "Well, this building has a water softener, which means you just poured a ton of sodium into two of my most high-maintenance plants." His eyes opened so wide that his lashes grazed his eyebrows as his mouth opened and closed as if to form an argument. "By the way," Brynn continued. "That 'little tree' is a fiddle leaf, which is also on its way to the compost now."

"From one time?" Jordan asked, jerking his fingers through his thick black curls.

"Probably!" Brynn shouted, throwing her arms out wide.

"I didn't know!" Jordan shouted back, his eyes darkening as he began to stand his ground. "I said I'm sorry, what else do you want from me?"

"Why would you just water someone's plants without asking?" Brynn said, ignoring his question as her pulse pounded in her ears. "Who would do something so stupid and selfish?"

"Wow, um, OK," Jordan said, his face stony as he pulled his gloves from his pocket and slipped them on. "Trust me, I won't make that mistake again." He rubbed his thumb and forefinger down either side of his mouth, throwing her an angry stare that Brynn could tell meant he had a lot more choice words he'd like to share. But instead of arguing with her or pleading for forgiveness, he beelined for the door. She watched him through the window as he stomped away through the flurries, now falling in fat, shimmering flakes. As the bell jingled simultaneously with the slamming door, Brynn bit her cheek. "Yeah, well, screw you too!" she shouted at the empty sidewalk.

"Was that a customer?!" Katie asked as she rushed past the curtain doors. "I couldn't' tell if I should expect to find you covered in blood or in the midst of a make-out session."

"Definitely not a customer," Brynn said through clenched teeth. "Just a huge jerk."

"If you say so," Katie said, eyeing her cautiously. "Do you care if we drive separately tomorrow? I have some errands to run."

"What's tomorrow?" Brynn asked, grateful for the change in subject as she angrily shoved her hair into a ponytail.

"The pancake breakfast," Katie said. "Remember? You're the one who volunteered us."

"Oh right, at the fire station," Brynn said, her heart rate slowing a little as she glanced at the wall calendar behind the counter. "I totally forgot. I couldn't say no to Mr. Danvers considering all he buys for the senior center."

"Plus, free pancakes," Katie said with a glint in her eyes.

"Plus, free pancakes," Brynn agreed, laughing a little despite her sour mood.

Once Katie left, Brynn plopped down on the thrifted rattan bench that faced the door, a ribcage-quivering sigh escaping her lips. She had never felt like such an idiot.

First off, she'd made a fool of herself, fawning over Jordan like a lovesick teenage girl. Then, she'd practically lost her mind when he dumped one plant and ruined another. Humiliation flushed her body as she remembered the hot tears that had filled her eyes.

Still, who acted like that? And after she'd told him what he'd done, he stormed out. She hadn't told him to leave, he'd ran away from her like a little wimp. And that's when it all became crystal clear: any guy that hot had to be entitled and way too into himself. She should have seen it coming.

The longer she sat, the more her breathing slowed and the storm clouds in her head began to part. No customers came. People must be staying in because of the weather, she reassured herself. A bitter wave of vague regret filled her mind, followed by a flash of Jordan's jaw clenched as he rubbed one hand in frustration against his sun-freckled neck.

She pressed her hands to her thighs and stood, shaking her head as if to clear his face from her mind. She wouldn't spend one more minute thinking about that man. Not then, not ever.

Her pocket vibrated and she could still feel the heat on her neck as she pulled out her phone, her eyes widening at the sight of Caleb's name. She took a deep breath and unlocked it, finding the message she'd been both longing for and dreading.

Hey, I'd love to catch up. Are you free tonight?

Saying yes would be a terrible idea. For months, she'd been mentally preparing herself for a moment like this, preparing the exact words she would use to shut him down. She should call Katie, who would remind her what an ass Caleb had been to her at the end. But she couldn't deny that she really, really missed him. After all, he said he just wanted to catch up. How bad could it possibly be?

SIX

"Earth to Jordan!"

Jordan blinked as Charlie waved him forward, already nearly ten feet in front of him as the line moved forward.

"Sorry," he mumbled, closing the gap as a woman behind him scoffed loudly.

"What's on your mind, Bubba?" Charlie asked, raising an eyebrow.

"I didn't sleep well last night," Jordan said. "Stayed up late running numbers."

Though finances were only part of what had kept him wide awake until nearly four, Charlie nodded and turned back to his conversation with the woman in front of them. Jordan couldn't remember her name, but he recognized her as a former volunteer firefighter from around the same time as Charlie. Avoiding the annoyed woman behind him, Jordan let his mind wander once more.

He couldn't stop playing back that scene at Planted in Twin. One minute, Brynn had been this charismatic professional that he couldn't keep his eyes off of, the next she had turned into this ridiculously irrational monster. Granted, he shouldn't have watered her plant without asking and it made sense she'd be upset that he dropped her plant. Jordan was typically a quiet guy, and he could count on one hand the times in his adult life he'd raised his voice, but then again, he couldn't remember ever having that kind of fury unleashed on him. Well, he was glad he'd seen her true colors before asking for her number.

"Where's your shirt?" the old guy at the firehouse door said to Charlie when they reached the front of the line.

"Still fits!" Charlie said with a grin, unzipping his cotton duck jacket to reveal a tight *Twin Falls Volunteer Firefighter* sweatshirt. Jordan chuckled as he shoved some bills into the donation bucket.

Hand drawn signs led them to the firehouse cafeteria and over half of the banquet tables were already filled. The mouth-watering smells of bacon and butter greeted them as they joined the long line for the buffet.

"It feels good to give back to my community this time of year," an all too familiar voice trilled from past the line and Jordan's stomach dropped. There she was, dressed in a candy cane covered apron, a spatula in one hand as she smirked with those perfectly red lips. Brynn. A volunteer in a hairnet was filming her on a cell phone while throwing her an encouraging thumbs up.

"Gross," Jordan muttered to himself. Of course, a woman like her would blast any kind of charitable work all over the Internet. As she continued on, he tuned her out, staring down at his scuffed boots as the line inched forward.

"You know her?" Charlie asked, lifting one brow as Jordan met his eyes.

"Nope," Jordan said. "And I don't want to."

"Right," Charlie said, narrowing those jolly eyes before turning to wave at some more of his old friends.

"You ever miss it?" Jordan asked as a firefighter delivered orange juices and coffee to a young family, posing for a photo with the two children before carrying his empty tray to the refill station.

"Nah," Charlie said, following his gaze. "I loved it, but just thinking about it now makes me tired. It's a young person's job, all those sleepless nights."

"I remember sniffing you ever time you came home from a call to see if I could smell smoke," Jordan said. Back when he'd thought all firefighters did was fight actual fires.

"I remember that too," Charlie said, laughing. "It didn't matter whether it was a kitten up a tree or what." He nodded and his gaze grew thoughtful. "You know, the farmer's got a lot of enemies between pests, drought, and disease. But nothing threatens our livelihood quite like fire. There's no better friend to us than a firefighter. Remember that."

Before Jordan could respond, Charlie gripped his arm and gave him a pointed look.

"Morning, Russell," Charlie said stiffly as Jordan turned to find the overly perfumed investor, his overly waxed eyebrows raised over a smug smile.

"Didn't expect to find my two favorite farmers here this morning," Sutkamp said, his grin revealing teeth so perfectly rectangular they had to be fake.

"Not today, Sutkamp," Jordan said, doing his best to hide his utter loathing from his voice. Though he wanted nothing more than to punch that pompous face, all he needed was the whole town to realize Evergreen Acres was in trouble.

"Whoa, whoa, whoa," Sutkamp said with a hollow laugh, raising his hands in the air as if being attacked. "I just wanted to come by and offer a truce."

"Uh huh," Charlie said flatly.

"I'm not as heartless as you might think," Sutkamp said, pressing a palm to his chest. "I was thinking it over and I'd love to offer you each a two-bedroom home in my new oasis free of charge when the time comes. I know you're a bit sentimental when it comes to the old homestead."

"Thanks, but no thanks," Jordan said through gritted teeth. "And if you don't stop harassing us, I'm going to get a lawyer."

"Tsk, tsk," Sutkamp said, pronouncing the actual words like the slime bag he was. "No need to get heated. I was just on my way out."

He stuck out his hand, a ruby ring glittering on his pointer finger, but Jordan pointedly turned away.

"I hate that guy," Jordan said, digging his fingernails into his palms once Sutkamp had finally left.

"Just be glad you don't have to live inside his lonely head," Charlie said with a chuckle, but Jordan could tell from his furrowed brow that Sutkamp had ruffled him more than he was letting on.

As they finally neared the front of the line, Jordan scanned the overflowing banquet tables. The first table was filled with pastries and Jordan recognized the stocky man restocking scones as the owner of Earlybird Espresso. Henry was what most people referred to negatively as "a Californian," the name for anyone who moved from a big city to Twin Falls. Some folks thought people like Henry were changing the town for the worst, but Jordan loved stopping at his shop for a black coffee and a corny joke.

The next table was lined with spatula-wielding volunteers Jordan didn't know, serving scrambled egg, sausage, and bacon. Locals showed up first to support the fire department, but they also came for a great meal. Jordan made a mental note to add more money to the donation bucket on their way out.

The line moved forward as the last table came into view, revealing Brynn and her coworker from the store. Great. So much for his plans to avoid her, though the spatula she'd been wielding in her obnoxious influencer mode should have been a clue.

Jordan registered someone waving from the periphery of his vision. As he turned, Mayor Tommy Lopez rushed toward them. A gregarious man in his late fifties, Lopez had been in office for as long as Jordan could remember.

"The Damon men!" Mayor Lopez exclaimed. "So good to see you."

"Likewise," Charlie replied as they all shook hands.

"I've already been through the line twice," the mayor said, keeping pace with them as the line moved. "A little tip? Ask for the blueberry syrup. Hattie Elroy made it herself."

"Will do," Jordan said. "Thanks, sir."

"Listen, fellas," Mayor Lopez said, lowering his voice confidentially as he stepped closer. "I saw Russell Sutkamp over here. He's been very...*vocal* about the financial situation at Evergreen Acres."

"I'm sure he has," Jordan muttered. So much for keeping it quiet.

"I wouldn't put much stock in Russell Sutkamp," Charlie said darkly.

"Oh, trust me, I don't," the mayor replied, waving a hand dismissively. "And it's certainly none of my business. But I wanted you to know I'm rooting hard for you."

"Thanks, Mayor," Jordan said, swallowing the knot in his throat. "That means a lot."

"Family businesses are what built this town and gave it a heart," the mayor said, scanning the crowd of locals. "I was hoping we could talk in more detail. Would one of you be willing stop by next week?"

"We'd be honored, sir," Jordan said. It wasn't cash, but having Mayor Lopez on their side gave him hope.

"Very good," the mayor said, backing away toward a table of senior citizens that had been trying to wave him over. "Call Beth and she'll set you up."

"Why don't you grab seats," Jordan said to Charlie as they neared the front of the line. "Let me guess...three pancakes, syrup on the side, extra sausage?"

"It's like you're my son or something," Charlie said, chortling at his own joke as he headed off. "Thanks, Bubba."

Jordan grabbed two Styrofoam plates and plastic utensil sets. He dropped a cheese Danish onto Charlie's plate, but his own appetite wasn't what it had been twenty minutes earlier.

Jordan felt panic ripple through his chest as he tossed a bagel on his plate. How could they make up the profits they needed this month? And if they managed to figure it out, what about next year? It was going to take a lot more than flyers if Evergreen Acres was going to make it to another Christmas.

"Mom, that's the plant lady!" a little boy whispered as Brynn slid two strips of bacon onto his plate.

"Derek! Manners!" the woman exclaimed as Brynn laughed. "I am so sorry."

"It's fine," Brynn insisted. "I like it. Come to the store and see me soon, okay?"

The boy nodded, looking relieved to avoid his mother's wrath as they shuffled further down the line.

Brynn's eyes felt heavy and swollen. She'd awoken in the middle of the night and hadn't fallen back to sleep until the first light was streaming through her linen curtains. When she'd finally crawled out of bed, all she could think about was the quickest and most effective way to inject caffeine directly into her body.

Even so, she'd been having fun ever since she clocked in for her shift. Everyone seemed to be in the holiday mood, even the firefighters who had just ended their rotations and would be heading to sleep after they cleaned their plates. Brynn had run into several customers already and had been introduced to countless locals promising to visit the shop. Not to mention, Katie had filmed some great content to add to the next video. Just as Brynn was brainstorming how to tie volunteer work to community gardens, Katie elbowed her in the ribs. Hard.

"Hey!" Brynn scolded, shooting her a look.

Katie looked right past her and subtly shook her head.

As Brynn followed her stare and her mouth fell open, snapping closed as Jordan sauntered to her station, his expression perfectly neutral.

"Well, look who it is," Brynn said evenly, her grip tightening on her set of tongs.

"Morning," Jordan replied gruffly as he nodded politely to Katie.

"Bacon?" Brynn asked, flashing a grin that reached nowhere near her eyes.

"Please," Jordan said, avoiding her start as he extended both plates.

"Eating for two?" Brynn quipped as she placed three strips on each plate. Katie snickered as Jordan blinked blankly at her.

"Listen," Brynn began. "About yesterday...I've been under a bit of stress lately, and—"

"Don't mention it," Jordan interrupted, turning to Katie and sticking both plates in front of him. "Extra sausage on this one, please."

"It's just that some plants are like people," Brynn continued, tossing some bacon onto the plate of the little old lady behind Jordan. "They can be really temperamental, and you can't just—"

"I said it's *fine*," Jordan said tightly, finally meeting her glare with his steely eyes.

Brynn's cheeks burned. She said nothing more as she plopped bacon onto one plate after another, and Jordan continued well out of earshot. She watched him fill a cup with syrup before he disappeared into the crowd. After the last 24 hours, she was about ready to give up.

"I'm surprised you guys didn't start making out right here on top of the sausage," Katie said, flashing Brynn a sly smile.

"That guy is the worst," Brynn muttered, scraping the last slices of bacon from her container into a full one that a volunteer she recognized from her mom's church shoved in front of her.

"So, you want me to believe he's not the reason you're still wearing the same dress as yesterday," Katie asked, pursing her lips as she skeptically narrowed her eyes at Brynn.

"What?!" Brynn exclaimed. "Absolutely not." She barely knew that guy. Still, she didn't have the emotional energy to fill Katie in on her unexpected night with Caleb just yet.

Last night had not gone as planned and Brynn was as much to blame as Caleb. What started as a cordial drink at Koto Brewing had turned into a night cap at his place. Which had turned into something that made Brynn's skin burn with electricity as she played back every sweaty moment. The sky was beginning to glow as she finally drifted off in Caleb's arms, his words of atonement and promises to change following her into a dreamless sleep. She had a lot to figure out before she could say any of that out loud.

"I'll be back," she said to Katie as she lifted an empty platter and headed to the kitchen. She averted her gaze as she passed Jordan, who was sitting at a table surrounded by several white-haired men, all laughing and slapping each other on the backs as they hooted like a bunch of old owls.

What a fake, she thought as Jordan laughed along with them.

"Perfect timing," Katie said when she returned to the buffet.

"I try," Brynn said, relieved to see only one familiar person in line before them.

"Morning, ladies!" Mr. Danvers said, his rheumy eyes twinkling as he reached their station. "Thanks so much for coming." The president of the Twin Falls Rotary Club stuck out his plate for bacon as he gave them a conspiratorial wink. "And feel free to take home as much food as you want."

"Thanks, we love free food," Katie said, and Brynn nodded enthusiastically. They had no shame when it came to a good meal.

"Well, guess I'll strike while the iron's hot," Mr. Danvers said, wiping a stray crumb from his wrinkled cheek. "Ever been to Donuts with Rudolph?"

"I haven't," Brynn said as Katie also shook her head. "But it's in the square, right? I've seen photos on the Twin Facebook page."

"Yep, after church on Christmas morning," Mr. Danvers said. "We could really use some extra hands. We're hoping it becomes as popular as the Festival of Lights. This year, we're raising money to build a garden for the senior center."

"Gardens are my love language," Brynn said, plopping an extra slice of bacon on his plate. "Count us in."

Katie subtly elbowed Brynn.

What? Brynn mouthed, but Katie just forced a smile.

"What was that about?" Brynn asked when Mr. Danvers had headed to a nearby table.

"The Homestead parade is on Christmas morning," Katie hissed.

"Oh, that's right," Brynn said. What was with so much planned on Christmas day? Most years, she never made it out of her pajamas after opening gifts. She considered for a moment, then shrugged. "Homestead is still a huge maybe. If I get the show, we'll ditch the donuts. They've done fine without us every other year. Honestly, it's a problem I'd love to have."

Katie pursed her lips as if she wanted to say more, but instead shoved a piece of bacon into her mouth.

As Brynn piled a few slices into a Styrofoam container, her mind played back the flood of events over the last couple days. From the phone call with Homestead's VP to Jessica's Brynn-bashing videos; from the ugly confrontation with Jordan, to seeing Caleb for the first since their breakup.

Caleb.

She swallowed as she remembered his fingers skimming her bare thigh as he whispered into her neck how much he'd missed her touch. How much he wanted a chance to make things right. She needed air and she needed it now.

As she slid plastic utensils into the container while managing to keep her expression relatively steady, her phone vibrated from her purse beneath the table. She glanced at the screen, gasped, and hurried to show Katie, who was stacking leftover muffins into grease-stained bakery boxes.

"Katie, look!" Brynn said, holding up her phone. "Grantway Market is going to have Monstera Albos tomorrow morning! I can't believe it! I've never seen any plant for sale in a supermarket for more than forty bucks!"

"Monsteras are the ones with the finger-shaped leaves, right?" Katie asked, tucking a blueberry muffin into her own container. "But don't you already carry those at the store?"

"Those are *regular* Monsteras," Brynn said, her voice getting higher in pitch by the second. "Albos are like, the rarest, trendiest plants out there. Kinda like the PPP, people will spend thousands for one plant!"

"What's a PPP?" Katie said, shaking her head impatiently as they carried the full pastry boxes toward the kitchen.

"Pink princess philodendron, remember? Like the one Jessica had?" Brynn said as they passed several volunteers cleaning up the rest of the buffet. Good thing she'd already made a doggy bag.

"Right, PPP," Katie said with a chuckle as they handed off the boxes and returned their aprons. "People are crazy. So, what, you could use it to grow more to sell?"

"In theory," Brynn said quickly. "But more importantly, we could show it off in a video! Jessica Southgate wouldn't know what hit her. This plant could single-handedly deliver me the show!"

Brynn looked at Katie who was studying her with a hesitant look.

"What?"

"I just- well, what Sofia said? They're looking at other things besides viewers. Your tone, your message—"

"What's your point, Kate?" Brynn interrupted as they crossed the emptying cafeteria and grabbed their purses. "That I should just sit around and wait for them to make a decision?"

"No, Bee, that's not my point," Katie said, gripping Brynn's arm to stop her. "But aren't you supposed to be decorating your mom's house with everyone tonight?"

"I mean, yeah, but I just won't stay late," Brynn said. "What does that matter?"

"I just don't want you to lose sight of what makes you...well, *you*, that's all. I don't think people love your show or your shop because of how fancy and impressive you are."

"Yeah, I know all that," Brynn said distractedly, scrolling her phone. "I guess it's part of a special holiday promotion..." She read the smaller print at the bottom. "Grantway will also have TV's, the hottest toys..." Brynn couldn't remember seeing Grantway's ads for Black Friday, but this looked like it could be really big. Which also meant a really big line.

Katie grunted a non-committal reply. Brynn didn't have time to make her understand, but Katie would see soon enough when that plant went viral for them.

"Would you mind wrapping up here?" Brynn asked, her eyes still on her phone. "I need to make a call."

"I guess so," Katie said, and Brynn couldn't miss the tightness in her tone.

"Thanks," Brynn said, flashing her a grateful smile as she pulled her coat from beneath the table and grabbed her carryout container. "I'll meet you at the store."

Once in her car, Brynn set her phone in its holder as she slammed the door closed against the biting wind. She quickly dialed as she blasted the not-yet-warm heat, blowing on her hands as loud ringing filled the car.

"Hi, can I speak to the nursery department, please?" Brynn asked as soon as someone picked up.

An instrumental version of "Silent Night" played for only a few seconds before she heard a click. "Grantway Market, garden department, this is Jon."

"Hi, Jon!" Brynn exclaimed, intentional flirtation on every word. "How's your December going so far?"

"Fine," Jon replied without taking the bait.

"Listen," she said, laying it on even thicker. "I heard you're going to have some new plants tomorrow?"

"Yes, ma'am, doors open at 6:00 a.m.," he replied in a curt tone. Okay, he clearly wasn't going to be charmed by her.

"Ooh, thank you for that," Brynn said, even though she'd already read the start time in the ad. "And in your expert experience, what's the best way to make sure I get one of those plants?"

"Well, last year, people started lining up at about five," he said. "Though that's no guarantee."

Oh, that wasn't awful, maybe just a little cold at that hour.

"So maybe 4:30 in the morning would give me an even better chance?" Brynn asked.

"Not morning, *night*," Jon clarified. "Tonight at five."

Brynn's eyes widened. People would sleep outside in this cold just for a good deal?

"Is there anything else I can help you with?" Jon asked, impatience creeping into his professional tone.

"I sure hope so," Brynn said. "I have an important...thing tonight and I'm seriously so desperate to get this one plant. Is there any way you'd consider setting something aside for me? Just one houseplant, something I really want to buy for my grandma?"

Brynn sent up a silent vow that she'd propagate one for Gram first.

"Are you talking about the Monstera Albo?" Jon asked, his voice every bit as bored as before.

"Yes!" Brynn exclaimed. "How did you know?"

"Fifteen hundred."

"I'm sorry?" Brynn asked.

"I will save it for you for fifteen hundred," he repeated.

"But I thought it was going for regular prices, like twenty bucks!" Brynn protested.

"It is," Jon replied. "At 6:00 a.m. tomorrow. You want me to make sure *you* get it, then the price is fifteen hundred."

"But it's just a plant!"

"I work in plants, ma'am," Jon said. "I know what that thing is worth, but I'd get fired if I bought it myself."

"You'd get fired if they knew you were extorting customers!" Brynn retorted.

"And who is going to tell them?" he asked. "You?"

"This is ridiculous!" Brynn sputtered.

"This is business, ma'am," he said. Brynn could imagine his smug self-satisfied smile on the other end of the line.

"Forget it," Brynn said coldly. "Thanks for nothing."

She hung up before he could respond. Now what?

She couldn't skip out on decorating. It was the one thing she never missed, and she'd promised. Anyway, her grandparents were mostly just there for moral support while Brynn, her mom, and her brother did the actual labor. They needed her. Not to mention, skipping tonight would be all the proof her mom needed that Brynn had lost control of her work life. She'd never hear the end of the nagging.

But then again, it was a *Monstera Albo*.

Think, Brynn.

She closed her eyes, rubbed the bridge of her nose before letting out a breath she didn't realize she'd been holding. Flurries swirled down from the gray sky, disappearing into droplets as they landed on the warm hood. She said a silent prayer that she could figure this out. At this point, prayer was the only shot she had.

SEVEN

The hollow chill was already seeping through Brynn's jacket as she sipped the last of her now-cold oat milk latte. As the sun tucked behind the giant square building, she slammed her car door closed with her hip and swung a backpack onto her shoulder. She slipped on knit gloves she'd picked up at the gas station before tugging a folding chair and sleeping bag she hoped she wouldn't need from the trunk.

She crossed the massive parking lot and, as she peeked over her overstuffed arms, her heart sank. The line was already at least thirty people deep. Most of them were probably there for the PlayStations and televisions, but she walked faster nonetheless. Regular customers were streaming in and out of Grantway Market's automatic doors as an orange-vested man with a walkie-talkie patrolled the area.

"Hi," Brynn said breathlessly as she approached him. "Where's the line for plants?"

"One line," he barked, looking over her head at a group of teenagers circling the parking lot on their bikes.

"The end's back there, dear," a grandmotherly woman offered from front of the line, where she was perched on a camping chair with knitting needles and a half-finished blanket.

"Got it, thank you," Brynn said, forcing a smile. Brynn's grin slipped into a grimace as a group of at least ten people join the end of the queue before she could reach it. This was going to make her plan that much more complicated.

She sighed, glancing at her watch as she hurried to beat a few others approaching the line from the parking lot, joining the line seconds before them. She tried to avoid staring at the person behind her, but she did her best to nonchalantly size her up. She was a short woman shaped like a square, her frizzy, brown hair in a thin ponytail atop her head. Did she look nice? Brynn couldn't tell.

In front of her, a group of Budweiser-wielding men in sports jerseys sat in a circle, laughing at something the bald one had said as they slapped each other on their backs. Maybe she'd have better luck there.

It was just after 5 and her toes were already tingling. She peered through the store window, watching a young mother and a chubby-cheeked toddler laughing hysterically as they looked through the cake catalog in the bakery department. Brynn blinked, her brain feeling as numb as her feet.

She hadn't figured out some magic solution to be in two places at once or hired a strong neighbor to hang lights in her absence. She was hoping for the kindness of her neighbors in line. Or if that didn't work, their desire to make a hundred bucks.

"Excuse me," she said to the burly man nearest her, who turned and narrowed his eyes suspiciously.

"Hi!" she said.

"Can I help you, lady?" he said, annoyance on his face as his friends crowded over a phone to watch some TikTok video.

"I sure hope so!" she said, smiling as she flipped her hair over one shoulder. The man just sighed and crossed his arms. Dang, her feminine charms sure didn't seem to be getting her very far today.

"Listen, I'll make this quick," Brynn said urgently as the man's buddies began to listen to their conversation. "I have to go see my mom. Is there any chance you'd hold my spot in line? Just for a few hours?"

He stroked his beard, looking uncertain as he peeked back at his buddies who shrugged. He hesitated and before he could speak, Brynn slipped a hundred-dollar bill from her pocket.

"Would this help?" she asked. "As a thank you for the hassle?"

"Hell, yeah!" he said, taking the bill from her and pocketing it. "Your spot is safe with me."

Yes! Finally, something was going her way.

Brynn grinned. "Thank you so—"

"No holding spots!" a gravelly voice croaked. She turned to find the squat woman who'd joined the line behind her, wagging her e-reader at them. "That's against the rules!"

"Aw, come on, ma'am," the man said, clearly on Brynn's side now that he was a Franklin wealthier than he'd been five minutes earlier. "It don't change anything for you or anybody else."

"It's against the rules!" she repeated, catching the eye of the security guard and waving him over. "This woman is trying to bribe people to let her cut!"

"That's not true!" Brynn protested. "I was just asking them to hold my place in line for a while, but this is my spot!"

The guard studied her as if she was one of the whooping teenagers still popping wheelies between the rows of parked cars.

"You step out of line, you're out of the line," he said coolly, planting a meaty fist on each hip.

"What?!" Brynn cried, searching for something, anything, to say. "But what if I need to pee?!"

He eyed her.

"No holding spots," he said before turning back to glare at the teens.

"Sorry, lady," the bearded man said, passing the cash back to her before turning back to his friends. Brynn shot an angry stare over her shoulder, but the woman behind her was already settled back into her chair, her face illuminated by her Kindle's white light.

Brynn stomped her foot in irritation as she tapped out a quick text to her mom. She knew she should call, but she was afraid Greta would hear the lie in her voice. A little niggling voice in her head scolded her for being a coward, but she had made up her mind. She needed that plant. She could make amends later.

Brynn craned her neck but could no longer see the line's end. *At least I got here when I did,* she thought, shivering as she unfolded her jacket's fuzzy collar to cover her bare neck.

She pulled out her chair, struggling to connect the little metal poles with her gloved fingers. As her phone vibrated against her stomach, she tossed the chair to the sidewalk in frustration, ignoring the loud scoff from the woman behind her. She pulled the phone from her coat pocket and tapped the screen. It was Greta: *How are you feeling? Want some soup delivered?*

Brynn swallowed, feeling suddenly light-headed. She pressed the phone's side button and said, "Text Mom."

"What do you want to say to Mom?" Siri trilled.

"I'm OK, thanks," Brynn said as the words appeared on the

screen. "It's probably just a cold. If you guys don't get finished with the lights tonight, I'll come help when I feel better."

She heard a snort from behind her.

"What?!" Brynn snapped, her blood boiling as she faced the Kindle-reading tattletale.

The woman said nothing, just rolled her eyes before staring back at her reading.

Brynn reluctantly slipped off her gloves and snapped the chair pieces into place. She sat, tugging out her sleeping bag and burying herself beneath its musty scent. She probably hadn't used it since Girl Scout camp circa the 2010s. She closed her eyes, determined to shut out the chaos around her. An image filled her mind's eye, Greta in only a robe as she climbed the shaky metal ladder, no one around to stabilize it from the ground. Brynn snapped her eyes open, her heart thudding. She swiped her phone and opened Instagram, not even registering the images as her bare thumb scrolled. This was clearly going to be a long night.

Brynn awoke to the sound of a hacking cough, her left hip throbbing in protest as she sat up. She yawned as the man two feet behind her cleared his throat in a guttural, mucous-filled bark, while the woman beside him blew her nose continuously into a wadded tissue. *Well, that's just great,* she thought. *Maybe my punishment for being a big fat liar would be to catch something worse than a pretend cold.*

Thankfully, the first glow of morning light was slowly fading the sky to a steely gray. She glanced at her watch and was relieved to see it was almost time for Grantway to open. All around her, people were packing up chairs and whispering excitedly.

Brynn rolled her stiff shoulders forward, then back. She was exhausted. Not only did the plague-filled couple talk at full volume until nearly two, but the frigid air that had arrived around midnight was barely muted by her thin sleeping bag.

When Brynn had finally drifted off, the jersey-clad men in front of her started streaming a Boise State game on their phones. Roars of disappointment, "Booyahs!" and expletives of every flavor had reverberated through the night, rattling Brynn over and over from a shallow dreamless sleep. Just as she silently swore to punch the next person who belched or crunched a can under their feet, she'd finally dozed off for good.

At least the night was finally over. During her sleepless hours, Brynn had come up with a plan: once she reached the door, Brynn would wiggle through the crowd in front of her and beeline for the nursery department. Most of them were at least twice her age and she'd seen more than one of them using a cane. She gulped slushie water from her slightly frozen bottle, popped a cube of gum, and tied her wild hair into a topknot.

Her heart began to thunder in anticipation as she repacked her sleeping bag and chair, tucking them out of sight behind a green metal trash bin. Nothing was slowing her down. As she tightened the straps on her backpack, a man emerged above the crowd, where he perched on a stepladder a bullhorn in hand.

"Good morning, friends and neighbors!" his voice boomed over their heads. "Welcome to the third annual Grantway Christmas Flash Sale!"

Some of the crowd cheered loudly, while most clapped sleepily.

"When we open these doors, you'll find our best deals of the entire year!" he shouted once they'd settled. Brynn's chest tightened as she eyed the front doors.

"Annnnnd—three, two, one—ho, ho, ho, happy shopping!" the voice boomed. As the doors flew open, the line began to form a frantic mob that in no way resembled the organized row of seconds before. It looked like every news segment of Black Friday footage Brynn had ever seen, but at least no one was pushing.

After the longest thirty seconds of her life, Brynn finally stepped into the brightly lit store. She hadn't been to Grantway in ages, so she scanned the ceiling for department signs. She thought the plants were to her right, but she didn't have time to take chances. Why didn't she try to get a layout of the store last night? She mentally kicked herself before rushing over to an employee beside a display of half-price blenders.

"Excuse me, where's the nursery department?" Brynn shouted over the shouts and squeals and the Christmas music that spilled out from two giant speakers on either side of the doors.

"Starts on aisle 42F," he said, pointing toward the back of the store. Brynn began to run, wedging her way through the instant mosh pit that had formed in the electronics department, spinning to avoid a crowd that was waiting to enter a raffle for some kind of cruise. Brynn couldn't believe her luck as she skidded to a stop next to 42F. This part of the store was almost empty.

But wait—

She frantically darted into the aisle. There were no plants, not even soil, just wet wipes and diapers. She ran to the next aisle but found only endless rows of colorful baby food jars and canisters of infant formula.

Oh no. No, no, no.

The guy thought she meant a *baby* nursery, not a plant nursery! She cursed, suddenly spotting a giant wall of windows on the other side of the store that looked like it opened to the outside. That had to be it. She ran, cutting a diagonal line through the jewelry department, then weaving around rack after rack of discounted sweaters and pajamas. As she burst out of the book aisle, she spotted the sign ahead: *Garden.*

As Brynn continued on, speeding past the hardware department, her foot caught on something soft, and she went flying. Her knees hit the linoleum with a sickening smack, catching herself with her hands as a sharp pain shot through her entire upper body. As she climbed to her feet, she tried to orient herself, searching the ceiling for the sign once more.

Suddenly, she heard a soft hiccupping sob from behind her. She turned and found a tiny girl curled into a ball, an overturned container of popcorn all around her. That's how Brynn tripped. On the girl. She must have been sitting on the endcap when Brynn rounded the aisle.

"I'm so sorry, honey!" Brynn exclaimed as she pulled the girl to a seat, shoving the empty popcorn tub into her hands. The girl continued to wail, scooting away from Brynn, who whipped her head in every direction looking for any sign of the little girl's parents. She could see no one that looked remotely related to the little pigtailed child.

"I'll be right back!" Brynn shouted as a stream of shoppers sped by them, not looking back as she joined the rush. A few panic-racked seconds later, Brynn finally reached the first aisle of the garden department, and she shouted apologies as she pushed past a crowd picking through a giant metal basket of pruning shears. She sped past a giant display of Miracle Gro, then past a pimply teenage employee scanning a watering can as an old man held a store circular up to his Coke-bottle-thick glasses. They both glanced at Brynn, but neither moved as Brynn tried to slow down.

"So sorry!" she yelled as she turned sideways and attempted to slip between them. Just then, the old man leaned closer to the worker and Brynn's chest collided with his head. His glasses skittered across the floor as the worker lunged for them, sending a stand of neatly stacked vases crashing to the floor where they shattered.

As Brynn's mouth widened in horror, she finally spotted a bright yellow sign:

Doorbuster Plants – Limited Supply!

"I'll be right back!" she called to the teenager, who was shouting into a walkie-talkie as she stood among hundreds of shards of broken pottery. Brynn cringed and felt a wave of nausea creep up her throat, but she couldn't stop now. Not when she was so close.

Brynn shoved an empty cart out of her way and sprinted to toward the sign, relieved to find a giant display of healthy, green plants beside it. Her eyes scanned the rows, searching for the Albo's signature green and white mottled leaves. She spotted several African mask plants just like the one Jordan had destroyed, along with black-stalked raven ZZ plants, bird's nest ferns and row after row of brightly hued Prince of Orange philodendrons. She rounded the display, finding several robust Monstera, but all were the full green *deliciosa* type she already owned. She frantically turned each pot, running her fingers over the split leaves, but nowhere did she see the marbled foliage of the Albo. Bile bubbled in her stomach as her heart threatened to thunder out of her ribcage.

Where is it!?

"Hey!" she shouted as an employee pushed a dolly past the aisle, but he didn't stop. "*Hey!*" she repeated, but he headed toward the warehouse and Brynn spotted a tiny pod sticking out of one ear. She rushed over and gripped his shoulder, trying to turn him to face her.

He jerked away, his face twisted in alarm as he pressed his hand to his shoulder. Had she grabbed him harder than she thought? She felt like her head was going to explode as she tried to catch her breath. She was running out of time.

"Where is the Monstera Albo?!" she shouted.

"The what, ma'am?" the man asked in a shaky voice, eyeing her like he'd just crossed paths with a poisonous snake.

"*Monster Albo!*" she shouted.

The man opened his mouth again, but quickly snapped it shut as he stared over her shoulder. Besides a jazzy instrumental of "Santa Claus Is Coming to Town," Brynn could only hear muffled whispers behind her. What had happened to the excited shouts of shoppers as they barreled around the store with squealing carts full of deals? She turned to follow his stare, finding a crowd of frozen shoppers, all watching her with varying expressions of disgust and alarm.

There, up front, was the swollen-faced popcorn girl, a thumb in her mouth now surrounded by adults who must be her parents. There was the old man with the circular, wiping his glasses on his shirt as he leaned against a shelf. And of course, there was Grumpy Kindle Woman, glaring in loathing at Brynn over an armful of paperbacks as she shook her head.

Brynn's throat plummeted to the floor as her hands flew to cover her mouth. She felt as if ice cold water had just been thrown across her face. What had just happened? *What had she done?*

"I—I—I'm sorry!" Brynn sputtered, turning toward the little girl. "Can I buy you a new popcorn?" she asked in a wobbly voice, trying for a smile as tugged the hundred from her pocket.

"Don't come near her!" the girl's father barked, stepping protectively between them like a guard dog.

"Okay. Okay!" Brynn said, raising her hands in front of her as she backed away.

"Can I help?" Brynn called as she headed for the gasping old man, but the pimple-faced employee appeared from behind him and blocked her path.

"You need to leave," she said, angry authority dripping from every word. Just then, a huge hulking man wearing a tight Grantway polo shoved through the warehouse doors, stopping less than a foot from Brynn. He crossed his meaty arms over his bulging chest as Brynn's chest tightened in panic.

They sent security. For me.

"I—yes, of course," Brynn mumbled as blood pounded in her ears. She avoided the scornful eyes of the watching shoppers as she headed toward the exit, the security guard keeping pace behind her. She felt dizzy and confused, almost like she might faint.

As Brynn passed two workers sweeping up the fragments of broken vases, she caught sight of a long, glossy black ponytail out of the corner of her eye. She whipped around, but saw nothing except the finally dissipating crowd. Brynn's insides turned to ice as she tried to reason with her rising hysteria. Jessica Southgate didn't live in Twin. There was no way that was her. As Brynn followed the gigantic security guard, she snuck one more glance over her shoulder. She saw no one that looked even remotely like the so-called Green Goddess. She tried to breathe.

Brynn's entire body vibrated with mortification. She had never acted like that before, not even the time she'd caught her high school boyfriend cheating on her with a cheerleader three years younger than her. As soon as she skulked past the registers and past the front doors into the cold morning air, she ducked her head and ran to her car.

She fell into the driver's seat, slamming the door behind her before locking it in case someone had followed her out of the store. She remembered her chair and sleeping bag in their hiding place, but nothing could make her show her face here ever again. She pictured the little girl again, curled in a ball, and one thought repeated in her mind:

I did this. I did this.

Only then did she start to cry.

EIGHT

"Morning," Jordan said as he tossed his staple gun and the remains of yet another stack of flyers on the Formica counter. He'd been canvassing the other side of Twin since dawn but drove twenty over the speed limit to try to make it back in time to help Gina. His stomach dropped when he pulled into the gravel lot, finding it just as empty as when he'd left.

"Mornin', Jordan," Gina said, flashing him a grin as she kept her eyes glued to the computer monitor. "Fresh pot's brewing in the back."

"Been slow this morning, huh?"

"So far, unfortunately," Gina said, her smile tightening as she shook her head. "Though we did get a few calls asking how late we're open tonight."

"Well, better than nothing," Jordan said, tugging off his knit cap and running his hand through his matted-down waves. "I think I've covered every business and telephone pole in a ten-mile radius of downtown. It's cold out there this morning."

"Only gonna get colder," Gina said, swiveling to face him. "Forecast is calling for a couple inches that might actually stick."

Jordan pulled a wadded-up paper from his back pocket before

unfolding it and tossing it on the keyboard in front of Gina.

"What's this?" Gina asked, sliding her glasses onto her nose as the attached gold chain draped loosely around her plump neck.

"It was on my windshield when I walked back my truck," Jordan said, his stomach churning as he crossed his arms over his chest.

"'Too busy to drive to a freezing tree lot?'" Gina read aloud. "'Tired of lousy selections and sky-high prices?'" She looked up at him, her eyes shining with fury. "What the heck!"

Jordan snorted. "Looks like they've got people on the ground now."

"Are you kidding me with this?" Gina asked, shooting Jordan a disgusted look.

"I wish I was," he said, biting his bottom lip.

"'Visit Tree-in-a-Box.com: one click, and the perfect tree comes straight to your door!'" Gina read in a mocking voice. "Absolute hogwash!" she groaned as she crumpled the paper and tossed it into the trash.

"It's one thing to see those Facebook ads and YouTube commercials, but this feels personal," Jordan muttered, blood pounding in his temples. "What they failed to mention is this so-called 'perfect' tree will arrive dry, smushed, and shipped from who knows what country."

"Preachin' to the choir, hon," Gina said, clutching her jingle bell necklace, her gaze wandering to the empty parking lot out the icy window as she tut-tutted in disapproval. Just then, low shouts erupted from the computer as she jerked her head back to the screen.

"Watching anything good?" Jordan asked, ripping open a vendor bill from a stack of mail.

"Oh, you know me," Gina said, waving her hand airily. "I love some good trash. Usually, I get it from my Housewives, but today it's my plant ladies spilling the tea."

"Spilling the what?" Jordan asked.

"Tea, you know, gossip. My nieces all say it. Anyway, look," she said, turning the monitor. "I've been watching this all morning."

Jordan had a list of outdoor chores a mile long, but he could never resist indulging Gina. She'd been like a second mother to him over these last several years, doting on him as if they were blood. Gina loved houseplants, loved to grow and especially loved to talk about them. She was the main reason the store had any non-evergreen foliage and the *only* reason any of it was still alive. She was always misting them with a little spray bottle, which Jordan couldn't help but find endearing.

He crouched down, watching shaky cell footage as a young woman barreled through a group of people, toppling over a display and nearly knocking an elderly man to the ground.

"What is wrong with people?" Jordan asked, his mouth twisting in disgust. "Is that a Grantway?""

"Kinda looks one," Gina said with a shrug. "That's the gal from *Planted*, my channel on the YouTube." Gina tapped a sparkly red nail against the screen. "She's usually the nice one! I would have expected this from the Green Goddess, but—ooh, look, here it comes!" Gina's eyes widened with glee. "Drama, drama, drama!"

Jordan watched as the petite woman shook a store employee before turning to the gathering crowd, her face ashen as her eyes darted around her. There was something familiar about that those wide eyes and messy, blonde ponytail... Was she an actress? As a very muscly man in a polo shirt escorted her away, the woman threw a look over her shoulder and right into camera. Jordan's jaw dropped open.

"Pause it!" he exclaimed; his mouth suddenly dry as Gina clicked. The woman froze, her beautiful round face suspended in an expression of shock.

No damn way.

"I would swear that's the woman from the plant store!" Jordan said, his nose almost touching the screen as if the closer he got the more he might be proven wrong. "The new one in town!"

"I remember Brynn saying she was from around these parts," Gina said, leaning back in the chair. "Such a shame. I really liked her."

Brynn. That was her name. As much as he'd like to forget he ever met her, he had a feeling she'd singed a permanent burn in his memory. He sighed, catching Gina studying him out of the corner of his eye before realizing he was still staring at the frozen footage.

"Anyway," he said evenly as he stood and cracked his knuckles. "Your text said you wanted to show me something?"

"Yep, almost forgot," Gina said, opening a new browser tab. "In fact, that's what I was looking at before I got sidetracked."

The familiar red of the Yelp website filled the screen, but as he scanned the page, Jordan's eyes stopped on a photo of Jordan and Charlie in front of the shop. Yep, there along the top was *Evergreen Acres.*

"You made a Yelp page?" Jordan asked.

"Not me," Gina said. "Charlie."

"Wait, my *dad* made a Yelp page?" Jordan asked, incredulous. He was less than tech-savvy than most millennials, but Charlie had never been any better.

Gina laughed. "It's really not that hard. I don't know why we didn't do it sooner."

She scrolled down to as Jordan's eyes scanned a blurb about the farm's operation and history. "I think he did a nice job. And look," she said, pointing to five red stars near the title. "There're three reviews already and I only wrote one of them!"

"Do you honestly think some review page is going to save this place?" Jordan asked, rubbing the bridge of his nose between his thumb and forefinger. Even he wasn't sure if he was genuinely asking or just being snarky like usual.

Jordan had always suspected that social media was little more than a passing trend. So many local businesses had come and gone, most failing in their first couple years. Those people had Instagram, Facebook Live, and all the other apps that Jordan didn't really understand. And what did they have to show for it? Evergreen Acres had been there long before those businesses, long before most of the buildings that had housed them had even been built.

"I wish I knew the answer, Jordan," Gina said gently as she hung her glasses around her neck, her usually bright brown eyes tinged with sadness. "But I do think we can move forward as the world does. You can change in small ways without changing the parts that truly matter. Growth is good."

Jordan jaw tightened as he nodded, no longer convinced of anything. Maybe social media would help. Or at least the Groupon idea. He was willing to consider anything at this point.

"I'm gonna refill," she said, patting his shoulder before heading to the storage room with her snowman mug. "Holler if you need me to ring someone up."

"Will do," Jordan said, plopping into the worn leather chair, his eyes resting on the ancient store phone as he rubbed the rough stubble on his jaw.

He missed his mom. Marissa's instincts about this place had always been spot-on. If only he could hear her voice one more time, he was sure he would know what to do. He pressed his head into his hands, but everything felt like a jumbled mess. One thing was crystal clear: Evergreen Acres wasn't going to survive on its own. Something had to change, and it had to change fast.

Brynn pinned a leafy vine to the top of the arch, barely registering the below freezing temperature. She had been so excited when she'd come up with the idea for the store entrance last week, so excited when she found the perfect wooden arch at the local hardware store. She had placed three trailing pothos on either side of the trellis, then wove Christmas lights and vines through the entire structure.

She gave a little wave to a huddle of preteen girls that had stopped to admire the display. One girl quickly looked down at her phone and whispered to the others. They all stared at the screen, covering their hushed whispers with their hands and giggling as they continued down the sidewalk and disappeared across the street. Brynn's chest tightened. They could have been watching the latest viral dance on TikTok, but she had a sinking feeling they had been watching her.

Brynn plugged the light strand into the extension cord and sat crisscross on the ground. The glittering bulbs among the ribbons of green leaves was every bit as gorgeous as she had hoped for, the houseplant version of a pine garland. Now, all seemed trite and pointless. She sighed, her vision blurring with tears for what felt like the hundredth time that morning.

Just then, a shadow fell over here as a bundled figure in bulky hiking boots stood over her. She wiped her face on her sleeve and hurried to her feet as the figure removed their hood. She knew that goofy, crooked grin anywhere.

"Tyler!" she exclaimed before launching herself into her brother's arms. His parka was ice cold against her thin sweater. "What are you doing here?"

"I was worried about you, sis," he said as she broke away. "I thought I'd better check on you after last night."

"Oh, right," Brynn said, suddenly remembering she was supposed to have a cold. Well, at least her puffy eyes and red nose wouldn't warrant explanation. "I'm doing fine today. It's sweet of you to check on me."

"Well, we got the whole front of the house finished, and I think it looks even better than last year," he said. "Those reindeer you bought for the yard are really cute. Even Mom loves them."

"I'm glad," Brynn said as guilt surged through her core.

"Still, I'd prefer to have *you* holding the ladder when we take it all down," he said with a grin. "You know how much Mom waves her hands when she's gossiping about the neighbors."

"It's a deal," Brynn said, busying herself with a loose vine. "Hey, Mom told me the park service gave you three weeks off this year? How'd you swing that?"

"We've got trees older than this country," Tyler said, waving his hand dismissively. "Things will be just how I left them. Besides, research is pretty limited when everything is frozen."

"You sure you're OK?" he asked, giving her shoulder a playful punch, his signature sign of affection.

"I took something," Brynn said, coughing a couple times for good measure. "Must have been a 24-hour thing."

"I meant about the video," Tyler said, eyeing her pointedly as chewed his lower lip. "At the market."

Brynn gaped at him, her cheeks burning. "I—I'm sorry, Tyler," she sputtered. "I didn't think you had seen that."

"Yeah," he said, his own face blushing a bit. They didn't usually talk about much beyond birthday gifts and the weather. "A buddy sent it to me this morning."

If her own brother had seen it that meant the video truly had gone viral. Brynn wanted to vomit. She knew that shiny black ponytail had belonged to Jessica, and she knew that Jessica had filmed everything. She just couldn't prove it.

But somehow, as much as Brynn tried, she couldn't bring herself to hate Jessica. Brynn had royally screwed up and it was her own fault. It just made it a thousand times worse knowing that the whole world could watch it on repeat.

She sighed. "I'm really not okay," she said, her voice wobbling. "This just really sucks. I don't know what came over me." She looked up at him and was relieved to see a tender affection in his eyes instead of judgment.

"Did you know someone made memes of me?" Brynn squeaked, and when Tyler studied his boots she knew he had already seen them.

"I'm just under a lot of stress right now, Tyler," she said. "That's all I can say to try to explain it."

"You don't need to explain yourself to me," Tyler said. "But I hate to hear things are so hard right now. Why don't I treat you to lunch this week and you can fill me in?"

"That would be lovely," she said, her eyes burning. She must finally be out of tears. She hesitated, then asked the question she'd been dreading: "Does Mom know?"

"No," he said, shaking his head firmly. "Her crowd doesn't tend to watch that sort of thing. I certainly won't tell her."

She wiped her sleeve across her face, glad she'd worn waterproof mascara that morning. "Thanks, Tyler."

"You know I got you, sis," he said, flashing her that crooked smile once more, the only feature that didn't quite mirror her own.

Just then, Katie rushed through the door, carrying a huge bag of potting mix. Her face lit up when she spotted Tyler.

"Dilworth, hey!" Tyler said, eyeing Katie's blue beret and tweed vest before grabbing the soil bag from her. "Here, let me get that for you."

They followed him to the back of the store where he carefully laid it on the potting table Brynn had inherited from her godmother.

"Sounds like you're in town for a good stretch this time, huh?" Katie asked Tyler.

"Yeah, finally," Tyler said, smiling like he had a secret.

"We should all go out for drinks or something while you're here," Katie said without a hint of her usual snark.

"I'd love that," Tyler said, and Brynn noticed his eyes never left Katie's. Feeling Brynn's scrutinizing gaze, he quickly looked away before adding nonchalantly, "We should all go."

"Sounds fun," Katie said with a shrug.

Brynn just stifled a laugh.

"Well, I'm driving Mom to choir," Tyler said, heading for the door. "See you gals later."

As they heard the bell jingle, Brynn plopped on the sofa and patted the cushion next to her. Katie hopped beside her, tucking her long legs underneath her.

"So, when exactly did my brother start looking at you like that?" Brynn asked, raising an eyebrow.

"What do you mean?" Katie asked, her face the perfect picture of innocence, other than her flushed scarlet cheeks.

"You know exactly what I mean," Brynn said.

"Well, if there's something on his end, it beats me," Katie said, twisting the stud in her nose. "Besides, I've been kind of seeing someone."

"Kate!" Brynn scolded. "You're not even gonna tell me?"

"I would have eventually," Katie said with a shrug. "When there was something to tell."

"You know literally every thought I've had about Caleb," Brynn reminded her, which was mostly true. While she'd endured some much-deserved scolding after filling Katie in on her wild night with Caleb, Brynn still occasionally let her thumb hover over his number in a moment of weakness.

"Look, it's just someone I met online," Katie said. "You'll be the first to know more, I promise."

Brynn wasn't totally satisfied, but she let it go. Only then did the memory of the night before flood her brain once more.

"Well, thanks for the momentary distraction," Brynn said, hugging a throw pillow. "I actually haven't cried in the last ten minutes, which is refreshing."

"Oh, Bee, I'm so sorry," Katie said, laying an affectionate hand on Brynn's shoulder.

"Lay it on me," Brynn said. She sighed. "How bad is it?"

Katie hesitated, then met Brynn's eye. "It's bad," she said, shaking her head slowly. "I'm sorry. It's really bad."

Brynn groaned and covered her face with the pillow.

"You've lost over a hundred thousand subscribers," Katie said gently.

Brynn groaned again.

"And Jessica Southgate just posted a 'Kindness in the Season of Giving' video with that stupid little winky emoji at the end of the title," Katie continued. "It opens with the shot of you bumping over that little girl, looping over and over. I don't recommend watching."

Brynn let out a shuddering breath and lowered the pillow from her face.

"I still can't figure out who runs the *Crazy Plant Chicks* channel that posted it, but it has to be Jessica," Katie said, pausing for just a moment before adding, "The original video has over two million views."

"I can't say I'm surprised," Brynn said weakly. She swallowed. Her lungs felt like they had been sloshed into her stomach. "This all seems on brand for the Green Goddess."

"I bet she started the hashtag, too," Katie added bitterly.

"The hashtag?" A fresh wave of panic flooded through Brynn's body.

Katie paled. "I'm sorry, I thought you knew."

"This is part of your job," Brynn said, wrapping her arms around herself. "Pretend you aren't my best friend. Let's hear it all." She had a feeling it couldn't get much worse.

"OK, then," Katie said. She scooted closer, resting one hand lovingly on Brynn's knee. "#CancelBrynn started yesterday, and unfortunately...it's trending."

Brynn said nothing, she just let out a sigh and gritted her teeth.

"Personally, I don't think it's very catchy," Katie said. "#BanBrynn has a much better ring to it."

Brynn glared at her.

"Sorry," Katie said sheepishly.

"And Homestead?" Brynn asked. And there it was, the question she'd been avoiding. Katie hesitated for only a moment tugging Brynn into a tight hug.

"I'm sorry, Brynn," Katie said softly, not letting go.

Brynn blinked as hot tears dropped onto Katie's shoulder. It seemed her crying reservoir had refilled in the last twenty minutes.

"Sofia reached out first thing this morning," Katie continued, finally releasing Brynn and lunging for the tissues on the side table.

"The network is not happy," Katie continued as Brynn took one and blew her nose. "Yes, you have less followers than you had before, but they're more concerned with how this...*situation* could hurt the Homestead brand."

"So, it's over?" Brynn asked, her voice barely above a squeak.

"Not necessarily," Katie said. "Sofia said the network wouldn't make a final decision until Christmas. So, in her words, there could be time for 'a highly unlikely comeback.'"

Brynn buried her face in her hands. How had she screwed up so badly? She might have lost the show to Jessica without the whole Grantway fiasco, but at least she could have walked away with her head held high.

Now, she'd been humiliated in front of millions of people. But the part that had kept her awake all day when she'd finally slunk home was that the video wasn't even inaccurate. She had plowed through all those people and acted like a selfish brat.

And while it didn't feel like she was watching her true self, her actions spoke loud and clear. Brynn had been burning the candle at both ends for so long that maybe she *was* this monster from the video.

"I have no idea how to make this right," Brynn said finally.

Katie said nothing, just waited.

"What am I going to do?" Brynn asked, rubbing the heel of her hand against her damp eyes.

"Are you okay?" Katie asked gently. "Forget about the show...I'm worried about *you*."

Brynn shook her head dismissively. Clearly, she didn't need to be thinking about herself any more than she already had.

"I know that plant was really special," Katie continued. "But in the video? Well, you just had this look in your eyes. It just didn't seem like the Brynn I know."

Brynn sighed. "All I could think about was that getting that plant would give me that little edge I needed to pass up Jessica Southgate. It was all I could see. It's hard to explain, but it was like I didn't even see that kid, or that old man. It felt like a dream, like it was happening to somebody else."

Katie nodded and waited for her to say more.

"I'm kind of freaked out," Brynn said, twisting the tissue between her thumbs. "I don't want to be that person."

"You *aren't* that person," Katie insisted. "But even the nicest person in the world can snap under too much pressure. Give yourself a break—if anyone can come back from this, it's you."

The bell jingled and they heard quiet footsteps coming from the front.

"Thanks, Kate," Brynn said. She cleared her throat and wiped her face once more with the tissue before shoving it in her pocket.

As Katie followed her through the saloon doors, Brynn saw the teenage boy from the other day standing at the counter, scrolling through his phone.

"Oh hey, you're back," Brynn said, summoning a smile. "What can I do for you?"

"Hi again," he said, flashing her a shy grin. If he noticed her swollen eyes, he was too polite to show it. His face was more relaxed than the other day, though he still carried the awkward edge that seemed universal to all pubescent boys.

"I'm Dylan," he continued. "I think I forgot to say that the other day."

"Nice to officially meet you," Brynn said. "I'm Brynn and this is Katie."

Katie gave a little wave and stretched out the crystal candy dish. "Mint?" she asked before unwrapping one and popping it into her mouth.

"Thanks," Dylan said as he took one and pocketed it. "And thanks for the other day, too."

"It's what we're here for," Brynn said. "How is that little rubber plant holding up?"

"Good!" Dylan said. "Well, I think so, anyway..."

He looked down and picked at his fingernail.

"It's just..." he continued, "I don't know, it's kind of silly."

"You can tell us," Katie said brightly. "Trust me, when it comes to plants, I've asked every silly question out there."

"It's not about the plant," Dylan said, hesitating before adding, "It's about a girl."

His ears had turned a deep purple red. "I don't even know why

I'm telling you this, I'm sorry."

"Don't be sorry," Brynn said, catching his eye. "You can trust us. It's like that saying—what happens in the plant store stays in the plant store."

Dylan chuckled but his eyes were uncertain as he looked from Katie back to Brynn. He let out a deep sigh.

"OK, so this girl...her name is Madison. She's a senior," he said, and then suddenly paled. "You don't know her, do you?"

Brynn and Katie shook their heads solemnly.

"Well, I'm only a sophomore," he continued. "She lives a couple blocks from here and she's like—perfect. But we haven't talked before. She doesn't even know I exist."

His face softened as his story found its rhythm. "So, one night, I'm walking home past her house, and I saw her sitting in her window reading. I couldn't tell what book it was, but I noticed this little spiky green plant on the sill. And it's always there." He took a deep breath. "So, that's why I came in the other day. I bought the rubber plant for her."

"What did she say?" Brynn asked excitedly and Katie shot her a look. Brynn tried to squash her enthusiasm. She didn't want to scare Dylan back into his shell. "Did she like it?"

"I didn't talk to her!" Dylan said, looking horrified. "I left it at her door."

"Did you leave a note?" Katie asked.

"Then she might have figured out it was from me!" Dylan sputtered, his face mottled and pink.

Brynn stifled a smile. He was adorable.

"The next time I walked by, there it was," Dylan said, and Brynn saw him truly smile for the first time. "It was in her window, next to the other plant."

"Oh, Dylan," Katie said, practically swooning. "That is so romantic."

Brynn nodded emphatically causing Dylan to blush even more ferociously.

"So, are you guys neighbors?" Katie asked.

Dylan shook his head. "We live out in Jerome." He gave a sheepish half smile. "I've been finding more excuses to hang out at my dad's shop lately."

She wondered where the Dylans of the world had been back when she was in high school. For their one-year anniversary junior year of high school, Caleb had bought her an ice scraper for her car with a glove attached.

"Yeah, well, anyway," Dylan said, still smiling softly as he stared at his feet. "I thought maybe I'd do it again. Get her another plant."

"Great idea," Katie said. "We've got your back."

"First off," Brynn said, coming around the counter, "we should figure out which plant she already has. Do you want to look around and see if you can spot it?"

"I already did, when I came in," Dylan said, eyeing the store uncertainly. "I can't tell. I feel like half the plants in here look exactly like it."

"Maybe I can help," Brynn said, leading him toward a display. "Tell me anything you can remember. She pointed to a pothos in a hanging basket. "Is it long and trailing, like one of these?"

He shook his head. "No, it stands upright."

"OK, let's see," Brynn said, scanning the shelves. She walked over to the table inside the front door. "Is it thicker and bushier?" She pointed to a snake plant. "Or more like this, with just a few straight stalks?"

"Straighter, I guess," he said. "But with some leaves on it."

"Hm, maybe a ZZ plant?" Brynn asked, pulling a tidy plant with small shiny leaves from the window display.

"I mean...maybe?" Dylan raised it to his face and studied it. "I'm sorry, I wish I knew about plants. I think they're really cool, I've just never had any."

Brynn grabbed a small heart leaf philodendron, its first vine just beginning to trail over the side of the pot. "This is probably a safe bet. It looks nothing like you described and it's just about as easy to take care of as the rubber plant."

Dylan took it, gently running a finger over one of the leaves. "They really do look like little hearts!"

"It's almost poetic," Katie called cheerfully from behind the counter.

"Before you know it, it will fill this little container and start trailing long vines down the side," Brynn said. "I have one at home and it always reminds me of Rapunzel's hair." She pointed to the vine-covered arch. "When that happens, she could string it up, like these pothos here. Or maybe..." She flashed him a playful grin. "Maybe she'll finally open that window and let it hang down."

"That's genius," Dylan said, his eyes shining in excitement. "Let's do it!"

As he handed the plant to Katie to ring up, he no longer looked the least bit nervous. Brynn rummaged behind the counter, digging through a basket of spare receipt rolls and paper shopping bags. She retrieved a few books from the bottom of the basket, dusting them off as she found one with the name Dr. D. G. Hessayon. She passed it across the counter to Dylan, who eyed the book with curiosity.

"*The House Plant Expert*," Brynn explained. "You can borrow it. I got this back in college, and I doubt it was new even then. Still, it's a great place to start."

"Thank you!" Dylan said with a grin as he flipped through the first few pages. "I'll be super careful with it." He considered. "Actually, I'll keep it at Earlybird to be extra safe."

"Earlybird?" Brynn said and suddenly she put it together. "Wait, are you Henry Lee's son?"

Dylan nodded.

"No way!" Brynn squealed. "I love your dad. And his espresso. Even his corny jokes."

"They're alright," Dylan said, but he was smiling.

"He wanted me to meet you, so make sure you tell him you've been here," Brynn said and suddenly Dylan paled. "I won't say a word about any girls. It's a part of my plant-client confidentiality."

Dylan laughed. "No wonder you like my dad's jokes."

"If you ever want to, you can come follow me around and ask questions," Brynn said.

"Really?!" he asked as Katie passed the little plant and his receipt across the counter.

"Anytime," Brynn said, returning his smile.

Dylan exited the store with a new buoyancy to his step.

"Someone is feeling awfully generous today," Katie said, shooting her a look.

"Maybe a little," Brynn said with a shrug. "I think at this point, I owe it to the universe." She popped a peppermint into her mouth as a group of three women carrying armfuls of shopping bags entered the store. "I hope he starts hanging around the shop. I'll teach him everything he needs to know."

Katie raised an eyebrow.

"It's partly selfish," Brynn said. "I wouldn't mind someone around here who actually likes talking about plants."

Katie chuckled.

"Welcome!" Brynn called, giving the shoppers a small wave. "Let us know if we can help you with anything."

"She wants someone who actually likes talking about plants," Katie said with a snort before heading into the back room. "I'm not even insulted."

NINE

Jordan inhaled, the crisp, morning air burning his nose as his jeans did little to keep the icy bench from chilling his legs. Even in the winter, he had always been most comfortable outdoors. Long after Megan had rushed inside to watch movies by the fire, a ten-year-old Jordan would still be contentedly sitting in the snow, watching a family of deer scurry by or catching tiny snow crystals on his gloved fingertips. No matter the weather, being outside invigorated him, much like the effects of a strong cup of coffee.

At the thought of caffeine, he grabbed his black coffee from under the bench, savoring the warmth as it rushed down his throat. He glanced around the empty town square, reveling in the stillness as his breath formed a mist in front of him.

It wasn't until Mayor Lopez suggested they meet near Perrine Bridge that Jordan realized how long it had been since he'd walked the canyon. Then again, he couldn't really remember a time in recent history he'd gone for a leisurely stroll. The farm was his work and his home, and he wasn't exactly a social butterfly. Sometimes, he'd grab a beer with a friend from high school or go on a date set up by a mutual friend, but he rarely felt lonely. Usually, he was just too busy.

As Jordan let out a yawn and leaned against the retaining wall, he noticed no one was jumping yet. Twin Falls attracted a very specific niche of tourist as Snake River Canyon had the only bridge in the US where it was legal for BASE jumping year-round. But as he looked closer, he saw dots of every color adorning the bridge. He'd forgotten about the tradition of tying scarves and gloves to the overpass, a community offering to those in need.

"Morning!" Mayor Lopez called from the steps behind them.

"Good morning, Mayor," Jordan replied as he stood, shaking the mayor's hand before passing him the other cup of coffee. "Thanks for taking the time."

"Appreciate the joe," Mayor Lopez said. "And the flexibility. I wanted to chat as soon as possible and I'm glad you agreed to walk the canyon."

"I haven't been here in ages," Jordan said, taking in the stark beauty of the craggy ravine. Though the canyon was devoid of color this time of year, minus the paved path and the bridge ahead, he felt like he was walking through a *Star Wars* set. "It's beautiful out here."

"I try to do a mile or so most mornings before heading to the office," the mayor said. "I find I do my best thinking here." He sipped his coffee, grunted his approval and nodded.

"Snake River Canyon is the core of Magic Valley history," the mayor said as they walked on. "Which is another reason why this seemed a perfect place to meet." He turned to face Jordan, his expression suddenly serious. "Evergreen Acres is a part of that history too."

Jordan didn't know what to say.

"We need businesses like yours," the mayor continued, his voice full of the conviction he was known for. "Family is the soul of Twin Falls, a part of our history. And if a millennial like you can't right things, it doesn't bode well for the places run by old folks like me."

Clearly, the universe was sending a hint. He silently resolved to search "Social Media for Dummies" when he made it back to Evergreen Acres.

"Well, you didn't come here this morning to get my Snapchat tips," Mayor Lopez continued, chuckling as he rubbed his hands and blew on them. "I have a thought. Next Saturday is the Festival of Lights," he said, referring to the yearly parade of homespun floats that headed down Main Street before ending in the square. "You probably saw the tree's not up yet."

Jordan made a non-committal sound. He didn't want to admit that he hadn't noticed.

"I think it's long past time we shop local and put our money where our mouth is, don't you?" Mayor Lopez asked, grinning.

"The tree?" Jordan asked, remembering the towering pines of years past. The lighting of the tree at the end of the parade was one of his earliest memories.

"You think Evergreen Acres can accommodate something that big?" the mayor asked. "Probably at least twenty feet tall?"

"Absolutely!" Jordan said eagerly as they stepped aside to let a jogger run past. "We've got trees that were planted long before Twin even had electricity. We never have demand for anything that size, so they just keep growing. And of course, we plant two seedlings for every tree we fell."

"We'll purchase it at fair market value, of course," Mayor Lopez continued as Jordan stood to toss their empty cups in the trash. "And I'll make sure we hang an Evergreen Acres banner in a prime spot."

"That would be amazing," Jordan said.

The mayor stopped and tugged out his phone. "Let me give you some ideas from the ones we've already received." He scrolled through photos of some of the banners as Jordan looked over his shoulder. There was one for KOOL 96.5 that played Christmas songs around the clock, another for one of the local Cub Scout troops. His eyes froze on an obnoxiously bright red and orange sign that featured an overly tanned model grinning back at him as she walked her dog outside of a generic McMansion: 'Merry Christmas from Sutkamp Luxury Home!' Russell Sutkamp seemed to be following Jordan, even way out here in the canyon.

"That brings me to my next question," the mayor said, as they walked. "Would Evergreen Acres consider being the Master of Ceremonies?"

"Us?!" Jordan asked. He had vague memories of posters for the parade, but they always seemed to feature some local celebrity.

"Sure," the mayor said, emphatically. "I can think of nothing better than a local business to remind the town how much community matters. We all get distracted by the commercialism this time of year."

"But..." Jordan trailed off, searching for the right words. "The whole town will be there."

"That's precisely my intention," the mayor said. "And it's early enough that plenty of people will still need a tree." He glanced at his watch. "I need to head back. I've got a meeting at nine."

"Of course," Jordan said, his mouth suddenly dry as they headed back the way they'd come. "This is such a big honor, but I'm no public speaker."

"That's part of the charm," the mayor said with a wink. "Just be yourself. I'll have Beth send you an outline of the night." He gave Jordan a fatherly pat on the back. "Trust me, you're the perfect choice."

"Thank you, Mayor," Jordan said. "We'll be there." Though gratitude and hot coffee warmed his insides, it was mingled with a cold doubt at the thought of such a big crowd.

They walked in companionable silence. As they passed the bridge, a petite ponytailed woman rigged a parachute as automatically as if she'd been taking out the trash. Jordan was instantly chagrined as the woman conferred with a man seated beside her; after all, speaking to a few hundred people had nothing on leaping from Perrine into thin air.

"Let's schedule the tree delivery for as soon as you're able," the mayor said once they'd climbed back to the parking lot. He flashed Jordan a smile. "I'm really rooting for you guys."

Jordan's mind was a jumble of chaos as he drove toward town, suddenly much more interested to see the square than he'd been the last time.

"Well, isn't this a nice surprise?" Charlie said, scraping the last bits of scrambled eggs from his plate. He laid down his fork and braced his arthritic hands on the table.

"Don't get up," Jordan said, setting a brown paper bag on the counter. "I should have known I'd be too late for the early bird. You've got bagels for tomorrow anyway, from that bakery in town."

"You know me, I like to catch my news early," Charlie said, nodding at the tiny television across from him on the linen-covered table. "I can always eat more!" He cleared a stack of newspaper from the chair beside him. "How about you pop a couple of those in the toaster and join me. Help yourself to some coffee."

"I just had some," Jordan said. "But I'll take OJ if you've got it."

"In the fridge," Charlie said.

Jordan poured a glass of orange juice as a tinny voice reported on the highlights of Friday night's state football game.

"I had that meeting with Mayor Lopez this morning," Jordan said.

"Oh, yeah?"

"They want us to provide the tree for town, the one at the end of the parade," Jordan said, pulling out a chair for himself. "Not only that, but he also asked us to be Master of Ceremonies."

"Wow," Charlie said, his eyes wide as he leaned back and clasped his hands over his broad belly. "Big morning for Evergreen Acres."

"I'd say."

"I knew we kept those old grandpa trees growing for a reason," Charlie said, smiling to himself as he tugged the crossword puzzle from the paper pile.

Jordan played back the conversation with the mayor as he spread a massive glob of cream cheese onto his bagel. Someone was always nudging Jordan to get Evergreen Acres online, so there must some benefit to it. Still, a part of him wondered if it might be too late.

"...reportedly knocked over shoppers and made quite a mess at Grantway, though no charges have been filed." Jordan's eyes flew to the tiny screen, recognition immediately banishing his swirling thoughts. Sure enough, there was the same clip he'd seen just hours before. "Yikes!" the pearly-toothed news anchor said, shooting a pointed look to her cohost as Jordan read the chyron running across the bottom of the screen: LOCAL PLANT SHOP

OWNER GOES VIRAL!

"Only time will tell what the fallout of this incident could mean for Callaway's blossoming career," the smooth voice continued as the clip zoomed in on Brynn's horrified face as she noticed the angry crowd. Jordan dropped his bagel back on the plate, the thought of any food suddenly much less appealing.

"Oh, that girl!" Charlie exclaimed, setting down the crossword. "I recognize her from the pancake breakfast." He twisted the volume knob all the way to the right.

"...with nearly a million subscribers to her channel," the anchor continued. "Callaway is the owner of Twin Falls' newest plant shop, Planted in Twin."

"*A million subscribers?*" Charlie gave a low whistle as the over-the-shoulder graphic morphed into a Boy Scout troop that had won some award. "That's impressive!"

"I think you missed the point, Dad," Jordan said, turning the volume back down.

"And she did all that from right here in Twin?" Charlie asked, his eyes drifting back to his crossword.

"Yeah," Jordan said, curling his lip in distaste. "So do your best to avoid her."

"You talked trash just like that about Jasmine Alvarado, too, you know," Charlie said with a chuckle. "Every day after middle school, you had some fresh complaint ready to file."

"Oh, please," Jordan said with a snort. Classmates since kindergarten, Jasmine had been Jordan's first real girlfriend in high school. Despite the memories of his middle school wrath, he'd fallen hard for her. Well, right up until she'd dumped him for the class president, anyway.

"No, that is—" Jordan sputtered, wiping his lips with a paper towel. "Brynn is actual bad news and I know firsthand."

"I'll bet you do," Charlie said, smirking as he studied Jordan with his narrowed eyes.

"Just eat your breakfast and leave me alone," Jordan said, laughing as he shook his head in resignation. He shoved a piece of his bagel in his mouth, waiting for Charlie to keep teasing him. But Charlie said nothing as he stared blankly at his puzzle, seemingly lost in thought.

"You okay?" Jordan asked.

"Yeah, I'm good," Charlie said, blinking a couple times. He pushed his reading glasses up his nose as he grabbed his pencil. "What's a six-letter word for an animal you can ride?"

TEN

"'We have close to seventy-five followers, which I think is pretty impressive,'" Katie read from the computer screen as Brynn picked at her pale pink nail polish. "'But it's going to take more than that. I hope you'll consider sharing your knowledge and experience with me.'"

"Sounds like a lonely old man looking for a date," Brynn muttered.

"Let me finish!" Katie said, holding a skeleton-ring clad finger up to silence her. "'If we can't catch up before Christmas, I'm afraid this year will be our last. Sincerely and gratefully, Charlie Damon.'"

Katie turned to Brynn, an expectant look on her face.

"What?" Brynn asked impatiently.

"I Googled Evergreen Acres," Katie said. "It's legit. This isn't some prank."

"Well, that's a nice respite after all the hate mail we've gotten this week," Brynn said, her voice dripping with snark.

"I'm serious," Katie said.

"What do you want me to say?" Brynn demanded. "If he heard

about me on the news, then why isn't he disgusted with me? I mean, I'm pretty disgusted myself!"

"He didn't say anything about the incident," Katie said with a shrug.

"So, what?" Brynn asked, planting a fist on her hip. "You want me to go have coffee with some old tree farmer?"

"I think you should go work there for the season," Katie said, preemptively raising her hands in defense.

"Are you insane?!" Brynn sputtered.

"Maybe just a few hours a day," Katie continued, running a hand through her emerald locks. "I can run the shop while you're gone."

"You've officially lost your mind," Brynn said, grabbing a box cutter and heading for the back room.

"Think about it!" Katie said, trailing closely behind. "The country could watch you save a beloved family-owned Christmas tree farm!"

Brynn pressed her lips together, ignoring Katie's pleas as she sliced open a cardboard box and began unwrapping ceramic pots wrapped in Styrofoam.

"They'll forget all about the video," Katie insisted as she scooped up the packaging, tossing them into the recycling bin as Brynn checked each pot for chips or cracks.

"I don't know anything about Christmas trees!" Brynn said. She plopped crisscross onto the wood floor, running her fingers over a pot with a hand-painted sunshine and the words *You Had Me at Aloe!* etched beneath.

"You literally grow plants for a living," Katie said, narrowing her eyes.

"*Indoor* plants."

"OK, I wasn't sure if I should say anything," Katie said softly, joining Brynn on the floor.

Brynn froze, her stomach turning to ice as she set down the pot. Katie never looked as serious as she did in that moment, her arched brown brows knitted together in worry.

"Tell me," Brynn demanded.

"One of my old coworkers called me, the one who works for Warner Brothers," Katie said, grabbing Katie's hand. "He said that Jessica Southgate was in Los Angeles yesterday... touring Homestead's stages on the lot."

"What?!" Brynn exclaimed. "Why?"

"Maybe she just showed up or maybe they invited her, I have no idea," Katie said. "But you said yourself it would take something big to climb your way out of this. Here you go! You couldn't buy publicity that positive."

Brynn sighed and pressed her palm to her forehead as she pictured herself hacking at a tree with an ax. Some Christmas tree farm was the last place she wanted to be, especially since the number of customers had suddenly doubled from the week before. Still, Brynn knew Katie wasn't wrong.

"Maybe this email isn't just a coincidence," Katie said, pulling Brynn to her feet as she stood and dusted off the back of her cargo pants. "Maybe it's a Christmas miracle!"

Brynn groaned. "Oh, please."

Katie pressed her lips together but didn't say another word.

When did I become such a cynic? Brynn wondered before the answer slapped her in the brain. It was probably about the time she burned her plant empire to the ground after acting like a complete moron in front of millions of people. Her stomach rumbled as the hanging Edison bulbs began to swim across her vision as she heard the doorbell jingle.

"You'll come back from this," Katie said over her shoulder as she headed to the front. "Just think about it."

Brynn braced her hands against the worktable, trying to push her exhale out her nose like she'd learned in the yoga class Katie had dragged her to. Brynn crossed to the tiny bathroom and flipped on the light switch. Her face blinked back at her, filling the ancient mirror that had come with the building. Other than the dark shadows under her eyes, she looked the same. Where had she gone wrong?

You'll come back from this.

Brynn wished she felt as confident as Katie sounded. She headed into the tiny office she had built in the old broom closet, flicking on the desktop computer she'd been using since college. She grabbed a canned coffee from the mini fridge, flipping through a stack of yesterday's mail as she waited for it to boot up.

A hand-addressed envelope with her mother's loopy cursive caught her eye. Why had Greta sent something to the store instead of her house?

She ripped open the envelope and saw her mother's decorated house, illuminated against the twilight sky. A grinning Tyler stood in the doorway as Gram and Paps each smiled through a window from inside. Brynn flipped the photo over and found a note:

Brynn,

Wasn't the same without you. Hope you're better. Sent this to the store since I know you practically live there these days! Please don't miss the real Christmas picture—and wear something festive!

XOXO, Mom

Brynn felt a tug deep inside her chest as she studied the picture again, noticing the woven wood reindeer huddled together in the front yard. She clicked open her calendar. Good, she'd remembered to save the date. After the wakeup call she'd just had, she couldn't miss the Christmas pictures.

She clicked a new browser tab and quickly typed *pine tree gardening* into the search bar, her screen immediately filling with forests and close ups of needles and bark.

She shook her head as she clicked on a photo of a strapping woman with a tree slung over one shoulder. Brynn could never carry something like that. A Christmas tree farm. Really?

She rested her elbows on the tiny desk and pressed her fingertips to her temples. She had told Katie she'd think it over, that she'd actually consider spending the next month on some farm instead of making content or working her store. But who was she kidding? Deep down, she knew the decision had already been made.

"So, let me get this straight," Jordan sputtered, huffing as he leaned on the metal handle of the snow shovel. "You hired some stranger you found on the Internet?"

Charlie chuckled as he unzipped his coat and wiped his forehead with his tattered handkerchief.

"Were you going to talk to me about it?" Jordan demanded. "And how do you plan to pay this guy?"

"This *gal*, and that's the best part," Charlie said, turning off the idling tractor. As usual, he'd managed to plow the entire parking lot before Jordan had finished shoveling the walk. "She offered to come for free."

"For free?" Jordan repeated. "Why?"

"Maybe she just wants to give back," Charlie said with a shrug. "'Tis the season and she's done very well for herself online."

"Nothing is every truly free," Jordan said, shaking his head. "I don't trust this for a second."

"And that's why I didn't ask you first," Charlie said. "But how about you blame me if it doesn't work out."

Jordan clenched his teeth, saying nothing more as he finished clearing the walk, feeling Charlie's eyes on him. He leaned the shovel against the wooden porch railing, cursing under his breath as he turned and met his stare.

"What do you want me to say, Dad?" Jordan demanded, crossing his arms over his chest. "Thank you?"

Charlie's smile wobbled and Jordan winced. He couldn't remember the last time he'd raised his voice at his dad.

"You said it yourself," Charlie said gently. "Evergreen Acres isn't just a farm. It's even more than our family. We are Twin Falls history. But you're the one who has kept us going ever since your mom died, even when you were too young to shoulder something so big."

Jordan pressed his lips together, but didn't argue. True, he had thrown himself into the farm, not because he felt obligated, but because he loved it.

"I asked for help, Bubba, because I'm not sure you know how," Charlie continued. "You have a blind spot for this place. You can be mad at me for now, but I think it will be worth it in the long run." He stiffly lifted one leg over the seat and climbed down from the tractor. "Would you go park this before you walk the North Ten?" Charlie asked, referring to the ten acres that held the farm's most mature trees. "I need to go make sure Gina put through that order for Neem oil."

Jordan could only nod. While he had been thinking more and more about advertising and social media, the idea of bringing in some stranger just didn't sit right. Especially not now, when they had such little time. Still, he could tell his dad was already convinced.

As Jordan crossed the gravel lot to the tractor, Charlie intercepted him, resting a leather-gloved hand on his shoulder.

"No one's gonna change Evergreen Acres," Charlie pledged, his eyes solemn. "But it's time the world finds out about us."

"We can give it a try, Dad," Jordan relented, offering a tight, weary smile.

Charlie pulled him close, and Jordan's shoulders slumped as he surrendered into the embrace. No matter if he was 35 or 65, Jordan would never be too old for his dad's hug.

"I guess I trust your judgment, Dad," Jordan said, flashing Charlie a reluctant smile as he swung his leg over the tractor, pressing the clutch as the John Deere whirred to life.

"I hope you remember that tomorrow," Charlie said, stomping the muddy snow from his boots on the porch steps.

Jordan chuckled. "Why?"

But Charlie simply waved his hand dismissively as he headed inside.

"Why?!" Jordan called again, but Charlie closed the door behind him and disappeared into the store.

Jordan shook his head as he shifted gears and steered the tractor toward the barn. What had his dad had gotten them into? The risk seemed small enough, no actual money was exchanging hands. But something about Charlie's smirk made Jordan certain there was something up his dad's flannel sleeve.

ELEVEN

Brynn tightened her grip on the peace lily she'd brought from Planted, her hand hovering above the doorknob as she willed the wooden boards underfoot to stop creaking. She needed a second to breathe before walking into...well, whatever Christmas tree mess she was walking into. She glanced at her watch, already knowing she wasn't going to like what it said. She had left her house with plenty of time to spare, but Waze had a hard time locating the exact address. That was certainly a problem....which now meant it was *her* problem. She sighed as she made a mental note to update the location in the app.

Just as Katie had made her promise, Brynn had reluctantly climbed out of bed before sunrise, her entire body shivering as she slipped into her subzero Honda Civic. There was no way her little blue hybrid would make it out to Evergreen Acres in bad weather, but luckily, the roads had been salted overnight. With an oat milk latte from the empty drive-thru line at Dutch Bros. between her knees, she'd almost enjoyed the scenic drive.

Katie had texted her last night, clearly worried Brynn was going to bail on the whole idea. Brynn was annoyed—she might be a bit scattered, but she always stood by her word. Still, she hadn't been completely convinced this was worth the effort.

A flash of movement through the window caught her eye as a grinning woman with black and silver-streaked hair waved plump fingers in Brynn's direction. How long had she been standing there? Heat flooded Brynn's cheeks as she swung open the door.

"You must be Brynn!"

Brynn turned to find an older man sitting in a well-loved armchair, a steaming coffee in one hand as he grinned, well-trenched creases framing his twinkling eyes.

"I am," Brynn said with a polite smile. "I guess that makes you Charlie?"

"Charlie Damon, at your service," he said, lifting his mug in a playful salute. "And the wizard behind the counter is Gina. Please forgive me for not getting up, my hip's not a big fan of snowy weather."

"No problem," Brynn said, giving Gina a little wave. Despite the eager, warm wave Gina gave in response, Brynn saw recognition in the woman's brown eyes. "I'm sorry, have we met?"

"Oh, I must be looking at you like the cat who got the cream," Gina said, laughing heartily as she clutched a hand to her chest. "It's just, I had no idea it was *you* who'd be coming to help us out."

"I think I missed something," Charlie said, pressing against the armchair to stand as looked curiously between the two women.

"Me too," Brynn said, a nervous chuckle escaping her lips.

"It's just, I'm *such* a huge fan," Gina said, her eyes gleaming with excitement. "I love your YouTube channel. If it wasn't for you, my begonia would have died faster than you can say 'overwatering.'"

"Glad to hear it," Brynn said with a weak smile as her stomach twisted. If Gina followed any other plant bloggers, she had surely seen the Grantway video. *Great.* Brynn certainly wouldn't be the one to bring it up. She did her best to mirror the happy faces in front of her as she set the peace lily on the counter in front of Gina. "Sounds like you're the right person to give this to...it's a 'thank you' for inviting me here."

"A thank you?!" Charlie exclaimed with a loud guffaw that shook his whole body. "Well, that's rich! I didn't dare hope for more than an e-mail with a few tips!" He squeezed her hand between both of his own. "I can't tell you what this means to me. You're a real, live angel, Brynn Callaway!"

"It's nothing," Brynn said, her thundering heartbeat slowing as Charlie and Gina blinked at her expectantly. Regardless of what they knew of Brynn, it was sweet that her presence clearly meant so much. Maybe the next few weeks wouldn't be so bad after all.

"Well, I should probably get to it," Brynn said, mustering as much enthusiasm as her double-shot latte would permit.

"Consider us your minions," Gina said, wiping the stray pine needles that covered the counter into her palm.

"Well, I thought I'd start by putting together some flashy posts for your social media accounts," Brynn said. "Can I get your logins?"

While Charlie cocked his head as if she'd spoken a foreign language, Gina snorted, an amused smile stretching across her broad face.

"You don't have any logins," Brynn confirmed, not entirely surprised. "Well, after today, you will. I'll need your customer database, ideally for the last five years." She took stock of the store around her, packed with fresh wreaths, tree stands, and every kind of Christmas knick knack imaginable. "Is it too much to hope that you've got email addresses?"

"Now that we can do," Gina said. "A few years back, the Scouts tried to get all the local businesses to go paperless. We've been giving the option for e-mail receipts ever since."

"Great," Brynn said as she plucked a glossy Evergreen Acres brochure from a plastic display and skimmed the hunter green script. "This will get me started." She glanced behind the counter. "I'm a little scared to ask about the Wi-Fi situation all the way out here..."

"Oh, it's great," Charlie said. "Gina talked me into that fiber optic business. Probably heard about it from one of her Housewives." He tossed Gina a mischievous grin.

"Oh, you hush, old man," Gina said, cackling.

Brynn couldn't help but laugh along with them. A database of email addresses and lightning-fast Wi-Fi? She couldn't believe her luck.

"I'll get you that list right away," Gina said with a wink. "No Internet password needed all the way out here. Would you like some coffee?"

"Thanks, but I had some on the way here," Brynn said, slinging her leather messenger bag off her shoulder. "Where should I...?"

"There's a table all cleared off for you in the back," Charlie said, nodding toward a set of old saloon doors.

The phone rang and Gina grabbed it. "Give me a few," she whispered before pressing the handset to her ear. "Evergreen Acres, how can I help you?"

"I'll set up and come back," Brynn mouthed quietly.

As she gently closed the swinging doors behind her, Brynn found a peeling office chair and plastic folding table wedged between two crates overflowing with red velvet ribbon. It wasn't exactly a corner office, but at least everything looked clean. As she set down her bag, she peeked inside a brown paper grocery bag, finding bottled water, a box of granola bars, and a long extension cord. How thoughtful.

She glanced at the snow-covered window, remembering how picturesque the farm had looked as she'd headed into the parking lot, like something from a Thomas Kinkade print. She definitely needed to generate some content to post, but the pine-covered beauty of Evergreen Acres should make her plenty of great photo ops.

As her laptop booted up, Brynn unfolded the flaps of a few of the boxes stacked against the wall, finding hundreds of glass ornaments, angel tree toppers, and light strands in every size and color. Brynn had a feeling it was Christmas year-round at Evergreen Acres. She pushed aside a garbage bag full of silver tinsel and found a plastic container covered in a thick layer of dust. As she lifted the lid and peered inside, her eyes widened. *Bingo*. Social media gold.

Brynn gripped the plastic container, pausing next to the saloon doors as a deep voice filled the room.

"FedEx just dropped the twelve-foot stands," the man said, sounding much younger than Charlie. Brynn hesitated. Where had she heard that voice?

She pushed past the doors, carefully adjusting her grip on the container as she glanced around the shop, finding only Charlie and Gina.

"Everything meet your needs?" Gina asked.

"Yes, thank you," Brynn said.

"Great," Gina said, then nodded to the counter. "List and coffee, ready to go."

"Cream and the sugar packets are in the back," Charlie said. He nodded to her arms. "Whatcha got there?"

"I was looking for some details to photograph for your Instagram stories," Brynn said, setting the box on the counter. "I hope you don't mind I was poking around?"

"Help yourself," Charlie said.

"What's the deal with this?" Brynn asked, lifting a large train car from the box, its paint shiny and pristine despite its vintage appearance.

"Oh," Charlie said, his eyes softening. "I'd wondered where that set had gone. That old thing was passed down through my wife's family."

Suddenly, a muscular arm reached over her shoulder, snatching the train from her grip. "That is *not* for sale," a gruff voice bellowed.

"I'm so sorry, I'm not-" Brynn sputtered, turning to find a pair of narrowed dark eyes beneath thick black eyelashes. Her jaw tightened as she realized exactly where she'd heard that voice before.

"What are *you* doing here?!" she demanded.

"Oh, no way!" Jordan's eyes widened, as he shot a horrified look to Charlie. "This in *not* who you brought in, is it!?"

Charlie shrugged, his brow furrowed in a look of amused confusion.

"Do you have any idea who she is?!" Jordan demanded and heat rushed to Brynn's face. "Dad, what were you thinking?"

"*Dad?!*" Brynn exclaimed before Charlie could reply. "Trust me, you're the last person I thought I'd see here!" She turned to Charlie. "He's your—?"

No way that nasty jerk could be this jolly old man's blood.

"This is our farm," Jordan said, ice in his voice. "The last thing we need is a train wreck like her around during the busy season."

"Can someone please explain what's going on?" Charlie shouted over top of them.

"I really should have read that flyer you stuck in my shop," Brynn said, laughing darkly, hardly hearing Charlie's question.

"I can't imagine you have time in your selfie schedule to read much of anything," Jordan retorted with a snort.

"*Excuse* me?!" Brynn sputtered. "You're the one who watered my Alocasia Polly with *tap* water and then ran out like a little baby!"

Gina just gaped at them, but the twitch of her lips suggested she was enjoying the spectacle more than a little.

"Jordan, I didn't know this train set meant so much to you," Charlie said, stepping between them.

"I don't care about the trains, Dad," Jordan snapped, though the care with which he set the little car back into the box suggested otherwise. "Besides, it doesn't even have an engine. I don't even know why we still have it."

"Why did you ask me to come here?" Brynn asked, shaking her head as she glanced from one confused face to the next. None of this made any sense.

"I didn't want anyone here at all, but in my wildest nightmares, I never would have guessed it would be you," Jordan said, his nostrils flaring as color flooded his chiseled, ruddy features. Brynn would have loved to punch those same full lips that had made her tingle the first time they met.

"I've been scratching my head since he told me, trying to figure out why anyone would offer to work her for free," Jordan continued. "Now it all makes perfect sense. After that little temper tantrum at Grantway, I bet you're looking for a charity case to redeem yourself."

Brynn's veins turned frigid. As she opened her mouth to retort, the phone began to ring once more.

"This was a bad idea," Brynn stammered. She fled through the curtain, scooping up her laptop and notebook as she threw her peacoat over her arm. "Sorry to waste your time," she called to Gina and Charlie, her voice quavering as she added, "Merry Christmas."

"Brynn—wait!" Charlie called as she stormed out the door and beelined for her car. She focused on keeping her thin, spiky heels steady as she hobbled over the gravel. A sprained ankle would really be the cherry on top of a great morning.

Her heart thundered in her chest as she dug her fingers into her jacket, but all she found was a gum wrapper and her phone in one pocket and a little bottle of hand sanitizer in the other. No keys.

"Crap!" she said, pressing the heel of her hand to her forehead to quell her growing headache.

She must have left her purse in the shop, hanging on the back of the metal chair. She blinked and tipped her head back, unwilling to allow even one tear to fall at this godforsaken place. She pulled her phone from her trouser pocket and a text from Katie lit the screen:

The comments on last night's videos are OUT OF CONTROL! People love you helping a small-town biz in need. How's it going? Saved Christmas yet?

She groaned as she shoved the phone back into her pocket. The last thing on Earth she wanted was to go back inside, but there was no way around it. She might as well get it over with.

She stomped back toward the shop, cursing her wardrobe choice as the chilly wind wrapped around her legs with each freezing step. She would head straight for her bag and then back to the solitude of her car without making eye contact with a soul.

She took a deep breath and flung open the door, crashing straight into the sturdy wall of Jordan, her nose colliding straight into his rock-hard chest.

"Ow!" she cried, batting him away as he reached for her.

"Oh, hey, I didn't—" Jordan began.

"*Excuse* me," she cut in coldly as she dabbed her hand against her nose. Thank goodness it wasn't bleeding. She pushed past him. "I forgot my purse."

"Wait," he said, firmly gripping her upper arm. "I—well, I'm sorry."

"Are you now?" Brynn asked sarcastically, tugging her arm from his grip and she spun to face him.

"I am," he said, his eyes now without the hardness of moments before. He looked like a scolded child. A six-foot-four, very muscular, perfectly scruffy scolded child. Brynn shook that thought from her head and allowed the anger to climb back up her throat.

"What exactly are you sorry for?" she demanded, raising an eyebrow.

"I mean," Jordan began, pausing as he scratched the back of his head. "I'm sorry for...being unprofessional. That was definitely not to my advantage."

"No, it sure wasn't," Brynn said, crossing her arms protectively over her chest. "Now if you'll excuse me, I'll get my purse and we can forget we ever met."

But Jordan quickly side-stepped, blocking her path.

"You really won't accept my apology?" he asked.

"Your *apology*?" she repeated.

He shrugged, but said nothing.

"You want to talk about an apology?" Brynn said, laughing darkly. "You physically block me and somehow think it's OK to touch me?! You better be grateful my pepper spray is inside my purse."

"You know, it's funny," Brynn continued as she glanced around the shop. "Gina and Charlie conveniently disappear, leaving only *you* with your half-hearted, sorry-not-sorry, so-called apology." She clenched her fist, willing herself not to slap that fake, eager smile from his cocky face. "It's almost as if someone *forced* you into an apology, then left you here to fix the mess you made with your rude, entitled, ungrateful behavior—but that can't possibly be what happened here."

"They grabbed lunch," he said, his brows furrowed. Was that a hint of amusement in those dark eyes?

"It's 9:30," she retorted.

"OK, let's be real here," he said, raising his hands in an irritatingly diplomatic way. "You clearly don't like me. If I'm being honest—"

"Well, that would be refreshing," Brynn interjected with a snort.

"—I don't care much for you either," he said, raising his voice to drown out hers. "But—I want to save Evergreen Acres. So, I'll do whatever it takes."

He watched her as he cautiously lowered his hands back to his sides as if she was a wildcat that was about to pounce. My gosh, the guy was dramatic.

"I have a feeling you really want to make up for that scene you caused in the supermarket, am I right?" he asked a moment later after she clearly did not, in fact, pounce.

Brynn just stared coolly.

"So..." he continued. "It seems our only option is to put up with each other for a few weeks, just until we can get out of our respective messes. Whether we enjoy it or not."

Brynn sighed as half her fury slid from her veins. As much as she hated to admit it—and she *really* hated to admit it—he was right. What other choice did she have?

"Is that all?" she asked finally.

"Uh...well, what else do you want me to say?"

"Maybe something about how you will stop being a complete asshole to me?" she said matter-of-factly.

"I can try, but I don't want to make any promises I can't keep," he said, a small smile tugging at the corner of his mouth.

"Right," she said.

"I'm a very honest person," he said with a shrug.

"So you keep saying," she said, a tired resignation taking up residence beside what anger remained. "OK, fine. I'll stay. For now."

"Great," Jordan said, his face even, but Brynn thought she glimpsed a hint of relief in those hickory-colored eyes. "Thank you," he added, the words clearly painful. "For giving it another go."

"You're welcome," she said. "But don't let it go to your head. You're literally my last option on the planet."

"Fair enough," he said, his laugh surprisingly warm. His breath smelled like coffee. Suddenly, Brynn shuffled back a few steps and Jordan stared at his boots as they both seemed to register just how close they were standing to each other.

"Well, let's get started, shall we?" he said, a little too brightly.

"Sure, I'll set up in the back," she said. "You can join me, but first I'll just be creating your social media accounts."

"I meant let's get started *outside*," Jordan said innocently, his eyes slipping from her bare legs to her black stilettos. "I assume you brought something other than those to work in?"

"Wait, what do you mean *work in*?" she repeated. "I'm here for branding. Advertising. Strictly indoor activities."

"And how exactly will you advertise us if you don't know anything about us?"

He waited, watching her with amusement as she racked her brain for a clever retort. She came up empty.

"Besides," he continued. "Everyone pitches in on the farm. You're a plant girl—you should be right at home, don't you think?"

"I didn't bring anything else," she said coolly, not about to give him a win that easily. "But you'd be amazed what I can do in heels."

"Gina's got a spare pair of muck boots by her locker," he said, pointing his thumb toward the back. "See if they'll work. As for a coat..." He was trying not to smile and doing a terrible job.

"I have a coat, thank you very much," she said quickly.

"Right," he said, eyeing her red wool peacoat. "Well, I'm going to grab some more coffee from my house if you want any," he said, raising his thermos. "I'll meet you at the barn in ten. If you head out the back door—"

"I'll find it," she said.

He nodded. "See you there."

"Can't wait," she said, flashing a toothy smile before storming off into the back room.

TWELVE

As Jordan waited for the little Keurig to come to life, he scratched Toby behind the ears, eliciting a sleepy groan from his old dog. Now that the weather had turned cold, Toby preferred to spend the day napping inside the toasty cabin rather than following Jordan around the property.

Charlie's face full of disappointment and confusion flashed across his mind, followed by to that feisty woman's penetrating stare, equal parts disgust and suspicion. He had to admit that he had underestimated her. Despite the frilly dress, Brynn was a force of nature. He still didn't like her, but admired the way she stood up for herself.

There was something else bothering him—the way she'd looked at him. Like *he* was the bad guy, like *he* was the one who had it all wrong. He couldn't remember anyone ever sizing him up with so much hostility, speaking to him with so much venom. He felt a sudden urge to prove her wrong that he quickly squashed like a bug.

He topped off his coffee and refilled Toby's water dish before zipping his coat and pulling the wool cap back over his messy waves. He stepped outside and slipped on his thick, leather gloves, not bothering to lock the door. He thought he was used to the winter chill by now, but shiver ran up his spine as the wind slapped his face.

As he trudged across the thin stretch of woods that separated his cabin from the work buildings, he saw Brynn leaned against the barn, her eyes glued to her phone. She wore fuzzy red earmuffs over a neat low bun and her perfectly tailored jacket was buttoned all the way up long neck. She reminded Jordan of a figure skater. Just then she looked up, and Jordan's throat tightened.

"Ready?" he said quickly as she tucked her phone into her pocket.

"As I'm gonna be," she said.

They walked up the rocky incline, still slick from last night's snow, as Jordan laughed, watching Brynn walk like an awkward duck in Gina's muck boots.

"You alright in those?" he asked.

"They're a little big, but nothing I can't handle," Brynn replied.

"We'll head for the seven-footer field," he said. "It's not far."

They trudged on. Jordan watched Brynn as she took in the property, her gold hoops swinging on her delicate ears with every step. He tried to imagine Evergreen Acres through her eyes, from the tree-encrusted rocky hillside above them to the fields of pines all around. It was easy to get used to this place, to forget its barely tamed beauty.

"You can't see most of it from the road, or even the parking lot," he said, lengthening his step to move in front of her. "But the best part is back here."

"I can't believe you live here," she said, breathless and he saw that a soft wonder had replaced her hard stare. "It feels like a whole different world from Twin Falls."

"It kind of is," he said. "There's a big elevation change—that's why it's so much greener."

They stopped outside a field of trees aligned in perfect rows. Jordan opened a steel locker outside the gate and dug out his leather tool belt. He could feel Brynn's eyes on him. When he glanced up, she looked away quickly. He slammed the locker and walked over to her.

"So...a Christmas tree farm," she said, crossing her arms over her chest. "What is there to do besides plant them and cut them?"

"You sell plants for a living," Jordan said, laughing. "Is that all you do?"

"Of course not," she said, cocking her head. "I water them, prune them, check for pests..." She rolled her eyes. "Okay, fine. I get it. So, what are we doing out here?"

"First, we tag trees," Jordan said, pulling rolls of brightly colored plastic ribbon from his tool belt. "I don't like to cut them until we need to—we pride ourselves on freshness." He unrolled the green ribbon, snipping several short strips. "So, I tie these around them. Green, which means sell first; yellow, which means give them another year to grow; or red, which means something is wrong and I need to inspect or treat it later."

"Seems very organized," Brynn said. "Is there some kind of tree school you go to in order to learn all that?"

"Maybe," Jordan said as he opened the gate and gestured for her to enter first. "I wouldn't know. My family has been doing this so long, they made up their own system along the way. If it ain't broke, and all that."

"You know," Brynn said, smirking at him. "It's ironic to see such a Grinch in the business of Christmas."

"Just because I don't like you doesn't mean I don't like

Christmas," Jordan said as he latched the gate behind them.

He turned to find Brynn staring at the ground, hands shoved in her pockets. "What you said in there," she began in a soft voice, "about my *temper tantrum*...I'm not usually like that. I don't know what happened. I just got—well, I don't think it was okay to act like that if it makes any difference."

Jordan said nothing, surprised at this sudden show of vulnerability.

"And you're right," she continued. "I do have something to prove now." She looked up at him and met his gaze, her long lashes skimming her perfectly groomed eyebrows. "But I also just want to help. It feels nice to be a part of something outside myself for a change."

As Jordan listened, he felt himself soften. She seemed genuinely remorseful. He tried to ignore the fact that he was acres away from the shop, standing alone with a beautiful woman. Really, she was a bit *too* good looking. In his experience, women like that always knew it and always got away with a little too much. He resolved to watch out in case she turned that hot-girl charm on him.

"So, you say you're here for the right reasons," he said. "In that case, let's get to it." He stopped next to the first row and pointed to a tall, full pine. "What color?"

"Green, obviously," she said immediately. "It looks healthy."

"Ooh, wrong, it's a yellow," Jordan said, screwing up his face into a look of mock disappointment. "We have too many seven-footers cut already. This one gets another year."

"Now, how am I supposed to know that?" Brynn protested.

Jordan smiled. "At least I know you were listening."

Brynn studied him and darted down the row, disappearing

behind the trees. Suddenly, she reappeared, grabbing his hand and pulling him toward an even taller tree at the very end. His stomach twisted at her touch, but he kept his face even as she stopped and held out her hand.

"Red, please," she said.

Jordan looked up at the full tree and shook his head. "That's not a red."

She put her hands on her hips and grinned. "Spider mites."

"Oh, you think you know fir trees now?" he said, scoffing as he stepped closer. As he reached for a branch, he could smell her perfume. It smelled like orange and cinnamon and something he couldn't quite place. He cleared his throat and focused on the tree. He lifted a branch and leaned closer. Sure enough, the thick telltale webbing that meant an infestation of aptly named spider mites.

"Beginner's luck," he said, slowly turning to face her.

"I'm far from a beginner when it comes to plants," Brynn said, that triumphant smile fixed on her lips as she did a little dance, pumping her fists and wiggling her hips side to side. She was like a toddler: adorable one minute; absolutely batshit the next.

"Looks like Charlie already got to these," Jordan said when they found the next row already tagged. "Guess it's time for the fun part."

"That wasn't the fun part?" Brynn teased.

Jordan led her down the hill to a second barn, which was much more state-of-the-art than the one behind the store. He felt a bit giddy bringing someone up here. This was always his favorite part of the day.

"Is that—Christmas music?" Brynn asked as they approached, and Jordan could hear the old radio droning from inside.

"Sure is," Jordan said, lifting the big wooden latch that kept the door barred.

Brynn chewed her lip as she eyed him with interest as her turned up nose turned redder by the moment. He'd enjoyed watching her pretend her jacket could stand up to the December wind, but he felt a pang of guilt as her body shivered. A completely irrational part of him wanted to wrap his arms around her petite frame; hold her against him until she stilled, and her color had returned. She might be hostile and bizarre, but she was beautiful, and Jordan was still a hot-blooded man.

"After you," he said, ignoring his caveman brain as he slid open the massive doors.

He followed Brynn inside, feeling for the switch through the warm, sweet-smelling dark. He squinted as fluorescent light flooded his vision, and "All I Want for Christmas Is You" became drowned out by a sudden cacophony. He bit back a smile as Brynn's mouth dropped open as she stared wide-eyed at each stall. The first housed seven or eight quacking, flapping white ducks; the next, a fat gray rabbit with floppy ears, and farther down, two black and white spotted pigs snuffing through their trough. There were six stalls along each side and all of them were occupied.

"I had no idea this was, like, a *farm* farm!" Brynn practically squealed as she rushed to pet a baby goat who'd stuck its head between the bars to bleat at them. "They're all so cute!"

She pulled off her earmuffs, sending wisps of golden hair unfurling down her back.

"You can pet them later," Jordan said, tossing a bucket under one of several different feed bins. "We've got work to do. I'll refill the feed and start mucking out the stalls." He nodded to a deep metal sink. "Can you refill water bowls?"

"Sure thing," she said, picking straw from her bare legs as she stomped across the barn in her oversized boots.

Jordan tossed the hens their feed before filling a bowl with kitten kibble. He still couldn't believe she was foolish enough to wear a dress outside in the middle of winter, but to her credit, she hadn't complained. And, as he pressed his lips together, forcing the image of those muscular thighs from his mind, he certainly wasn't complaining either.

Brynn made her way from stall to stall, humming along with the Pentatonix as she filled each bowl. To her delight, each animal greeted her at the gate and was happy to be pet, even a little three-legged raccoon. As she rinsed the last bowl, she glanced over to where Jordan was scooping a stall with a pitchfork, his white long-sleeved tee pulled tight across his strong shoulders.

She stared at the water dish, trying not to spill as she set it beside a tortoise the size of a Rottweiler. She wasn't the type to get flustered by a few extra muscles, but this was the first time she'd seen him without his coat. There was no other word to describe him besides *jacked*.

"What can I do next?" she asked, her heart beating in her ears as Jordan pushed the muck-filled wheelbarrow.

"Teddy could use some fresh cedar," he said, nodding his head at a skinny black miniature horse. "The bedding is all behind you."

She nodded and turned to find stacked bales and a big cube of shavings that had already been ripped open. Jordan held out a shovel, but didn't immediately let go when she tried to take it from him.

"Thank you," he said, holding her gaze.

"Got it," she said briskly, snatching the shovel from his grip. She'd already allowed her thoughts to wander too far in some dangerous directions.

Though it couldn't have taken more than five minutes, Brynn's arms felt like sandbags as she scrubbed her hands in the wash sink.

"Not bad," Jordan said, lowering himself onto a hay bale as he passed her an unopened water.

"Yeah, you did okay too," she said, opening the bottle and downing nearly the whole thing. "So, what exactly do you do with these animals?" They clearly weren't eating them, unless raccoons were their idea of a snack.

"They're all rescued," Jordan said as she followed his shining eyes to the nearest stall. "Bartholomew has been here longer than I have."

"That giant turtle?"

"*Tortoise*," he said. "My mom had a soft spot for pretty much all living things, so we've always ended up with strays."

Brynn blinked. *His mom had a soft spot. Past tense.*

"Don't you run out of room?" she asked. She wasn't sure how many more animals could possibly fit.

"We work with a couple rescues and veterinarians," Jordan said. "When they get the unusual hard-to-place creatures, they call us. Sometimes, we get wild animals waiting to heal, but most get adopted eventually."

"Then what's with the kittens?" Brynn asked, scooping a tiny tabby onto her lap. "Unless they're baby panthers, I'd hardly call them unusual."

"Maybe I'm just a cat person," Jordan said, widening his eyes into a look of innocence. She doubted that, but they were pretty hard to resist. As if on cue, the little orange bundle burrowed her nose into Brynn's elbow and began to purr.

"The kittens kind of took over that stall after we released the deer that was staying in there," Jordan continued. "Our neighbor found her and called us after they saw her limping on what turned out to be a broken leg." He tugged out his phone and scrolled before passing it to Brynn. Sure enough, there was a selfie of a grinning Jordan and a full-grown doe. "The vet set the bone free of charge and she lived in here for a few months. We call her Debbie. She still hangs around. I keep a dish filled with fruit and oats down by the store."

"That's the story you need to be telling the internet!" Brynn said. "Family-owned Christmas tree farm finds forever homes for rescued animals?" She shook her head at him. "My wallet is practically screaming as we speak!"

"I guess that's why you're here," Jordan said, chuckling as he threw on his coat. "Tell the world—just don't mention Bartholomew. He's not up for adoption."

"Fair enough," she said, buttoning her jacket as she followed him outside. This place was content gold. Brynn would have to drag her ring light up there before she left for the day.

"When it's warmer, I open the stalls to the outside," Jordan said, his eyes shining as he latched the door. He clearly loved the animals as much as his mom must have. "In this weather, even the sheep prefer the barn."

Suddenly, a floppy tan blur charged through the muddy grass, planting its paws squarely on Brynn's skirt as it began furiously lick her hand. The little dog let out a yip, then swept a circle around her feet before jumping on her once more.

"Down, Toby!" Jordan scolded, shooing the dog with one hand. "Sorry," he added, eyeing a dirty smudge on her otherwise pristine outfit. "This guy will laze around all day, but he acts like a puppy around anyone new."

"He's sweet," Brynn said, laughing as he sped past her legs once more. "Is he yours?"

Jordan nodded. "Charlie must have let him out. So much for a fearsome guard dog."

"He seems like a great judge of character to me," she said with a smirk as Toby rolled over at her feet, inviting a belly scratch she was happy to oblige.

"Well, we should get back," Jordan said, glancing up at the sky. "If we're lucky enough to get a morning rush, it will be starting anytime."

"Sounds good to me," Brynn said as Toby hopped to his feet and began sniffing the perimeter of the barn. "The sooner I can get these social media accounts up and running the better."

Jordan groaned. "You aren't going to force me to twit, are you?"

"It's called a *tweet*," Brynn said, bursting into giggles.

"It should be called Tweeter then," Jordan said grumpily.

"No one even uses Twitter anymore," Brynn said, trying to stifle her laughter. "We're going to get you all over Insta and TikTok, my friend."

She was still smiling as she followed Jordan down the embankment, muddy now that most of the overnight snow had melted. Despite being stuck with the most self-righteous man she could think of, Brynn had to admit she might actually be enjoying herself. Maybe.

THIRTEEN

"He is beyond obnoxious," Brynn mumbled, a roll of Scotch tape in her teeth as she held the popcorn garland in place.

"I just can't believe it's the same guy," Katie said, waving as a couple shop regulars passed by the window.

"I felt like I'd been set up on some hidden-camera show," Brynn said, stepping back to admire the garland on her newly decorated counter. "Should I drape it or hang it tight?"

Katie peered out over the computer. "Drape. Definitely drape."

"The frustrating part is that Evergreen Acres is, like, some watercolor Christmas card," Brynn said, sticking on a couple extra pieces of tape for good measure. "But the only people who know about it are all locals who've been going there since they were kids. Jordan seems absolutely clueless when it comes to advertising."

"You've only been there one day," Katie said, pulling a stack of papers of the printer and stapling them together. "Give it some time. You really know your stuff."

"Could you tell that to Jordan?" Brynn joked. "That guy hates me."

"Hate is a strong word," Katie said. "It's probably more of a general dislike."

"Hilarious." Brynn huffed.

Yesterday still seemed like some kind of fever dream. She'd hardly spoken to Jordan once she'd settled into her makeshift office, but she just couldn't reconcile the jerk she'd encountered too many times with the warm, teasing animal lover. It was like two different men with the same face.

"Well, you could quit," Katie said as Brynn tossed a handful of leftover popcorn into her mouth. "But your subscribers are already coming back. Soon enough, maybe they'll forget about Grantway altogether."

"I can't quit," Brynn said, ripping open a ream of paper. "For a million very good reasons, but the biggest one being that I wouldn't give that man the satisfaction." She grabbed a chunk of pages, filling the printer tray before gently sliding it closed. "Besides, Charlie is kind of growing on me."

"The old guy?" Katie asked.

Brynn nodded as she watched two college-age girls peruse her collection of succulents. "You know, it was kind of nice to be outside; nice to get a break from commenting, 'like and subscribe!' every five seconds."

"Did I just hear that right?" Katie asked, breaking into a purple lipsticked grin. "Brynn Callaway is enjoying the Great Outdoors?"

"Oh hush," Brynn said, elbowing Katie playfully. "Speaking of the Great Outdoors, do you have, like, a *coat* coat? I think my coat might actually be more of a jacket."

"You did not wear your little red peacoat to the farm, did you?" Katie asked with a laugh.

Brynn shrugged. "What would you have worn?"

"At least a puffer!" Katie said.

"You know me," Brynn said, tapping a manicured nail on the counter. "A puffer isn't exactly my style."

"A puffer isn't exactly anyone's style, you city slicker," Katie said, laughing so hard tears began to stream down her face. "It's just warm. And I'd put down money that you wore heels."

Brynn groaned in response and Katie lost it, tossing her head back in silent hysterics as the two young women carried plants to the counter.

"I'll ring you up," Brynn said to them, smiling and shaking her head as Katie grinned and swiped at her eyes.

"I got it," Katie replied, still grinning as she grabbed a box from beneath the counter. "You've got somewhere to be."

Brynn would never stop being grateful to have her friend by her side. She had no idea where she'd be personally or professionally without her Kate. She took a deep breath and exhaled slowly. She was ready for day two.

"That woman clearly never stepped foot on a farm before," Jordan declared, raising his mug just as the waitress walked over with a full pot.

"I'll kindly remind you, that woman isn't charging us a dime," Charlie said, scooping up the loose muffin crumbs that had tumbled to his plate.

"Don't think for one second this is from the goodness of her heart," Jordan said. "That girl cares way more about being some influencer than she does about Evergreen Acres."

Charlie studied Jordan through narrowed eyes as he wiped his mouth and took a sip of orange juice.

"What?" Jordan asked.

"I saw Brynn trudging up the mountain yesterday," Charlie said. "She must have been freezing. I'm surprised you didn't scare her off a second time."

"First off, she insisted on helping," Jordan said, tossing his napkin onto his empty plate. Charlie blinked, skepticism all over his grizzled face.

"Fine," Jordan said. "I was trying to make a point: how can she sell us if she doesn't know who we are?"

"You sure that's all you were doing?" Charlie asked, cocking a bushy eyebrow.

"What else would I be doing?"

Charlie shrugged. "Pulling her pigtails before recess?"

"Yeah, right, Dad," Jordan said, catching the waitress's eye and beckoning her over. "I am tolerating her. That's it."

"Well, how about you let that poor woman work on the computer where we need her," Charlie said. "And please show her courtesy and at least a little gratitude."

Jordan raised his hands in mock surrender as the waitress approached.

"Can I get you fellas any more coffee?" she asked.

"No thanks, just the check," Charlie said. "Lori, please tell the kitchen everything was delicious as always."

"Will we be seeing you at Evergreen Acres this year?" Jordan asked. Lori was close in age to Jordan, and as kids, they'd often sneak off to play hide and seek while her always growing horde of siblings ran from tree to tree, picking their favorite. Now that she had kids of her own, Lori had kept the tradition going, though now it was her boys running through the woods, taking turns hiding from each another.

"I really want to," Lori began, looking at the table and shifting uncomfortably. "I love bringing Ellie and Noah, it's just...I think I might do one of those tree-in-a-box deals this year?"

As Jordan opened his mouth to reply, she added, "I'm working longer shifts to make some extra money for presents. It makes it hard to find a time to get out there, you know?"

"Sure, we understand," Charlie said kindly. "Sounds like a busy time."

That seemed to be the one thing everyone could agree on. Somehow the world seemed to feel busier and busier with every passing year. Jordan rubbed his stubbled jaw.

A busy time. Maybe there was something there.

"What if I threw in free delivery and brought it over after your shift one night?" Jordan asked.

"Oh!" Lori said. "That's so generous, but I wouldn't want to put you out."

"I'd be happy to," Jordan said. "And you'd be doing us a favor by staying a customer."

"Well, sure," Lori said, her surprise easing into a small smile. "Thank you. I'd much rather buy from you. It's tradition after all."

"Same size and type as last year?" Jordan asked. "We keep good records."

As they made plans for delivery, Jordan's heart swelled. True, it was only one sale, but it was something he could see. Some tiny hint of progress. Lori promised to call Gina with her payment info as Charlie unfolded a few bills and tossed them on the table.

"Thanks for treating," Jordan said as he finished tapping out a text to Gina.

"That was a nice gesture," Charlie said, downing his last swig of juice. "Free delivery."

"What she said about tradition," Jordan said excitedly, as he tucked his phone back inside his jacket. "it's got me thinking. *We are* tradition. We're family. We're a face. We're town history."

"I'm not sure I follow," Charlie said.

"I'm still working it out, but there's something there," Jordan said as he glanced out at the clear blue morning sky. "Sure, we need to let the world know about us, but we also need to reach out to our customers here. Their lives are changing just as fast as the tree prices."

The same old scents of stale coffee and vanilla air freshener wafted through the drafty cab of the old truck, and the Winona track blaring from the CD player told Jordan the tunes hadn't changed either. It had been ages since his dad had driven him anywhere—there was never reason to—but Charlie had called the night before, offering to pick him up and treat him to breakfast before work. Jordan studied his dad's creased face, his narrowed eyes fixed on the road as his hands never wavered from ten and two.

"Doesn't look like snow, though they said its coming," Charlie said, nodding through the windshield where thick white clouds swirled in the clear winter sky. "I expect we'll get the double whammy."

"I'll take it," Jordan said, with a tight chuckle. The 'double whammy' was their shorthand for the rush that came after a snowfall. On one hand, it put people in the holiday mindset and reminded them time was running out to buy a tree. On the other hand, lots of snow meant more work around the farm and a more precarious trek to the outer fields.

The sky was deepening to yet another shade of cerulean when they pulled into the driveway at Evergreen Acres twenty or so minutes later. The hunter green Jeep Cherokee was parked in its usual spot, typical for Gina who liked to get through the administrative work before the first customers arrived. As they passed between the towering twin ponderosas that framed the parking lot entrance, Jordan spotted a familiar blue car.

"Looks like she came back," Charlie said, his eyes twinkling as he backed into a corner spot. He smacked his palm against the dashboard. "Oops, forgot to grab the mail. I'll meet ya inside."

As Jordan stomped his boots clean on the porch steps, he saw the back of a familiar head through the window, and his eyes followed the wild yellow waves that cascaded nearly to her waist. He pushed the thought aside, looking away as he swung the door open.

Jordan took three automatic steps toward the register before freezing in place.

What the hell?

There was that messy blonde hair he'd spied seconds earlier, but he had obviously missed the rest of her. Brynn turned to face him, all grins as she gestured to herself like Vanna White. Replacing the impractical dress of the day before, was a red and green elf costume, complete with pointy plastic ears.

"Cat got your tongue?" Brynn asked with a smirk, shaking a bell-fringed boot cover.

"You look ridiculous," Jordan said, stifling a laugh.

"Ho! Ho! Ho!" Gina called, her cheeks pink with excitement as she danced her way through the saloon doors wearing a long, red, velvet dress. Jordan watched, open-mouthed, as she pinned a white wig in place. "I'm ready for my North Pole photo shoot!"

"Well, doesn't this beat all," Charlie said, laughing merrily as he closed the door behind him, a stack of mail tucked under one arm. "I must have missed the memo."

Gina responded with a deep curtsy as Charlie roared.

"Don't worry," Brynn said, tossing a paper shopping bag to Charlie. "You're next."

He tugged out a clear, slim package with a photo of an old-fashioned Santa Claus on one side.

"I had a feeling I'd be getting typecast," Charlie said, grumbling, though his creased eyes told Jordan he was loving every minute of this.

"I thought a photo of Santa visiting Evergreen Acres would be the perfect first social media post!" Brynn said, jingling as she stepped towards Jordan. He had to admit, she looked absolutely adorable as an elf, her rosy cheeks flushed with excitement. Costumes had never been his idea of a good time, but he had to admit her idea wasn't half bad.

"Well, good luck guys," Jordan said, grabbing the mail from Charlie.

"Where do you think you're going?" Gina asked, blocking the saloon doors as she crossed her arms over her ample chest.

"Uh, to open the mail in peace," Jordan said. No way he'd be caught dead dressed as some kind of reindeer. "If you're thinking I can take the photo, you'd be better off asking Toby. I'm a terrible photographer."

"First of all, I happen to remember a great photo you once took outside my shop," Brynn said, cocking her head and blinking coquettishly as Gina shot Jordan a curious glance. Clearly, Brynn was not above flirtation when it came to getting her way. "Second of all, you are the face of Evergreen Acres, and we need all hands on deck."

She tossed a bag to Jordan, but he wasn't about to open it while they all watched. It didn't take a genius to figure out what ridiculous outfit was inside. It was just a matter of *how* ridiculous.

"You're head elf," Brynn said as if reading his mind.

"You're already an elf," Jordan retorted. "I don't think we need another one."

"I just thought if I joined in, you might have a harder time saying no," Brynn said, smiling coyly. "I'll be the one taking the picture." She pressed her hands together in the universal symbol of begging.

Jordan had to laugh. This woman had absolutely no shame. Still, he had never worn a pair of pantyhose, and didn't plan to start anytime soon.

Before he could reply, he saw Charlie waving from behind Brynn's line of sight.

Be nice, Charlie mouthed, widening his eyes urgently in Jordan's direction as he flared his nostrils. Jordan much preferred Charlie's usual kicked-back nonchalance over whatever this silent messaging was.

But as Jordan opened his mouth to refuse, he caught a glint of something in Brynn's amused eyes. Was that victory? *Of course.*

Shutting Brynn down was exactly what she expected from him.

A low yip sounded from the back room as an antler-clad Toby scurried into view. He shook his head furiously, bucking so that his little brown felt sweater flapped up and down behind him.

"I guess he realized we took advantage of his nap time," Gina said with a snort to a giggling Brynn.

"See?" Brynn said, cocking an arched eyebrow at Jordan. "Even your dog is a good sport."

Jordan groaned. He clearly wasn't getting out of this, but that didn't mean he had to smile about it.

"I hope you got an extra-large," Jordan muttered as he reluctantly tugged the costume from the package.

"Obviously," Brynn retorted as Jordan bit his lip, pretending to be embarrassed. He loved nothing more than watching as Brynn cringed in realization, following his suggestive line of thought. "You know what I meant!" she added, but Jordan just shook his head in mock offense.

As he headed for the bathroom, he snorted, trying to hold in his laughter. He'd never seen anyone turn that deep a shade of crimson, and he was loving every minute of it.

"Big smiles!" Brynn called, centering the photo on a beaming Charlie as she zoomed in tighter. Not surprisingly, Charlie's twinkling eyes and thick gray eyebrows made for a perfect storybook Santa Claus. Gina, on the other hand, had gone fully method after regaling them with funny stories from her summers spent in stock theatre in college.

"Cheese and crackers!" she called in a thick British accent as she flashed Brynn her best Mrs. Claus smile.

"I guess the North Pole is in England," Jordan muttered as Brynn snapped away. It was easy to ignore his grumpiness when he was wearing red tights and a green tunic that barely covered his nether regions.

Even Toby was sitting patiently on Gina's lap, having forgotten to attack his antlers as soon as Gina began slipping him bacon-shaped dog treats.

Brynn sighed and crossed her arms over her own tunic as she leveled her gaze at Jordan. "You know, if you would just smile a little, this could over a whole lot sooner," she said.

Jordan shot her a murderous stare before plastering on a half-grimace, half-smirk.

Brynn would take what she could get. She snapped several shots in a row before tapping her camera roll to review them.

"That last one is the winner," Brynn called to them as she zoomed on Toby's open grin. "I think we've got it."

"No, we don't," Charlie said. "We need you in here!"

"Yeah, get over here, girl!" Gina chimed in, waving her over.

"OK!" Brynn said, setting the camera timer. While she would never turn down a chance for good content, she genuinely wanted to remember this moment of ridiculousness. Besides, it wasn't every day she got to rock elf ears.

"Everyone say 'tree'!" she shouted as she jogged over and tucked behind Gina.

"Tree!" they all exclaimed in unison, and this time, even Jordan joined in as the camera snapped several shots in a row.

Brynn ran back behind the tripod, flipping through the shots as Gina and Charlie argued jovially about whether Will Ferrell's *Elf* could now be considered a Christmas classic. Her gaze hovered over the last photo, their banter becoming white noise as Brynn realized she'd finally caught a genuine smile from Jordan. So, that's what he looked like on his better days. Her stomach flip-flopped a little as she zoomed in tight on his face. His eyes were softer, crinkling at the corners with apparent joy. He was absolutely ridiculous in that costume, but for a second, all she could see was his stubbled jaw, his pink-tipped nose, his thick, full pink lips.

Gina suddenly hooted in response to something Charlie had said. Brynn locked her phone and tore her focus back to the group, where her gaze collided with Jordan's. Had he been watching her? She swallowed and looked away, inwardly reprimanding herself for the heat that suddenly coursed through her veins.

"OK, guys, that's a wrap!" Brynn said, sliding her phone into her pocket as she collapsed and folded the tripod. "Thanks for being good sports."

"And thank you for ruining any chance of a future career in politics," Jordan said, fluttering his eyelashes cheekily while pointing to his pantyhose.

Brynn groaned.

"Get used to it," Charlie said, his voice light as he tugged off his velvet hat and ran his thick fingers through his salt and pepper hair. "That boy was born stubborn."

"Watch it, Old Man Christmas," Jordan teased.

"Well, that stack of wreaths isn't gonna put pinecones on itself," Gina said, affectionately patting her wig with no indication she was in a hurry to change out of her own costume. Brynn, who appreciated a good accessory herself, bit back a smile. This woman was easy to like.

"Could you use a hand?" Charlie asked.

"Only if you keep that outfit on," Gina said, a playful glint in her eye.

Charlie laughed, but he tugged his hat back over his hair and followed Gina up the steps and into the shop. As Brynn watched them go, she couldn't help wondering if there was something more between them than simply being coworkers. Well, she'd have to wonder. She certainly wouldn't be asking Jordan to spill the Evergreen Acres tea.

As Brynn sorted her favorite shots into the newly created folder on her iPhone labeled "Evergreen Content," she could feel Jordan silently watching her.

"Did you need something?" she asked, ignoring the way her pulse began to rise. Her body really needed to spend more time talking to her brain.

"Um, not really," Jordan said quickly, looking less than his usual confident self. "I just wanted to say that I watched one of your videos. Last night." He cleared his throat. "The one about soil-borne illnesses."

"And?" she asked, with intentional impatience.

"And..." he replied begrudgingly, "you really know your stuff."

"You're surprised," Brynn said, returning her eyes to the phone. She'd be damned if she'd let him see how that compliment gave her a little surge of pride.

"A little," Jordan admitted. "I remember when we were planting test saplings of Chitalpa hybrids and were having acidity issues, and no one had a clue what I was talking about."

"Well, okay, Bill Nye," Brynn said with a laugh, glancing back at him. "Did you major in trees or something?"

"Botanical science," he said without his usual hint of sarcasm. "But I didn't finish. What about you?"

"PR," she said. "My mom is always muddling some mixture of homegrown herbs, but otherwise, I'm self-taught."

"Huh," Jordan said, and Brynn wasn't mad to see some newfound respect in the way he looked at her. "Well, scrolling through your channel, got me thinking," he continued. "Specifically, about this internet advertising business. Maybe all these newfangled ideas aren't that crazy after all."

Brynn snorted. "Did you just say 'newfangled' with a straight face?"

"Oh, hush," Jordan said, but his lips curled into a tiny smile. "What I'm trying to say is, you're clearly much smarter than I gave you credit for, and I'm sorry." He shrugged and that tiny smile turned sheepish. "We don't have much time to turn things around. I'm going to try my best to stay open and to trust you."

"You trust me?" Brynn asked, raising an eyebrow in amusement.

"I said I'm going to *try* to trust you," Jordan clarified, but those deep brown eyes were dancing.

"I'll take it," Brynn said softly. She swallowed, but neither of them looked away. She hadn't noticed those tiny freckles on his nose before.

"Well, I better go in so I can upload these faster," Brynn said, all too aware of her sweaty grip on her phone as she clumsily waved it in the air.

"Can I come?" Jordan asked, his face unreadable. "I should probably learn how to log in at least, right?"

"Sure," Brynn said, annoyed at how her heart kept pounding. "It's already working, you know."

"What is?" Jordan asked.

Brynn opened Instagram and tapped a post. It was a selfie of her from the day before, grinning as she embraced one of the plastic life-size snowmen decorations on the Evergreen Acres porch. "This one already has almost 500,000 likes."

Jordan's eyes widened as she passed him the phone and he

began to scroll the comments, a smile tugging the corners of his mouth. "Who are all these people?"

Brynn shrugged. "Mostly my followers. But once we get the Evergreen Instagram up and running, I'll direct folks to follow your page."

Suddenly, Jordan's entire face turned steely as his eyebrows knitted together.

"You OK?" Brynn asked.

"Yeah," he said, but she couldn't ignore the ice in his voice as he passed her back the phone. "Why don't you go ahead without me?" He stared blankly somewhere over Brynn's head. "I need to check the animals anyway."

"Sure," Brynn said, confused. "Maybe we can go over the socials later?"

"Yeah, maybe," Jordan said coolly. "When you have some extra time for charity."

Brynn chest constricted and her pulse went from racing to thunderous. She watched as Jordan trudged across the parking lot without a single look back. Her throat tightening and she frantically refreshed the post. What comment had upset him so much?

But she was on the very edge of the WiFi range, and Jordan was a tiny speck in the distance by the time the post refreshed. Her throat caught as her thumb hovered not over the comments, but the caption: *Feels so good to give back! #charity #helpthelessfortunate #blessed*.

She groaned as her pulse now throbbed in her temples. How could she have been so ignorantly callous? She'd only used those hashtags because they were so popular, making it more likely people would who didn't already follow her would find it.

Suddenly, she saw it in a new light. An out-of-touch, entitled, completely insensitive new light. No wonder Jordan had stormed off.

"Jordan, wait!" she called to him, hobbling across the lot in the cowboy boots she had swapped for her stilettos. "I'm sorry! I'll change that caption, but please let me—"

"I couldn't care less," he called over one shoulder, not slowing in the slightest. "I've got work to do." He stuck his fingers in his mouth and let out a high-pitched whistle. "Come on, Toby!"

Chagrined, Brynn teetered back to her tripod, tucking it under one arm as she carefully climbed the porch steps. She took a deep breath and forced a smile as she entered the warm shop and headed for the back room, snapping a photo of Mr. and Mrs. Claus finishing wreaths as she went.

FOURTEEN

"And if you like, you can spread the rest of those pebbles in a thin layer across the top of the soil," Brynn said, flashing her best camera-ready smile into the lens. "Not only will this keep your plant watered, but you can also match it to your home's aesthetic!"

She tipped the pot towards camera, knowing Katie could be counted on to zoom in for a close up. Though the filming lights were blinding, she could just make out Katie's silhouette flashing her a thumbs up.

As Brynn set the little begonia aside, she stole a glance at the little stopwatch that was tucked just out of view of the camera. Almost fourteen minutes. *Perfect.*

Brynn peeked at her notes, finding the information she had written for the end of her video:

Stones can be used for drainage, to line a pot, or for decoration.

How to find stones in your hometown.

Comment below and share your favorite rocks for top dressing.

"Begonias are great, right?" Brynn said briskly, folding the paper and tucking it in her pocket as she leaned closer to the camera. "And some rare ones, like this polka dot variety, feel like winning a prize when you find one. But nothing gets my heart beating faster than the one plant no one can hunt down."

Katie's shadow leaned around the camera and Brynn didn't need to see her expression to know her friend noticed she'd gone off script.

"We are all just one nursery stop away from that super rare plant," Brynn continued, gaining momentum as she started to feel as if she was outside herself, watching it all. "The one we scoop up for twenty bucks in a forgotten corner. The one we'll be able to sell cuttings from for a hundred dollars each. The one that will make all our friends green with envy...pun intended!" She laughed, but even to her own ears it sounded tinny and nervous.

"It's the dream, right?" she continued, as the LED lights swam through her vision. "I collected Beanie Babies when I was little. I'll never forget finding this super rare blue elephant at a flea market when I was eleven. How I felt when I turned it over and found its tag in pristine condition. And then when the stall merchant charged me five dollars!? Well...that rush, that exhilaration, can sometimes make us blind to anything else."

Katie was now standing off to the side, her hands on her hips as she watched Brynn with a thoughtful expression. Brynn took a deep breath, imagining Gina from Evergreen Acres watching this video.

"Sometimes I wonder if it's even worth it," Brynn said. "Like, if I get that blue elephant of a plant, can I even keep it alive?" The words had taken on a life of their own, spilling over from somewhere deep and uncharted. "Do I even like the blue elephant?" Her voice grew louder. "Or maybe I'm just hoping my blue elephant will impress people." A dull weariness spread through her body as the turmoil of the last week engulfed her brain, no longer dormant. Brynn couldn't tell if she hoped

Katie would put her out of her misery, or if she wanted to keep indulging the primal satisfaction of purging her guts to almost a million people. "Sometimes I wonder if I've spent so long keeping up, and trying to win, and get more, more, more—that I don't even know what the hell I like anymore." Her shoulders slumped as she braced herself against the table, a vision of Jessica's smug face getting the call from Homestead flashing across her mind.

Katie cleared her throat softly and Brynn blinked as she saw that the little red recording light was still flashing.

"Anyway!" Brynn said quickly, straightening as she plastered on her best attempt at a camera-ready smile. "Thanks as always for joining me. If you liked the video, please click that like button and comment below!"

"Aaaaaand...cut!" Katie called, and Brynn could swear she heard cautious hesitation in her voice. As the red light disappeared, a dull ringing thundered in Brynn's ears. She rubbed her palm against her temple and turned to Katie.

"Sorry," Brynn said weakly.

"For what?" Katie asked.

"Going off script," Brynn said as a hysterical giggle escaped her lips. "Word vomiting all over it. I could keep going."

"It's your show," Katie said, pulling Brynn into a quick hug. "We can always edit or reshoot, though I think viewers might really appreciate your honesty." She released Brynn and flashed her a secretive smile. "Besides, we have a little wiggle room now; your subscriber number has officially passed a million!"

"But, how?!" Brynn sputtered. Her numbers had dropped by over two hundred thousand after Grantway, but she'd been too busy to look at anything that past week. "All because of the Christmas tree farm?"

Katie shrugged. "Well, it obviously must have helped!"

"I wonder what Jessica's numbers look like," Brynn said, mostly to herself, barely catching Katie's almost imperceptible wince.

"What?" Brynn asked, a knot of dread forming in her stomach.

"Well," Katie said carefully. "She's close to three million subscribers now."

"*Three million*?!" Brynn sputtered. "What did she do, buy a small country?"

"We probably don't want to know," Katie said with a laugh, but her brows were knitted together in thought.

Brynn sighed. "Well, it looks like I'll be putting my elf hat back on tomorrow, figuratively speaking, anyway." She stifled a yawn. "Just upload the damn video as is before I change my mind." She glanced at the wall clock. "I better go. My mom will disown me if I stand them up tomorrow morning."

"I'll lock up after I upload this," Katie said as she popped the memory card out of the camera and headed for the office.

"Thanks, Kate."

A dull hollowness spread through Brynn's stomach as she maneuvered through the darkened store, carefully stepping around each display from memory. She pressed her lips together and squeezed a palm against her chest as if it might steady this sudden flood of anxiety. She missed the early days of her channel. Back then, when a store of her own was still just a pipe dream, everything had seemed so much simpler.

Not that she'd give up Planted in Twin for anything, but she never envisioned spending her waking hours counting likes and trying to impress a million strangers on top of running a brandnew business. She took a deep breath and braced herself against the door frame, the frigid night air penetrating the wood and stinging her hands.

Before she could stop herself, she shot off a quick text to Caleb. She still couldn't wrap her head around getting back together, but just then, she didn't want to be alone.

By the time she fell asleep a few hours later, she was both disappointed and relieved that he never wrote back.

Brynn silently congratulated herself as she avoided the ice patches that had formed overnight on her mom's front steps. She hoped Greta had her usual pot of coffee warming in the kitchen. After another restless night of worst-case-scenario dreams interrupted by long stretches of staring at the dark ceiling, Brynn was actually glad to have an excuse to wear makeup.

"There she is!" Gram called as Brynn hung her jacket in the entryway. She tucked her emerald green turtleneck into her high-waisted trousers and followed the muffled voices into the living room.

"Just in time," Paps said warmly as Brynn grabbed a cookie from the coffee table and plopped into the armchair next to Gram, who was applying lipstick in a compact mirror.

"You both look nice," Brynn said, recognizing her grandfather's wool cardigan as the one she'd given him for Christmas last year. "Where's the rest of the crew?"

"Oh, you know your mom," Paps said, easing back into his chair as he settled his sock-clad feet onto the ottoman. "She's probably in the yard showing the photographer what kind of mushrooms to forage for this time of year."

"Sounds like I have time for coffee," Brynn said, rising and heading for the kitchen.

As Brynn sipped her coffee, her mother's animated chatter suddenly droned in from the kitchen.

Tyler entered the room first, clean-shaven and sharply dressed in a tailored plaid button down shirt as he sipped from a ceramic Santa mug. He shot Brynn a quick covert look that gave Brynn a two second heads up that their mother was in a mood.

"Where were you?" Greta asked with a laugh as the photographer trailed behind, but Brynn saw genuine hurt hiding in the corners of her mother's eyes.

"I've been here since nine," Brynn said, confused. "We've been waiting for *you*."

"We ready to get started?" the photographer said before Greta could reply. He rifled through his camera bag, oblivious to the subtle tension forming around him.

"I'm just glad we're all here," Gram said brightly as the crew made their way to the backyard.

"She thought you weren't coming," Tyler whispered, catching up to Brynn as she dusted cookie crumbs from her pants.

"Why would she think that?" Brynn asked.

Tyler gave her a pointed look.

"OK, well unless something has changed, she thinks I actually was sick that night," Brynn hissed.

"You know Mom," Tyler said with an amicable shrug. "She's a sensitive creature." He studied Brynn's face as the photographer placed Greta, Gram, and Paps in front of the gazebo. "You OK, sis?" he asked, gently gripping her shoulder.

"Just tired," Brynn said, patting his hand, and she was relieved when he didn't press her further.

Once Brynn and Tyler tucked in beside their grandparents, and all five Callaways were positioned to the photographer's satisfaction, Brynn realized how much she'd missed having everyone all together. If she lined up every Christmas card her mom had sent since she was born, she'd have a timeline of her life, a flipbook of the people she loved the most. As much as she and Tyler shared eye rolls at the photo shoot Greta insisted on every winter, Brynn was grateful her mother truly made family traditions a priority.

When the photographer was satisfied and began packing up his gear, Brynn and Tyler left the others chatting in the backyard as they snuck back to the kitchen. As Tyler refilled both their empty mugs, Brynn plopped a business card on the counter in front of him.

"What's this?" he asked, eyeing the card as he grabbed a cold piece of bacon from a platter Greta had set out.

"Guess the photographer is single," Brynn said. "And Mom made a point to tell him that I was too."

"He slipped that you just now?" Tyler asked.

Brynn nodded. "When Mom seized his camera to scroll through at the pictures."

"Mom means well," Tyler said, laughing as Brynn groaned.

"Sorry, Greg," Brynn said, glancing at the card once more before tossing it in the trash.

"I'm surprised Mom didn't ask him to reshoot when the snowflakes started to fall," Tyler mused.

"I just don't know what she wants from me," Brynn said, shaking her head as she set her mug on the counter and popped a bagel in the toaster. "It's like, she thinks I'm throwing my life away because I work so much. And yeah, I'm tired, but I like working. I don't see what is so wrong with me."

"Have you told her that?" Tyler asked.

"Not in so many words," Brynn admitted.

"She just wants to make sure her kids are happy, as annoying as that can be," Tyler said.

Brynn offered a non-committal shrug. She was too tired to get into it.

"Mom aside—how are you doing?" Tyler asked as he passed her the blueberry jam, and she knew in that way that siblings have that he was referring to the incident at Grantway.

"I'm fine," Brynn said breezily.

He narrowed his eyes.

"I'm figuring it out," Brynn amended. "Katie's been a big help."

"So...are you happy?" Tyler asked, shoving the last piece of bacon into his mouth.

"I don't even know what that means," Brynn said, chewing her bagel as she watched the snow fall in fat flakes outside the garden window.

"Whatever you want it to mean," Tyler said.

Brynn blinked, not sure how to answer as she wiped a glob of sticky jam from her cheek.

"There better be some bacon left!" Gram called, her voice reaching them just as she, Paps, and Greta hurried in from the back deck.

Brynn and Tyler shared a look over the now empty plate.

"Come on," Brynn said, laughing, despite the weariness that she couldn't seem to shake these days. "You refill coffee and I'll fry up some more bacon."

As she rifled through the fridge's deli drawer, Tyler's question echoed through her mind.

Are you happy?

She felt her phone vibrate in her pocket and saw a text from Katie:

You have to see this. Scroll to the end. Love you. I'm so sorry. Call me as soon as you can!

Brynn's stomach plummeted as she slammed the fridge door, grateful that Tyler was preoccupied as she stepped into the hallway and clicked the link. She didn't know if she could handle any more bad news.

The Green Goddess YouTube channel filled her screen and Jessica Southgate appeared, seated primly on a tufted velvet loveseat behind a Lucite coffee table filled with exotic houseplants, her signature high ponytail draping over one shoulder.

"We goddesses know that plant ownership is a *privilege*," Jessica flashing her neon white grin at the camera. "Take this Euphorbia for example."

Jessica lifted a petite cactus from the table in front of her, its fin-like top encrusted in what looked like small beads.

"Some call this a Mermaid Tail," Jessica said, before laughing like a Disney villain. "Stop using nicknames. If you want to converse with the great plant minds of the world, you must master the universal language. I've been studying Latin since I was five."

Brynn groaned, but she couldn't figure out what she was supposed to be noticing that was so offensive.

"Brynn?" Tyler called.

"Be right there, taking a quick call!" Brynn yelled back. Then she reread the text from Katie and scrubbed to the last sixty seconds of the video.

"—and I couldn't do any of this without his help!" Jessica was saying when, suddenly, a tall man with sandy blonde hair entered frame and sat on the couch inches beside her. Brynn nearly choked as her blood ran cold.

"No, no, no, no," she gasped and turned the volume to full blast.

"—to my new cameraman, Caleb Whitaker!" Jessica's voice blasted from the speakers and even though there was no doubt about his identity, hearing his name confirmed knocked the air right from Brynn's lungs. Caleb gave a shy wave.

So, Caleb was Jessica's videographer? It seemed impossible. And yet, it clearly wasn't.

As she noticed Jessica's knee rub against Caleb's thigh, it all began to make more sense. He'd hated running camera for Brynn there at the end, but he hadn't seemed to mind before they started having problems. Brynn felt sick. No wonder Caleb had never texted her back.

But as she took a deep breath and headed back to the kitchen, she realized something: though she felt completely disgusted and more than a little betrayed, she wasn't jealous. And in that moment, she knew that she was never getting back together with Caleb.

FIFTEEN

Thwack! Jordan hammered the final nail into the porch handrail. After shaking the new rail and finding it sturdy enough for his liking, he checked his watch and turned the volume up on his headphones. Though he'd been outside since sunrise, the morning had flown by, thanks to Willie, Waylon, and the mind-numbing rhythm of nails piercing wood. He stood back and admired his work. It wasn't bad, but it would look much better once the snow stopped and he could stain it to match the rest of the porch.

He felt the floorboards shift and turned to find Brynn tiptoeing toward the door.

"Morning," he called, pausing his music.

"Oh! Morning," Brynn said, flashing him a sheepish smile. Had she been trying to sneak past unnoticed? He couldn't blame her.

She'd finally had the sense to wear pants today, though he hoped she had a coat in her car to go over that green top. His gaze lingered for only a split second, but not before he had a chance to admire the way the thin material hugged her slim curves.

"Well, see you in there," Brynn said curtly as she reached for the doorknob.

"About yesterday," Jordan said, sliding his hammer into his tool belt as he leaned against the damp railing. "I might have overreacted to that photo caption."

Brynn said nothing, just pursed her lips together and waited.

"Fine, I *definitely* overreacted," he said, rolling his eyes dramatically. "Better?"

"Much," Brynn said, her face softening into an unexpected smile that brought a wave of relief over Jordan. "But it was bad taste on my part. I'm sorry too. I changed the hashtags as soon as I realized."

"I noticed," Jordan said, as Brynn casually took a single step closer. She had flecks of amber and gold in her green eyes. His stomach clenched. Something about those eyes seemed to see straight through him. He swallowed. "You're doing so much for us, and, well, what I'm trying to say is, thank you."

"You're welcome," she said, looking out at the mountains as she joined him against the railing. His chest thundered, feeling every fiber of her sleeve as it brushed against his bicep. He followed her gaze over the ivory horizon, broken only by the blacktop of the road where the snow had already melted.

"I've been thinking," Jordan said after a moment. "I offered to deliver to a past customer who works late. It was just one tree, one person, but it felt good to make her life a little easier. Maybe I should be offering that all the time."

"Delivery?" Brynn asked. "That's a great idea, but wouldn't it require more manpower than we've got right now?"

We.

"On a large scale, definitely," Jordan agreed, suppressing a smile. "But I'm happy to do it in the evenings, especially if it helps some of our busier customers. Depending on where folks live, I could probably manage a few deliveries a night with the truck, more on weekends when we open later. I think most people would throw in a tip that would at least cover gas."

"That's very generous of you," Brynn said, studying him thoughtfully. He felt his jaw clench as he checked his watch again, not even registering the time.

"I could reach out to my friend who's a web designer," Brynn said, scrunching her nose in a way Jordan was beginning to recognize as her thinking face. "Maybe we could get your inventory online. Then, if someone wants a tree delivered, they can see what you have from home."

"That's a great idea," Jordan said.

"Thank you," she whispered, a small smile curling on those full, pink lips.

He resisted a sudden strong urge to touch the blonde wave had come loose from her topknot and draped softly against her smooth jawline.

"What are you doing tonight?" Jordan asked suddenly, trying to keep his breath even.

"No plans," Brynn said, narrowing her eyes. "What's up?"

"Do you want to come over?" Jordan asked. To his relief, his voice sounded nonchalant despite the fact that his chest was tied in knots. "You could show me Facebook, Instagram—what's the clock one?"

"TikTok," Brynn said, laughing. "Sure, I'll come. I just need to run to my store first and go over an order."

"Great," Jordan said. "I'll tell Gina and my dad to meet us. Do you know where to go?"

"Pretty sure I can find it," Brynn said, smirking as she nodded toward the little house, perfectly visible through the cluster of bare maple trees.

"I guess you can," Jordan said, running a hand against his warm neck. "How does eight sound?"

"It's a date," Brynn said brightly.

Jordan's mouth went dry.

"Well, not a *date,*" Brynn said quickly. "But you know..."

"It's a saying," Jordan said, biting back a smile as she blushed.

It was nice to see her flustered for a change.

"I better see if I can help Gina with your socials," Brynn said, snipping the tension. She turned and fled inside before Jordan could say another word.

He unbuckled his tool belt as he watched Gina and Brynn talking with their hands through the window. Why was he acting like such an idiot around her? Sure, she was hotter than hell, and if he had just met her, he probably would have been completely infatuated. But he already knew too much. Brynn was superficial and unstable, and besides a loosely overlapping love of plants, they had nothing in common. She was an obligation, he reminded himself. A temporary obligation.

Still, a hidden part of him couldn't help picturing her coy smile awash in the golden glow of his fireplace, as she splayed her muscular legs across his worn, leather couch. He clenched his jaw, cursing to himself as he gathered up his tools and headed for the storage shed.

Tiny ice crystals grazed the tips of Brynn's lashes as she carefully navigated the slick stone steps that led to the weather-beaten farmhouse, balancing a plant wrapped in craft paper under one arm. She was glad she'd had a last-minute thought to swap her turtleneck and peacoat for a comfy fleece and Katie's spare puffer coat.

Brynn knocked and peeked into the frosted glass window beside the front door. She could hear muffled piano music, but no one came. She turned the icy brass knob, the door swinging wide open as she hesitantly stepped inside.

"Hello?" she called, gently closing the door behind her as Frank Sinatra crooned from what sounded like a record player. The house had a rustic feel, with beams across the ceiling and chestnut wood walls that matched the hardwood floor. Despite the architecture, it was surprisingly modern, with recessed lighting and a flat screen TV mounted above the fireplace. Huge twin skylights stretched across the ceiling; two pitch black rectangles encrusted in frost. She could smell a mixture of Pine Sol, cinnamon, and something else...the buttery, mint scent she could now recognize as Jordan's own. Her heart began to drum so loud she could hear it.

"Hello?" she called.

She heard a scuttling sound as a warm body pressed against the back of her legs and began sniffing her. She grinned as she found Toby panting up at her, his tail wagging so hard his whole body twitched back and forth like a metronome. She bent down and scratched his ears, prompting him to heft himself onto his back and stretch out his belly, inviting a good scratch.

Brynn laughed as she obliged. "Quite the ferocious guard dog, aren't you, Toby?"

"I'd say his bark is worse than his bite," Jordan said from behind her. "But he doesn't seem to be much good for either."

Brynn stood and turned, finding Jordan leaning against the doorway as he dried his hair with a towel. She forced herself not to stare at the damp gray thermal that hugged every muscle in his torso.

"I didn't hear you come in," Jordan said, draping the towel around his shoulders as Brynn caught the scent of soap and aftershave.

"Sorry," Brynn said, feeling awkward. She shoved the plant into his hands. "For you."

He bit back a smile. "Are you on a mission to convert everyone to the dark side?"

She snorted and shrugged. "I had a feeling your place needed some greenery." As she peeled back the paper, a couple of vines tumbled out. "Plants help clean your air and this one isn't toxic for Toby." She smiled. "This is a heart leaf philodendron, which was my first ever plant. In fact, it's still alive."

Jordan gazed back at her, his brown eyes glittering with amusement. "I bet it lasts a week before I kill it." She swallowed as he subtly bit his lower lip. It was unfair how attractive this man was. What a waste.

"Sorry to tell you, but it's pretty hard to kill," Brynn said with a smirk.

"Sounds like a challenge," Jordan said. He unpeeled the rest of the paper and set the plant on the windowsill. "Why don't you catch up with Toby, and I'll mix us a couple drinks?"

"Sounds great," Brynn said. She handed him the wine. "We can open this later or you can just keep it."

"Nice choice," he said as he scanned the label. "Thanks."

"Sure," she said. She peeled off her coat and hung it on the coat rack as he headed down the hallway.

Brynn could hear the clinking of ice cubes as she wandered deeper into the living room. She walked to the mantle where two stockings hung from heavy hooks. She leaned closer to a picture frame, the fire below warming her face, as she gazed at a black and white photo of a bright-eyed young woman with big teeth and horn-rimmed glasses.

His mother, maybe?

Beside it, she found a delicate tarnished snow globe. She picked it up, gently shaking it as two ice skaters twirled around a glass pond, tiny white flakes swirling around them. She was gently setting the little globe back in its spot when the record crackled, and the music stopped.

She found the record player sitting on a wooden credenza in the dining room, the open cabinet filled with more vinyl than she could count. She thumbed through a stack of Christmas records, finding everything from John Denver to the Trans-Siberian Orchestra. She slipped the Sinatra record back into its sleeve, swapping it for the *White Christmas* soundtrack. Just as the opening bars of the title track filled her ears, she heard Jordan approach.

"Great choice," he said, handing her a glass filled with a thick white liquid.

"White Russian?" she asked, sniffing the drink.

"Eggnog," Jordan said, a childish grin spreading across his lips.

She laughed. "That's a little on the nose, wouldn't you say?"

He shrugged. "You might have called me a Grinch, but I happen to love Christmas."

"Did you make this?" she asked, pausing as she raised the glass to her mouth.

"I didn't poison it," he said with a chuckle, taking the glass from her and drinking from it before placing it back in her hand. She bit her lip, her gaze drifting to the faint smudge where his lips had been, before taking a hearty swallow. It was sweet and creamy, and the liquor instantly warmed her stomach. As she lowered her glass, she caught Jordan's eye.

"Surprisingly, it's not bad," she said, the words barely betraying the heat in her throat.

"Glad it meets your approval," he said, a soft smile dancing in those chocolate eyes.

Her phone chirped.

"Sorry, I thought I put it on silent," she said. Before she could toggle the volume switch, her eyes caught a notification and she groaned.

"Everything OK?" Jordan asked.

"Oh yeah, it's just a YouTube notification." She turned the phone so he could read it: *Green Goddess has posted a new video!*

"I don't think I have the whole story on this rivalry you've got going on," he said.

She rolled her eyes and quickly filled him in, telling him everything about Jessica's online aggression and their competition for the Homestead show. Well, almost everything.

"Wow, the show sounds like a really big deal," Jordan said.

"It is." Why hadn't she told him the show was in Los Angeles? It's not like he would care. "I love all these Christmas albums," Brynn said abruptly, changing the subject as she gestured to the stack. "I had a record player when I was a kid, but nothing this classy."

"These all belonged to my mom," Jordan said. "She was basically the queen of all things Christmas."

He straightened the stack with tidy efficiency, but Brynn

couldn't help noticing the distant look in his eyes.

"Should we sit down?" he asked.

She followed him back to the living room, sinking down into the comfy loveseat as she steadied her glass. As Jordan passed the obviously empty armchair opposite Brynn and sat down beside her, Brynn's stomach twisted into a pretzel. She cringed as she swallowed a huge gulp of eggnog, regretting not eating a proper dinner. She leaned over and patted Toby as he curled up on the floor between them.

"I was surprised you didn't have plans tonight," Jordan said, almost in her ear, as he scratched Toby underneath his collar.

"Why is that?" she asked, her pulse throbbing in her wrists.

"You know," Jordan said, his ruddy cheeks flushing. "Saturday... date night and all that."

"Do I have a boyfriend I don't know about?" Brynn asked, mortified as a nervous giggle escaped.

"Confession time," Jordan said, raising his hands in mock surrender. "I was trying to get the hang of Instagram and I looked through some of your posts. I saw you with someone on there, I think a camera guy."

"Oh, Caleb," Brynn said, willing her voice to stay steady. "We've been broken up for a while now."

"Sorry to be so nosy," he said and for once, he didn't seem to be mocking her. "Must be the eggnog."

"It's okay," Brynn said quickly. "Weren't Gina and Charlie joining us?" She set her glass aside as she focused on picking the lint off her trousers.

"They should be here any minute," Jordan said, glancing at his watch. "I actually asked them to come a bit after you because I wanted to ask you something."

"Nothing bad, I hope?" she asked as her heart began to pound against her ribcage.

"Not at all," Jordan said. "I wanted to tell you that Evergreen Acres was asked to be Master of Ceremonies for the tree lighting this year."

"That's huge!" Brynn said. Everyone went to the Festival of Lights parade, lining Main Street and even watching from inside the local businesses. When she was a kid, she'd even ridden on a kitschy float for the dance studio her Gram had owned. "I'd love to take pictures, though I'm sure the newspaper will."

"I was hoping you would do it with me," Jordan said, and Brynn could see that beneath the flickering glow of the fire, he was actually nervous. What was he up to?

"Me?" Brynn asked. "They asked *you*."

"They asked Evergreen Acres," Jordan said, a pleading smile in his eyes. "This year, that includes you."

That includes you.

Brynn wanted to slap herself at the surge of pride she felt at his words.

"Charlie won't do it," he continued, wiping a hand across his brow. "And I'm just not good at this stuff. And..." He looked down and began to pick at his calloused hand. "I would like you to be there, if you want to."

"Yes," Brynn said quickly.

Wow, way to sound smitten.

"I mean," Brynn said, reassuming her even expression, "I would be happy to."

But now he was gazing straight at her, his eyes betraying the same thoughts she was working so hard to banish. He must have registered her awareness, because he suddenly sprang to his feet.

"I'll get you some more," he said, reaching for her empty glass.

"No!" she exclaimed, more forcefully than she intended. "I mean, I'm driving so I better not. How much liquor is in there, anyway?"

"I don't measure," he said with a shrug. "I just taste it as I go."

She laughed. "That could be dangerous."

"Maybe, maybe not," he said, and she felt that devilish twinkle all the way down her torso. "How about some tea instead?"

"That would be perfect," she replied, half pleased and half disappointed that they were finding their way back to safer ground.

She didn't trust herself to drink more, not tonight. Not after that starving, voracious gaze he'd been laying on her all night. She must have been hallucinating or something. Or maybe he was just the clichéd booty call type.

The door swung open as Charlie's stout frame crossed the threshold, stomping his boots against the frame as he stepped inside and kicked off his boots.

"Oh, you beat us!" Gina said to Brynn as a broad smile spread across her weathered face. "What did we miss?"

"I hope not the eggnog!" Charlie said, scratching Toby as he threw his little, tan body on the threshold.

"There's plenty more!" Jordan called from the kitchen.

"Your face is pink from the fire," Charlie said, clapping Brynn on the shoulder before beelining toward the kitchen. "I'll tell that boy to watch how many logs he piles on."

Gina plopped down next to Brynn and immediately started

filling her in on a housewife who had just announced she was filing for divorce. Brynn wasn't sure if these were the New Jersey wives or the Atlanta ones, but she nodded along anyway. Soon, Charlie and Jordan joined them, each taking one of the armchairs. Jordan's rough fingertips brushed Brynn's as he passed her a teacup, but she pretended not to notice as Gina droned on.

"So," Brynn said once the small talk had waned. "Are we ready for Advertising 101?"

"Girl, I was born ready," Gina said, pumping a fist in the air. "Give me flash sales, give me Groupon, I want it all!"

Brynn laughed and she saw Jordan stifle a cringe.

"Well, I'll make this as simple as possible," Brynn said. "I thought tonight we could stage a few activities and I'll take pictures that we can use for posts. Nothing complicated, maybe even one of you guys sitting here enjoying some eggnog."

"Seems easy enough," Charlie said. He tossed a throw pillow at Jordan, who caught it just before it knocked over his eggnog. "Isn't this overtime? We really aren't paying her enough."

"We aren't paying her *anything*," Jordan reminded him.

"My point exactly," Charlie said, shooting Jordan a meaningful look.

"I'm here because I *want* to be," Brynn insisted. "This stuff isn't always fun, but it can make a big difference."

"I'm not the most photogenic, but I'm sure you've got some fancy editing skills?" Jordan asked, but Brynn thought he was only half joking.

"I brought my ring light and I promise to make you look good," Brynn said.

"Count us in," Gina said, pointing a look at the men as if daring them to argue.

"Great!" Brynn said. "First, let's go over some basics. At some point, I won't be around to post for you, so I want to be sure you can do it on your own."

"I hope Evergreen Acres is around that long, period," Jordan said, and the room grew quiet as his words penetrated the atmosphere.

"One step at a time," she said, rallying a smile. "Let's say a customer shares a photo and tags you in it. How do you repost it?"

She looked expectantly from one blank face to the next.

"Not the foggiest," Charlie said with a chuckle.

"Don't worry," Brynn said, offering a sympathetic smile. "Ten-year-olds do this stuff every day."

She showed them how to download an app they could use to repost photos. All three seemed relieved when it proved to be as simple as she claimed.

Next, she taught them to find popular hashtags and local users that they message. She showed them a free program to generate newsletters and suggested they leave pamphlets at the county schools and libraries.

Brynn glowed as Charlie took eager notes in a blank notebook and Gina pulled up aforementioned websites on her laptop. Throughout the lesson, Brynn thought she felt Jordan's eyes on her as she stuttered more than once.

Of course his eyes are on you, you ding dong. You're the one talking.

"Any questions?" Brynn asked, closing her computer as Charlie scribbled notes furiously.

"Not me, I'm just excited!" Gina said, clapping her hands together. "Let's get Evergreen Acres on the freakin' map."

"I might have questions tomorrow," Charlie said with a smile as he peeked up from his page.

"And you?" Brynn asked Jordan, who was standing by the window and gazing into the dark woods.

"Hm?" he asked, turning back with wide eyes.

"Do you have any questions?" Brynn repeated, studying him.

"No," Jordan said, his voice cool. "All sounds great."

Brynn forced a smile, smoothing her fleece as she assembled the ring light and set it up next to the undecorated tree.

"Where's an outlet?" she asked, scanning the wall behind the tree.

"Here," Jordan said, extending his hand. Brynn handed him the cord and watched as he ducked behind the tree, his face scrunched in focus as he felt around the wall. As he stretched forward, his tee rose, exposing a sliver of the dimples of his tanned hips. She exhaled and turned back to Gina and Charlie, just as the glow of the ring light illuminated the tree.

"I say we start this little photo shoot by hanging some ornaments while I take pictures," Brynn said as she tightened her phone to the tripod. "Sound good?"

"Lights first," Charlie said, his joints popping as he climbed to his feet. "Ornaments second, candy canes third—"

"—And no star on top until Christmas Eve," Jordan finished, he lips twisting into a soft smile. He caught Brynn's stare. "That's how my mom always did it," he added with a shrug.

"Then that's how it should be done," Brynn said, not breaking his gaze.

"I'll unravel lights!" Gina said, springing to her feet.

"Jordan, you still keep extension cords in the closet?" Charlie asked.

As Charlie left the room, Jordan's hand hovered over a box of ornaments as he glanced back to Brynn, his gaze narrowing as he searched her eyes. His fingers grazed her elbow, eliciting tiny sparks of electricity that shot through her body.

"Thank you," he said quietly, his eyes never leaving hers. "For everything you're doing."

All Brynn could do was nod as he released her and tugged a big plastic container from a towering stack.

As Brynn swiped open her phone's camera, she tried for the millionth time that night to focus. Nearly every part of her knew Jordan was No Man's Land; selfish and moody with a temper that exploded without warning. Clearly, her body wasn't getting the message. She couldn't wait to go home, shower, and scrub off the day.

Brynn grabbed her empty cup and headed toward the kitchen, flipping the record to the B side as she went. Behind her, Gina called, "Get a move on old man, we need power!"

She squeezed her eyes closed for a just a moment, setting her glass on the small kitchen island before gripping the edge of counter. She took a deep breath, slowly exhaling every wisp of air from her lungs before turning to the stove, her hand hesitating over the kettle. Nope, more tea was *not* in the cards tonight. She opened the fridge without a second thought and filled her cup with eggnog.

She relished the distracting burn as the warm cream slid down her throat. She felt a little woozy as she headed back to the living room, though she doubted the alcohol could hit her that quickly. She swallowed a smile as pressed her palm against the spot on her arm where Jordan had been touching her just moments before.

SIXTEEN

Jordan's eyes snapped open, and he was suddenly wide awake. He stared at the dark wall, stretching his toes against the soft warmth of Toby's sleeping body before glancing at the clock: 4:00 a.m.

He tried to recall the dream that had awakened him, but all he could see were flashes: muscular legs stretching playfully across his lap, the night sky dancing with constellations, the snow around him illuminated like neon. He groaned as he rolled onto his back, the only other sounds the whirring of the heat and Toby's rhythmic breathing.

He interlaced his fingers behind his head, gazing up at the pitch black skylight above his bed. He needed sleep: the tree lighting was the following night. But the more he willed himself to drift off, the more his mind wandered.

He hadn't decorated a tree since he was a kid. Later, Brynn had posed them in other parts of the little farmhouse as they staged different holiday activities: Jordan pouring eggnog, Gina staring out the window at the falling snow, Charlie reading a Christmas card as the others looked on.

Then, Gina had insisted on jumping behind the tripod as she

ordered Brynn to sit by the fireplace, shoving *'Twas the Night Before Christmas* into her hands. Next, Gina had tugged Jordan into the shot, positioning him just behind Brynn.

His mouth had been mere inches from her bare neck as he half-listened to Gina's instructions. Even now, he could still smell the jasmine that had radiated off her skin.

He groaned as his fingers involuntarily brushed against his own neck. Warmth spread through his entire torso as his breathing grew ragged. He swallowed, willing his eyes to close.

He laid still for a long while, finally dropping into unconsciousness as the heat of his skin was slowly replaced by the coolness of the night air.

Brynn had just started watching the Green Goddess's video when she saw something that made her groan in fury—a beautiful green and white marbled Monstera Albo. Any remaining doubts that Jessica was the one who took the video at Grantway instantly dissolved into utter frustration.

Her fingers paused over the laptop keyboard as a stack of red envelopes with white embossed snowflakes appeared on the table beside her. She glanced up to find Gina standing behind her, arms akimbo with a triumphant grin on her broad face.

"What's this?" Brynn asked, returning the smile as she fingered an envelope.

"Have a look," Gina said, pulling a folding chair to the table beside Brynn.

Brynn slid the card from the top envelope and laughed as her eyes scanned the photo.

Season's Greetings from Evergreen Acres! was printed across the bottom in sage metallic scroll as the Clauses and their elves beamed back.

"These are so cute!" Brynn squealed, touched that she'd been included in the card as she flipped it over and read a handwritten message of good tidings.

"You inspired me," Gina said, patting Brynn's knee affectionately. "I'm sending these out to all of our past customers and the other Twin Falls folks I have in my address book. Thinking outside the box, right?"

"Right," Brynn said, a genuine grin splitting her face. "Great idea, Gina."

"Everyone loves a Christmas card," Gina said proudly, before noticing the graphic on Brynn's screen. "What's that?"

"I just got back the coupon sample from my web designer friend," Brynn said, clicking the image to enlarge it. "What do you think?"

Brynn loved the way her pal Trent had used the Idaho mountaintops behind the Evergreen Acres logo. And since she'd offered to plug his services on her Instagram, it wouldn't cost the farm a penny.

"So classy!" Gina said, snapping enthusiastically. "And I feel like adding the bit about local delivery might bring in tons of last-minute folks."

"I hope so. And the best part is he made the text super easy to edit." She clicked the expiration date and deleted it. "See?"

"Foolproof is my love language," Gina said, nodding her approval. "Can I send it to the paper? We could sneak it into the next issue if we submit it today."

Brynn emailed the files to Gina before helping her seal each Christmas card with a damp sponge. She didn't mind it; there was something heartwarming about the simplicity of it all.

"Why are we the only ones here?" Brynn asked, too aware of Jordan's absence for her liking. "I thought Sundays were all hands-on deck."

"They usually are, but we all got a late start after last night's eggnog," Gina said, chuckling as she stifled a yawn. "Charlie's at the end of the drive fixing the sign. I guess the wind blew it crooked."

Brynn nodded and grabbed another stack of envelopes.

"What?" she asked when she felt Gina's eyes on her.

"Don't you want to know where Jordan is?" Gina asked, a playful glint in her eyes.

"It doesn't really matter," Brynn said, keeping her expression even as she sealed the cards.

"Mm-hm," Gina muttered, still smirking.

Brynn said nothing, but after a few moments of feeling Gina's eyes boring into her, she looked up.

"Out with it," Brynn said, sighing as she set down her sponge.

"I just couldn't help noticing a few little things," Gina said with feigned innocence. "Pink cheeks. Clearing throats. Averted eyes. Made me wonder if we had interrupted something, is all."

Brynn's mouth dropped open. "No! Absolutely not."

"You don't find Jordan attractive?" Gina asked, her eyes innocently wide.

"I mean," Brynn sputtered. Damned if she did; damned if she didn't. "Of course, he's attractive, that's obvious. What does that matter? He's a complete asshole."

Gina tipped her head back and cackled. "Truer words."

"Plus, if I get my way, I'll be in Los Angeles soon," Brynn said as Gina raised her brows. *Where did that come from?*

But Gina's soft eyes encouraged Brynn as she filled her in about Homestead's search for a new host, consciously omitting the part that led to her arrival at Evergreen Acres.

"That does sound like a great opportunity, though we sure would miss you around here," Gina said, straightening a stamped pile of cards before setting them on the growing stack. "What a great idea for a show! I'd definitely have it on my DVR, even if I didn't know you." Gina squeezed her into an unexpected side hug. "I'm rooting for you, Brynn girl."

"Thanks, Gina," said Brynn, swallowing her emotion as she hugged her back. "We'll see what happens."

They continued to seal cards in comfortable silence, as Brynn glanced to the door. It was still early, but she hoped the next couple hours would bring in the rush of customers they desperately needed.

"I noticed you still haven't mentioned where Jordan is," Brynn said finally.

"I knew you'd take the bait eventually," Gina said with a giggle, not looking up from her stack. "He's down at the square, making sure the tree gets set up properly while he chats up the mayor."

"He's doing all that himself?" Brynn asked.

"Oh, heavens no," Gina said, waving her hand distractedly. "The town hired a construction crew to handle lighting and ornaments, complete with an apple picker with a sixty-foot reach."

"Well, that's good," Brynn said a little too brightly.

"I bet Jordan could use some help down there," Gina said,

barely bothering to disguise her amusement. "A woman's eye to make sure it looks good, that the tree's even, that kind of thing."

"You think someone should go help?" Brynn asked.

"I do," Gina said. "And I can't go. You don't know the register codes. Why don't you go?"

"Me?" Brynn asked as her throat tightened with possibility.

"Sure," Gina said breezily. "Besides, if Jordan botches that tree it will be the opposite of good publicity. He wasn't even going to decorate his own Christmas tree for crying out loud!"

"That's a good point," Brynn said, tucking her bangs behind her ear. "Well, if you're sure..."

"You'd be doing me a favor," Gina said, not looking up as she shooed Brynn with her free hand. "Now, go on, time's a-wasting."

Brynn quickly shoved her computer and papers into her messenger bag. As she passed through the doorway, trying to ignore Gina's quiet chuckling, she spotted a sprig of mistletoe that she could have sworn hadn't been there the day before.

SEVENTEEN

Brynn tucked her scarf into her coat as she braced herself against the icy wind that whipped through in sudden, sweeping gusts. Normally, she'd have no problem parking in town, but today the nearest spot was a quarter mile away. Several intersections were already blocked off in anticipation of the parade and the sidewalks were packed with locals staking out the best spots.

Before Brynn could even glimpse the town square, she could see the tree, towering several stories above the tallest buildings downtown. She warmed as a thrill of ownership shivered through her. She was kind of with the tree, after all.

The square was lined with red-and-white striped canopies, sandbagged into place against the biting wind. In one booth, a man secured zip ties through a wooden sign boasting the best hot almonds in the state. In another, college-aged kids were unloading giant cardboard boxes beneath a banner that read *Glo Accessories – 2 for the price of 1.*

Brynn hadn't been to the Festival of Lights since high school, though her mom and grandparents went every year. In past years, she'd avoid the crowds with Caleb and some friends at Big Papa's Grill or Whiskey Creek Saloon, but last year she'd been so wrapped up in work that she forgot all about it until she saw the trash crew hauling everything away the next morning.

She remembered weaving through the crowds as a kid, a churro in one hand as she gripped Tyler's in the other, catching as much candy as she could carry from the floats they passed. Paps, much spryer back then, would hoist her onto his shoulders as they raced to the square in time for the tree lighting. Gram always bought the kids candy from the peddlers who hawked everything from Big League Chew to candy cigarettes. Twin Falls seemed like a whole different place at Christmastime.

Brynn forced a deep breath as she crossed the square, a twinge of nostalgia tickling her ribcage as she retraced her old footsteps. Then, all at once, there it was—the beautiful 60-foot Norway spruce. Though Brynn could see long strands of dormant lightbulbs encircling the tree from top to bottom, only the bottom half had been decorated with ornaments so far.

She spotted Jordan squatting at the base of the tree, unscrewing bulbs and presumably replacing them with fresh ones.

"Ho, ho, ho," Brynn called, raising a bag of wrapped gift boxes. Jordan stood and turned toward her, his eyes crinkling into a smile as he dusted his hands against his flannel jacket.

"I feel like I recognize those," he said, a bit winded as he eyed the sack of presents. "Are these the sad, empty boxes you were posing with when I met you?"

"No emptier than your soul," Brynn teased. "I thought you could use these under the tree."

"That's actually not a bad idea," Jordan said, taking the bag and carefully arranging the packages beneath the branches. "Folks will see where to put the gifts." People were encouraged to bring unwrapped toys to donate to the hospital's children's wing.

Brynn crouched beside him. "Does it ever make you sad?" she

asked. "Killing something you grew?"

He followed her gaze to the giant severed trunk, secured in the center by a steel spike.

"As far as the environmental impact, we plant at least two saplings for every tree we sell," he said.

Brynn rubbed a few of the needles between her fingers before standing. "How long does it take for a tree to get this tall?"

"30 years, give or take," Jordan said, climbing to his feet.

"I hardcore cry when one of my plants die," Brynn said, and Jordan thought he saw a tear glittering in her eye. "Especially if it's one I've had for years."

Jordan scratched the back of his head. "I guess I never thought about it like that." She looked so wistful that he had a sudden urge to hug her. "But maybe it's more like growing flowers."

She looked at him sideways under those thick lashes.

"You cut them and enjoy them and then you grow more," he said softly.

She nodded and a tiny smile curled one side of her lips. "I can get behind that." She sighed and they watched a man atop the crane hook a candy cane the size of a small dog to one of the branches.

"Can I help you with anything?" Brynn asked.

"I'm pretty much finished," he said, his brows knitting together as he stepped back and gazed up at the towering tree.

"It's beautiful," Brynn said, stepping closer to him as they both peered skyward.

"It really is," Jordan said softly, and Brynn flushed as she felt him glance sideways at her.

"Gina said to tell you to get some lunch and not rush back,"

Brynn said.

"I take it this morning has been slow?" Jordan asked, running a hand through his thick, dark hair.

"I mean, yes," Brynn said. "But it was still early when I left."

Jordan sighed and she had a feeling he was sending up a silent prayer that the tree lighting might send some much-needed customers their way.

Brynn chewed her lip, feeling more than a little useless. "If there's nothing left to do, I guess I'll go check on Planted in Twin."

"Wait," Jordan said, resting a hand against the small of her back. A chill raced up her spine as her stomach tightened. "Bill over at the nut stand promised me a complimentary coffee. Do you have time to join me?"

"Sure," Brynn said, a little too enthusiastically. She could never resist another round of caffeine. At least, that's what she told herself. Her dislike of Jordan had repeated in her head like a mantra for the past couple weeks, but despite her best efforts, that voice had slowly grown quieter.

"Great, wait here," Jordan said.

She watched him walk away, her heart still thundering as a gust of wind threw his thick hair over his eyes. Brynn forced her eyes back to the tree, recognizing more than one familiar decoration as she watched the crew in the apple picker continue their ascent, a giant net bag hanging over the side. She removed her glove and ran her bare fingers over one of the ornaments, a metallic teddy bear the size of a small watermelon.

"How about VIP seating?"

She turned to find a grinning Jordan, a coffee in each hand, one foot perched on top of a green metal bench.

"VIP?" she teased, taking one of the cups and sitting on the bench beside him. Despite the cold that immediately leeched to her legs from the metal seat, she wiped a bead of sweat from her upper lip.

"People are going to be staking out this area long before dusk," Jordan said, his stubbled cheeks flushed pink with cold as he crossed an ankle over his knee and turned to her. "And we'll say we had it first."

Brynn could swear his gaze slipped to her lips for just a millisecond before fixing back on her eyes. She swallowed, fighting a sudden irrational urge to lean into his body.

Instead, she forced herself to look away and sip the scalding hot coffee. After a few moments of electric silence, Jordan pulled a paper bag from his pocket and offered it to her.

"Bill's best," he said, waiting until she grabbed some almonds before taking a handful of for himself. "They aren't the warmest, but he said he just made them last night."

"Thanks," Brynn said, popping one into her mouth. "Yum." They might not be hot, but they were a sugary cinnamon dream.

Though neither spoke, the tension slowly eased to a comfortable quiet, keeping pace with Brynn's finally slowing pulse. They sipped their coffees and watched as the last few ornaments were fixed to the tree with sturdy wire. Brynn's gaze wandered across the white banners that hung from the retaining wall, recognizing ones boasting of Evergreen Acres and the fire department as sponsors. Suddenly, her eyes froze, and her mouth dropped open as she leaned closer to the vinyl sign nearest the tree.

An all too familiar beautiful, veneered smile stared straight back at her.

Jessica Southgate.

Her stomach flip-flopped as she narrowed her eyes, but it was definitely her. Even printed on plastic, she still looked perfect, mid-laugh as she posed with a moving box in her arms.

"What's wrong?" Jordan asked, raising an eyebrow as he followed her line of sight. "Do you hate that man as much as I do?"

"Um, no, *woman,* actually," she said, slightly confused as she pointed at the banner. "I know her."

"Oh, that model?" Jordan said, and suddenly it all made more sense.

Jessica had become famous for her modeling career after all, though if she was posing for local businesses, she'd definitely taken a step down from New York Fashion Week.

"I thought you meant the guy who owns the business," Jordan continued.

"Sutkamp Luxury Homes," Brynn read aloud, registering the hardness in Jordan's eyes. "Is that...?"

"The ass who wants to turn Evergreen Acres into some concrete subdivision?" he said bitterly. "One and the same." He gestured to the banner. "How do you know *her?*"

"Well, remember when I told you about that influencer Jessica Southgate?" Brynn said. "In addition to being my biggest competition and an all-around pain in my ass, she also happens to be a model."

"What an evil duo," Jordan said, and Brynn was relieved to hear some of the playful teasing return to his voice as he laughed.

"Seriously," Brynn agreed. The sign's designer had most likely found Jessica's image on some stock photo site, but Brynn preferred to imagine their mutually empty souls had drawn them together. "We could steal it," Brynn whispered, her eyes shining as she pictured a covert midnight operation with her going for the kill while Jordan kept lookout.

"Nah," Jordan said, though not without a little reluctance. "Sutkamp paid for the sponsorship fair and square, and all that money goes to the hospital."

Brynn groaned in response, but definitely would have still been up for the heist if Jordan had been on board.

"Besides," Jordan continued, "he strikes me as someone who would love to make a paper headline as the victim of some crime against his reputation."

"Fair enough," Brynn said, tossing her empty cup and narrowly making it into the trash bin.

Jordan inched closer and Brynn nearly jerked away when his knee pressed against hers. A jolt rushed through her body as she suddenly became aware of every molecule where they connected.

"Wherever I go these days, I feel like Sutkamp's always there," Jordan said, seemingly unaware of this new breach in their distance. "Seeing him reminds me that I'm one step away from losing everything."

He looked straight at her, his dark thoughtful eyes no less than a foot from her own as she recognized his painful longing. She held her leg perfectly still as her heart became a kick drum.

"Well, you have one thing on him," Brynn said, cocking an eyebrow as she ignored the way he bit his lip and waited. "You are the Master of Ceremonies of the best tree lighting in America, and quite possibly, the entire world."

Jordan laughed. "Co-master, might I remind you."

"Right," she said, and couldn't help but giggle. "Speaking of," she continued, glancing at her phone. "I should start getting ready soon, for tonight."

"Getting ready?" Jordan asked blankly.

"As in a cute dress, hair," Brynn said, grimacing before adding, "makeup."

"So, you like wearing dresses all the time, but you don't like makeup?" Jordan asked, looking understandably confused. Brynn was used to this question.

"I don't mind wearing makeup," Brynn said. "I just hate having to wash it all off!"

"Right," Jordan said slowly, and Brynn was willing to bet he'd never spent much time thinking about what goes into the average woman's skincare. "But you're not wearing that?" Jordan asked, gesturing to her turtleneck and trousers.

How could he be so clueless? Brynn stifled her laugh this time, noting the innocent confusion that filled his eyes. "Have you ever been to the parade?"

"Every year," Jordan said.

"And you don't know how they dress for the tree lighting?"

Jordan looked to the sky as if searching his memory before shrugging. "No?"

"Such a stereotypical man," Brynn said, shaking her head as a rueful smile spread across her face. "I haven't been in ages and even I know all the presenters get dressed up."

"Looks like I better go find Gina," Jordan said, his eyes settling on his scuffed work boots.

"You'll be just fine," Brynn said, and before she knew what she was doing, she was patting his denim-clad thigh. Should she jerk her hand back? That would just draw attention to it. It's not like he'd tensed up, but still, it was weird. She snuck a glance at him, but once again, he seemed oblivious. She'd wait for a good moment, then act like she had to scratch her nose or maybe that her phone was vibrating. But before she could do any such thing, Jordan gripped her fingers, gently placing his thumb against her sweating palm. Her heartbeat went from racehorse to rocket ship in a split second.

"Thank you," he said, his deep voice even huskier than normal. "For doing this with me."

"You bet," she said, trying and failing to steady her words. Her cheeks were on fire, but neither of them let go.

"Anyway," she said, a little too chipper as she reluctantly pulled her hand away and made a show of grabbing her gloves and slipping them on. "I'll see you in a bit."

"See you in a bit," Jordan said.

She could still feel his eyes on her as she busied herself with her purse, but she avoided looking at him as she stood and headed in the direction of Planted in Twin, easily imagining the sounds and smells that would fill the air that evening. Suddenly, a thought occurred to her, and she stopped.

"We don't need to have, like, a speech written or anything, right?" Brynn called back to Jordan. "I feel like I remember the master of ceremonies saying something."

"Oh no," Jordan said, his perpetually tanned face suddenly going as pale as the gray sky. "I completely forgot. The mayor mentioned I needed to say something."

"Did he say how long it had to be?" Brynn asked, more gently this time. She felt bad for Jordan. Not knowing what to say in front of hundreds of people was a waking anxiety dream.

"I think he said to keep it simple, but still," Jordan said, his breath as shallow as a trapped animal. "I've never spoken to any kind of crowd. I have no idea what to say."

"First of all, breathe," Brynn said, offering him an encouraging smile. "Just mention you're with Evergreen Acres, wish them a Merry Christmas, and get the heck of out there."

"You're right," Jordan said, his lopsided smile less than convincing. "I'll figure something out."

He gave her an absent-minded wave as she retraced her steps, feeling every bit as discombobulated as Jordan looked. Her lungs felt a bit too small, the coffee sloshing in her stomach, as she remembered the warm, insistent grip of his fingers on hers.

When she reached the corner, the urge to look back finally overtook her, and her chest clenched as her eyes fell on the empty bench. But then she saw him, standing beneath the tree, running his hand over the same teddy bear ornament she had been touching when he brought her the coffee.

"Twenty minutes," Mayor Lopez said, smiling as he extended a Styrofoam cup of brown liquid to Jordan. He arched an eyebrow in appreciation as he clocked Jordan's navy-blue suit. "You clean up alright, son."

"Thanks, sir," Jordan said, taking the cup.

Before he could raise it to his lips, the mayor placed his hand over the top of the cup and whispered, "Officially, hot chocolate. Unofficially, hot *bourbon* chocolate."

"Even better," Jordan said. He could definitely use something strong to take the edge off his nerves.

"Here's to Twin Falls," Jordan said as they both raised their cups.

"Here's to Evergreen Acres," the mayor said, shooting him a

meaningful glance he couldn't quite read.

"I'll drink to both," Jordan said, wincing a bit as the liquor warmed his throat.

"Where's your cohost?" the mayor asked. Jordan glanced at his watch before surveying the crowd. Just as he reached for his phone, he spotted someone in a familiar red jacket. There was Brynn, waving from behind the fence that was being secured by the local police department.

"There she is," Jordan said, waving back to her before gesturing that he'd be over in one minute.

"Brynn Callaway?" the mayor asked. "I didn't know you knew each other."

"She's been helping out at Evergreen Acres," Jordan said.

"Ah," the mayor said, nodding in approval. "Any idea if her mother's coming tonight?"

"I'm not sure," Jordan said, unable to miss the mayor's sudden interest.

"Well, go get her past security," Mayor Lopez said, affectionately patting his arm. "I'm going to go warm up my speech."

My speech.

He patted his pockets automatically, knowing full well he'd find them empty.

"You're looking a little green," Brynn said once Jordan had brought her backstage.

"I'm fine," Jordan said, mopping his forehead with the back of his hand as he guided her to stand beneath a temporary propane heater. "I'm just really second guessing my decision to speak from my heart tonight."

"You mean, you didn't write anything?" Brynn asked and he

appreciated the lack of accusation in her eyes as he shook his head.

"I tried, but everything I wrote down just sounded worse and worse." His churning stomach was suddenly not in favor of the liquid courage he'd just downed.

"Well, that's OK," Brynn said a bit too brightly. "Just do what we talked about—get in, get out, and let them start the countdown."

"Right," Jordan said weakly as bile rose in the back of his throat. "Would you do it for me?" he asked, and though he meant for it to come out as a joke, he sounded as serious as death.

"It's your baby, both the tree and Evergreen Acres," Brynn said, her voice warm with concern. Jordan's pulse throbbed in his throat as she reached up and straightened his tie. "They should hear from you."

It was then that Jordan finally saw her, truly saw her, and he had to stop himself from doing some kind of cartoonish double take. Her golden hair was twisted back on one side, her wild waves tamed into shiny curls that spilled over one shoulder. Those plump, curved lips were stained a glossy red and her perfectly carved cheekbones glistened under the stadium lighting. Jordan swallowed, his mouth suddenly dry. All that and she still hadn't even taken her jacket off.

"You look very dapper tonight," she said, her kohl-rimmed eyes meeting his, seemingly unaware of the battle going on inside his body.

"Thanks," he said steadily as the scent of jasmine nearly sent him over the edge. "You look great too."

She smiled. "Figured I'd wait until the last minute to freeze my booty off."

"Still, the…" He gestured feebly to her head.

"Hair? Makeup?" She laughed as he nodded. "Thanks."

"So, any tips from the on-camera queen?" Jordan asked before downing the dregs of his chocolatey bourbon.

"Well..." Brynn said, scrunching her small, freckled nose as she glanced at the growing crowd. She placed a reassuring hand on his sleeve and beamed up at him as Jordan's heart began to drum. "You said your plan was to speak from your heart. I don't think you can ever go wrong with that."

"You're right," Jordan said, but he knew he didn't sound convincing. Still, the pressure of her fingers against his bicep was a very welcome distraction.

"And I'll be there," Brynn said softly, her tightening grip sending electricity through his torso. "I've got you."

Her thick cherry lips were level with his chest; her eyes never wavered from his as he felt an overwhelming desire to tip her chin towards his face. But just as he was about reach for her, he heard Mayor Lopez's booming voice growing closer.

"Sorry to interrupt," the mayor said as he joined them. Based on the playful glint in his eyes, Mayor Lopez knew exactly what Jordan had been thinking.

"Not at all," Jordan said as breezily as possible. "We were just discussing our game plan."

"Right," the mayor said, his amused grin saying it all.

"Hi, Mayor," Brynn said, reaching out one perfectly manicured hand. Jordan noticed her fingernails were the same hue as her lips. "I'm not sure if you remember meeting me before, but... "

"Brynn, it's great to see you," he said, shaking her hand warmly. "How's your mom?"

"Oh, um, she's great," Brynn said, sounding a bit flustered.

"She's out there somewhere with my grandparents."

"Well, tell her I said hello, will you?" the mayor asked, and Jordan could almost swear he was seeing that man blush for the first time.

"I sure will," Brynn said, shooting a tiny look to Jordan. Clearly, she was surprised by this too.

"Well, three minutes till blast off," the mayor said after glancing at his watch. "I'll see you kids in a few." He winked as he headed over to chat with the guy running the sound equipment.

Jordan took a deep breath, trying to calm his nerves as he repeated Brynn's advice from earlier. *Say Merry Christmas. Say why you're here. Say what it means to you.* He could do this. And, hey, one silver lining to his panic was that it left him very little brain space to consider what was happening to him around Brynn with annoying, increasing frequency.

"She's going to take photos for us," Brynn said suddenly, pointing toward the front row where Jordan saw Gina and Charlie huddled together, waving enthusiastically at them. He waved back and grinned as Gina pointed a phone in his direction. "That's why I was a few minutes late," Brynn continued. "I helped them squeeze to the front and gave her my phone since it has a newer camera."

Then, as the mayor climbed the stage, Brynn slid her jacket off, thousands of tiny goosebumps covering her smooth bronzed shoulders as Jordan fought the urge to stare. As she looked for somewhere to stash her coat, he let his eyes roam freely. Her dark green strapless dress hit just below her knees and hugged her soft curves as though it had been sewn right onto her body. It was classy in an old-Hollywood kind of way, as if she had stepped out of some black and white holiday musical. Jordan clenched his fists against his thighs as his gaze settled on her naked collarbones.

"Great turnout, huh?" she asked, apparently clueless about the effect she was having on him as she flashed him that dimpled smile. "You ready?"

The Twin Falls Municipal Band began marching in front of the stage playing a very enthusiastic, very *loud* rendition of "Jingle Bells." Brynn laughed and sang along, and Jordan couldn't help but smile as hundreds of joyous faces beamed back at them. When a second song ended and the band dissolved into the crowd, the mayor finally stepped forward and grabbed the microphone.

"Good evening, Twin Falls!" He bellowed into the mic and the crowd roared back. "There is no greater honor than to be here tonight, kicking the winter season off with the best folks in the Magic Valley!" Even more jubilant shouts and applause echoed back. "I want to take a moment to thank our platinum sponsors tonight, Channel 13 News, Milner's Gate Craft Brewery, and Sutkamp Luxury Homes!"

Jordan couldn't hold back a giggle as Brynn quickly pursed her lips in disgust as he helped her climb the stairs. The announcement of the platinum sponsors was Jordan's and Brynn's cue to join the mayor onstage.

"We have another special sponsor tonight," the mayor said, nodding to Brynn and Jordan, who had quickly replaced their grimaces with big smiles. "Evergreen Acres provided this beautiful tree—" he gestured to the towering giant that loomed above them in the dark sky, "—but also supervised the decorations and lighting in preparation for tonight's big moment." Mayor Lopez flicked two fingers back toward his chest, motioning them closer. "Why don't you two come join me at the mic."

The crowd was deafening now. Jordan's innards turned to ice as Brynn tugged him into position. Charlie flashed him two enthusiastic thumbs up and Jordan managed a weak smile in return.

"Evergreen Acres has been a part of our town's legacy for a century," the mayor continued, his earnest voice booming across the night. "Small businesses are a big part of what keeps this place magic." As Jordan listened, his gaze drifted over the rapt crowd, hanging on every word as they tossed out cheers of encouragement. Mayor Lopez let the fervor briefly settle before continuing. "I thought it only fitting to ask Evergreen Acres to be our masters of ceremony tonight." The mayor locked eyes with Jordan. "Help me welcome them as they say a few words before the countdown."

The crowd complied with a deafening cacophony, and the mayor stepped back, gesturing for Jordan to take his spot. Terror gripped Jordan's chest as he clutched the microphone stand. He forced his eyes to stay open as the flood lights blinded him. A heavily made-up reporter pointed a camera at him as Brynn's enthusiastic cheers registered somewhere deep in his mind. He took a deep breath and began.

"Hi...everyone," he said, and feedback screeched through the square as several people cringed and covered their ears. Tiny specs were appearing in his peripheral vision as he took a step back and forced a laugh.

"Merry Christmas," he said, trying again, and thankfully his voice carried clear and true across the crowd. He stared only at Charlie's warm eyes, trying not to think about how many people he probably knew out there. "I've lived in Twin Falls my whole life," he said, no idea what was coming out of his mouth next. "Evergreen Acres is my whole life, too, and I...I'm so thankful for..." His mouth turned to ash and acid rose threateningly in his throat. "For..."

Everything in his brain went empty. He looked back at Brynn who mouthed *keep going* as she gave him an encouraging nod.

"I'm thankful for..." he repeated once more, but it was like the hatch had busted on his mind and everything that had ever filled it had been sucked out into some great abyss. "I'm thankful for..." the crowd began to swim before his eyes, but he could swear he could hear muffled laughter. "Brynn Callaway."

Oh my God, did I really say that?

Jordan froze, his lips flapping dumbly as he turned to find a red-as-a-tomato Brynn. But before he turned back to the silently watching crowd, Brynn stepped forward and squeezed his hand.

"I got you, remember?" she whispered before shouldering him aside to take his place at the microphone.

Her color had begun to soften as she inhaled and plastered a wide, bright grin across her face. Despite this waking nightmare, he couldn't help wondering how anyone could pay attention to anything other than Brynn in that dress.

"Happy Winter, Twin Falls!" Brynn shouted, raising a fist in the air, grinning as the crowd hooted and clapped obligingly. "Jordan often works behind the scenes, trying to make his neighbors smile. Neighbors like you." She bumped her hip against his thigh in an almost imperceptible nudge, and a swell of warmth penetrated his entire lower body. "Trying to give these neighbors memories they will never forget. Never taking credit for how much of his life he has devoted to this town." She tossed him a cheeky wink. "So that's where I come in! To shout it to the treetops, pun intended."

She laughed as the crowd whooped and clapped. "Twin Falls needs Evergreen Acres as much as Evergreen Acres needs us!" she shouted as the cheering became an explosive roar. "With your support, and a little holiday magic, we can make sure we get to keep Evergreen Acres for another hundred years!" Now she was pumping both fists as Jordan let the earsplitting applause wash over him. "So, let's shop local, share with our neighbors, and give a little extra to those need it." The crowd was at a fever pitch now, pumping their fists along with her. "'Tis the season! Here's to the best Christmas ever!"

Thank you, Jordan mouthed as Brynn turned that electric smile on him once more, both of them stepping aside as the thunder of whistles and hoots continued.

Mayor Lopez stepped forward to the mic. "Well, I think you know where the Lopezes are getting our tree this year!" he shouted over the noise, clapping Jordan on the back. "And now it's time for the big moment." He gave Brynn and Jordan a nod: *go ahead.*

Jordan followed Brynn to the edge of the stage where a giant cartoonish red switch sat atop a small table. The switch was just for show—Mayor Lopez had told them that the lighting crew would illuminate the tree the second they flipped it—but Jordan's heart thundered in his ears, nonetheless. Once more, he felt the eyes of the town upon him, but at least this time, he wasn't alone. He hoped he wasn't shaking as he gently took Brynn's hand and placed it on the switch, her slender fingers completely disappearing as he placed his on top. Her skin felt like cold marble beneath his palm.

"Everyone all together now!" the mayor shouted as Jordan took a deep inhale. "Ten! Nine! Eight! Seven!"

Brynn's lips parted into a honeyed smile as she met Jordan's gaze.

"Six! Five! Four! Three!"

He glanced at Charlie and Gina, who were grinning up at them, phones in hand, like two parents watching their toddler take his first steps.

"Two! One!"

Together, they flipped the switch, and the square became as

bright as morning. The crowd gasped and pointed as all sixty feet of the tree were illuminated at once. From somewhere in the distance, the band began to play, this time a jolly rendition of "Joy to the World." It had only been a second, but Jordan suddenly realized he was still trapping her hand beneath his.

"Sorry," Jordan said, swallowing as he jerked his hand away and stuck it in his pocket. Brynn didn't respond as he followed her gaze to the glowing tree. "It's pretty special, isn't it?" he whispered.

"It's beautiful," Brynn said, and he could see the reflection of those thousands of lights in those green eyes. "I want to freeze this moment in my memory forever."

Jordan forced himself to squash a sudden urge to press his mouth against hers, crowd of people be damned. He tipped his head ever so slightly closer to her, inhaling the perfume that emanated from her long, slim neck.

Suddenly, she jerked away.

"That's it," she muttered.

"*What's* it?" Jordan asked, puzzled as he followed her stare back to the tree.

"Nothing, just thinking," she said quickly, turning to him before once more flashing that delicious smile. "But I think we better join in and start singing, co-master. Even you must know the words to this one."

He laughed, his tense muscles finally loosening as they began to sing along. His voice lost in the hundreds of others, he began to feel more like an anonymous part of the mob, and less like the guy whose speech had just crashed and burned. His eyes traced every bough of the towering silent giant he had known since childhood. He wondered which of these branches had stared down at his great-great ancestors; which of these branches only knew Charlie and Jordan. His gaze wandered until it landed on the tree's illuminated crown, and it was almost as if it stretched all the way to the stars, an evergreen bridge between Twin Falls and the heavens above.

EIGHTEEN

"Do you need me to sign?"

Brynn blinked as the bald man in front of her, eyed her with slight concern. His arms were outstretched, and Brynn suddenly realized she was still holding the spiky dracaena he'd just purchased.

"Sorry," she mumbled apologetically, gently sliding the plant across the counter. "No signature needed." She circled the number at the bottom of the receipt. "Be sure to call if you have any questions about its care."

The man thanked her, the polite smile returning to his face before he reached the door and disappeared down the street.

She rubbed her temples and groaned. Normally, talking to customers was her favorite part of the job, but today her mind was far from houseplants. She had the beginnings of an idea, and her mind was rattling with so many possibilities she barely heard the keys rattling in the back door. She pulled up Google, but before she could type a word, a familiar gleeful shriek erupted from the back room.

Before she could investigate, the curtain was pushed aside as Katie rushed over, shoving her cellphone into Brynn's face.

"Merry freakin' Christmas, Bee!" Katie squealed, as Brynn took the phone and glanced at the open YouTube app. There was Brynn's homepage, her headshot, her handle.

Just as she was about to ask what Katie was so worked up about, Brynn's eyes rested on her subscriber count. Brynn's mouth fell open and her hands began to sweat as she took in the number—all seven digits of it.

"Three *million*?!" Brynn barely squeaked out. "When? How?!"

"Well, for starters, the tree lighting got coverage all over the country! Apparently, Twin's is the closest to Christmas of any major city, and, I don't know, maybe it was a slow news day on the Today Show."

"But there was only one reporter there!" Brynn sputtered, tugging down the page to reload it. Yep, the number was real.

"Who knows?" Katie said, shrugging dismissively. "It's the age of the internet. It was probably on the AP Wire or whatever." Brynn guessed that was some sort of PR thing, but before she could ask, Katie wiggled her fingers theatrically. "It gets even better! You know Homestead's morning show?"

Brynn nodded. Of course, she did. Her lungs felt like they might burst against her ribs.

"They did a whole segment on it!" Katie squealed.

"They did not!"

"Yep," Katie said, beaming as she typed something and handed the phone back to Brynn. "They called you the Houseplant Queen."

There was the headline: *The Houseplant Queen joins the Christmas Tree King just in time to save the family farm.* As she scrolled, a muted video of her and Jordan played, hands intertwined, gazing up at the tree. She had to admit, they truly did look like some kind of royalty up there, impeccably dressed with hundreds of people cheering them on. A knot in her stomach threatened to drench her thrill as she wondered if Jordan had seen the story yet. She wouldn't soon forget how he reacted to her Instagram "charity" post.

"I bet Jordan will be thrilled," Katie said, as if reading her thoughts. "Evergreen Acres is officially in front of millions of eyeballs."

"Let's just hope it's the right eyeballs," Brynn said.

Katie narrowed her eyes. "This response is a bit less climactic than I was hoping for."

"Sorry," Brynn said. "I'm so thrilled! I promise. My mind's just a bit scattered this morning."

Before Katie could reply, a familiar ringtone of singing crickets emanated from the back room.

"The work cell!" Brynn exclaimed as both their eyes widened in excitement.

Katie sprinted to the back. A few seconds later, Brynn heard, "Katie Dilworth speaking," just as her friend burst back through the doorway.

"Oh hello, Mr. Barnes!" she said, shooting Brynn a pointed look before silently mouthing, *Holy shit!* Brynn swallowed. The actual CEO of Homestead was calling them?! "Yes, we have been in talks with Sofia," Katie continued. "Absolutely. One moment, please."

She handed Brynn the phone, wild incomprehension on every inch of her elfin face.

Brynn heart was thundering, and she briefly wondered if she should put the cell on speaker, but there was no way her violently shaking fingers could do anything of the sort.

"Brynn Callaway, speaking," she said finally and was delighted to find that her voice wasn't betraying her impending nervous breakdown.

"Brynn! How are you?" the deep voice with a hint of a Boston accent replied.

"Doing well, thank you, Mr. Barnes," Brynn replied as she eyed Katie who was doing a silly happy dance. Brynn swiped her hand across her neck, giving her the sign to chill out.

"Please, call me Mark," he said. "I'm sure you know you've been on our radar for quite some time. Everyone at Homestead has been delighted by your recent content, and that lighting ceremony last night was nothing short of ratings gold."

"Thank you," she replied, searching and failing to find anything more original to say.

"We were hoping to tempt you into touring our studios here in Los Angeles this week or next," he said as Katie huddled close enough to Brynn to hear the conversation. "What do you say? Would you like to trade in that cold Idaho weather for some sunshine?"

"Oh, wow!" Brynn said, still unable to form complex sentences and Katie gripped her arm so tight it was almost painful.

"First class, all expenses paid, of course," Mark added quickly in the silence that had followed. "It would be chance to get to know us and see this incredible city. Sofia and I would love to take you around town ourselves."

"That sounds amazing," Brynn replied, her elation growing as she wiped her sweaty forehead against her cardigan sleeve. The network must be seriously considering her if they wanted to wine and dine her on the company dime.

"Maybe three or four days, if you can take the time away?" he continued. "And feel free to bring Jordan Damon with you if you want.

Jordan.

The image that flashed across her mind wasn't the one from last night, clean-shaven and gorgeous as hell in that snug suit that so perfectly hugged his muscles, though she'd replayed that one countless times while staring at the ceiling around midnight. No, it was the image of Jordan on his farm, oblivious that his threadbare Carhartt jacket was now trendy, three days of rugged stubble contrasting with those boyish, chocolate brown eyes. He would never leave the Evergreen this time of year, not with so much at stake. And neither could she. She sighed.

"I'm honored, Mr—er, Mark," Brynn said. "But this is an important time for Evergreen Acres. I won't be able to travel anywhere until after Christmas."

Katie studied Brynn with what was either total admiration or utter confusion. The line was silent for an endless moment. Brynn had the feeling that men like Mark Barnes didn't hear 'no' very often.

"I understand," he said finally. "Though I hate to be the bearer of bad news to a board room of excited colleagues, it's nice to see a young person with some integrity."

"Thank you," she said, hoping she didn't throw up before this phone call ended.

After they'd hung up, she spun to a slack-jawed Katie, who was shaking her head in wonder.

"They invited me to LA," Brynn said numbly.

"I heard," Katie said. "Can I go instead?"

Brynn groaned.

"I'm just trying to cheer you up," Katie said, pulling her into a side hug.

"Did I just blow it?" Brynn asked weakly.

"No," Katie said a little too forcefully. "You heard him. Mark likes your integrity."

"I don't know," Brynn said. It was true, but it could also have merely been a polite response.

Just then the crickets chirped again.

"Same number," Katie hissed. Brynn thought her fried nerves would kill her before either of them could answer. Katie swiped to answer, then tapped the icon for speakerphone.

"Brynn Callaway's office," Katie chirped with remarkable breeziness.

"Hi Katie, Mark again," he said, sounding a bit breathless. "Is Brynn still around by chance?"

"I'm here, Mark," Brynn said, clutching the counter so hard her already pale knuckles turned a sickly white.

"My assistant just had a thought," he continued. "Was I told that you are an Urban Farm fan?"

"A huge one," Brynn said, raising her eyebrows at Katie, who just shook her head and shrugged.

"Well, Urban Farm is about to celebrate its fiftieth episode, and the network is hosting a brunch on Georgina and Paul's Utah compound. Homestead's whole board will be in attendance, as well as lots of talent from our other programs. Is Salt Lake City far from Twin Falls?"

"Not far at all," Brynn said, excitement growing. No need to mention the drive was at least three hours each way. She would drive much farther than that to meet the Urban Home stars, let alone schmooze with the entire Homestead executive team. "I'd love to come! When is it?"

"Next Monday," Mark said as Katie grinned and pantomimed clapping. "And bring Jordan. You remind us of a younger Georgina and Paul, you know."

Before Brynn could correct him, Katie clapped a hand over Brynn's mouth.

"All sounds great, Mark!" Katie said quickly. "I'll be sure it's on the books."

Once Mark promised to have his assistant send over the details and they'd said their goodbyes, Brynn shot Katie an incredulous look. "He thinks we're a couple!"

"Well, there's no reason to correct him!" Katie said, raising her hands in defense. "You're welcome."

Before Brynn could name any of the many reasons to correct Mark Barnes, the bell on the door jingled and Tyler pushed open the doorway, giving her a pointed look as he crossed his arms over his chest.

"Ty! I'm so sorry," Brynn said, glancing at the phone's clock. "I totally blanked."

"Too big of a celebrity now?" he asked, the glint in his eyes betraying his scowl.

"Hardly," Brynn said before turning to Katie. "Want to join us? I'll just lock up."

Katie glanced at Tyler's earnest smile as she ran black enameled fingernails through her cropped hair.

"You go ahead," Katie said after considering. "I want to publicize the crap out of this while the iron is hot. Bring me the southwestern salad?"

Twenty minutes later, Brynn and Tyler were huddled together in a shivering bundle beneath the café's awning.

"Trust me, it's worth the wait," Brynn chattered.

"I'll survive," Tyler said. "I do work in a forest after all. It's at least ten degrees colder in northern Maine today."

"That sounds miserable," Brynn said, her breath visible on every consonant. "How's work going, anyway?"

"Busy," Tyler said, his face lighting up as he spoke. "Actually, reproducing this new method to spread the pathogenic fungus and the baculovirus is proving to be more difficult than we expected, partly due to the summer drought, but—" He shrugged as if anything he'd just said was comprehensible. "—I think we're close to getting the grant."

Brynn laughed. "The fifteen percent of that I actually understood sounds very exciting."

He snorted. "I'm used to it."

"You should meet this guy I'm working with right now," Brynn said, as casually as if she were commenting on the weather. "He's a tree junkie like you. He might even be able to translate all that."

"Mm-hmm," Tyler said, his lips that looked so much like her own twisting into a wry smile.

"What?" Brynn asked.

"Well, I saw you two at the tree lighting," Tyler continued. "Do I really need to say more?"

"Uh, yeah, considering I have no idea what you're talking about," Brynn said, her voice rising despite her best efforts to sound indifferent. "What you saw was a mutually beneficial professional arrangement." She said each word slowly as if that might make Tyler more likely to believe her.

Instead, he dramatically closed his eyes and made loud snoring sounds.

"Ugh, whatever, Tyler," she said, lightly punching his shoulder as he cracked up at himself.

"Hey, don't get mad!" Tyler said softly amidst his laughter. "Maybe it's just hope on my part."

She narrowed her eyes quizzically at him and he shrugged.

"I'd love to see you find someone," he said, looking a little uncomfortable. "You know, after what happened with Caleb."

"What do you mean, 'after what happened with Caleb'?" she repeated. "We both know I work too much to be with anyone except myself." Her mom had been right for once: she'd seen Caleb's growing frustration long before Brynn did. And despite Greta's advice to make more time for their relationship, Brynn had ignored her.

"Is it possible you didn't do anything wrong?" Tyler asked, cocking his head. "Maybe you and Caleb just weren't right for each other."

Brynn opened her mouth to argue, but hot unexpected tears poured out instead of words.

"Aw, come here, sis," Tyler said, pulling her in to a gentle hug.

"Callaway, party of two?" a teenaged host called, poking his head out the door.

Brynn swiped at her face as she and Tyler were led to a cozy corner table. It wasn't like her to cry in public, but that morning had already been such an emotional rollercoaster that it kind of made sense.

When Tyler brought up Caleb, Brynn suddenly realized that not only had her ex never replied to her texts after that steamy night they'd spent together, but she'd also forgotten all about them. Still, the sting of guilt and failure clearly hadn't faded much since their breakup.

Maybe her brother was right; maybe they hadn't been right for each other. Either way, Brynn didn't have time to dwell on it. Not on Caleb, with his hurtful words and his ghosting and the way he'd breathlessly muttered her name into her neck that night. She didn't have time to dwell on any man, not even the one who had begun to inspire a paralyzing heat every time he looked her way.

She was back in the race for Homestead, and if Katie had her way, this publicity might lead to more customers for Planted in Twin as well. Though she couldn't remember a time she'd ever felt so much pressure, she was in the home stretch. Maybe in January she could start thinking about a personal life again. Maybe from Los Angeles. A fresh wave of anxiety pummeled her chest at the swirling spider web of her thoughts.

After a half-hearted protest about working hours, Brynn agreed to be Tyler's accomplice in the two-for-one Bloody Mary lunch special. Brynn felt a tiny surge of pride as her out-of-towner sibling nodded in approval at the menu. Less than an hour later, Tyler proclaimed himself a new fan of the craft burger joint, even promising their waiter he'd be back for trivia night the next week.

"Whatcha doing there, sis?" he asked, sliding back into the booth after using the restroom. He furrowed his brow, his eyes scanning the upside-down notes Brynn was scribbling on the back of the placemat across from him.

She rotated the paper and slid it across to him, watching his face as she savored the last olive from her glass.

"Petting zoo…ice skating…ring toss?" he read before looking up at her. "What is this?"

She took a deep breath and decided that test driving her idea on someone other than Jordan might not be a bad idea.

"What do you think about a Christmas carnival?" she asked.

Despite Brynn's promises to leave the store unlocked, Jordan was half-surprised when the door easily swung open. He moved carefully across the darkened shop, keeping his elbows tucked against his body to avoid knocking anything over. Blue security lights beamed across the floor and the giant, leafy shadows they cast made Jordan feel like he was in a funhouse. The damp, warm air softened his joint's icy stiffness as he made his way toward the register's looming silhouette.

"Brynn?" he called.

"Back here!" her voice called back.

Using his phone as a flashlight, he stepped past a table full of cacti as he batted away dangling vines that tickled his neck. When he shoved past the gray curtained doorway, he found several bright square lights aimed at a vintage-looking table against one white cinderblock wall.

"Brynn?" he called again.

"Down here!" came the reply. It was coming from behind the table, though he still couldn't see anyone. He carefully stepped onto the makeshift set and found Brynn sitting crisscross on the concrete floor.

"There, that feels better, doesn't it?" she said quietly as she clutched a squirt bottle in one hand and a striped rag in the other.

"What feels better?" Jordan asked, throwing a glance over his shoulder to see if Katie was still there.

"I wasn't talking to you!" Brynn replied cheerfully, and now Jordan could see the glossy, giant leaves of the plant she was apparently conversing with. "I'm washing leaves," she added, and she lifted the rag in his direction. "Look how much dust just came off this rubber plant."

"Do you always talk to your plants?" he asked, chuckling. It was kind of cute, in a kooky cat lady kind of way. He mentally corrected himself—kooky *plant* lady.

"Not always," Brynn said, his throat tightening as she flashed that full-lipped crooked smile at him. "Just when I have something to say."

"Got it," Jordan said, looking everywhere except at the bare collarbone where her oversized sweater had just slid off one shoulder.

"Begonia Rex," Brynn said, gesturing to a second smaller plant with purple leaves as she stood and tucked a plant under each arm. "Pretty, isn't?"

Jordan watched as Brynn crossed the room, setting both plants on a long wooden shelf. She lengthened a chain that was attached to a long tube-shaped light, lowering it until it was near the top of the rubber plant. Then she tapped a tiny humidifier, and a fine mist began to disperse around the begonia.

"What is all that?" Jordan asked, incredulous.

"Just the standard," Brynn said breezily, grabbing the spray bottle and misting a box of tiny sprouts.

"*That's* the standard?" he asked.

"For a sub-tropical plant, it is," Brynn said, squinting at the soil in each small pots. "If I want to get the full expression of color, the begonia needs consistent temperature, no direct sun, and tons of humidity." She narrowed her eyes at his amused expression. "It sounds more complicated than it is."

Despite the way Jordan smirked, he had to admit he was impressed. This was the first time he had seen her truly in her element. It suited her, though he doubted he could repeat back those care instructions if she asked him to. He could never imagine fussing with a tree that much.

Jordan studied her as she turned a dial on the light cord and the color tone instantly became cooler. "Seems to me if you have to work that hard to fit in, maybe you're just not meant to be there," he said.

"Are we still talking about plants?" Brynn asked, raising an eyebrow as she adjusted the hue.

"Plants. Definitely, plants." He laughed, stepping closer and gently smoothing the leaves of one of the tiniest seedlings. "They seem so fragile," he said, his words catching a bit as he felt her eyes on him.

"They're tougher than they look," Brynn said softly. "But compared to Christmas trees I guess they are pretty delicate."

She was so close to him. Jordan could feel the heat of her shoulder as it lingered inches from his fingertips. Her sweet, minty breath grazed his neck with every exhale.

She searched his face a moment longer and Jordan allowed himself to drink her in. A flash of disappointment tugged at him as she finally broke their gaze. She unzipped a big Canon camera from its case and expertly affixed it to a sturdy industrial-looking tripod.

"Are you ready for this?" she asked.

"I kind of hoped you'd forget why I came," Jordan said, feeling a bit panicked at the thought of that giant camera lens pointing at him.

"Oh, come on, it can't be worse than last night!" Brynn said, and Jordan suddenly wondered how he'd ended up in yet another terrifying public speaking situation.

Before he could remind Brynn just how poorly his speech had gone, she grabbed his arm and dragged him behind the brightly lit table. He ignored the breathless longing that filled his chest as her hand warmed inside his own.

"You're going to be great," Brynn said, smiling as she positioned him over a white taped X on the concrete floor. "I'll make sure of it."

"OK," Jordan said weakly before taking a deep breath.

Brynn dragged a white glittery bundle of fabric out of a trunk beneath the table. As she unrolled and then flattened it, the tabletop transformed into a sparkling landscape of snow.

"I figured you were too busy to think about set decoration," Brynn said a little coyly as she stretched a string of tiny white Christmas lights around the table.

"So festive," he said, running his hand approvingly over the scratchy white fabric. She was right, of course; not once had set decoration even remotely crossed his mind. "Thank you."

"Oh, I almost forgot!"

She ducked beneath the table once more, this time pulling out a wispy foot-tall Norfolk pine. She placed the immaculate terracotta pot on the table in front of Jordan and flashed him a reticent smile. "I know it's not quite like your pine trees, but I couldn't resist this little guy."

"It's perfect," Jordan said, and for a moment, he forgot all about the camera. She had truly thought of everything.

"Here we go!" Brynn said, with as much enthusiasm as any kindergarten teacher as she hurried behind the camera. She eyed him through the viewfinder, making a few quick adjustments that Jordan could only guess at. "Let's do this!"

He nodded and forced a smile, but as he braced himself on the fabric-covered table, his vision began to swim.

"Remember," Brynn said, locking eyes with Jordan as she peered over the camera. "It's just you and me. I can edit anything. You can start and stop, and even do parts over again if you want."

He made another attempt at a smile as he took a deep breath. Brynn gave him a thumbs up gesture as a little red light began to blink. Was she filming already?

"I started rolling, but no pressure," Brynn said, obviously registering the panic in his expression. "Take your time."

"Is it OK if I move?" Jordan asked, demonstrating by leaning from one side to the other.

"As long as you don't get any taller," she said, laughing. "What are you, six-two?"

"Six-three and a half, actually," he said and he felt a surge of satisfaction as Brynn's eyes widened.

"I made notes." Jordan's mouth was dry as he pulled a few creased index cards from his chest pocket. He wasn't about to repeat the mind-numbing blankness that had swept over him the night before.

Brynn said nothing as she watched him through the viewfinder, but he thought he could make out a small smile amidst the blinding filming lights.

Jordan glanced at the first index card, then tucked the tiny stack under the table and out of the camera's view.

"Hi, everyone, and Merry Christmas," he said, staring right at Brynn.

Before he could go on, she shook her head and pointed to the camera, before dragging her index finger in a quick silent air circle: *Go again.*

As he adjusted his eye line to the dark gaping lens, his chest felt like it might explode.

"Hi, everyone, and Merry Christmas," he repeated, his mind now empty of what he'd read ten seconds earlier.

Now what? His mind droned with an empty hum. He sighed and peeked at his cards once more. Should he start over again?

"I'm Jordan Damon," he said, deciding to keep going as he blinked at the lens once more. "And I'm from Evergreen Acres, an Idaho Christmas tree farm that's been in my family for over a century."

He knew it was time to dive into the substance of the video. He'd planned to teach any willing viewers how to extend the life of their Christmas tree; the same information he repeated to every customer who came to Evergreen Acres. But when he opened his mouth, all his tips for choosing the best tree spot in any home froze on his lips. His tongue suddenly felt like it was filling his whole mouth as he peeked down at the cards once more. A droplet of sweat dangled from his forehead before darkening a tiny circle on the denim shirt that Gina had so generously ironed for him that afternoon.

Thanks for watching, he read silently. Wrong card. He shuffled his notes with shaky hands as he tried to keep smiling, his jaw twitching as he finally faced the camera once more.

"Do you ever get your Christmas tree home?" he mumbled, the words swimming through his mind with absolutely no meaning. And why did his voice suddenly sound like he'd been drugged? He feebly pressed on. "Do you wonder what to do? Well, today—"

"Cut!" Brynn called as the red light mercifully stopped blinking.

"That was a disaster," Jordan said, catching the box of tissues Brynn tossed to him. He tugged one free and mopped his sweaty face, wondering for the first time how people did this sort of thing wearing makeup.

"It was your first time," Brynn said, and he couldn't help but appreciate the calming sweetness in her voice.

"How do you do this?" he asked, studying her with a newfound appreciation.

"You get used to it," Brynn said easily. "You know what helps me?" She walked over to Jordan, and leaned her chin on her fists and her elbows on the table, almost like they were two friends just having a drink at a bar. "I think of a specific person, and I picture myself talking to them. Like, for example, there's this retired plumber who always comes in to buy plants for his screened in porch. I doubt he had much use for YouTube, but he's someone I use a lot. When it works, I forget all about the camera."

"I could try that," Jordan said weakly. It was not like he had any better ideas.

"Can you think of a customer you told this to recently?" Brynn asked.

"Pretty much every single one of them," Jordan said with a nervous chuckle.

"Then what do you need cards for!" Brynn giving him a good-natured whack in the chest. "Just say what you know and pretend you're talking to one of your regulars."

Jordan chewed his cheek. "Mrs. Pfeffer," he said after a moment of contemplation. "She's been coming in since before I was born." He would know her wrinkled smile and silver-streaked curls anywhere. "At this point, she knows the spiel, but she asks every year anyway. Probably just to make me feel good."

"She sounds perfect," Brynn said. Her lingering gaze was doing nothing to help his erratically beating heart.

"One other thing," Jordan said quickly. "Doesn't it feel weird to make a video that is, I don't know...all about you?"

Brynn chewed her lip and tied her hair into a messy topknot as she seemed to consider. "Do you think Evergreen Acres is a special place?" she asked a moment later.

"Of course, I do," Jordan said.

"Why?" Brynn asked.

He raised his eyebrows in a look that clearly said, *what's your point?*

"Why?" Brynn repeated with more insistence.

"Because—because it's survived world wars, for one thing," Jordan said. "And because it's a living example of a simpler time." The words began to find each other and more came behind them. "And because it brings families together, and a thousand other reasons."

"Perfect," Brynn said, her eyes shiny up with excitement. "This video isn't about you at all, see? It's about *Evergreen Acres.*"

Her argument mostly hinged on semantics, but she had made her point.

"When you look into this camera, tell Mrs. Pfeffer all she needs to know," she continued, smiling with encouragement as she walked backwards toward the camera. "Tell the whole damn world."

"Let's try again," Jordan said, a genuine warmth spreading to his own cheeks for the first time that evening.

"Annnnd...rolling!" Brynn called as her face disappeared

behind the camera once more.

Jordan tucked the cards into his pocket and took a slow, steadying breath.

Mrs. Pfeffer. Mrs. Pfeffer.

"Hi, everybody, and a very happy holiday season from all of us at Evergreen Acres," he said, relieved to hear his voice sounding less strained. "I'm Jordan Damon, fifth generation Christmas tree farmer, and I can't wait to share my tips for getting the most out of your natural tree."

Mrs. Pfeffer nodded along eagerly in his mind's eye, never interrupting as she patiently listened.

"First off, choose your spot wisely," Jordan continued, feeling like he was finally back in his body. "A shaded spot away from your fireplace and heat vents can easily add weeks to the life of your tree..."

And just like that, the words began to flow from deep in Jordan's well of inherited expertise, just like they always did at Evergreen Acres. Somewhere in the time between describing different tree additives and reemphasizing the importance of fresh water, he realized he had actually begun to enjoy himself. Soon, he had wrapped it up with a snappy outro, and the red light stopped its previously ominous blinking.

"Not too shabby, huh?" he asked, unable to suppress his proud grin.

"You were great!" Brynn exclaimed, clasping her hands to her chest.

As Brynn slid the batteries off the back of the lights, returning them to their charger, Jordan found himself rambling on about ideas for future videos. Brynn chuckled to herself as she listened and popped out the camera's memory card. He followed her to a tiny office he'd mistaken for a closet and watched as Brynn popped the card into the desktop, scrolling her phone as she waited for the files to import.

"So, what's next?" he asked.

"Well, I'll edit this tomorrow and figure out some hot keywords, and then you can put it on Evergreen Acres's new YouTube channel," she said, a glint in her eye as she tapped away on the keyboard. "We'll promote it on your other social media pages. Eventually, you could buy ads, but that costs money I don't think we want to be spending."

We. There it was again. A week ago, he would have been annoyed by the implied ownership of her words. Today, it made his stomach drop as if he'd somehow just missed a stair.

"Do you think anyone will actually watch it?" Jordan asked.

"I know they will," Brynn said, "because I'm posting it on my channel too."

"Really?" Jordan asked, touched beyond measure as the significance of this gesture fully sunk in. Her videos were getting millions of views. "Thank you."

"Turns out, you're a natural," Brynn said with a coquettish shrug. "If you'd tanked, I wouldn't have offered."

Jordan laughed, though he was starting to suspect that Brynn wouldn't have let him leave until he had a video to be proud of.

"So, for the next video," Jordan said, fully aware he was still grinning like a fool. "We should do one about the different kinds of trees. You know, compare look and scent, longevity and—"

"I've created a monster," Brynn said with a groan, but she was smiling too as she pulled out her phone and tapped out a quick message. "Just remember, you also promised to film me tonight?"

"Trust me, I'm good for it," he said. "Is everything, OK?" He gestured to her phone.

"Oh, yeah, sorry," she said, sounding flustered. "Work stuff. Other work, I mean." She tucked her phone back into her pocket. "But there is something I meant to tell you," she continued. "My web-developer friend sent over HTML code and some kind of app for that real-time inventory tracker. You might not be ready for it until next season, but it should be perfect for what you need."

"You really are amazing," Jordan said softly, and she beamed up at him, her cheeks flushing a dusky peach.

Once Brynn had assured Jordan that his footage was safely stored in the cloud, she showed him how to operate the camera. She had already adjusted the settings, so all he had to do was push a button and let her know if she ever looked out of focus in the viewfinder. The minutes flew by as he watched Brynn play to the camera, unable to take his eyes off her as she bounced her way enthusiastically through a lesson about propagating plants. She was amazing. Plus, Jordan didn't mind an excuse to stare at her without coming off as a weirdo. The timestamp on the screen told him they'd been filming for nearly fifteen minutes when she motioned for him to cut, but every second had flown by.

Jordan helped Brynn tidy the area, zipping equipment in protective cases and plugging the batteries into chargers. Once they'd finished, Brynn snapped off the wall lights and Jordan followed close behind her as they maneuvered through the shadow-filled store and out onto the slush-covered sidewalk. The frigid wind howled by them as Brynn locked the door, but the sheltered alcove they shared remained still.

Jasmine.

His chest tightened as he quietly savored the scent that had so quickly become synonymous with this charming, fiery, driven woman. She turned, now only inches away, and her eyes bored into his as if asking a question. Neither of them spoke as they huddled close in the dark bay. She stood on tiptoe and reached toward his head, pulling a pine needle from his hair before handing it to him.

"I hope it wasn't there the whole time," he murmured.

"Trust me," she said, softly, her eyes now full of something that looked like hunger. "I saw everything."

She stepped impossibly closer, and he could feel her breasts press against his stomach beneath her too-thin jacket. She shivered, though nothing but heat permeated from the exposed skin of her ivory neck. Her eyes flicked down to his lips then back up again, and his stomach twisted as he fought a sudden urge to wrap her into his own jacket.

Suddenly, her pupils constricted, and she stepped back, picking at an invisible piece of lint on her sleeve. He mirrored her movement and gave her as much space as the alcove would allow as he tried to keep his expression even. What had just happened?

"Do you want to see the video before I upload it?" she asked, a brisk professionalism on every word.

"No, I trust you," Jordan said, and as he said it he realized he meant it. "I'm sorry I took so long to get it right. Especially with tomorrow being your only day off at the farm—"

"I had fun," Brynn said, stopping him with a dismissive wave as she looked over her shoulder at the street. "I wanted to do it."

"Can I walk you to your car?" he asked, trying his best not to sound too eager at the prospect of spending a few extra minutes with her.

"You kinda already did," she said, nodding to the Civic parked a few feet away.

"Right," Jordan said, tugging his own keys from his pocket. "Well, goodnight then."

"'Night," she said, her expression unreadable as Jordan stepped into the biting wind and headed toward the public parking lot.

"Jordan!"

He turned back as Brynn caught up to him, no small feat in those dangerously high heels she always wore.

"Do you have plans tomorrow night?" she asked, a bit breathless.

"Free as a bird," Jordan said, biting back a smile. The glow of the streetlight made her hair look as if it was streaked with gold.

"My family does this cookie decorating night every year," she said, talking just fast enough that Jordan thought she might actually be nervous. "Just silly fun. But my brother will be there, and I think I mentioned he's also weirdly obsessed with trees, so I thought you two might hit it off. If you like cookies, I mean." Jordan couldn't stop himself from every inch of her suddenly flushing cheeks.

"Count me in," Jordan said.

"Yeah?" She sounded relieved.

"Yeah," he said.

"Great. Do you want to meet at the shop at seven and we can drive over together?"

"It's a date," he said, a teasing smile boldly poised on his lips. Though she narrowed her eyes in response, she didn't correct him. "Remember when you said that to me?"

"Yeah," she said, laughing softly. "I remember."

Jordan watched as she walked away, holding her hair in place with one hand as the wind whipped at her face. Once he saw her headlights cut through the dark street, he headed for his truck.

He slammed the door behind him and sank into the freezing leather, everything suddenly too cold and too quiet. He gripped the wheel and started the engine, blasting both the heat and the radio as he pointed his truck away from town.

He knew it was only natural he would be feeling something for Brynn. She was probably the most beautiful woman he'd ever met in real life, and they'd been spending so much time together. True, they'd gotten off to a horrific start, but Jordan was starting to see he'd been at least partly wrong about her. He'd never felt so magnetized to someone, especially someone he barely knew.

Still, he had always listened to his brain first, but especially before listening to any organs below his shoulders. Sure, that meant he'd never had a textbook intimate relationship, at least, not one where they connected much beyond a physical connection. But looking back, from the sloppy one-night stands to the longer-term women he would actually claim as exes, he had no regrets. That pragmatism had saved him from losing a piece of himself to women who, in hindsight, were not right for him at all, and, in at least a couple cases, were utterly toxic.

But buried far beneath this certainty was a quieter understanding. Even without the therapy that Gina always encouraged him to try, he knew that everything about how he loved—or didn't—had probably started there. This understanding was weary and broken, but as permanent and firm as bedrock. It reminded him how fragile love could be; how it could nearly destroy a person if it was suddenly ripped away.

He'd seen it firsthand, not once, but twice. Half of Charlie's sparkling joy had never returned after Jordan's mom passed, and Charlie had actually met with one of Gina's therapist recommendations. And then there was Megan, Jordan's beautiful big sister, who was just beginning her fairy tale ending when her husband disappeared in the blink of a drive home. A drive she'd made hundreds of times, just like the drives to the South Hills Jordan had made hundreds of times. Odds mean nothing when the worst-case scenario happens. Jordan would never forget that. A blink. Gone.

NINETEEN

A frustrated sigh escaped Brynn's lips as she stared at her equally dissatisfied reflection. She unzipped her dress, tossing it onto the growing pile on her bed, as she shook loose a few of the tighter curls she'd added to her natural frizz. She was trying too hard, and she knew it.

She flicked through dozens of hangers, finally pulling out a crisp, ivory blouse. She held it beneath her chin and narrowed her eyes at the full-length mirror. She wore that shirt all the time, but it hadn't let her down yet. It would do.

Brynn dressed quickly, resolving to put away the mountain of clothes later. She sprayed her perfume, walking through the sweet-smelling mist as she assessed her outfit once more. She tugged on her vegan leather leggings, grabbing her favorite black booties before clumsily fastening her gold hoop earrings as she thundered down the stairs. The afternoon had slipped away as she made one call after the other. She was late.

She saw Jordan before he saw her. He was leaning against his pickup truck parked a few feet from Planted in Twin's front door, a soft smile relaxing above his perfectly square jaw. Brynn couldn't help but notice the dark brown shadow of his whiskers, which must have already reappeared after Jordan's clean-cut dapper appearance the other night. He would dart his eyes every so often to the front door of Planted before going back to watching some commotion across the street. He clearly expected Brynn to come out of the shop as Brynn herself had intended before turning into a mad woman who had no idea how to dress.

She followed Jordan's gaze, where she saw a hunched old man slowly guide a tiny white-haired woman down the street. Suddenly, the woman stopped shuffling and frantically turned a wobbly circle as she seemed to scan the sidewalk. The man bent low and patiently retrieved her dropped handbag, inches from where the woman stood. Though Brynn couldn't hear their words, there was no mistaking the scolding smack on the hand the old lady administered as she snatched her purse and placed the strap pointedly over her shoulder. Despite the reproach, her companion simply offered his arm to her once more and they continued down the pavement. Even from where she stood, Brynn could see the elderly man's wrinkled smile and a subtle twinkle of amusement in the woman's rheumy eyes.

"Sorry, I'm late," Brynn said finally, breaking the spell as Jordan turned to her with an easy grin. Was it her imagination, or had those dark eyes actually lit up when they'd grazed over her face?

"I wasn't sure what to bring..." Jordan said, blushing ever so slightly as he passed her a bulging grocery bag. Brynn peered inside and her eyes widened as she bit back a giggle. She quickly counted at least ten tubes of icing, as well as several containers of sprinkles in every color of the rainbow.

"You didn't have to bring anything at all," Brynn said as Jordan sheepishly took the bag back and slung it over one shoulder. "But I'm sure my mom will put all of that sugar to good use."

"I guess I got excited," Jordan said with a laugh as held open the truck's passenger door for her. "I haven't decorated cookies since, well, since my mom was around. Besides, I can't meet your family for the first time empty-handed."

Meet your family. For the first time.

A girlish flutter rippled through Brynn's stomach as they walked side-by-side down the empty sidewalk. Though she was sure he was just making an offhand comment, her body seemed to believe otherwise. Brynn still couldn't believe she'd asked Jordan to come to her mom's house in the first place. There was no way she could pretend this was work-related. Pure and simple, she had wanted Jordan to be there. And he had said *yes*. Her brain was still trying to untangle what it all meant, but she was done ruminating. She had more pressing things to think about.

The truck cabin finally started to warm as they reached the edge of town, though Brynn could still see tiny puffs of her breath in the darkness. She swallowed as she watched Jordan tap his thumbs against the steering wheel, in rhythm with some vaguely familiar rock song that was filling the cabin at a polite volume.

"I'm glad we have a few minutes to talk," Brynn said lightly, after giving Jordan the first few driving directions. "I have an idea to run by you."

"Oh, yeah?" Jordan said, his eyes crinkling in the corners as he shot her a curious sideways glance.

"The tree lighting the other night was packed, right?" Brynn began, sitting on her hands as much to still her nerves as warm her tingling fingers.

"It was a great turnout," Jordan agreed as he headed out toward the canyon.

"It got me thinking," Brynn continued, summoning her courage. "What if Evergreen Acres hosted something like that, but maybe more like a...Christmas carnival."

"I'm not sure I follow," Jordan said, squinting as he split his focus between Brynn and the slick blacktop.

"You know," she said quickly, "Games, treats, winter activities. Maybe Santa Charlie could make an encore appearance. Besides the mall, I don't know anywhere local kids can meet Santa."

"Sounds like a lot of work," Jordan said noncommittally, and Brynn had a sinking feeling that he was already dismissing the idea. Well, that was what she had expected.

"Well, it might be a lot of work at first," Brynn said, infusing her words with extra optimism. "But every year it would get easier, and maybe even grow. I bet we could get a lot donated, which would keep costs low." Any false gaiety had quickly morphed into true enthusiasm as she shared the ideas she'd been devoting every free minute to. "It could definitely bring in revenue for Evergreen Acres. Think of it: a family could buy some pizza slices or hot chocolate, give Santa their wish list, and then buy their Christmas tree. A one stop shop. I bet you guys could sell out the lot."

Jordan chewed his lip as the song ended and the silence that filled the cab in the seconds before the next song played felt infinite.

"It's not a bad idea," Jordan said finally. "We could bring the customers to us, get them to think of Evergreen Acres when they think of holiday fun." He blinked and shook his head as a tiny wry smile twisted his lips. "Your mind is incredible."

He sounded like he was teasing, but Brynn's neck burned, nonetheless.

"Too bad we won't have you around next season," Jordan said before adding automatically, "I mean, if there *is* a next season." He chewed his lip thoughtfully. "I doubt we've got the creativity to pull something like that off without you."

"Yeah...see..." Brynn began. "I wasn't thinking next year—I was thinking much, *much* sooner."

The car swerved a few inches to the right as Jordan shot her an incredulous look. "As in...?"

"As in this weekend?" She flashed Jordan her most confident smile, but her stomach felt like jelly.

"*This weekend*?!" His jaw fell slack and his eyes widened impossibly bigger. "Are you out of your mind?!"

"I might be," Brynn said before adding quickly, "But I know we can do it."

Jordan's mouth wordlessly opened and closed as he gripped the wheel, throwing her a sideways look as if she might be joking.

"Jordan," Brynn said, her tone turning more urgent as she dared to place one comforting hand on his arm. At her touch, he froze. "I know we can save Evergreen Acres, but it's going to take something big."

He sighed, and his body seemed to soften as her passionate words reached his ears. After a moment, he shook his head.

"We don't have money," he said. "Things like carnivals cost a lot of money."

"I have it all figured out," Brynn said, much more confidently than she felt.

"How?" he asked, his forehead knitted as he narrowed his eyes dubiously.

"Well, you would just have to trust me on that," Brynn said, holding her breath as she tried to read the internal struggle that vibrating from his rugged features.

Her heart drummed faster as his eyes darted to his arm, where her hand still rest against him.

"I'll think about it," he said finally, his husky voice barely above a whisper.

"I'll take it," she said, a peal of relieved laughter escaping her lips as they rounded the corner into the quiet subdivision. Brynn pointed to her mother's ranch-style house, and Jordan parked beside the charming white picket fence. Jordan crooked his head to look past Brynn and smiled as the illuminated reindeer heads raised and lowered as if beckoning them to the front yard.

"Didn't you tell me your mom was kind of new age?" Jordan asked.

"Yeah, why?"

"Well, the beautifully decorated and manicured front lawn," he said, giving it an approving nod. "Not exactly what I was picturing."

"Well, if you saw the herb garden in the back, you might think differently," Brynn said, laughing as she pictured the tangles of oregano and rosemary her mom kept covered during the winter months. "My mom is a tough one to stick in a box. You'll see."

They wiped their slick boots on the welcome mat, the tinkling of "Carol of the Bells" floating between them as they entered the warm foyer. As Jordan chivalrously hung both their jackets on the hooks, Gram's head poked around the doorway to the living room.

"Gram!" Brynn said, walking into her outstretched arms as she rested her chin atop Gram's short, white hair.

Gram looked positively miniature next to Jordan's towering frame as Brynn introduced them.

"Well, isn't this nice surprise?" Gram replied, stepping closer and lowering her readers. "You're even more handsome up close!"

Jordan laughed. "Thanks for making room for me."

"Oh, please," Gram said, waving her hand dismissively. "You should see the mountain of cookies in there!"

As Brynn followed them into the living room, Paps appeared from behind the newspaper's finance section. As he shook Jordan's hand, her grandfather snuck a wink at Brynn, which she pretended to ignore as she felt her cheeks flush.

Just then, Tyler emerged from the pantry, their mother close on his heels.

"Careful with those, Ty, they're older than you," Greta barked joyously as Tyler hefted a box labeled *Platters* onto the counter.

"Brynn," Greta said as she noticed her daughter's arrival. "You made it! Can you grab—?"

She stopped mid-sentence, her eyebrows subtly raising as she discovered Jordan standing by the doorway.

"Oh! Hi there," Greta said, with a humiliating amount of friendliness before shooting Brynn a pointed look. "I didn't realize this handsome fellow was the guest you were bringing."

Greta wiped her hands on her holly-patterned apron before extending one to Jordan.

"What's up, man?" Tyler said with a grin, as he hurried over to join the introductions.

"I heard we might have a few things in common," Jordan said politely.

"Any friend of the forest is a friend of mine," Tyler said in his dorkiest voice, before pretending to notice Brynn. "Oh, and any friend of my baby sister's, of course."

She elbowed him, but she couldn't help smiling as the two men immediately fell into a heated discussion about programs offered for tree replanting.

"Sorry we're late," Brynn whispered to Greta. "That was my fault."

"I'm sure it was," Greta said, a slight coldness in her voice. Clearly, Brynn still wasn't forgiven for missing the decorating night.

"Anyway," Brynn said, grabbing a festive mug from the dish drainer and filling it with hot water and a tea bag. She raised the cup in Jordan's direction, but he shook his head.

"You haven't missed a thing," Greta said, resting her hands on her hips as she glanced around the kitchen. "This batch is still cooling, and I need to set the table."

"Can I give you a hand?" Jordan asked.

"Oh, that's sweet of you, but we've got it under control," Greta said, gesturing to Gram who was grabbing a stack of plates from the cabinet.

"Want to have a beer and help me split some wood?" Tyler asked Jordan.

"Absolutely," Jordan said.

Tyler pulled two bottles from the fridge, prying off the caps before handing one to Jordan. He took an appreciative sip, then, seeming to have just remembered his grocery bag, he set in on the butcher block counter in front of Greta.

"I'm no cookie expert, but I brought a few things," he said with a self-conscious smile.

"This is the same brand I use!" Greta squealed as she peered into the bag. "How thoughtful of you."

"A *few* things?" Greta whispered to Brynn once the boys were safely out of earshot in the backyard. "We could open our own bakery with all this."

"He said he was just excited," Brynn said with a shrug as she forced her expression to stay level.

"Jordan seems like a great guy," Greta said with false nonchalance as Brynn sipped her tea and pretended not to notice. "Maybe this is the one," she added once Brynn refused to take her more subtle bait.

"It's not like that," Brynn said quickly. "We're working right now, and I guess..." Brynn searched for the appropriate term to describe their relationship and came up empty. "I guess you could say we've become friends."

Greta snorted. "I know how friends look at each other, my dear daughter. I might be old, but even I can see that."

Before Brynn could protest, the door swung open as Jordan followed Tyler in, both men bearing armfuls of logs.

"That was quick," Greta said, and Brynn could hear a note of disappointment. Brynn on the other hand, was relieved to escape her mom's cross-examination.

"There was more wood already cut out there than I thought," Tyler said, as he headed for the living room. "It's a good thing; it's freezing out there."

"Ladies," Jordan said politely, lifting one hand from his load in an adorable mock salute. Brynn rolled her eyes as Greta giggled, but Jordan didn't seem to notice as he followed Tyler, his beer bottle tucked under one arm.

Brynn followed them into the living room, plopping onto the loveseat beside her Gram, who was watching flurries swirl through porch light beam outside the bay window with a soft smile on her face. Brynn couldn't help but laugh as Paps distractedly hummed along to Mariah Carey, now buried deep in the sports section.

Tyler poked at the fire as Jordan stacked the rest of the logs in the antique iron basket beside the hearth. Brynn bit back a grin as caught snippets of their quiet heated conversation—something to do with the migration patterns of invasive insects.

Jordan looked right at home as he settled into the empty recliner. Brynn watched as he politely accepted Paps's finished newspaper sections, her mother's words echoing obnoxiously through her mind.

Greta was wrong. She had to be. They *were* friends, weren't they? Just two adults enjoying each other's company, with no obligations; no strings attached. She set her cup on the coffee table, blaming the tea for the heat that flooded her chest since she'd arrived. She was done thinking. Whatever this thing was between them, something about having Jordan there just felt right.

Jordan braced his hands on the porcelain sink and blinked at the dark circles that seemed to have taken up permanent residence under his eyes. He had told himself that coming here tonight would be good for business. They could pose for a couple photos to post, maybe even talk about Instagram algorithms or some other such nonsense. He had told himself that Brynn's mom might still need a tree. He had told himself lies and he knew it.

As Gram headed back into the kitchen, Jordan fought the urge to take her spot on the loveseat. Instead, he stared at the paper, sipping the remainder of his beer as he softly tapped his foot to the Christmas pop radio station. Suddenly, Tyler peered over the paper, yanked the empty bottle from his hand and passed him a new one. Tyler was proving to be an easy guy to like.

"OK, cookie time!" Greta called. "Come on in!"

"Everyone can fill a plate!" she said with giddy excitement once they'd assembled in the kitchen. She gestured proudly to several piles of festively shaped sugar cookies.

"I call a reindeer!" Brynn shouted, seconds before Tyler yelled, "One of those reindeer is mine!"

"I take it Brynn didn't warn you," Greta said, laughing as she noticed the confusion on Jordan's face. "Those two get quite competitive with the reindeer."

"Poor guy didn't know what he was walking into," Gram said as she patted Jordan warmly on the back.

"When I was little, Tyler always made the solitary Rudolph cookie," Brynn explained, her cheeks flushed pink with excitement as she piled cookies onto her plate. "When I got old enough to decorate, I wanted to make one too—"

"And I always reminded my dear sister that only one reindeer can lead Santa's sleigh." Tyler finished.

"We finally settled on a little friendly competition," Brynn added, smirking at her brother. "Anyone can decorate as many reindeer as they want, but only the best gets the red cinnamon candy on its nose."

"You're in luck," Greta said, passing Jordan a plate. "I made extra reindeer."

"I think I'm going to stick with the trees," said Jordan with a chuckle.

"Wise man," Paps said, shooting Jordan a knowing look as he bit into an icing-less angel cookie.

"Paps!" Brynn scolded playfully. "You have to decorate it first!"

"It's better for the old waistline," he retorted, accepting a peck on the cheek from Gram.

Suddenly, Greta clapped her hands together. "Jordan should be our guest judge!"

Jordan felt himself blanch. "I don't know..."

"It's all in good fun," Tyler said with a mischievous grin. "We promise this will be nothing like the 2001 Christmas cookie night."

Jordan was almost afraid to ask. "What happened in 2001?"

"Let's just say the fire department showed up and leave it at that," Brynn said, winking at him, eliciting a hot tingle that flooded his stomach. "Please?" she begged with wide, pleading eyes as she stuck out her bottom lip.

"Okay, fine," Jordan groaned, but this time, he didn't bother holding back his smile. This family was fun.

Greta turned up the music up as everyone began decorating except Paps, who nibbled unabashedly at the finished cookies when no one was paying attention. Brynn and Tyler had immediately begun sorting through their supplies with the matched intensity of someone diffusing a bomb. Jordan, on the other hand, could barely keep the icing within his cookie's perimeter, let alone make any kind of discernible design.

"You need an icing tip," Brynn said. "See?" She held up her own tube, pointing to a tiny plastic funnel over the opening.

He watched as she scrawled Noël in beautiful red lettering across a bell-shaped cookie, her brow furrowed in concentration. He twisted an unclaimed cap onto his own tube, but the star he attempted looked like a yellow jellyfish.

Gram and Tyler passed icing back and forth like a practiced team. Jordan smiled. He loved spending time his dad, but his sister was rarely around, and their gatherings seemed much tamer in comparison to the Callaway's.

Eventually, Jordan had iced all the cookies on his plate, though he thought it would be a stretch to call them 'decorated.' As he rinsed his spatula in the sink, Brynn sidled up to him, his pulse quickening as she playfully bumped her hip against him like she'd done the other day. She reached for him, turning his palm upwards as she set a little pickup-truck shaped cookie on his hand. A sugary pine tree stuck out of the red truck bed and could just make out the words *Evergreen Acres* in tiny perfect script on the door.

"Well?" she asked.

"Pretty good," he said, fully aware he was grinning like a fool. "Am I allowed to eat it?"

She laughed. "Of course. I already snapped a photo in case you want it for later."

She leaned against the sink, her arm pressing against his. He felt her muscles tighten against his sleeve, but she didn't pull away and there was no chance he was going to. They stood there, an unspoken tension rippling between them, for what could have been thirty seconds or an hour.

"Ten minutes until judging!" Greta called, finally breaking the spell.

"I better put the finishing touches on Rudolph," Brynn said, glancing at the closed pantry where Tyler was presumably holed up with his reindeer cookie in secrecy. "Don't give away my hiding spot," she whispered before heading into the living room.

As she left the kitchen, Jordan released a low, shuddering breath he hadn't known he was holding. He wanted to be in the same room with her, a room where they could do whatever it was they had just been doing. He needed to feel her warmth against his body again. An image of grabbing one of those full red lips between his teeth danced across his mind.

"Care for some cocoa?" Greta asked brightly, shattering his tantalizing vision.

He cleared his throat. "No thanks, I'm good."

"I could use another beer," Tyler called, clearly listening to the conversation as he stepped out of the pantry. "Top secret artwork in there," he added when he noticed Jordan's amused smile. He strode across the kitchen and pulled a beer from the fridge before pointing his finger at Jordan.

"Sure," Jordan said, though in reality, he would have preferred something much stronger to settle whatever thoughts kept churning dangerously inside his mind. Still, a beer was for the best. He had to drive them back after all. Not to mention, he couldn't afford to say something to Brynn he would regret in the morning.

He pulled up a chair next to Brynn's grandmother, who was hunched over her plate. Her face was screwed up in concentration as she placed tiny candy pearls in clusters around a cookie wreath. As he took a closer looked, he noticed that the green foliage was also made of the little balls.

"Beautiful," he said, when she looked up at him and smiled. "It's like a little piece of art."

"You're the one who brought the nonpareils," Gram said, her eyes shining as she scooted over so he could take a closer look."

Jordan laughed. "Not only do I have no idea what that word means, I also have no idea what I bought. That aisle was a blur."

"A man with an eye for detail," Gram joked, wagging a finger playfully at him.

"Definitely not," Jordan said, laughing as he gestured across the table to his own messy plate of cookies. "But I do appreciate detail." He nodded at her cookie art. "When someone goes the extra mile just because they want to."

"So, you have a soft spot for passion?" Gram asked, her wrinkled mouth curling into a sly smile. "I happen to know a young lady who is very passionate."

He sipped his beer as he fumbled for a reply, but just then, Greta shouted, "Thirty seconds!"

A frantic squeal carried from the living room and Jordan laughed as he pictured Brynn frantically sprinkling her cookie.

"Three, two, one...TIME!" Greta yelled gleefully. "Icing down!"

Jordan joined the gathering Callaways at the kitchen island as everyone placed their plates on the counter. From the soft muffled snores floating in from the living room, Brynn's grandfather must have dozed off. Un-iced stacks of cookies still piled around them, though they must have collectively decorated over a hundred.

"We'll get to those," Greta said, following his gaze. "We just finish those at a more regular pace."

"Look at these!" Gram exclaimed, wiggling her fingers excitedly over the plates. "I think this is the best year yet!"

"You say that every year, Gram," Brynn said, giving Gram a fond squeeze.

"My friends in the choir are going to be over the moon with the extras," Greta said, as Gram nodded in agreement.

"Yeah, yeah, all that's great," Tyler said lightly. "But enough Christmas cheer." Everyone followed his gaze as it settled on a suddenly uneasy Jordan. "It's the moment of truth," he added with a grin. "Who gets Rudolph?"

"Give him some space!" Brynn said, spreading her arms wide. "He can't get a good view."

"This feels dangerous," Jordan said, wary as he stepped closer, but the family was chattering too excitedly around him to hear.

The cookies weren't exactly decorated to bakery perfection, but they were much more complicated than anything Jordan could do. Tyler's reindeer sported a little top hat and a bowtie made of icing, whereas Brynn had painted eyelashes and hearts in each of her doe's cartoonishly wide eyes. Both cookies were cute, but despite those minor differences, they were the same brown reindeer cookie. He laughed as he noticed the serious way the siblings' eyes bored holes into him, almost looking like twins as they crossed their arms over their chests expectantly.

"I better confer with my colleagues," Jordan said irreverently, eliciting good-natured complaints as he pulled Gram and Greta into a peppermint-scented huddle.

"So, who wants to be the bad guy?" Jordan whispered. Both mother and daughter immediately protested, laughing as they reminded Jordan of his sworn duty.

"Looking good, guys," Paps said, stifling a yawn as he entered the kitchen.

"You're on your own, kid," Greta teased as she crossed to the table and began twisting lids back onto the icing.

"I think you know the winner here," Gram whispered, narrowing her eyes conspiratorially. "The right choice is always a young lady."

Jordan couldn't help but laugh at this suggestion, though he didn't disagree. He had a feeling Tyler would forgive him.

"Paps!" The horror in Brynn's voice was unmistakable even Jordan turned to see what had happened.

"What?" Paps blinked blankly at his granddaughter, wiping crumbs from his lips as he clutched the remains of a cookie in his other hand. A cookie that had once been a girlish reindeer, but was now a headless, eyelash-less reindeer.

"Ha, ha, yes!" Tyler said, genially as he clapped his grandfather on the back. "I win! Thanks, Paps!"

"That's not fair!" Brynn protested, trying to keep a straight face.

"That cookie didn't have the candy on its nose!" Paps protested innocently. "I thought it was fair game!"

Suddenly, Brynn, now laughing so hard that tears streamed down her cheeks, grabbed Tyler's reindeer and shoved the entire thing into her mouth.

"Brynn's always been a bit competitive," Greta said to Jordan as a fresh wave of giggles surrounded them.

"It's a side of her I haven't seen before," Jordan said, chuckling as Brynn wrestled her plate from a roaring Tyler.

"I hope that doesn't scare you away," Greta said, inserting herself into the hushed conversation.

"Not at all," Jordan said, feeling a sudden irrational urge to defend Brynn. "In fact, I admire drive like that."

"Well, it's helped her in her professional life," Greta said, and he thought he heard a touch of resentment in her words. "I assume she told you about the show she's being considered for?"

"Homestead TV," Jordan said, nodding. "Sounds like a huge opportunity." He sipped his beer. "That could really put Twin Falls on the map."

"I'm not sure how," Greta said as Jordan watched Brynn hand her phone to Paps to take a picture of her and Tyler. "I can't even see how she'll be able to keep the store running from Los Angeles."

Jordan's bottle froze mid-swig.

Los Angeles?

"You know, Brynn hasn't had much luck in the romance

department lately," Greta said, winking at her daughter as she joined them with a glass of red wine in one hand.

"Wow, thanks, Mom," Brynn said, but she was smiling. "Just the topic I had hoped to walk into."

"Relax," Greta said. "I haven't shown your new boyfriend any embarrassing childhood photos yet, but the night is still young."

"He's not—" Brynn said quickly, shooting an apologetic look to Jordan. "We're not dating."

"Definitely not dating," Jordan repeated quietly, and he could feel Brynn's eyes on him.

"Well, that's too bad," Greta said, looking between them with an unreadable expression. She shrugged. "Maybe men and women truly can be friends." She looked as if she was about to walk away, but she opened her mouth once more. "I do worry about you, Brynn, you know that. I just don't want you to work your whole life away and end up alone."

"With all due respect, Mrs. Callaway," Jordan began, something sparking in his chest. "I think anyone Brynn ends up with will admire her work ethic just as much as I do."

Out of the corner of his eye, he could see the corners of Brynn's mouth twitching upward.

"Well, of course, my daughter is wonderful," Greta said, blinking a couple times as she twisted her crystal necklace with one hand. "All I mean is, well, I just want what's best for her."

"Hey, I forgot to congratulate you on the tree lighting!" Tyler said, and Jordan exhaled as Tyler joined their circle. He hoped he hadn't made Brynn's mom angry. He wasn't sure why he had felt the need to defend her, but then again, he would guess he spent the same percentage of his days working as Brynn did. As the conversation continued on, the awkwardness of the moment blessedly passed, and Jordan helped Brynn and Tyler stack iced cookies into little waxed cardboard boxes as Greta grabbed her own glass of wine.

"I'll throw a couple more logs on the fire," Jordan said to no one in particular, avoiding Brynn's searching eyes as he passed.

So, Brynn was planning to move to Los Angeles. As if he didn't already have enough reasons to keep his growing feelings for her to himself. He could see the end before anything had even begun. He opened the grate and sparks flew as the log landed on the still-glowing pile. He told himself this was a relief. All his attention would be where it belonged, back on Evergreen Acres. Despite the clenching in his chest, a part of him was relieved to have some kind of closure of his inner turmoil. Or at least that's what he told himself as he rejoined the others in the kitchen.

TWENTY

As Brynn twisted side to side, her tight back muscles pinching in protest, she heard the now familiar sound of someone stomping their mucky boots on the porch. She stifled a yawn, wrapping her sweater around herself in the drafty back room as she glanced at her phone. How was it 8 a.m. already?

"Why are you here so early?" Jordan asked, catching her eye as he entered the store and walked over to her makeshift desk.

"There's just so much I want to get done," Brynn replied, barely glancing up from the screen. She didn't add that she had been there since it was still dark outside.

Just as Jordan braced his hands on the back of her chair, Brynn clicked onto the Evergreen Acres Facebook page, blocking the other open browser windows from his view.

"Last night was really fun," Jordan said, leaning over her shoulder to peek at the screen. "It was sweet of your mom to send me home with so many cookies."

Brynn's throat dropped into her stomach. If she leaned back a single inch, her back would be touching his belt.

"You were doing us a favor," Brynn said, proud her voice sounded calm as she looked up at him. "No matter how many she gives away, we're usually stocked until Valentine's Day."

His eyes were adorably puffy, his hair flopping in an unruly mess like a kindergartner who had just woken up from a nap. That irresistible lazy stubble that peppered his smooth jaw, however, screamed hot-blooded man. She swallowed as she felt her mouth go dry. "I'm surprised we didn't scare you off for good."

"Nah, you're lucky," Jordan said, stretching as he rubbed his hand over his tousled locks. "I love how close you guys seem."

"Yeah, I guess we are pretty close," Brynn said. As much as her mom's nagging could drive her up a wall, Brynn loved the traditions her family held close each year. As she watched Jordan scroll the newest comments on Facebook, she wondered what his Christmas usually looked like. She thought she remembered him mentioning an out-of-town sibling on one of her first days at Evergreen Acres.

Jordan's eyes lowered to Brynn's as her face burned hot. Her heart was pounding against her ribcage, but she didn't look away.

"Thank you," Brynn said after a moment. "For standing up for me to my mom. She can be very opinionated when it comes to what I choose to do with my life."

"Well, I meant it," Jordan said, his voice now low and rough. "Any guy would be lucky to be with you, just as you are."

The air whooshed out of her as she struggled to conceal the raw need that permeated her body. She wanted him to kiss her, what he meant be damned.

But just as suddenly, Jordan cleared his throat, tearing away his eyes as he glanced at his phone with unusually intense interest. Despite Brynn's discomfort, the corners of her mouth twitched. So, this is what Jordan looked like when he got flustered.

"Anyway," Jordan said, stretching out the word with badly acted indifference. "I've been doing some thinking. You've had some pretty out there ideas, but you seem to know your stuff." He took a deep breath, appearing to consider his words carefully before continuing. "If you think a carnival—a very small, very simple carnival—is a good idea, consider me your soldier." He smiled and the sight of his nearly invisible dimple made Brynn's breath catch once more. "If anyone can pull off a Christmas miracle," he continued, "I'd put money on Brynn Callaway."

"You said yes!" Brynn squealed, beaming as she clapped her hands together and threw herself against Jordan in a sudden embrace that caught them both by surprise.

Honk, honk!

The deep bellow of a horn froze the smile on her lips as Jordan's head whipped toward the parking lot. She cringed as she glanced at her phone. They were early.

Before Brynn could say a word, Jordan had darted through the saloon doors toward the front. She hurried after him and found him staring agape through the window as two tractor-trailers filled the lot's entire length. Her chest clenched as she braced herself and waited for him to put it all together, waited for him to become furious. But seconds later, Jordan tossed his head back in a throaty laughter that shook his whole body. Brynn took a breath as a relieved chuckle escaped her lips. Jordan wiped his eyes before pushing past her to the back room once more, returning a moment later with both of their coats in hand.

"Bold move, Callaway," he said, and the impressed smile on his face sent a warm glow through Brynn. She took her coat and followed him onto the porch, relief filling every excited step. As the drivers stepped down from their cabs, Brynn threw them a friendly wave. Jordan simply watched the scene unfold, his eyes twinkling as he looked at her and shook his head.

Jordan directed the drivers to park in the patchy grass field beside the storage barn. As they cleared the parking lot, Jordan stopped mid-step as the long driveway was suddenly revealed. Ten or so vehicles sat bumper to bumper, idling on the driveway. Who were these people?

He shot a questioning glance to Brynn, but she was too busy waving the cars forward to notice. People of all ages began to pile out of parked SUV's, station wagons, even minivans. Some of them he recognized from town, but many others he'd never seen.

Still frozen, he watched as Brynn grabbed a stack of orange cones off the porch. She jogged over to the far corner of the lot, blocking it off with the cones as she waved to the driver of a flat-bed truck that was bringing up the rear. As its loud engine drew closer, Jordan glimpsed what looked like a pink horse peeking out from under a black tarp.

"Is that a...?" Jordan began. He could now make out the animal's bared teeth, its eyes rolled back in a permanent stare.

"I think you're looking for the word Merry-Go-Round," Brynn said, laughing as she hurried over to the driver, calling back over her shoulder, "Or do you guys call it a carousel?"

Just then, a woman waddled over to Jordan with two stuffed trash bags, and he hurried to take one from her.

"Thought you could use these to decorate the trees up front," the woman said with a sweaty grin as she pointed to the pines that lined the road. "Leftover ornaments from the town square."

"Thank you," Jordan said, truly touched as he took the other bag and jogged back to the porch to set them down. When he returned, only the woman's lower half was visible, sticking out she tugged at bags onto the gravel in the back of a Volkswagen SUV.

"You can lean the canopies against the shop!" he heard Brynn shout. "All non-perishable food and drinks can go on the back porch," she yelled to someone else, pointing them in the general direction.

She breathlessly hurried over to Jordan, planting her gloved fists on her hips as she gazed proudly over the packed lot. Her breath formed a tiny cloud in front of her lips, and her nose had begun to turn as red as Tyler's reindeer cookie. She turned to Jordan, breaking into a somewhat apprehensive grin when their eyes met.

"How did you do all this?" Jordan stammered as even more cars rolled closer, parking along the driveway when they saw the filled lot. "Who are all these people?!"

"I called in some favors, put out a blast out to my followers—nothing too major," Brynn said breezily, but he could see in her eyes she was loving every minute of this. "Oh, I also called our new friend at the local news station, the reporter from the tree lighting. She made sure the carnival was mentioned on last night's broadcast." She laughed as she noticed how pale he'd become. "I wasn't exactly stealthy. I'm amazed you didn't catch wind before now."

"And if I had said no?" Jordan asked.

"You wouldn't," Brynn said with boastful confidence.

Jordan narrowed his eyes.

"Well, okay, the possibility did cross my mind," Brynn admitted. "But I hoped that once you saw how much everyone wanted to help, you'd change your mind." She paused to tuck a stray curl into her messy bun before continuing. "Some of these people drove hours just to be here."

He slowly shook his head again, but he couldn't suppress a huge smile of astonishment. Based on the sheer number of volunteers that were now swarming his property, this woman was impossible to refuse.

Gina's Jeep Cherokee pulled to a stop in front of the walkway, emergency blinkers flashing as Charlie hopped out and hurried to open the hatch. Jordan couldn't help but laugh as Charlie and Gina tugged human-sized candy canes from the back, each throwing one over their shoulder before heading their way.

"Where to, kiddo?" Charlie said to Jordan, but not before he threw Brynn a theatrical wink.

"You guys were in on this?!" Jordan huffed. Next thing he knew, a clown car would pull up with every teacher he'd ever had in school.

"In on it?!" Gina scoffed, though she was nothing but grins as she pointed behind them. "That's my cousin Cliff over there setting up the ice rink."

"How about standing a candy cane on each side of the gate over there?" Brynn said as she pointedly ignored Jordan's open mouth, grabbing the decoration from Gina as Charlie followed close behind.

"Ice rink?!" Jordan finally repeated, as a man in a driving cap that shared Gina's chocolate complexion directed a crew of teenage boys to unroll what looked like a house-sized tarp.

"Don't worry, you've got no grass left to kill," Gina said brightly. "He'll find the perfect level spot. Don't know if you saw it set up over at the Baptist church last winter, but it was a real crowd-pleaser."

"When you two are finished gawking, we should really get to work!" Brynn called, glowing as she weaved her way towards them through the growing mob.

Just then, Mayor Lopez emerged from the crowd, a folding table in each arm.

"Where do you want these, Brynn?" he asked, his broad face as jubilant as ever.

"Here, let me take those," Jordan said as he reached for them.

"There's more in the van," the mayor said, zipping his coat to the top of the collar as a brittle gust of wind swept the walk. "Why don't you set those somewhere and help me bring in the rest."

Jordan counted fourteen tables by the time he and Mayor Lopez had unloaded the rest from the back of a cargo van with *E Street Community Center* stickered in a big decal on the side.

"Where to?" the mayor asked. Jordan scanned the crowd and saw Brynn emerge from the shop.

"I have a strong feeling that woman plans to give us orders," Jordan said, and the mayor laughed along with him when he followed Jordan's gaze. "Thanks for lending the tables, Mayor."

"Happy to," the mayor said. "But I'm also lending myself for the day, so use me how you need me."

"You don't need to get back to work?" Jordan asked as Brynn joined them, a clipboard in hand.

"This *is* work!" the mayor replied as he hurried over to offer an arm to a woman Jordan recognized as Susan Lindle, the retired librarian from his elementary school. *Not too far off the clown car,* Jordan thought as he bit back a grin. Susan passed Brynn a Tupperware of what looked like brownies as Jordan joined the mayor in helping her up the porch steps. "Look around, Jordan," Mayor Lopez continued. "Half of these people are your neighbors."

Sure enough, Jordan saw the owner of the coffee shop unloading cases of sound equipment from a weathered camper van. Mr. Wykle, Evergreen Acres's insurance salesman, was passing around a pack of name tags and a Sharpie. And everywhere Jordan looked he saw the beaming faces of his own customers; some he hadn't seen for years.

Jordan blinked his eyes clear before turning to Brynn. "I don't even know what to say."

"Well, you've got plenty of time to think about it," Brynn said, chuckling as she dragged a polished fingernail down her clipboard and circled something in pen before glancing up at him. "We have our work cut out for us."

"Tell me what to do," Jordan said, still trembling at the scene before him. "Anything."

"Right this way," Brynn said, grinning as she looped her arm through his and guided him behind the shop.

He liked the way her slim arm fit in his; liked how people smiled at the two of them as they unpacked boxes of popcorn seeds and hot dog buns. He would never admit this out loud, but he even liked the way she was bossing him around. They worked side-by-side for what felt like hours.

Finally, the sky cleared, and people shed their coats as Jordan refilled their coffee cups. A giant stainless steel carafe had been perched on the porch, Styrofoam cups and boxes of donuts stacked beside it.

Jordan helped the mayor set up the pop-up canopies as several other volunteers unfolded tables beneath each one. Jordan paused to take a breath, munching on a cruller as he snuck a glance at Brynn. Her round ivory cheeks glowed in the sunlight as she passed out copies of her hand drawn carnival map to everyone she saw. He watched as she clapped her hands over her mouth, squealing in delight as an overall-clad man led two real reindeer down the ramp of his horse trailer, eventually releasing them in a temporary pen that had been constructed earlier by a pair of Eagle Scouts.

Just then, "Grandma Got Run Over by a Reindeer" blasted from a car stereo. Jordan pressed his lips together, unable to look away as Brynn sang and danced while she wove lights around the fence. Suddenly, she caught him watching and her face broke into a giant rosy-cheeked grin.

He reminded himself she was moving. He reminded himself he'd sworn her off just the night before. He reminded remind himself not to fall for her. Not to fall for the vivacious, passionate woman who had rallied the entire community to his aid. He swallowed, the knot of desire growing with every carefree giggle, every toss of her messy hair. Staying away from Brynn Callaway was going to be much easier said than done.

TWENTY-ONE

Brynn gave the black scrolled "L" a final stroke with her paintbrush before climbing to her feet and stepping back to inspect their work: *Evergreen Acres's Christmas Carnival: Dec. 18-20.* A pine tree with cartoon eyeballs pointed readers up the drive.

Perfect.

Dylan Lee, her new favorite Planted customer, had shown up in the afternoon with his dad Henry, loaded up with scones and muffins from Earlybird Espresso. Dylan seemed to help, especially when he learned his art club experience was desperately needed. Not only had he spent over an hour outlining the professional-looking lettering on the giant plywood sign, but he'd spent two more creating the adorable tree graphic. Next, it was time for him and Brynn to carefully apply three coats of paint.

The sun had nearly sunk behind the hills when the Lees begged off to go to his piano lesson, but Brynn could tell he would have liked to stay longer. She was delighted to learn he'd caught the houseplant bug, and she'd eagerly answered a bottomless list of gardening questions as the hours sped by. After reassuring him that she could handle the paint touch ups on her own, Brynn practically begged him to hang around the store more often. It wasn't every day someone was just as excited as she was to discuss organic methods of indoor pest control.

Today had been an even bigger success than she'd hoped for. Between the surprisingly warm afternoon and the Girl Scouts' generous donation of handmade sub sandwiches, more than fifty volunteers spent the day cheerfully working side-by-side. And although Brynn knew better than to believe such an impossible thing, the sun had even seemed to set extra late just for them.

And then there was Jordan.

Even when he was out of sight, she swore she could feel his presence almost like radar. Anytime he came close, she found herself hyperaware of his every breath. Of where he put his hands. Of the way his eyes narrowed in polite concentration when he spoke to anyone, even the youngest kids who had tagged along with their parents that day.

And then there was the way he looked at her—his jaw softening, the way he leaned in as a look of craving filled his gaze. It was almost like his body had forfeited a game that his words still played. Brynn knew that game all too well. She wondered if Jordan could see through the chipper, professional façade she kept wearing when he approached, see past the bulwark she'd created with her clipboard and borrowed walkie talkies.

As Brynn wiped the paintbrush clean in a paper towel, she couldn't help wondering what he was doing at that very moment.

"No driver in all of Idaho could miss that beautiful sign."

She smiled. There he was.

"Think these will be enough?" Jordan asked when she'd rearranged her expression to something more appropriate and turned to face him. She followed his nod to the massive bag of stuffed bears thrown over his shoulder like Santa's gift sack, though she could never imagine Santa being so muscular and rugged.

"That's perfect," Brynn said, pulse racing as she pulled out her phone and snapped a couple shots. She zoomed in on the last photo. *Absolutely adorable.* She tucked her phone into her pocket and put on her best carnival director face. "How's the game section coming?"

"Locked and loaded," Jordan said, his eyes crinkling at the corners. "Gina is stocking the rolls of tickets as we speak."

"Great!" Brynn said, scanning her list for any unfinished tasks. "Oh! Your dad came by and asked me where to put the generators? I'm glad Mayor Lopez made that call for us. I guess I didn't realize how much electricity something like this would need."

Jordan chewed his lip as he considered. "I think the West Twenty would be best, as long as the cords are long enough. It's the driest spot on the property, though it's been a pretty dry year all around so far. Still, better to play it safe." He nodded. "Yeah, let's say the West Twenty."

The what now?

"I'll talk to my dad about it," Jordan said with a chuckle as Brynn blinked at him like he was speaking Russian.

"Perfect," she said gratefully, checking off another item on her dwindling list as she heard the shop door jingle.

"I'm coming back tomorrow for my tree," Mayor Lopez said jubilantly as he bounded down the porch steps to join them. "I'm dying to test drive the skating rink, but I think that might end badly. My knees have seen better days."

"Well, we sure appreciate your help, Mayor," Jordan said.

"My pleasure," the mayor said, giving Jordan a paternal clap on the shoulder as his gaze wandered thoughtfully over the pine-scented woods. "What you've done with this place..." He seemed lost in thought, but a moment later he cleared his throat and looked square at Jordan, his eyes shining as they reflected the porch lights. "Your mother would be very proud of you."

It was then that Brynn remembered Jordan telling her that his mom and the mayor had graduated college together. They must have been friends. Her eyes shot to Jordan, but it was too dark to read his expression.

"That means a lot, sir," Jordan said finally, his voice thick with emotion.

Mayor Lopez smiled, clapping Jordan's shoulder once more, before lowering his voice in a conspiratorial tone as the few remaining volunteers passed by on their way to the parking lot. "There's something else I meant to tell you earlier," he said, as Brynn inched closer to listen. "I forgot, what with all the festivities."

"Sure," Jordan said. "Is everything OK?"

"Maybe better than OK," the mayor continued, and even in the darkness, his grin was impossible to miss. "This morning, we had the county commerce meeting, and I told everyone about your holiday carnival. Later, Laurence Krebs pulled me aside."

"Why does that name sound so familiar?" Jordan asked.

"Probably because he's the Krebs of Krebs Mall," the mayor said, his grin widening impossibly bigger as Jordan's eyes widened in recognition.

"That's a good friend to have," Brynn said. She'd seen his name all over the Magic Valley; not just at the mall. There was a Krebs Cineplex, a Krebs sports arena, and she'd heard the tycoon had ties to several charities around town.

"He said the mall's usual tree supplier had fallen through..." Mayor Lopez continued, adding suspense as he paused. "And he wondered if you could handle a last-minute order. One for the entire mall."

"What?!" Jordan stammered, and Brynn could practically see the excitement pouring out of him. "I mean, of course! Absolutely! Thank you!"

"I've been to the mall at Christmas," Brynn said, shaking her head in amazement. "They go all out. They put cute displays all over the parking lot and if you turn your radio to a specific station, they light up in time with the music."

"Well, I'm glad to connect you," Mayor Lopez said, chuckling at Jordan's sudden speechlessness as he headed for the community center van. "Good night!"

"Night, Mayor!" Brynn called, giddy as she turned back to the thunderstruck man standing next to her. "Krebs Mall?! That's huge! I bet I've seen thirty trees there between the ones in the lot and the ones inside."

"Well, let's just wait and see," Jordan said calmly, but his eyes shone with excitement. "Thirty trees won't save us, but it sure would help."

"It's OK to believe it will all work out," Brynn teased. She climbed the porch steps, ducking behind the rocking chairs and flipping on a power strip. Suddenly, everything glowed as a thousand lightbulbs lit up the railing and bushes around them. As she stood on the edge of the porch, she could see as far as the edge of the forest, everything illuminated as brightly as dawn. She stole a glance at Jordan as she shoved her clipboard into the handbag she'd stashed behind the railing that morning. He stood perfectly still, his hands in his pockets, his crooked smile growing as he cocked his head and met her gaze. Everything inside her twisted and strained as she forced herself to look away, tugging her keys loose as she descended the steps.

"Well, today has been a blast," Brynn said, somewhat reluctantly as she noticed the now empty parking lot, well, empty except for the Civic tucked into the shadows. A tiny thrill of anticipation rippled down her spine.

We're alone.

As Jordan shifted the bag of teddy bears to his other shoulder, Brynn cracked a smile. "I'm pretty sure those stuffies are out past curfew," she said. "And I should probably get home too."

"You can't leave just yet," Jordan said, those lips twisting into a playful smile as he stepped into her path. "You heard the mayor— there's one more job to do."

"There is?" Brynn asked, but before she could tug the clipboard from her bag, Jordan grabbed her hand.

"Come with me," he said.

She had to laugh as he pulled her along, the stuffed bears staring with blank smiles as they bounced on Jordan's back. Where was he taking her?

He shot her a self-conscious look, which melted into that boyish grin when he caught her already smiling up at him. In that moment, Brynn would have followed him anywhere.

The sky glittered with a million tiny crystals as Jordan pulled Brynn onto the ice. The rink was small but seemed was surprisingly sturdy. Gina's cousin Cliff had left a plastic trunk full of skates of all sizes, and he promised to return the next day with more supplies.

"Are you sure it's okay we're out here?" a pink-nosed Brynn

asked, her knees wobbling as she struggled to right herself.

Jordan shrugged. "It looks frozen to me."

The brief warmth had faded along with the afternoon sun, and Jordan was glad Brynn had agreed to wear a faded parka with a furry hood he'd pulled from the storage closet. He wasn't sure why, but he hadn't mentioned it once belonged to his mother.

Brynn gazed up at him, her smile both wary and trusting as she gripped his hand tightly. Once they'd circled a few times, Jordan flipped around and grabbed her other hand, pulling her along as he skated backwards. As he picked up pace, resisting the urge to whip her around the tight corners, Brynn shrieked in what could have been terror or glee. Soon, Jordan's cheeks were numb from a combination of the winter night air and the fact that he couldn't stop grinning like a fool. As they slowed, Brynn let go, her gait growing smoother as she started to get the hang of the movement. Jordan tipped his head back, inhaling the woodsy breeze as the pearly moon waxed above them.

After a time, Brynn gripped the side, resting her chest against the plastic railing.

"You okay?" he called from across the rink.

"I haven't skated since I was a kid," she said breathlessly. "My ankles are killing me."

"I can help you," he said, and he could feel her green eyes following as he finished the lap. He skidded to a stop beside her and extended his hand. "I'll hold onto you."

She eyed him, but lifted her arms as he moved behind to embrace her. Jordan began to skate, bracing her weight against him as he pushed them along. He was hit with the sweet scent of strawberries as wild strands of yellow hair blew across his face. His toes were tingling as the temperature continued to drop, but all he could focus on was the way Brynn surrendered her body against his, her back to his stomach, as if she had melted into him.

"Night is so much darker out here," Brynn said a few minutes later, pulling away from his grip and heading for the rail. "You can see so many stars."

Though Jordan's back ached and he was thirsty, regret surged through him as the night air once again chilled his torso. He skated next to her, mirroring the way she leaned against the rail. He could almost feel her pulse as they both tipped their heads back and gazed at the sparkling sky.

"I don't stargaze much," Jordan said, acutely aware of each inch between them. "Sometimes I get too caught up in work and life to see what's right in front on me."

"I know that feeling," Brynn said softly, and he could feel her eyes on his face. An image resurfaced of her bare collarbone as her sweater dripped off her shoulder. He willed his mind to picture anything else, anything to redirect the pressure growing in his jeans. He didn't trust himself to return her stare.

"Earlier this week, you could see the Aurora Borealis just a bit north of here," Jordan said, swallowing as he guided himself to safer territory.

"I'd love to see that one day," Brynn said, hesitation sneaking into her words as she laced her arm through his.

The silence stretched between them. The only sounds to fill Jordan's ears were the rustling of the wind through the trees and his walloping pulse.

"I have a favor to ask," Brynn asked, her face glowing as he looked down at her. "Have you heard Urban Farm?"

"The show with Georgina and Paul?" Jordan asked.

Brynn raised her eyebrows and bit back a curious smile.

"I leave it on in the background for Toby," Jordan said. No need to add that he'd marathoned two full seasons when he'd been sidelined with the flu that past February.

Brynn gave a little smirk, but Jordan could see apprehension clouding her eyes.

"Well, what's this favor?" Jordan said, nudging his hip against hers, just like she had done to him in her mother's kitchen.

"So, Urban Farm is in the same network that is considering me for a show," she said, studying the dark woods around them.

The show in Los Angeles, you mean.

"They invited me to this luncheon on Monday and all the higher-ups will be there," she continued. "I was hoping...maybe you'd come with me?"

Jordan's breath caught in his throat. She wanted him there with her?

Brynn spit out the rest in a blur. "It's all the way in Salt Lake City, so I understand if you can't take the day off."

"I'll come," Jordan said without hesitation. Sure, he wanted to support her, but the idea of spending a few hours alone with her in a car was too much to resist. "It sounds like fun."

"Just one other thing," Brynn said, and her smile no longer extended to her eyes.

"What?"

She winced. "The network thinks we're a couple—not because of anything I said!" She pressed her hand to her chest. "I guess they just assumed after the tree lighting..." Her face was even redder. "Anyway, if that makes you uncomfortable, I totally get it."

"I'm honored to go," Jordan said, leaning on his elbow so that his face was level with hers. "Even as a pretend boyfriend."

She smiled that cherubic smile and Jordan felt the last bars of his reluctance begin to warp and bend every time she blinked back at him.

"Maybe we should have a dress rehearsal," he said. "You know, so we're convincing."

"Good idea," Brynn replied softly, and her face so close to his, it took everything in his power not to stare at those glossy red lips. "What exactly did you have in mind?"

"How about dinner at my place tomorrow night?"

"Lovely," she said, and despite those little voices inside him shouting in protest, he inched even closer. God, her eyes were gorgeous.

He swallowed and his throat felt sticky as he finally let his eyes drift to her mouth.

He felt his phone vibrate a split second before he heard it ring. Before he could silence it, Brynn touched his cheek with one cold, ungloved finger.

"See who it is," she said.

He nodded, but when he looked at the screen, he didn't recognize the number.

"Hello, this is Jordan Damon."

"Hi Jordan, my friend Rick Lopez told me about you." Before he continued, Jordan's blood turned to ice as he realized who was calling. "This is Laurence Krebs." Jordan could hear a cacophony of voices, beeping and whirring machinery, as if the man was calling from a factory or construction site.

"Hi Mr. Krebs," Jordan said, fighting to keep his voice steady. "Mayor Lopez told me you might call."

Brynn's eyes widened as she excitedly clapped her hands over her mouth.

"Please," the man's warm voice replied. "Call me Larry."

And Jordan knew in that moment that things were going to go his way.

Larry explained that the tree suppliers they'd used in the past had major shortages this year. As soon as he said they shipped from the South, Jordan suspected they'd been hit by blight or root rot, two destructive diseases that had been rampant that year. Jordan told Larry that Evergreen Acres had produced several disease resistant species.

But what Larry said next almost caused made Jordan drop his phone.

"I'm sorry, can you repeat that?" Jordan asked as time slowed around him.

"I need three hundred trees," Larry repeated. "Or as many as you can spare."

Brynn didn't seem to be able to hear what Larry was saying, but as soon as she took in Jordan's peaked face, she gripped his arm in a way that sent heat back through his body.

"All four of my malls are without trees," Larry continued. "I'm hoping to fill them in the next few days." Jordan's ears began to ring as he fought to make sense of what he was hearing. "I know it's late in the season, but next week is our busiest of the year."

Brynn mouthed a question, but Jordan held a finger up to ask her to wait.

"We can do that," Jordan said, though his voice seemed to be coming from somewhere outside of his body. "I'll make it happen."

After a giddy, blurry few minutes spent discussing details, they wished each other a Merry Christmas and the call was over.

Brynn watched him and waited; her hands clutched tightly under her chin in earnest anticipation.

"He wants three hundred trees," Jordan finally muttered once he was able to form a sentence. He gripped the railing as the night seemed to spin around him.

Brynn gasped. "No way! Do you have that many?!"

"He said he didn't care about size or species, so yeah, we do," Jordan said numbly. "It will basically empty the west field and half our cut inventory. It won't deplete our stock much for next year, but I couldn't accommodate much bigger of an order." He gripped her shoulders before he could even register he was touching her.

"We're going to be OK, Brynn," he said, drinking in every inch of her rosy face, finally settling his gaze on the two juniper orbs as they glowed back at him. He raised one bare hand and slowly skimmed his fingers along her smooth alabaster jaw.

This time, he knew exactly what he was doing.

He pressed his lips against hers, their teeth colliding roughly as he gripped her neck. Her body stiffened for only a second, before she began to press his face against her own with the same hungry need. He tugged one cherry lip between his teeth, just as he'd imagined so many times, savoring the taste. Somehow, it was even more intoxicating than he'd fantasized on more than one sleepless night.

Her arms clenched back over and over as if she couldn't get close enough. A throbbing warmth penetrated every inch of Jordan's body as she folded perfectly into his embrace. When they breathlessly broke apart, wild-eyed and disheveled, he was relieved to see a giant grin on that beautiful face.

Brynn Callaway.

One look at those swollen lips and everything else faded into nothing. He couldn't feel the cold. He couldn't see the stars. Not even Larry's phone call could reach him. A part of him knew he was officially done for, two feet planted where he'd sworn he'd never go. But as she tiptoed and brushed a tender kiss against his pulsating throat, he was far too drunk on Brynn to care. Los Angeles be damned.

TWENTY-TWO

"Did you triple your latte or what?" Katie asked.

"What do you mean?" Brynn asked, biting her lip as she adjusted the phone against her shoulder, a paper-wrapped plant on one hip as she navigated the crowded sidewalk.

"You sound extra chipper this morning," Katie said, suspicion thick in her voice. "By the way, sorry I didn't make it to Evergreen Acres last night. I got your text saying you were finished right as I was locking up the shop."

"I can't tell you grateful I am for all your help," Brynn said. "Thanks to you, it's like I can be in two places at once."

"Well, I *am* the one who made you go to Evergreen Acres in the first place," Katie said. "And it's not like I'm working for free."

"We both know I don't pay you nearly enough!"

"Maybe not," Katie teased. "But I'm exactly where I want to be."

"I have some exciting news," Brynn said, watching through a window as a saleswoman adjusted a mannequin.

"Do tell!"

"On my nursery run today, I hit the jackpot," Brynn said, barely able to contain her excitement. "The store order is being delivered later, but right there at the counter I found...a Monstera Obliqua!"

Katie gasped. "Monstera Obliqua! Isn't that the one you said you'd never even seen in person?!"

"It was forty bucks!" Brynn practically squealed.

"No way!" Katie said, and for a second, silence filled Brynn's ear. "Wait, is that the same one you tried to get at—"

"Nope," Brynn said, cutting her off before she had to hear the rest of that sentence. "This is the one that looks like Swiss cheese. Not the one with white leaves."

That memory of that day at Grantway felt like a black hole, and Brynn was not about to let it ruin his moment. She peeled back the corner of the butcher paper, admiring the gaping lime green foliage that was finally hers.

"Can you propagate it?" Katie asked.

"Listen to you!" Brynn said. "Slinging that plant vocab around. I'm so proud."

"It's probably Stockholm Syndrome," Katie said with a snort.

"Well, you're welcome," Brynn said. "And to answer your question, yes, propagating should be easy."

"I bet you could sell those babies for a fortune!"

"I have a better idea," Brynn said. "What if we do an online raffle? We make a video, have folks tag their friends—"

"—show off a rare-as-hell plant and get a million more followers in the homestretch!" Katie finished, sounding impressed. "Love, the idea, but then you won't get to keep your new baby."

Brynn shrugged. "If I get the show, I'll buy myself another."

She continued past Kit's Knick Knacks, where the windows were dressed to look like an antique living room on Christmas Eve. Red and orange tissue paper served as the hearth's fire as tiny paper snowflakes were into the air by a tiny machine.

"Still on for tonight?" Brynn asked as she absent-mindedly gazed at the tiny artificial tree, barely registering the dolls, wooden games, and tin cars beneath it. "I'll rewrite the video outline to include the Obliqua."

"Sounds good," Katie said.

Suddenly, a shiny red train engine caught Brynn's eye and her breath caught. She knew where she'd seen that train.

"Katie," Brynn said quickly. "I'll be there soon. I just need to make a quick stop."

As she dropped her phone into her purse, a woman in the store caught Brynn's eye and wiggled her fingers in invitation.

Twenty minutes later, Brynn held open the door as two middle school girls hurried out of Planted in Twin, smiling as she caught pieces of their chatter about the snake plants they'd just purchased. Brynn beelined over to Katie, who was tapping away on her laptop behind the register. With a dramatic flourish, Brynn placed the paper-wrapped plant on the counter and carefully peeled back the wrapping.

Katie gasped. "It's so ugly, it's almost pretty!"

"Be nice, it can hear you," Brynn said, laughing as she headed into the back to drop her bags.

"By the way, can we reschedule your taping Friday night?" Katie asked. "I have a date after the carnival."

"Oooh, who's the lucky guy?" Brynn asked before correcting herself. "Or gal?" Katie's long dating history had included many dates of both genders.

"Gal," Katie said, and Brynn was surprised to see her blush. "This one might be pretty special." Before Brynn could ask, Katie held up a hand. "If there's anything more to report, you'll be first to know. I just don't want to jinx anything."

"You got it," Brynn said, joining Katie behind the register. She pulled up the store's email and gave it a cursory scroll. "How are sales?"

"Getting busier every day," Katie said. "I think Twin Falls is starting to notice this place."

Brynn felt a surge of pride that mingled with a pang of guilt. This was exactly what she wanted—for her store to grow. But at the same time, she felt bad at how neglectful she'd been lately as she'd poured herself into Evergreen Acres and making sure her channel had as many subscribers as possible.

Katie turned her laptop so Brynn could see the screen. *The Green Goddess* YouTube channel was pulled up and a video posted the day before was cued up to play. Jessica's threateningly shiny ponytail swung aggressively as Brynn watched her gesture to the camera with perfectly gelled nails. Just as Brynn was about what she was supposed to be looking for, her eyes fell on the video's title. Her mouth fell open as she registered the words: *The Hunt for the Elusive Obliqua.*

"Merry early Christmas," Katie said, grinning as she crossed her arms over her chest.

"Shut the front door," Brynn said, shaking her head in disbelief. "This could not be better timing."

Brynn scrolled through the comments, which were a mixture of encouragement, trolling, and suggestions on where to find the rare plant.

Suddenly, Katie poked her in the stomach.

"What?" Brynn demanded, slapping her away, as she skipped past a comment from a supposed Nigerian prince.

"Welcome!" Brynn called over her shoulder, excitement growing as she scrolled and scrolled. This plant might be exactly what she needed to take the lead. "Let us know if you need help finding anything," she called distractedly.

"Oh, I will."

Those husky words seemed to freeze midair as Jordan stepped up to the counter. He tugged off his wool cap, his floppy hair falling in a tousled mess over his forehead. Her eyes grazed over his thick eyebrows knotted in amusement, hover his extra stubbly chin, finally resting on the dimple framed lips that had devoured her less than twelve hours earlier. Her heartbeat thundered in her throat as she shot a look at Katie, who shrugged as if to say, *I tried to warn you.*

"Morning ladies," Jordan said smoothly, setting a cardboard drink carrier on the counter. "Brought you a couple coffees. Splash of cocoa, a little trick I learned from Gina."

"Yeah, thanks," Brynn said quickly. "I didn't know you were coming by."

"Well, it's not entirely selfless," Jordan said, and for a heart-stopping second Brynn prayed he'd come for her. "I wanted to ask if you would help me with another video soon. Customers are always asking me the best way to get rid of a dead tree... What do you think?"

"I probably could have just called," he blurted after Brynn blinked dumbly back at him for a moment.

Why didn't he just call?

"Sure," Brynn said, finally finding words as she ignored a giggle from Katie's direction. "I need help with a video myself. Apparently, Katie's got a hot date on Friday—"

"Shocking, I know," Katie interjected between sips of coffee.

"I totally get it if that's too much," Brynn said. "It would have to be after the carnival that night,"

"I'm in if you are," Jordan said, holding her gaze for just a moment longer than normal.

"Definitely," Brynn said, her face growing hot as Katie snorted just loud enough for Brynn to hear.

"Still on for dinner tonight?" he asked with a small smile.

"Can't wait," she said, not daring to glance at Katie's face.

The bell clanged once more, and Brynn glimpsed a familiar teenager weaving his way through the plants.

"Dylan!" Brynn said, waving him over. "How's it going?"

"Hey guys," Dylan said, giving a little wave before turning shyly to Jordan. "I didn't meet you yesterday, but I helped Brynn make the sign."

"Helped me," Brynn said. "Don't let this kid food you—he drew the whole thing."

"Wow, I can't believe you drew that," Jordan gushed as Dylan beamed and turned scarlet. "Please thank your dad for all the pastries he brought."

"I sure will," Dylan said, already backing up a few steps. "If you're busy, I can come back another time."

"Not at all," Brynn said. "Are you here for plants or girl trouble?"

Dylan hesitated and shot a look at Jordan, who was tactfully studying his fingernails.

"Oh!" Brynn exclaimed, suddenly understanding. "Jordan, you need to swear an oath of secrecy." She winked at Dylan. "Plant-client confidentiality, remember?"

"On my honor," Jordan said, placing a hand over his chest.

"Girl trouble," Dylan finally confessed as his shoulders relaxed slightly.

"Preaching to the choir," Katie said, shrugging when Brynn shot her a look.

"Dylan has been leaving plants for a special young lady," Brynn explained to Jordan.

"I just walked by her house on my way over," Dylan said, looking terrified. "She has *both* plants in her window." He rubbed a nervous hand over the back of his neck. "I was just standing there, smiling like a dope when- *she saw me*! I mean, I ran, obviously, but she one hundred percent saw me."

He groaned and pressed his palms to his forehead as Brynn bit back a smile.

"I don't know what to do!" he said.

"I once had this huge crush on another camp counselor one summer in high school," Jordan said. "Every week, I swore I'd ask her to the Friday night mixer, but every week I chickened out. Everyone had a crush on Nicole. I had no reason to think she might be interested in me."

Brynn would have liked to disagree, but didn't say a word.

"Let me guess," Dylan said glumly as he pulled his hands from his face. "You finally worked up the courage to ask her out and now you're married."

Jordan laughed. "Hardly. Summer ended and we all went home."

"Is that supposed to make me feel better?" Dylan asked with a grimace.

"That fall, I ran into another counselor at an away football game," Jordan said. "She told me that Nicole had a huge crush on me and had waited all summer for me to ask her out." Jordan crossed his arms over his chest. "Before I could ask if she was at the game, her friend told me she'd moved to Maine."

"Bummer," Dylan said, considering. "But why didn't she just ask you out?"

Jordan raised an eyebrow.

"Yeah, yeah, I hear you," Dylan said, chagrined. "I need to make a move before the moment passes, right?" He paled. "I can't think of anything more terrifying. Like, horror movie level terrifying."

"That fear is what kept me from making a move," Jordan agreed. "But take it from me—the regret of never trying was ten times worse that that fear ever was."

"Have you ever tried to look her up?" Dylan asked.

"Nah," Jordan said, waving a hand dismissively. "I doubt I'd even recognize her if I saw her on the street," He smiled, locking eyes with Brynn. "I think the reason I met her was to teach me something, something that's taken me a long time to understand."

"What's that?" Dylan asked, rapt.

Jordan didn't look away from Brynn. "That you should never wait to tell someone how you feel about them."

Brynn resisted an urge to leap over him and pummel Katie in her smug grin. Brynn was never going to live this down.

"I agree with Jordan," Brynn said, focusing on Dylan as she tried in vain to tame the lava churning through her insides. "You need to tell her. Worst case scenario? She doesn't like you back and you're in the exact same spot you are in right now. But best case? Well, I have a feeling you've imagined that already more than once."

Dylan's face was practically purple as he considered. "I'll think about it," he said finally.

Brynn grabbed a tiny bird's nest fern from the counter and shoved it into his hands. "This one's on the house," she said, running through the curtain and returning with her coat. "This is not a time for thinking. Let's go."

"Wait," Dylan said, panic spreading across his face. "*Now?*"

"I'm in," Jordan said, eyeing Brynn as he pulled his cap back over his ears. "Don't worry, Dylan. We'll hang back and offer moral support."

"You mean, you'll make sure I don't wimp out," Dylan said, narrowing his eyes as he swiped at his sweating neck.

"That too," Jordan said with a devilish grin.

"What Jordan means to say is that you should only do it if *you* want to," Brynn chastised, shooting Jordan a scolding look. "But we'll be there to cheer you on either way."

Dylan took a deep breath before a hesitant smile spread across his face. When he smiled, he was really quite handsome, although Brynn had a feeling it would be a few more years before he realized it.

"Let's do it," he said, his voice cracking.

"That's my man," Jordan said, clapping Dylan on the back before gesturing toward the door. "Ladies first!"

"I'll man the store!" Katie said. "But I expect a full report. Good luck, Dylan!"

Jordan peeked over the fence, trying to guess which unassuming split-level housed Dylan's crush.

"I can't do this," Dylan said in a whisper, tucking himself back against the wooden fence as his face took on a particularly ashen shade of gray.

"You can," Brynn said, her eyes narrowed with determination as she looped an arm around Dylan's shoulders. "We'll be right here the whole time."

"Remember," said Jordan. "You have nothing to lose, but a whole lot to gain."

Dylan gazed back longingly in the direction from which they'd walked.

Brynn gestured to the little plant gripped between his white knuckles.

"Name?" she prompted.

"Bird's nest fern," Dylan replied, automatically.

"Water?"

"Consistently moist soil," Dylan said in the same monotone.

"Air?"

"Humidity," Dylan said, his eyes now fixed on a yellow house at the end of Retreat Street.

"See?" Brynn said. "You got this."

Dylan didn't seem convinced, but he heaved a sigh and headed down the street.

As he approached the house, Brynn and Jordan tucked themselves lower behind the fence. In order to watch the scene unfold, they had to press their bodies close to share the tiny gap between two wooden planks. Jordan carefully leaned over top of her, and every so often, Brynn's head pressed against his chest as she silently readjusted. He could feel the damp heat every time she exhaled. He had never been close to her for this long, not even the night before. A vision of her desperate eyes fixed on his lips flashed through his mind and he stifled a groan as he shifted his weight. Did she have any idea what she was doing to him? If so, her stillness gave nothing away.

Dylan gingerly stepped onto the small stoop once he finally reached the yellow house. He snuck a look back over his shoulder, and both Brynn and Jordan popped up just long enough to give him some emphatic thumbs up. He raised his hand to knock, but hesitated, instead reaching for the doorbell.

Before he could press the button, the door swung open, and a mass of fiery red curls filled the doorway. Madison was tall— at least two inches taller than Dylan. She sported a baggy tunic over leggings and wore wayfarer glasses, giving off the vibes of someone who marched to her own beat.

Though Dylan's back was facing them, Jordan could hear muffled voices and see Madison's lips moving. Her arms were crossed, but her face was too distant to read her expression. Just then, Madison took a small step closer, throwing back her head in laughter, a hearty sound that echoed down the quiet street. Brynn looked up at Jordan with wide eyes that seemed to ask the same question he was thinking. Was that a happy laugh or a mean one?

Jordan looked back through the crack in the fence just as Dylan handed Madison the little fern. He shoved his hands into his pockets and ducked his head as he retreated. When he drew closer, Jordan's stomach dropped as he noticed his sullen eyes.

"Dylan!"

All three of them looked back as Madison's voice rang out across the lane.

Madison trotted down the steps and quickly intercepted Dylan, bending down as she planted a quick kiss on his cheek. As Jordan's eyes became as big as saucers, Jordan's heart leapt for this kid he'd only met an hour before. He lowered his hand to meet Brynn's in a silent high five.

Once the door to Madison's house had closed behind her, Dylan sprinted over, a goofy grin plastered on his flushed face.

"So?!" Brynn exclaimed.

"She asked if I want to drive around at look at lights this weekend," Dylan said, looking stunned as he mopped his forehead with his sleeve.

"I knew you could do it!" Brynn said, pulling the lanky teenager in for a hug. "You should bring hot cocoa. That's what we did on dates when I was in high school."

But Dylan was too dumbstruck to squeeze her in return, in fact he was too dumbstruck to say another word.

TWENTY-THREE

Jordan blew out the match, watching as black tendrils of smoke curled the air as the smell of sulfur filled his nose. He took a deep breath grateful he'd held on to the unused scented candle Gina had gifted him last Christmas. He sniffed in the general direction of his underarms, relieved to smell nothing but his deodorant. He could use a drink.

Headlights suddenly beamed through the kitchen window, and Jordan hurried to flip the Michael Bublé record, his heart hammering. He waited until she knocked to approach the door, and when he finally swung it open, there she was, arms full, confetti-like flurries swirling around her perfect face.

"Hi," Brynn said, her eyes crinkled in a smile. Either her lips were redder than usual or the ruby shade of her sweater dress made them seem that way. He forced his eyes to stay on hers and away from her bare legs.

"Perfect timing," Jordan said, as she stepped through the doorway. "I hope you're hungry."

"I'm *always* hungry," she said before sniffing the air. "Mmm. It smells great."

"What's that?" he asked, gesturing to her armload. "You didn't need to bring anything."

"I can't help myself," she said. "First, some entertainment options." She pulled out a DVD of *A Christmas Story*. "Always a classic."

"DVD's, huh?" Jordan said. "How very 2004 of you."

Brynn laughed. "Says the guy who never had an Instagram and listens to records instead of Spotify."

"I'll take that as a compliment," Jordan said. "And besides, the WiFi in here makes streaming kind of hit or miss."

She handed him the bag and he peeked inside, quickly counting more than ten movies.

"Exactly how long are you planning to stay?" he teased.

"Very funny," she said, rolling her eyes but he was pleased to see she was blushing.

"And what's behind bag number two?" Jordan asked with a smirk.

Brynn grinned and handed him the package.

He peeled back the paper to find a shaggy little plant that reminded him of a character from Fraggle Rock. He cocked an eyebrow. "I haven't even killed the last one yet."

She laughed and clocked the philodendron in the windowsill. "I had a feeling it might need a friend." She tapped a handwritten label on the side of the pot. "Spider plant. Super easy and I wrote down how often to water it."

Jordan snickered. "You're relentless."

Jordan locked the door behind her as she followed him into the living room.

"So, what's in the final bag, Santa Claus?" he asked.

"A little surprise for after," she said coyly, bending down to scratch a wagging Toby.

Jordan snorted and shook his head.

"Why don't you pick something for us to listen to next while I pour some wine," Jordan said. "Do you like pinot noir?"

"I'm an equal opportunity wine drinker," Brynn said.

He returned with an open bottle and two empty glasses as an orchestral version of "O, Holy Night!" filled the tiny farmhouse.

Brynn was standing in front of the fireplace, gazing at a photo on the mantle, and Jordan noted it was the last family photo that had been taken of all of them together. He filled a glass and passed it to her.

"You and your sister could almost be twins," Brynn said, smelling the wine as she swirled it in the glass.

"I'll try to take that as a compliment," Jordan said. "Though I like to think I've filled out a bit since then."

"That's her husband?" she asked, and he was glad she didn't look at his face when told her it was.

"And that's your mom?" Brynn asked, her eyes finally resting on his as she turned to face him.

He nodded.

"She was stunning," Brynn said. To Jordan, she had been the most stunning woman in the world.

He poured himself some wine, then set the bottle on the mantle before raising his glass. "To the woman who saved the farm."

She chuckled and shook her head, peering at him through those thick dark lashes.

"We both know I had nothing to do with Laurence Krebs," she corrected.

"Haven't you heard that a cricket could cause a tsunami thousands of miles away?" he teased as he stepped closer. "None of this happened until you showed up. You're the cricket."

"I don't think that's quite how that saying goes," Brynn said with a small smile. "How about...to Evergreen Acres and all the world's crickets."

"Cheers," he said with a laugh.

As they clinked their glasses, the oven began to beep.

"Be right back," he said. He took a big swig of wine as he headed back to the kitchen.

As he spooned homemade sauce over the baked fish a few minutes later, he felt a satisfied glow spread through his whole being. It was nice to cook for someone; nice to share a decent bottle of wine and a meal that didn't come in a greasy bag.

Who was he kidding? Having this delicious woman standing inside his home was more than just nice. He let out a long shuddering breath as he scooped caramelized Brussel sprouts onto each plate.

He carried the dishes into the dining room where Brynn sat watching him, her round chin resting on one delicate fist.

As he set a plate in front Brynn, her eyes widened.

"You weren't kidding!" she said with clear approval. "This really is a gourmet meal."

"Striped bass with toasted shallot vinaigrette," Jordan said proudly, spreading his napkin onto his lap.

"And how exactly does a tree farmer become a fancy chef?" she asked, inspecting every inch of her food.

"My roommate in college," Jordan explained with a shrug. "He studied culinary arts and taught me a lot." He couldn't help but smile as Brynn stuck a Brussel sprout in her mouth and made an appreciative groan. "I don't usually cook much since it's just me," he continued. "Plus, my dad would pick a stack of ribs from Barbie's anytime over an ingredient he can't pronounce."

"So, you went to college," Brynn said, and he couldn't tell if it was a statement or a question. She pierced a piece of the flaky fish with her fork, gently placing it on her tongue. He stared as she closed her eyes with a decadent smile and Jordan bit his cheek as he swallowed.

"I started college, but never finished," he said, sipping his wine. "After my mom passed."

"We don't have to talk about it," Brynn said quickly. "If you don't want to."

"It's okay," Jordan said. "I think about her every day, but I just haven't talked about it in a long time."

"You must have been, what?" Brynn asked. "Late teens?"

He shook his head. "Few years older. I was a 'non-traditional undergrad,' as they called us on campus. I started working here when I was fifteen. My sister took off as soon as she turned eighteen and I didn't feel right leaving Mom and Dad alone at on the farm."

"Your sister took off?" Brynn asked, her brow crinkling in concern.

"Oh, not in a bad way," Jordan said. "She wanted to be a teacher and she got a full ride to the University of Cincinnati. I just always felt like I owed it to my mom and dad to make sure things kept running around here."

Brynn listened patiently, nodding at all the right moments, but Jordan wished he knew what she was thinking.

"Eventually, my parents hired a couple of high schoolers,"

Jordan continued, remembering the way they'd say him down, almost as if it was an intervention. "I was finally convinced they'd get by without me. My dad never went to college, and I think they were worried they were holding me back, which wasn't true. I always came back to work summers and the Christmas rush."

He could still remember what it felt like, turning onto the gravel drive in his little blue pickup after being away for months at a time. Evergreen Acres was always his home.

"Can I ask what happened to her?" Brynn asked softly.

"Her heart," he said, twisting the stem of his wine glass between his fingers. "Massive heart attack, my junior year." As the words came out, he forced the memories of that day to stay tucked somewhere deep and detached. "I was drafting grant proposals for the environmental club and didn't end up making it home for Thanksgiving. She died the next day."

"I'm so sorry," Brynn said, touching her fingertips to his as she stretched her graceful arm across the table.

"I'll never really forgive myself for that," Jordan said quietly, swallowing the lump in his throat.

"You had no way of knowing—"

"It doesn't matter," he murmured as he began to stroke the palm of her hand, back and forth. "I should have been here. This is where I belong." He bit his lip and focused on the warm pressure of her fingers. "I won't make that mistake again."

Brynn's lips parted as if she wanted to say something, but she remained silent.

"Between then and now, I convinced Dad to semi-retire," he continued. "I moved into the farmhouse when Dad got a place in town. He didn't like living here without her."

Jordan glanced around the room, shadows of family dinners

and birthday parties flickering in the periphery of his mind.

"Oh, Jordan," Brynn said softly. "So now you do it all by yourself?"

Jordan shook his head. "Dad can still do a lot, and I still give him most of the say around here. I hire some extra hands in the spring when we have the most pruning and such to do, but we haven't needed anyone besides Gina in the winter." He once again felt steady enough to meet her eyes. "I hope now that might change."

He had told himself all kinds of things back then so he could keep moving, keep breathing. Other people had lost more. Then, he felt numb as he remembered what happened next. He tugged at his collar in a vain attempt to breathe more freely.

"I've always wondered if it's worth it." Jordan shook his head as the familiar fingers of grief wrapped tightly around his ribs. "Risking that kind of pain? You never know when someone will get ripped away from you."

"I don't know if you can help falling in love." Brynn said, her lips parting into a smile.

"Well, I've dodged that bullet so far," Jordan said, letting out a dark chuckle that sounded too loud to his own ears.

"And how's that working out for you?" Brynn narrowed her eyes as she leaned across the table.

"Can I top you off?" Jordan asked, pulling his hand from under hers as he raised the wine bottle. She eyed him thoughtfully as she dabbed her napkin at the corners of her mouth. As Jordan sipped from his glass, the flakes swirling beyond the window caught his eye. Now they were the size of small leaves. He felt the edge of her shoe press against his own. He didn't move his foot away, but he also didn't meet her eye. "You might need the refill for the next part of my story."

She opened her mouth before closing it again quickly. "What?"

Jordan pinched the bridge of his nose and sighed before his shoulders heaved in a sardonic, shuddering laugh. "I've already taken you this far. I promise I had no plans to go this dark tonight."

"Darkness doesn't scare me," she said, and he looked at her just in time to see her encouraging smile.

"My brother-in-law?" he began as his stomach began to churn.

"The guy in the picture," Brynn said.

He nodded. "Eric." He took a deep drink from his wine glass before continuing. "They finished each other's sentences. He thought Megan's neurotic personality was adorable." He shook as he remembered tagging along with Eric to a college poker night—how cool he'd felt as he pretended to be an adult. "They couldn't get enough of each other." A sad smile curled his lips. "Now that I think about it, they were the first people I ever saw actually fall in love."

"Oh no," Brynn said, almost inaudibly as she realized the direction the story was heading.

"The other driver fell asleep at the wheel," Jordan said quickly, having no desire to build suspense. "They were heading to some bed and breakfast a couple of hours from their place in Ohio. The car crossed the median and Eric didn't have time to swerve." The room was silent, and Brynn seemed to have frozen in her chair. He took a deep breath and continued. "Megan had a broken wrist and a concussion, but otherwise, she walked. The other guy walked away." He pressed his eyes shut. "Eric didn't. They said it happened instantly."

"Oh my God," Brynn said, her hand hovering over her mouth.

Jordan shrugged. "I don't know how Megan survived it." He glanced at Brynn and felt something tense as he saw her eyes brimming with tears.

"I don't think you ever really get over something like that," she said in a whisper.

"I look at the world differently now, that's for sure," he said before downing the rest of his wine. "They only had each other for four years and now she has a lifetime of pain. I mean, is it even worth it?"

"Have you asked Megan if it was worth it?" Brynn asked gently.

Jordan shook his head. "At the time, we were all too broken, and now...well, now that just seems cruel."

"I'm sure it must not seem like it after all you've been through, but things like that don't happen every day," Brynn said, reaching across the table as if she meant to grab his hand, then slowly resting it back under her chin. "Most people have long, happy lives together."

Jordan chewed his lip and mentally kicked himself. This was not how he saw this night going. He wanted to blame the wine, but a part of him knew there was something about Brynn that made him want to tell her everything. He scraped his fork through the thick sauce on his plate as the record ended once again.

He flipped it over, and when he returned, he noticed Brynn's empty plate.

"There's plenty more where that came from," he said, trying to muster a smile and shake off the weariness that had settled over him.

"Oh, I'm stuffed," she said, patting her stomach for emphasis. "But it was delicious. Truly."

He nodded as he sat back down, forcing forkful after forkful into his dry mouth. A tension filled the air, and the only sounds were the classical music and the crackle of the fireplace in the next room. He waited for her to make an excuse about a stomachache or an early morning, and if she did, he certainly wouldn't blame her.

"I hope you saved some room for dessert?" Brynn asked when he had finally set down is fork. Despite everything, her face was as warm and open as ever.

"I always have room for dessert," he said with a laugh, hearing the relief in his voice as he stacked her dish onto his own. "What do you have in mind?"

"Don't worry about it," Brynn said as she cryptically pursed her wine-stained lips. "Do you have some old newspaper?"

He raised his eyebrows, intrigued, but simply nodded.

"How about you meet me in the living room with the rest of the wine," she said, mischief igniting in her eyes. "I'll get the movie ready."

"What does dessert have to do with a newspaper?" Jordan asked with a laugh.

She laughed. "You'll see," she said in a singsong voice as she carried a glass in each hand and sauntered out of sight.

Brynn blinked as she laid out the supplies on the coffee table, her mind a million miles away. Between the good wine and the deep heart-to-hearts, she had so many questions she wanted to ask, so many things she wanted to say.

She had no idea Jordan had been through so much. She felt a little guilty and very lucky when she thought of her own crazy family. Sure, she grew up with a single mom, but she hadn't ever felt traumatized or abandoned. After her parents broke up, her dad married a woman he met on a cruise ship, moved to Puerto Rico and now had a second family. Their dad felt more like an uncle than a father; he sent gifts, called on birthdays, and always reminded her and Tyler that they had an open invitation to visit. But even though he never visited the states anymore, when you factored in Gram and Paps, Brynn had grown up with plenty of family.

A wet nose shoved its way under her arm, snuffling the top of the coffee table before yawning and curling up against her leg. She scratched Toby as she sipped from her nearly empty wine glass.

Snow stacked on the windowsill, though there'd been no mention of a winter storm in the forecast. She thought Jordan would probably offer to drive her home if the roads got slick, but a tiny part of her couldn't help but picture being stuck in the farmhouse overnight, snowed in with a stunning lumberjack. Not to mention, a lumberjack who could cook.

She pulled out the drawer on the side table and found three remotes. She pointed the one with the most buttons at the TV and pressed the power button. Nothing. She repeated the process with the other two remotes, but finally groaned and gave up.

Jordan crept into the living room, a stack of newspaper under an arm. When he saw the cans of icing and bags of gumdrops, he burst into laughter.

"This is your surprise?" he asked.

"Worried your skills can't compete?" she teased as she took the newspaper and spread it under the pre-made gingerbread squares. "I mean, you saw what I can do with a cookie."

"I'm mostly worried you won't let me eat it afterwards," Jordan said, his eyes sparkling with amusement as he knelt beside Brynn, scratching Toby's belly until he rolled over.

"Of course," she said. "That's the best part."

He nodded toward the dark TV. "Change your mind?"

Brynn scoffed. "I'm convinced it's impossible to operate anyone else's TV," she said. "It's one of those rules of the universe."

"I can set it up," Jordan said, still smiling.

She considered. "How about in a few minutes. We have some gingerbread house ground rules to discuss, after all."

"Fair enough," Jordan agreed.

As Brynn grinned like a complete idiot, she wondered if he knew what passed through her when he bit his lip like that.

"Are these supposed to fit together like LEGOs or something?" Jordan asked, grabbing two of the biggest gingerbread squares.

"No, the icing is like glue!" Brynn said. She cut open the corner of her icing bag and dragged a neat line of white down the edge of one piece. "See?"

He cocked an eyebrow and stared dubiously at his own bag of icing.

She laughed. "Maybe we should build them together?"

"That sounds much better," he said, his eyes meeting hers.

"Here," she said. "Hold these together." She passed him two of the little wall pieces as she dug around for another piece of gingerbread.

She kept waiting for him to mention the night before, to bring up the kisses and touches that replayed in her mind on a loop. But he said nothing, and she didn't dare.

Once all four walls and the roof seemed sturdy, they repeated the process with the second kit. They worked in an easy, yet charged silence, him holding the pieces together while she sealed them with icing, her stomach clenching every time their hands brushed.

"OK, let's see here," Brynn said, holding the instructions higher in the dim firelight. "It says wait twenty minutes before decorating."

"You think we need to?" Jordan asked, ripping open a bag and popping a gumdrop into his mouth.

"I guess it depends if you want your new home to have structural issues or not," Brynn said with a shrug before playfully yanking away the candy bag.

"Vicious," he scolded, but his mouth twitched at the corners as he threw his hands up in surrender. "Twenty minutes it is."

Brynn wiped her sticky fingers on a paper towel, only noticing the record player's silence as she climbed onto the sofa.

"More wine?" Jordan asked, standing and reaching for her glass.

"I better not," she said reluctantly. "Driving might be tricky enough tonight."

"It sure would be a tragedy if you had to stay," he said, following her gaze to the frosted window.

"Sure would," Brynn agreed holding his gaze.

"Kind of like 'Baby It's Cold Outside', huh?" he mused.

She snorted.

"What?" he asked a little defensively. "I like that song."

"Have you ever really paid attention to the lyrics?" she asked. "The guy in that song is one roofie short of felony."

"What?!" he protested, but she saw him squint and guessed he was running through the lyrics in his mind.

"Told you!" she said when he cringed suddenly.

As Toby snored from the floor beneath Brynn's feet, Jordan

settled onto the couch a polite distance away. She was acutely aware of the inches between her leg and Jordan's hand, which rested beside him on the cushion. As he stared into the crackling fire, Brynn watched him from the corner of her eye. The fire cast an amber glow across his face, nearly concealing the pensive look in his eyes. Brynn didn't move a muscle.

He looked over at her. "Twenty minutes, huh?"

"Twenty minutes," she repeated softly.

He tipped his head and narrowed his eyes. "You have icing in your hair."

"What?" she asked, patting the crown of her head. "Where?"

"By your..." he pointed to her brow.

"Did I get it?" she asked, swiping frantically at her forehead.

He laughed. "No, here. I'll get it." He shifted closer so that his knee pressed against hers.

She shuddered as his fingers brushed against her temple.

"Here," he whispered, and she wondered if there was ever any icing in her hair in the first place. As his eyes bore through her own, she felt as if he could see every single thought she was hiding from him. Her breath hitched in her throat, her mouth like sandpaper. She suddenly wished she had said yes to more wine.

Jordan tore his gaze back to the fire and Brynn could tell he was rallying himself to say something important.

"This show is in Los Angeles?" Jordan asked finally, though his eyes stayed on the hearth. How had he found out? "Your mom told me," he added, as if he could hear her thought.

Brynn nodded and swallowed. "If I get it, yeah, I'll be moving."

"Ah," he said, staring into the fire.

"It would be a big change," she said quickly, feeling an

involuntary need to explain herself. "I worked so hard to get my shop. And Katie is only here for me, so it's not like I can ask her to run it." She pressed her fingernails into her thighs. "I mean, I don't really like the cold, but this is home, you know?" She knew she was rambling, but she could do nothing stop it. "I'm sure I could get used to it. It's worth it, right, to have my own show, to teach people all over the world how to care for plants?"

"It sounds like a big opportunity," Jordan agreed. "I've never seen a show about houseplants." He sounded perfectly diplomatic, but Brynn couldn't ignore the way his shoulders sagged as he nodded toward the fire. "I hope you get it," he said softly.

"Thank you," she said.

He cleared his throat. "I feel like I've really laid it all out there tonight, so how about making it your turn."

Her stomach tightened as she waited for him to continue.

"What's the story with your ex?" he asked with just a tad too much nonchalance.

"I mean, I don't know that it's much of a story," Brynn said, brushing a loose strand from her face. "We were high school sweethearts. We broke up twice total: once in college, once for the last time." She shrugged. "He's a cameraman for a news station, so he used to film all my videos for me."

Jordan quietly waited, and Brynn knew she owed him something of actual substance.

"I definitely made some mistakes," she admitted, pressing her lips together and letting out a weary sigh. "Caleb wanted to come home, have dinner with me, talk about anything *except* work. But all I thought about was plants and starting a business."

Jordan narrowed his eyes at her, his expression unreadable and Brynn suddenly felt embarrassed.

"He gave me more than one chance to put in the work," she continued. "But what I had to give and what he wanted weren't even in the same galaxy."

"I'm sorry," Jordan said, and he sounded like he truly meant it.

"Yeah," Brynn said, forcing a wry smile. "I'm sure I could have worked less. I just didn't want to." He nodded and the way he cocked his head as he listened made her wish she could crawl right onto his lap.

"So, what about you?" she asked. "Do you have 'the one that got away'?"

"I go on dates here and there, but I don't get out much," he said. "Evergreen Acres is my life. You can bet on a woman getting a conveniently timed migraine or a phone call about a sick pet by dessert. By the time I mention a prehistoric fossilized pine tree being discovered in the area, she's yawning."

"Funny you say that," Brynn said with a smile. "The kind of ferns I sell were growing here before the dinosaurs went extinct."

Jordan chuckled. "See, how can anyone find that boring?"

"I think we just reached a whole new level of geekdom," Brynn said, laughing along with him.

Jordan kept smiling as his gaze flitted to her mouth and back up again.

"What am I going to do with you?" Jordan asked in such a low voice, that Brynn could barely make out his words. Brynn's breathing grew ragged as he slipped his fingers through her hair and pressed his forehead against hers, his lips parting as he leaned impossibly closer, and she silently begged him to keep going.

When his mouth finally met hers, an explosion surged through her body, like a million little fingers tickling her from the inside. His mouth was deliciously soft, and he tasted like wine and coffee and something else that was uniquely him. She was desperate for more. She pressed her mouth hard against his as a quiet moan escaped his lips. She felt his scratchy cheeks lift into a smile as he pressed his arm against her lower back, driving her even closer.

She felt feverish as he pressed his tongue against her teeth, the tender warmth igniting something primal in her as his fingers gently explored her back. She thought she might explode as he tugged her roughly onto his lap, and Brynn groaned as he pressed her entire torso against his. She wrapped her arms around his neck, clasping her hands behind his head, desperate to connect every inch of herself with his body.

He pulled away, his lips red and swollen, his breath ragged and hot on her face. His eyes burned as he drank her in. First her face, gently dragging his fingertips down each side of her cheekbones as he studied every contour. Then her neck, tipping her head to one side as his fingers continued down, igniting an unbearable heat that rippled between her legs. She gasped as his fingers trailed each shoulder, but when his teeth found her neck, she nearly ripped off her dress. His breathed hovered outside her ear, his soft tongue caressing it a moment later.

She hesitantly ran her hands beneath his sweater, then beneath his undershirt, until her fingers found his warm, firm back. He raised his hips against her, a whispered grunt slipping from his lips in reply. His skin was smooth and electric, and Brynn wanted every part of him.

Jordan lifted both shirts over his head, his eyes never leaving hers as he tossed them to the floor. As she ran her hands along his muscular shoulders, she tasted blood on her lip. Whether it had come from him or her, she didn't know. It didn't matter. She pressed her lips to the thin black hairs that curled across his chest, dragging her mouth to the soft down that traced the hard V of his heaving stomach until her kisses met his belt. His body was absolutely breathtaking.

He suddenly pulled her back roughly, gripping her torso with both hands, his tongue forcing her lips apart once more as he reached for the hem of her dress.

"Is this okay?" he asked, panting. "Wouldn't want to reenact that Christmas song without your permission."

She answered by crashing her teeth against his, tugging off the dress herself and tossing it on the floor beside them.

"Oh my God," he moaned, tucking a finger under each of her bra straps as he stared at her exposed skin. He carefully dropped one strap, then the other, as if she were made of glass.

As he reached for her chin, tipping it toward his face, his eyes were needful and desperate.

I'm the one he looks at like that, she thought. *Me.*

This time when he kissed her, his lips were cautious and delicate, and his eyes stayed fixed on hers. She'd never kissed anyone with her eyes open before. She wrapped her knees around his stomach, never close enough. He dragged one calloused finger up her bare spine, sending shivers that reverberated through her entire body. Her thighs shook as she unfasted her bra, watching his enchanted eyes as a fresh wave of goosebumps down her arms.

Over his naked shoulder, Brynn caught sight of the tiny gingerbread house and couldn't hold back a giggle.

He followed her gaze. "Maybe we should have set a timer," he said, panting as he turned his hungry eyes back to hers, and she knew there would be no more crafts that night.

"I can't stop thinking about you," Jordan confessed, one hand cradling her head as he gently guided her onto her back. "I'm keep trying to stop, but I can't."

"Don't stop," she said, realizing she meant it in more ways than one.

He balanced his toned body above hers, careful not to crush her under his weight as he lowered himself. His lips stopped when they brushed hers, his breath wet and frenzied. She arched her back, desperate to bring him closer.

He held her gaze a moment longer before engulfing her with his entire being, the stillness shattered as their fingers and mouths gripped each other with a ferocious need. Just as abruptly as he'd begun, he stopped. He sat back with a devilish smirk.

Before she could protest, he traced his mouth over her stomach, his lips and tongue grazing every exposed inch. The room started spinning as she lost herself in every touch, in every kiss.

Jordan paused, out of breath as he rested his rough cheek against her belly.

"Please don't leave," Jordan mumbled as his eyes found hers. "Not yet."

She shook her head as she wrapped her fingers through his sweaty hair. She wasn't going anywhere. A quiet whimper escaped her lips as Jordan's tongue found the spot between her belly button and elastic of her tights. She watched him as he lifted her hips and peeled off her tights. She would memorize every inch of his body. The DVD could wait.

TWENTY-FOUR

"...and cut!" Katie called, and Brynn let out a low whistle.

"That was a long one," Brynn said, wiping her brow with the back of her hand as Katie popped out the memory card.

"Great stuff though," Katie said.

"I hope I can keep this thing looking good until the giveaway," Brynn said, gently thumbing a slightly brown-edged leaf on the Monstera Obliqua. "This gal is high maintenance. It looks like it's been in the desert, even with a humidifier running 24/7."

"I hope so too," Katie said. "We've already gotten over forty thousand entries."

Brynn's mouth dropped open. "What? Just from that one post?"

"Yep," Katie said, grinning. "And each of them tagged two friends."

"Wow," Brynn said, pressing a palm to her forehead in disbelief.

"You've officially passed Jessica Southgate," Katie said, flipping the stereo dial as folksy Christmas music played once more through the store. "Though she was a big help: her numbers dropped." She shook her head. "Why would she switch to posting once a week now? You think she'd be pushing more content, not less."

"Probably has to go walk the runway somewhere exotic," Brynn said with a snicker. "Speaking of, did I tell you she is the model that Sutkamp guy used on his logo? I saw it in the square."

"Oh my gosh, that's her?" Katie said. "I know exactly who you're talking about. I saw his billboard on the highway!"

"What are the odds, right?" Brynn muttered as she swept some loose topsoil from the counter into her hand.

"Like attracts like, I guess," Katie said, grinning as she cocked her head toward Brynn. "But more importantly? There's no way you're not getting that show."

"I better," Brynn said, yawning as she stepped out of her stilettos and tugged a fuzzy wool sock over each tender foot. "This whole process is exhausting."

"Speaking of exhausting," Katie said, a glint in her eye. "How'd the date go last night?"

"I wouldn't exactly call it a date," Brynn said, focusing her eyes on a thread that was coming loose from her sock.

"Oh, yeah?" Katie said, and Brynn knew she wasn't going to let this go. "Was there dinner? Did you kiss? Because if you did, that's a definite date."

Brynn pressed her lips together, lacing her boots much slower than she normally would.

"You little hussy!" Katie squealed. "What happened?!"

"A lady does not kiss and tell," Brynn said demurely.

"Well, I don't see any ladies in here!" Katie said with a scoff. "Did you guys…?" She wiggled her eyebrows at Brynn in a gesture that spoke for itself.

Brynn rolled her eyes.

"I knew it!" Katie yelped.

"Where's the footage?" Brynn asked evenly, but she knew her face was red and mottled. "I'll upload."

"I think it's great," Katie said, an apologetic note in her voice. "I like him."

"Well, I appreciate that, but it doesn't matter," Brynn said briskly, opening and closing her palm, but Katie clutched the memory card to her chest. "Hand it over, please."

"Why doesn't it matter?" Katie asked, clearly holding the footage hostage.

"I think it's pretty obvious," Brynn said, sighing as she crossed her arms.

"Not really!" Katie said, looking bemused.

Brynn clenched her jaw, trying to still the frustration that was only partly caused by Katie's interrogation. "First of all, I'm moving," Brynn said. "Second? I suck at relationships. Third? Not only is he never leaving Evergreen Acres, but he's got some *major* abandonment issues." She put up a hand to stop a protest that Katie didn't deliver. "Not that I can blame him. The guy's been through a lot."

"Fine," Katie said with a reluctant groan. "But things can change."

"*Footage*," Brynn hissed, sticking her hand in Katie's face.

Katie passed it over with a weary sigh before plopping on the couch with her laptop. As Brynn tucked the memory card into her pocket and repacked the camera case, she wondered if things would ever be less complicated again.

"I'll take that, thank you very much," Jordan said, sliding the bill his side of the table.

Megan snorted and rolled her eyes at him, but she tucked her wallet back in her purse. As she topped off their coffee mugs from the carafe, Jordan wondered which Megan hated more: not paying her own way or being reminded her baby brother was all grown up.

"Pie a la mode at the Lonely Pine," she said wistfully as she admired the kitschy snowmen and elves that decorated the windows. Charlie once told Jordan the diner's tattooed cook painted all the window art himself. "I can't remember the last time we did this."

"It certainly brings back memories," Jordan agreed, stirring his half-and-half until it blurred his coffee into a milky tan.

"Well, next time is on me," she said. She patted her mouth with her napkin. "How's your schedule look next month?"

"You're visiting again so soon?" he asked, raising an eyebrow.

"Nope," she said, before breaking into a huge grin. "I'm moving back!"

"What?" Jordan dropped the stirrer. "Are you serious?"

As far as he knew, Megan had always wanted to leave Twin Falls. When she hadn't moved home after Eric died, Jordan assumed she'd never be back.

"It's time," Megan said and there was an unmistakable glow in her eyes. "Over the last couple years, I've really come to miss this place." She shrugged. "Maybe I needed to go somewhere else before I could appreciate it. When they posted an opening at Twin Falls Elementary, I decided it was fate. I'll be teaching third grade."

"That's great," Jordan said, still trying to wrap his mind around it.

"But how are you doing?" Megan asked. "I can tell Dad is sugarcoating the farm's finances quite a bit."

"Sounds like Dad," Jordan said. "We're doing what we can."

"How about this houseplant woman?" she asked and from the way her eyes glittered she knew Charlie had said more than he would have liked. "You two seem like a perfect match."

"It's good for the cameras," Jordan said noncommittally as he scraped the last of the lemon cream pie from his plate.

"I don't know if you can fake chemistry like that," Megan persisted.

"Maybe I'm a better actor than you think," Jordan said, chewing slowly as he met her stare.

Megan flattened her mouth in that way that Jordan knew meant she wasn't buying it.

"What do you want me to say?" Jordan crumpled his napkin and tossed it on the table, annoyed at the frustration he heard in his voice.

"I can't remember the last time I saw you so heated," Megan teased, but her voice had softened.

"Whatever," Jordan said, shaking his head dismissively.

"You always had girlfriends in high school," Megan mused. "First Jenna, then Stephanie, then that one girl who interned at the farm, what was her name?"

"Georgia," he said, not looking up.

"Right, Georgia," Megan said. "But after everything happened with Mom and Eric..." She hesitated for a split second before continuing. "I haven't seen you with another woman in a long time."

"You're here two weeks a year," Jordan scoffed. "How would you know?"

"Am I wrong?" she raised a skeptical eyebrow. Damn big sisters.

"Why does it matter?" Jordan asked. He sighed. "I thought you of all people would get it."

"Get what?" Megan asked.

"You think I want to put myself in your situation?" Jordan asked, the bitterness in his voice surprising him as Megan's eyes widened. "I'm not an idiot. Not only is she moving, but she has stated more than once that she's not looking for a relationship. This story has no happy ending, and unlike you, that's not a chance I'm willing to take."

As soon as the words had left his mouth, he wished he could take them back. Neither of them spoke for a charged minute.

"You really think that?" she asked quietly. She looked as if she'd been slapped.

Jordan clenched his jaw and waved the waitress over, shoving the bill and his credit card in her direction.

"Yeah, it's been hard," Megan said once the waitress was out of earshot. "The hardest thing I've ever gone through, but life goes on." Tears filled her eyes and Jordan felt like a monster.

"According to who?" Jordan shot back. It certainly didn't feel like life went on, especially not when he caught his dad in the fields, eyes glazed, and Jordan knew Charlie was lost in the pain of the past.

"According to me!" Megan said, her voice rising. "Look, I cried, I drank, I damned the whole universe." She flipped three fingers at him like she was crossing off a list. "Then, I went to therapy. I got my new life together and I *moved on*." She let out an exasperated sigh and ran a shaking hand through her chin-length hair. "Jordan, part of the reason I'm moving back is because I met someone."

"You *met* someone?" Jordan repeated.

"Yes, online," Megan said, nodding. "It's- well, it's nothing like being with Eric, but I'm happy in a different way. I'm here. I'm still alive."

Jordan stared at her, unable to find a coherent reply.

"It's still early on, but we've been talking for a while, and I want to see where it goes," she added, but he just shook his head.

"What?" Megan asked, and a flash of uncertainty crossed her eyes. "Am I not allowed to be happy?"

"No, all I want is for you to be happy," Jordan said earnestly. "I guess...well, I just don't understand how you could choose to put yourself in that position again."

"Who do you think you are to just- opt out?" She narrowed her eyes, her neck flushing red in anger. "Take it from me, life means nothing without other people. Friends, family, husbands, wives. That's all there is." She watched him sadly as she swiped at her cheeks. "Don't act like you're somehow above all that. It just makes you look like a coward."

Now it was Jordan's turn to feel like he'd been slapped. "I'm sorry," he muttered.

"Eric would want me to live my life. For both of us." She let out a shaky exhale and pulled a wrinkled packet of tissues from her purse. "I know it might sound crazy to you, but I talk to him sometimes. I tell him everything."

Jordan reached across the table and grabbed her trembling hand. "I love you, sis," he said, his own voice thick with emotion. "And I'm happy if you're happy." He bit his lip to keep back a smile. "Just so long as you don't tell me that Eric talks back."

"Shut up!" Megan said, standing and reaching across the table to smack the back of his head, but she was giggling between sniffles. "Jordan, I would do the same life over again in a heartbeat if I had the chance." She paused to blow her nose. "Even if I couldn't change the ending. It was worth it."

Jordan didn't know what to say, so he just squeezed her hand tighter.

"There are worse things in the world than heartbreak," Megan said, clearing her throat and swiping at a streak of mascara under her eye. "Love is a good thing. Period. For any length of time. Always." She smiled. "This *feeling*?" She clutched her chest with both hands and Jordan realized she no longer wore her wedding ring. "It's what life is all about."

Her words hung in the air for a few quiet minutes as Jordan knew she was waiting for him to digest her sisterly wisdom.

"So, when do we get to meet this new mystery man?" Jordan asked as they threw on their coats and headed to the door.

"I promise you will sometime this trip," Megan said, her eyes shining with hope and something else Jordan couldn't place as they stepped out into the dry, frigid afternoon. "I have a really good feeling about it."

"Then I have a good feeling too," Jordan promised.

"I'm keeping an open mind," she said as they reached the nearly empty parking lot. "I need you to do the same."

He gave her a peck on the cheek as he opened her car door and waved as she pulled out of the lot. But instead of climbing into his truck, he headed back toward the sidewalk. Walking outside in the deepest of winter had always been how he'd done his best thinking.

TWENTY_FIVE

"Over here, honey!"

Brynn struggled to see over her armload of poinsettias as she followed the sound of her mother's voice. The tangy scents of incense and fifty years of wood polish reminded her of all the childhood Sundays her mom had taken them to mass.

The already ornate church looked extra festive with red ribbon bows at every pew and pre-lit garland framing each ten foot stained glass window. These days, much to her mother's chagrin, Brynn only went to church on major holidays. Brynn always felt a bit guilty when she ran into Father Luke, but he always greeted her with warm small talk.

She made a mental note to ask where the church bought their greenery. She'd have to ask Greta to put in a good word for Planted in Twin.

"Oh, goodness," Greta said, tugging two plants from the top of Brynn's teetering stack. "Let me take these."

"Thanks," Brynn said. "Where do you want the rest?"

"Anywhere around the pulpit," her mother said, leading the way.

Brynn recognized most of the choir members as they chatted in the first few pews. A few of them noticed her and offered enthusiastic waves.

"Can you stay?" Greta asked after they'd arranged the last of the poinsettias. "We love an audience."

"I wish I could," Brynn said, bracing herself for her mother's disappointment. "I have to get back to work."

But Greta simply nodded and gave her a quick hug before Brynn headed up the aisle.

"Wait," Greta called.

Brynn turned as her mother hurried to catch her.

Greta shifted her weight between her clogs. "I owe you an apology."

Brynn waited, but said nothing.

"I feel really bad," Greta said, and Brynn was stunned to see her blink back emotion. "I should be the one standing up for you, not someone else. I'm sorry."

"Thank you, mom," Brynn replied in a quiet voice.

"I know I can be hard on you," Greta continued, clearing her voice as she dabbed the corner of her eye with her thumb. "It wasn't easy being a single mom. I just don't want you to end up alone."

Brynn blinked. It was true Greta had never remarried, but Brynn always assumed that was the way she preferred it. Maybe, she had been lonely. Brynn felt a pang of guilt as she realized she still didn't always see Greta as more than a mother and a daughter. She was an adult woman, after all.

"I saw how hard you worked to provide for us," Brynn said, grabbing her mom's hand. "Thanks to you, Gram, and Paps, Tyler and I never felt alone."

Brynn opened her mouth to say more, but Greta raised her hand to silence her.

"That's not my point," Greta said. "I realized that whatever life you decide to build, my job isn't to weigh in. I'm going to do my best to respect your decisions from now on."

"Even if I'm a workaholic?" Brynn asked, raising an eyebrow.

"Even then," her mom said, finding a small smile. "You know what you're doing, Brynn.

"It's five past!" a male voice called before clapping his hands to round up the choir.

"I really do have some errands to run," Brynn said before Greta could walk away. "But can I come back and give you a ride home? It's really too cold to walk."

"Thanks, but I'm catching a ride with Carl," Greta said.

"Carl?" Brynn asked.

Greta nodded as a face in the assembling back row of the choir met their eyes and raised his hand in a friendly wave. Stunned, Brynn forced herself to wave back.

"Mayor Lopez?" Brynn asked, hissing a whisper through her clenched smile.

But Greta simply shrugged, a wry twinkle in her eye. "See you at the carnival," she said coquettishly before hurrying to join the choir.

"The volunteers should start showing up any minute," Jordan

said, handing Charlie a fresh lightbulb.

"Did you see what Brynn did with the decorations in the office?" Charlie asked, eyeing him sideways as he worked.

"Not yet, I've been tagging all day for the Krebs order," Jordan said, spotting another dead bulb further down the string.

"I got it!" Megan said, the lightbulb from Jordan's hand and hurrying down the porch.

"Never thought that one would be out here in the cold with a smile on her face," Charlie said with a chuckle.

"I can hear you!" Megan shot back, but she was smiling.

Jordan's sister did seem different. She was somehow lighter, more engaged with everyone and everything around her than she'd been the last time he'd seen her.

A low hum pierced the silence, and Jordan glanced up as a caravan of vehicles led by a familiar blue car wove its way up the long driveway. Just before reaching the parking lot, Brynn pulled over and threw on her hazard lights. She quickly jumped out, signaling for the other drivers to wait, before her eyes finally landed on Jordan. As her lips curled into that full cherry smile, something inside him twisted ferociously.

"Where do you want the volunteers to park?" Brynn called, cupping her hands around her mouth.

"By the barn!" he called back.

She flashed him a double thumbs up and directed the vehicles to the empty grass.

A bit distracted, Jordan glanced back to the string of lights, only to find Megan studying him with a smirk.

He scoffed and shook his head, but his attempt to hold back his dopey grin failed miserably.

"I can't believe how many people showed up on a Friday afternoon!" Brynn said, a bit breathless as she jogged over to meet them.

Before he could squash it, an image flashed through Jordan's mind. Of a different kind of breathless. Of smooth, ivory skin and tangled hair splayed across his pillowcase. He swallowed. This was not the time.

"I'm going to man the carousel," Mayor Lopez called from the parking lot. As he passed by, he saw Brynn's mother had her arm looped through the mayor's.

"Hey, Jordan!" Greta called as she waved at him.

"Hey, guys," he managed. "Thanks for coming out!"

As they disappeared behind the shop, Jordan shot Brynn a questioning look.

"Your guess is as good as mine!" she said, but she was smiling.

"The infamous Brynn Callaway!" Megan said, wiping her hands against her jeans as she walked over to join them.

"And you must be Megan," Brynn said, shaking her hand. "I recognize you from—well, from the fact that you look just like your brother."

"At least people don't think we're twins anymore," Megan said with a good-natured laugh before nodding to the clipboard under Brynn's arm. "I hear you're the boss this weekend. What can I do?"

"Would you mind helping Gina handle sales?" Brynn asked, scanning her list. "I have a hopeful hunch she's going to be busy."

"You got it," Megan said, throwing Jordan an almost imperceptible wink as she hurried into the shop.

Just then, Brynn's face turned to stone. Jordan followed her gaze, grimacing as Russell Sutkamp approached.

"Mr. Sutkamp," Jordan said diplomatically, though he could think of no one he'd rather see less. "Didn't expect to see you here."

"Well, I didn't want to miss out on the fun," Sutkamp said. He attempted a friendly smile, but his face barely moved. He leaned forward conspiratorially. "Besides, you never know, I might meet some locals in the market for a new home." He laughed as though he'd said something funny before turning to Brynn. "Can I run a game?"

She warily scanned her clipboard. "I guess ring toss could use another person."

"I'll take it," Sutkamp said, his nose wrinkling as he scanned the decorated porch.

"I don't trust that man one bit," Jordan said once Sutkamp was out of sight.

"I'll make sure to count his cash box myself," Brynn said with a snort. An old Ford Escape pulled into the lot, idling a few feet away. The tinted window rolled down to reveal a grinning Dylan who waved quickly before the car headed to park by the barn.

Moments later, Dylan reappeared, hand-in-hand with Madison, as they hurried over with matching grins.

"Hi guys!" Brynn said, a little too brightly.

"So glad you could make it," Jordan said, clapping Dylan on the back. Clearly, they couldn't wait for the weekend to hang out with each other.

"It's Christmas break, so why not?" Madison said cheerfully.

"Dad will be here once he closes up," Dylan added. He leaned closer, and his neck was flushed as he lowered his voice. "I introduced Madison to my dad."

Jordan and Brynn both flashed him a covert thumbs up and pink crept all the way to his ears. That boy was smitten.

"We could use you both over at the prize wheel," Brynn said, throwing Jordan a meaningful glance. "And maybe keep an eye on the guy running the ring toss next door."

"You got it, boss!" Dylan said and the two of them sprinted up the hill, never letting go of each other.

And then, it was only Brynn left standing with Jordan.

"Well, that is just the most adorable thing I've ever seen," Brynn said, still looking in the direction the teenagers had gone.

"You did good," Jordan said, trying to pretend his stomach wasn't in a million knots.

"*We* did good," Brynn corrected, flashing him that smile, and all Jordan wanted to do was find an excuse to take her back to the farmhouse. "How'd you sleep last night?" she asked, feigned innocence dripping off every word.

"Like a baby," he said, playing along. "You?"

"Can't complain," she said, her cheeks a delicious shade of pink.

And as she bounded down the porch stairs to check in the rest of the volunteers, Jordan let out a deep shuddering breath he didn't realize he'd been holding. He was a liar.

Jordan had stared at his dark ceiling for hours when Brynn finally left, long past midnight. He had pressed his nose into his sheets, drinking in everything she'd left behind. He'd replayed every second, every inch of her smooth skin, until first light, when he'd fallen into a dreamless sleep.

The parking lot was nearly full as Tyler Callaway began to spin a brand-new custom playlist of Christmas tunes. When he'd asked to volunteer, Brynn knew exactly where to put her brother. Before he was saving the forests, he'd paid for college by DJing every wedding and school dance that would have him.

She handed a volunteer the last of the walkie talkies as Gina greeted patrons in the parking lot, gesturing enthusiastically to the festival behind them. Megan, sporting a bright orange vest from Gina, had temporarily abandoned her post inside to direct parking. Soon, they'd have to park people on the side of the driveway.

Brynn shook her head in amazement. When Mayor Lopez had offered up his van to shuttle overflow from the church parking lot down the road, she thought he'd been adorably optimistic. But at this rate, she'd be asking him soon to set it up, and it wasn't even yet dark.

Brynn walked from tent to tent, ensuring everyone had stocked cash boxes and answering their questions. Was there an age limit on kiddie games? Were the animals in the petting zoo up for adoption? Did they have dairy-free hot chocolate? She plastered on her best YouTuber smile and answered as best as she could, while adding to a running list of things to address for next year.

Next year.

It was starting to look more and more like Evergreen Acres would make it another season. A few weeks ago, she would have been happy for them—glad she'd completed her unofficial community serve. Now, she felt nauseous imagining the end of this place, with its endless fields and hillsides blanketed in pine. And a small part of her was ready to admit that she had needed this place too.

And then there was Jordan. Heat flushed her hips as she skipped down the hillside, remembering the night before. The sweat, the skin, the insatiable desire to fold his body into hers. The way his eyes never left hers. Never. She could still smell him, all wood and vanilla and sweat. She sighed as she looked to the sky, gunmetal gray on its way to onyx.

This place couldn't be her fantasy. Not this farm, not this man unlike any she'd ever laid eyes on. She shouldn't complain. She was on track to get everything she wanted, and she knew she'd done her job here at Evergreen Acres.

Brynn sighed, refocusing on the jubilant scene unfolding all around her. She pressed her lips together, willing herself to get a grip as she watched the growing crowd. She made a note to circle back and check if any booths were running out of prizes.

Greta passed out water to volunteers while recruiting passersby to try out some games. Madison was busy spinning the game wheel as Dylan handed out ornaments to the winners. Sutkamp wasn't about to win volunteer of the year, but he dutifully handed out ring after ring as squealing children looped the target.

Brynn climbed the hill to the skating rink.

"Looking good up here," Brynn said to Katie, who was tying a young boy's skate laces. A line several people deep waited to take their turns.

"Okay, remember what I told you," Katie said to the boy a sweet voice. "Keep your weight forward and go slow."

"If you're a girl why does your hair look like that?" the boy asked, narrowing his eyes.

"Because it makes me happy," Katie said brightly. "Does short hair make you happy?"

His eyes were wide as he nodded.

"Well, there you go!" Katie said as if that settled the matter.

"Green hair would make me happy too!" the boy said, but his mother hurried him onto the ice before Katie could say another word.

"With the twenty-minute limit per person, we should be able to get everyone through," Katie said, standing up and pulling her gloves back on. "Megan had the brilliant idea to take reservations if things start getting backed up."

"That's a great idea," Brynn agreed. "When did you meet Megan?"

"I saw her in the parking lot before I came up here," Katie said, passing skates to a couple who had just dropped cash in the jar. Katie turned to count the line and Brynn suddenly felt like she was in the way.

"I'll bring up some bottled water," Brynn called as she stepped away from the crowd.

She stopped at the edge of the rocky hilltop, careful to brace her weight in case any of the rocks beneath her came loose. She needed a second to breathe. The entire carnival spread out below her, its bright colors and sounds glowing like a kaleidoscope. She could see Charlie in his Santa costume, taking photos with anyone who asked. Mayor Lopez was manning playing security at the upper barn door, probably making sure none of the baby goats snuck out more than anything. There was a snaking line at the hot chocolate booth, and Brynn smiled as she saw Mr. Danvers chatting up a customer and looking at a phone screen that was probably filled with pictures of his kids and grandkids. Down in the parking lot, Jordan was tying a tree to the top of a station wagon, and at least three cars waited, presumably to take home their own trees.

At that moment, Los Angeles seemed a million miles away. She tugged her phone free and snapped some photos, then hurried back down the hill to resume her duties. Tyler was handing over the DJ booth to a college-aged girl with dreadlocks, and Brynn thought he'd be just the person to help Mr. Danvers at the cocoa booth.

"Brynn? Do you copy?" Gina's voice chirped through the walkie.

"Copy!"

"Do you have eyes on Jordan?" Gina asked.

"Last I saw he was loading trees in the parking lot," Brynn said. "Is everything OK?"

"Sure, except we might run out of pre-cuts tonight," Gina said.

"What?!"

"I can think of worse problems," Gina said with a chuckle. "We can always send them out to cut their own."

"I'll find him," Brynn promised.

It took much longer than she expected to reach the parking lot as person after person stopped her along the way. The basketball game needed more prizes. Someone recognized her from the tree lighting and wanted to take a selfie. A dad with a few small kids gushed about how much fun they were having. As Gina had said, there were worse problems.

Brynn felt a lightness in her step as she peeked at the food prep station behind the shop. She may have been too busy to really *do* Christmas, but it seemed Christmas had come to her anyway. It was impossible not to feel festive as she watched all those bundled-up smiling faces, dancing along to "Rudolph the Red Nosed Reindeer". Just then, something wet landed on her cheek and she swiped at it: a snowflake.

Once she finally made it to the parking lot, she found Jordan waving at a tree-topped minivan as it disappeared into the inky darkness. He tipped back his head and stuck out his tongue to catch a snowflake. Brynn couldn't help but smile. He was perfect.

"Hey, you," she said, sticking her hand in her pocket when she noticed it was trembling. "Gina says you're almost out of trees."

"I'm not surprised," Jordan said, his wincing face glowing in the yellow porch light as he rolled his shoulder back and forth. "I'll talk to her. We can take pre-orders and I can go cut more tomorrow."

"Congratulations," Brynn said, unable to take her eyes on his chiseled face. "I think Evergreen Acres is gonna make it."

"I'm afraid to jinx it, but I think you're right," Jordan said, his eyes finding hers as he stepped closer. He gently took her clipboard and set it on the railing behind them. His breath became ragged as he grabbed her hands and wrapped them around his back, pulling her chest against him. He gently tipped her face toward his, grazing her cheek with his lips as his whiskers tickled her skin.

"I told you we could pull this off," Brynn said softly.

Jordan smiled before putting his mouth beside hers. "I'm learning never to doubt you," he whispered.

"There you are!" Mayor Lopez's voice boomed from the shadows.

Brynn broke free of Jordan's embrace just as he reached them.

"How's it going at the petting zoo?" Brynn asked breezily, glad it was dark enough that the mayor wouldn't be able to see her face.

"Great!" he said, passing a stack of papers to Jordan. "I ran out of adoption interest forms, so it's looking like your barn might be a whole lot emptier. Except for that grumpy old tortoise. No one even asked about him."

"I prefer it that way," Jordan laughed. "He and I have too much history."

"A couple of Principal Massey's kids just took over, so after I gave them the rundown, I figured I'd go spend some cash myself," the mayor said. "But I was hoping I'd run into you guys."

Brynn smiled politely and waited.

"Are you guys coming to the firefighter ball?" the mayor asked.

"I never miss it," Jordan said. "I've been going since I was a kid, back when Charlie was still a volunteer."

Brynn hadn't thought about the event in years, but she nodded anyway.

"Well, you may have heard that country star Deana Carter was supposed to be there to sing a few songs and give the Christmas wish," the mayor said, shaking his head. "Sadly, she got stuck in the snow while touring up in Fargo. She's not going to be able to make it in time."

"Oh, that's too bad," Brynn said. "Gina mentioned how much she was looking forward to it."

"It is too bad," the mayor agreed. "But she promised to do a special concert in Twin this spring. But now I'm left without anyone to deliver to the Christmas wish."

He blinked, waiting for them to follow his line of thinking.

"You can't mean us," Brynn said.

"I do!" the mayor said, his eyes twinkling.

"We can't sing!" Jordan sputtered, then realized he didn't know if Brynn was musically included. "Well, I can't anyway."

Mayor Lopez laughed. "I've got our choir lined up to perform, yours truly included." He winked at Brynn. "Not quite Deana Carter, but your mother does have a lovely solo. And while I thought about stepping in for the wish part, I think this town hears my voice more than enough."

Jordan flicked his eyes nervously toward Brynn.

"You could make it about anything you want," the mayor added quickly. "Anything you think might bring a little peace, hope, and love to the town."

"So, why us?" Brynn asked.

Mayor Lopez grinned. "You're practically Twin famous now. And your journey has really brought this town together." He swept his hand behind him toward the hillside. "Look around."

Brynn gazed over the crowd, her eyes flitting from the giggling children to the enthusiastic volunteers; from the teenagers on dates to Santa Charlie taking a cocoa break. There were nearly as many people at the carnival as there had been at the tree lighting, and they still had two more days to go.

"I'm okay with it," Jordan said, resting a protective hand on Brynn's back that sent electricity through her spine. He looked down at her. "Assuming you are."

"It would be an honor," she said as evenly as she possibly could while being touched by this brilliant man.

"Excellent!" the mayor said, clapping his hands together. "Well, I'm off to get some popcorn before my next shift starts."

Once he'd rounded the corner, Jordan's eyes settled on Brynn. He picked a snowflake from her hair, and Brynn's pulse began to thunder.

"I wish we could sneak away," he said softly.

"Me too," she said, and she became liquid as his eyes flicked to her lips.

They breathed that way, as if daring the other to break first.

Brynn held still as he stared deep inside her, and she forgot all about the prizes and the popcorn and the ice skating.

"Um, Brynn," a tentative voice called from the lot. She winced at the interruption and Jordan chuckled.

She turned, plastering on her professional smile, reluctantly ready to get back to work. But it wasn't a volunteer who was walking towards her.

Brynn's lips froze a man with painfully familiar blue eyes smiled back, holding hands with a beautiful tall woman with a jet-back ponytail.

No effing way.

But it was.

Caleb. And Jessica Southgate.

TWENTY-SIX

Based on the way the blonde guy stared far too intimately at Brynn, Jordan instantly knew it was her ex. Jordan's jaw clenched as his gaze drifted to the elegant woman that clung to Caleb's arm. She had that rail-thin model vibe, all angles beneath a generically symmetrical face, but she wore way too much makeup for his taste.

"Jordan, this is Caleb," Brynn said stiffly.

"Hey," the man said, flashing Jordan a shy smile.

Jordan replied with a curt nod.

"What are you doing here?" Brynn asked, an unmistakable note of hysteria in her voice.

"Jessica told me about the carnival," Caleb said, a look of apprehension on his boyish face.

"Did she?" Brynn asked, sharp edges on her words. Brynn clearly knew more about this woman than Jordan did.

"So precious," Jessica cooed, clapping a hand to her tanned throat for emphasis. "We had to come support."

As Jessica flashed her blindingly white teeth, Jordan was reminded of the white barn cat that stalked the mice around the barn.

"Well, welcome to Evergreen Acres," Jordan said as cordially as he could manage. He reminded himself that not only had Caleb done nothing to him, but he'd also brought a date. Nevertheless, Jordan's pulse vibrated through his skull as he extended a hand, attempting to summon his manners.

Caleb's hand was smooth, and Jordan suddenly felt self-conscious about the ripped callouses that crisscrossed his own fingers.

"Nice to meet you," Brynn said tightly to Jessica.

"Officially," Jessica said and threw her an over-the-top wink.

"Right," Brynn muttered. "Officially."

Jordan felt sick. Brynn must be jealous of her.

"So adorably festive," Jessica said approvingly, nodding toward the garland wrapped archway that marked the entrance to the carnival.

"Thanks, but it was all Brynn," Jordan said, resisting an urge to wrap a possessive hand around her waist.

"I'm on my break!"

Someone called from up the hill and Jordan saw Sutkamp stomp toward the porch. He glanced up and his eyes skipped across them, settling on Jessica.

"You know Russell Sutkamp, right?" Brynn asked Jessica.

She jerked her head to the porch and shrugged. "That guy? Why would I know him?"

"I saw your picture on a banner for his company," Brynn said, and Jordan could tell that she hated to admit it. "I just assumed."

"Oh, right," Jessica said with a hollow giggle. "I've seen the billboards. It turned out cute. I don't know him, though."

Jordan was not about to offer to introduce them.

An awkward silence stretched between the foursome as Jordan silently hoped both Jessica and Caleb would turn around and go home.

Jessica turned to Caleb. "Baby, I'm going to snag a selfie," she said in a syrupy voice. "Catch up in a few?"

Caleb nodded, and Jordan felt a sick satisfaction as he noticed he was blushing.

A tense silence blanketed the parking lot as the snowflakes dissolved midair around them. Caleb kept shooting furtive glances at Brynn, and Jordan got the feeling he wanted to speak to her alone. He swallowed a knot in his throat, not wanting to walk away, but feeling like he should.

"I'll go see if Gina found the extra register tape," he said as breezily as he could manage.

"Oh, okay," Brynn said, and the hint of disappointment in her voice made his heart soar. "Do you want me to—?"

"Nah, I've got it," Jordan interrupted.

He hurried up the porch steps, as a crisp gust bit at his bare neck. He willed himself not to look back, not to listen, but Caleb's hushed voice carried over the on the wind.

"Can we talk?" Jordan heard him ask. "In private?"

Jordan hurried inside, acid burning his throat as he slammed the door much harder than he'd intended. Gina looked up, watching him with curiosity over the heads of the people in line.

"Sorry, the wind caught the door," he said, his neck still burning. "You still need register tape?"

"Nope!" she said, her glittering eyes telling Jordan all he needed to know about how business was going. "I found some at the bottom of the supply closet."

"Good," Jordan said, running a distracted hand a display full of tree toppers.

"Everything okay out there," Gina asked, her eyes betraying a hint of concern as she passed a ponytailed man his change.

"Everything's going great," he insisted, forcing his mind back onto the trees. "We've got about four six-footers left, one ten-foot, and a few miscellaneous shorties. Everything else, I'll need to cut tomorrow."

"Roger that," she said, ringing up the next customer. "Hey, if you see Brynn would you tell her I'll send her some photos in a bit that she might want to post?"

"Yep," he said, heading for the back door without looking over his shoulder. "If I see her."

He passed beneath the blinding fluorescent lights, swinging open the storm door as he lost himself in the giddy crowd. Everywhere he looked, parents were shuffling children from one booth to the next and lines weaved between every tent.

And yet, he wanted to throw up. It felt like a fist was squeezing all the air from his chest. He pressed his eyes closed for a second as he forced himself to unclench his jaw. It was none of his business what Brynn and Caleb were doing out there, but images of the night before forced their way into his mind; but this time, he saw Caleb drawing her smooth thighs closer. If he was alone, he could have punched something. But whether he lost Brynn to her ex-boyfriend or lost her to California, the undeniable truth was that this thing between them was going to end the same way.

He let out a slow exhale, pinching the bridge of his nose as he slowly regained control of himself.

It's for the best.

It's for the best.

It's for the best.

"You rang?" Dylan asked, holding up his walkie talkie as he jogged around the building. He eyed Caleb with curiosity, but said nothing as he waited for Brynn's instructions.

"Would you mind taking over for a few minutes?" Brynn asked, passing Dylan her clipboard.

"Of course," Dylan said, his ears turning pink as he registered Brynn's trust in him.

"Just remember, the general channel is two," she said, twisting the dial on her own walkie. "I'll keep four open in case you need me, but I won't be long."

"No worries," Dylan said eagerly. "I'll check in at the booths and see if anyone needs anything."

"You're the best," Brynn said, watching Dylan hurry off before she turned back to Caleb.

"I can give you ten minutes," she said levelly.

"I'll take it," Caleb said, and Brynn felt a wave of nostalgia at the way he watched her. He fiddled with his plaid scarf, a souvenir Brynn had bought for him when they'd gone to his cousin's wedding in Montana.

"We can talk over here," Brynn said, and he followed her to the tree lot beside the shop.

The yard had been packed an hour before, full of people competing for the rows of pre-cut pines. Now, only a few customers milled about, looking through the remains for trees without "sold" tags dangling from their branches.

Brynn stopped in an empty aisle, the rows of pre-sold firs forming a slender forest on either side. She'd helped choose these trees herself, trees that would be transported to the local malls the following morning. Though she didn't particularly want to be alone with Caleb, she thought it best to talk without curious eyes on them, and Brynn was not about to let her mom see them together.

"What can I do for you, Caleb?" she asked, crossing her arms over her chest as she kept a respectable distance between them.

"I miss you, Brynn," he said, reaching a hand towards her, then thinking better of it and shoving it in his pocket. "We haven't talked much lately."

"Well, not that it matters," Brynn said coolly. "But you're the one who never texted me back."

"I know," Caleb said, chewing on his bottom lip as his eyes searched hers. Her face burned as she ripped her gaze away and stared at the sky, barely registering the innumerable stars as a faraway chorus of "Silent Night" drifted past them. "I tried to stay away, but I can't stop thinking about that night."

"You think the night we hooked up meant something?" Brynn snorted. "It was a mistake."

Caleb looked as if he'd been slapped, but Brynn wasn't going to take it back.

"Caleb, why are you here?"

"Something about you seems different," Caleb said, ignoring her question, his eyes filled with trepidation as he smiled at her. "I still love you."

Something in those eyes told Brynn that he meant everything he said.

"Still the same workaholic," Brynn said impatiently. "Or have you forgotten when you said that all I seem to care about is making money and getting famous?"

And that's when she realized she was no longer blaming herself for their breakup. She had finally moved on.

"I have a confession," Caleb said as he stepped dangerously closer. "I didn't just come here to support a good cause. I was curious about you and this tree guy."

"His name is Jordan," Brynn said with an edge to her voice.

"Right. Jordan," Caleb said, chewing on the consonants.

"Well, you seemed to have moved on just fine," Brynn said, doing her best to ignore his proximity. "I had no idea Jessica even lived near Twin Falls until I saw you pop up in one of her videos."

"We've gone on a few dates, but it's nothing serious," Caleb said, and she batted his hand away as he tried to tuck a loose wave behind her ear. "She's no Brynn Callaway, but she's a sweet girl."

Brynn was proud of herself when she suppressed a snort.

"How's the old YouTube going these days?" Caleb asked, searching her face.

"Better than ever," Brynn said, wrapping her arms tighter. "Katie runs video now and we have millions of followers." She was hoping to see this land on him, but his expression never wavered, and she had a feeling he knew exactly how many followers she had.

"I'm not surprised," Caleb said. "I knew it was only a matter of time before the rest of the world realized you were so special."

Brynn smiled, but the knot in her stomach kept growing.

So special.

How many months had she longed to hear these words? This

affirmation from the man she'd loved for most of her adult life; from the man who had shattered her heart into pieces. It wasn't that he was insincere—his wide blue eyes and boyish grin had never told her lies. Still, something about this scene felt hollow and empty.

"Listen, Brynn," Caleb said, tugging her hands close and pressing them between his own. She didn't jerk away, but she wanted to. "I know I've already wasted too much time." Brynn had never seen him cry, but his eyes were glistening with tears as he continued. "I thought I needed someone who would focus more on me, but I have that now. Jessica tries in a way you never did."

Before she could say a word, he brushed his lips against her forehead.

"I feel bad even saying this, but it's just not the same," he murmured into her hair. "I miss you; I want *you*." She felt trapped, like a cornered animal, but she was frozen as he pressed her close.

"Caleb, listen," she said, finally untangling herself from his embrace. "You're a great guy, Caleb," she continued, "but we're just not right for each other." She swallowed and took a deep breath. "But you were right about a few things, and it's taken me some time to understand. "

"This whole YouTube persona is exhausting," Brynn admitted. "And sometimes I feel like a total fake, like it's all pathetic and maybe these videos aren't even worth it." Tears stung her eyes as every thought spilled forth, never before said aloud. "I spend half of my time looking for some plant I've barely heard of, pretending to be an expert on it just to get a few more followers." She laughed sardonically. "I know they're probably going to kill it anyway, because I'm going to kill it too!" She angrily swiped at her nose. "I barely have time for my actual customers because I'm spending every moment tap dancing for a few more views from countries

I've never even heard of. It's exhausting."

She took a deep breath, depleted, and looked up to find Caleb studying her.

"But at the end of the day, I read the emails from fans who say I've helped them, I see where I've made a real difference, and I know I'm on the right track," she said. "I am pursuing my dream, as cheesy as that might sound. And yeah, I'm still figuring out how to make it all work, but I will never stop. Not for you, not for anyone."

She wiped her face with her sleeve once more. She felt sick, but she meant every word.

"I miss all of it," Caleb said, brushing a hand against her cheek before she could stop him. "Even the work talk." His eyes gleamed with fervor and Brynn could tell he would never understand. "It's just this stage of life. We have plenty of time to slow down when we're older."

A flash further up the aisle caught both their attention and Brynn seized the chance to pull away. Was someone watching them? But as she pushed the still quivering branch aside, a little wren hopped to the snow, shaking its feathers clean before flying off into the night.

How long had she been standing there alone with Caleb? Panic gripped her chest as she pictured Jordan seeing Caleb's lips against her forehead. She needed to get out of there.

She was just turning back, an excuse poised on her lips, when he pressed his mouth hard against hers. His lips were slick with Chapstick as they began to move in a choreography she could have remembered in her sleep. She could smell his cologne; the same one he'd been wearing since high school. She went limp in his fevered embrace as her body automatically remembered his touch. But then, just as suddenly, a cold terror seized her insides.

She pressed her hands against his chest and shoved as hard as she could.

"Whoa!" Caleb said, raising his hands defensively in front of him as he stumbled backwards.

"What are you doing?!" Brynn exclaimed.

"I'm sorry," Caleb sputtered, his eyes wide in bewilderment. "I guess I thought you would want me to kiss you." His shoulders slumped and his hands lowered to his side when it was clear she wouldn't shove him again.

"Did you think I was just waiting for you, hoping you'd give me another chance?"

Brynn hugged herself protectively as she backed further away.

"I guess things are more serious with the tree guy than I thought," Caleb scoffed, running an agitated hand through his shaggy hair.

"This has nothing to do with Jordan," Brynn said, feeling years of anger bubble to her lips. "I'm happy just the way I am."

"You're not dating him?" Caleb asked, looking dubious. "Look, I probably shouldn't say anything, but Jessica really wants this show. She already signed with a modeling agency in LA."

Brynn willed herself not to stick her finger down her throat and gag.

"Sometimes she's like a bull seeing red with this stuff," Caleb said, and he hesitated for a moment before continuing. "Jessica told me that she will do whatever it takes to ruin *both* you and Jordan."

Brynn paused. What could Jessica possibly have against Jordan? She could feel a headache forming deep inside her temples and dread flooded her stomach as she pictured Jessica tearing apart

Evergreen Acres on her channel.

"Not that it's any of your business, but I'm not dating Jordan," Brynn said, choosing each word carefully. "The stuff online is all for show." Her mouth was dry as sand as she continued, but she kept going. "He is nothing to me, and after Christmas, it wouldn't surprise me if I never see him again. Please tell Jessica to leave him alone."

"Just be careful," Caleb said, genuine concern in his eyes. "I'm sure Jordan can handle himself."

"I'll say it once more, Jordan has no part in this!" she said, her voice rising as she stepped closer. "The fans love it, okay? I'm bringing him more business, and he's bringing me more followers. That's all it is."

He leaned toward her, and that's when Brynn realized he had confused her rejection of Jordan as an invitation. She raised her hands in front of her before he could move any closer.

"That is what I need you to tell Jessica," she said, a steely edge in her voice. "Make her back off. Make her leave Jordan alone."

"I don't understand," Caleb said, looking around as if she was telling some joke he didn't quite get.

"In my heart, I do want to be with Jordan, okay?" she said. It was time she put on her big girl pants. "He gets me in a way you never did," Brynn said, as his eyes flashed with pain. "I'm not saying this to hurt you, Caleb; I'm saying this to set us free. I deserve someone who loves all of me and so do you."

"I see," was all Caleb could manage.

"Promise me you'll get Jessica to leave Jordan alone, *please*," Brynn said.

Caleb watched her with sad eyes before tossing her a resigned nod. "I guess I better go find her, then."

"Thank you, Caleb," Brynn said, and this time when Caleb pulled her close, she let him hold her for a long while. She knew this time was goodbye.

"You're sure this is what you want?" he asked in a small voice when she finally pulled away.

She nodded, feeling exhausted and a little guilty. She had loved him once and she knew she had just hurt him badly.

As he stepped out of the center of the aisle, a cold chill shot down her neck. There, in Caleb's place, was Jessica, watching them with horror from a few yards back. Brynn tried to say something—*anything*—but no words came forth. Caleb followed Brynn's panicked stare and spun around.

"Jessica!" he sputtered, but she was already hobbling toward the parking lot, awkwardly traversing the gravel in her stiletto-heeled boots. He caught up to her quickly and Brynn willed herself to ignore Caleb's hushed pleas of understanding and Jessica's primal screeches. She resisted the urge to follow, resisted the urge to call out, "it's not what it looks like!" like some character in a bad movie.

This wasn't her business. And if the tables were turned, she was sure she wouldn't want Caleb to run after Jordan. She sighed and closed her eyes as a frigid gust of wind whipped a loose tendril across her neck.

The crowd had thinned considerably as she trudged up the slick embankment to the porch. Watching several young families load into SUV's and minivans, she realized it must be later than she thought.

"Dylan, do you copy?" she said into the walkie.

"I copy," the voice replied. "I see you—keep walking this way,"

Dylan had been cornered by Russell Sutkamp, who was

gesturing emphatically. As Brynn approached, Dylan threw her a discreet look. *Save me.* As she carefully stepped across the loose gravel, she could only hear pieces of their conversation before the brisk wind transformed it into white noise.

"Too bad I can't be here tomorrow," Sutkamp was saying. "I made them so much money. Did you see the line at the ring toss?"

"It was a good turnout tonight," Dylan said diplomatically as he handed off a package of bottled water to Charlie, who carried it toward the booths.

Without realizing what she doing, Brynn tucked herself out of Sutkamp's line of sight so she could hear the conversation better. She'd need to rescue Dylan soon, but at the same time maybe she could catch Sutkamp saying something, anything, they could use against him.

"Can't believe they managed to put something like this together out here in the boonies," Sutkamp said with a chuckle. "Though it's been very interesting to see that people don't seem to mind the drive." Dylan said nothing, but Brynn didn't need to see his face to know he would have rather been anywhere else.

Gina's laugh suddenly carried down the hillside, quickly followed by muffled cheers near the games. Sutkamp droned on and on, first suggesting that they hadn't pulled the right permits, then criticizing the carnival's limited menu.

Brynn bit back a sigh. It's not like Sutkamp was going to say something incriminating to Dylan. And, as much as she hated to admit it, it was nice that the guy had given up his evening to help. There was a difference between being generally unlikeable and being an actual criminal.

"They're about to blow every fuse in this place if they haven't already," Sutkamp was saying as Brynn approached. "Can you imagine the electric bill?"

"They have a couple generators," Dylan said with a shrug, waving eagerly as Brynn climbed the steps to join them.

"Interesting," Sutkamp said, but his tone suggested otherwise as he craned his neck toward the flow of people heading to their cars, always on the lookout for someone with something to offer him.

"Thanks, Dylan," Brynn said, pointedly taking her clipboard back as she joined them. If ever she was in a position to hire an assistant, she would beg him to take the job.

"Miss Callaway," Sutkamp said, flashing those veneered teeth at her. "Charlie said he'll close up the ring toss." He cupped his hand conspiratorially around his mouth and chuckled. "Between you and me, he seemed a bit suspiciously that I might tamper with the cash box."

"Duly noted," Brynn said flatly as she tugged a stack of flyers free from her clipboard. "Dylan, would you go stand at the exit?" she asked, splitting the stack and passing half to Dylan. "You can hand folks a coupon as they leave."

"You got it, boss," Dylan said, looking relieved as he jogged for the exit.

She turned to Sutkamp, who was already slinking away, and held up the remaining flyers. "Would you mind sticking these on the windshields of people who are still here?"

She waited for his him to refuse, but instead, his eyes lit up as he snatched them from her hand. "It would be my pleasure!" She wasn't sure what to make of his sudden Christmas spirit, but she would take what she could get. She'd just have to make sure he didn't harass anyone heading to their cars with promises of low interest rates.

Back at the food tents, volunteers were loading drinks into

coolers, though Brynn wondered if they might stay colder outside. She looked around for a place to pitch in, but everyone seemed to have found a methodical rhythm as they chatted and laughed. As she adjusted her scarf, she looked down over the parking lot, countless headlights and taillights cutting through the night as people came and went.

Dylan's red cap was just a speck, but she could just make out the bright green papers he handed to each driver. The lot was half empty now, though the volunteer parking was still completely packed.

A flash of movement caught Brynn's eye in the far corner of the parking lot. It was Sutkamp, making his way through the remaining cars just as she'd asked. All of a sudden, he beelined out of the lot, glancing at the empty porch before unceremoniously tossing the stack of flyers in a trash can and disappearing behind the shop.

"Seriously?" Brynn muttered. Clearly Sutkamp was still Sutkamp.

The crunch of kicked-up gravel drew her attention back to the lot, where an all too familiar Range Rover was speeding toward the exit. She could picture it now: Jessica screeching from the passenger seat, while Caleb begged for forgiveness.

A long shadow fell across her face, and she turned to find Jordan, his eyes following the same vehicle.

"Glad they didn't hit anyone," Jordan said with a snort. "They could have at least bought a tree." He looked as if he was going to say more, but instead bit his lip and kicked the dry ground distractedly with his toe.

"Are you okay?" Brynn asked, unsure whether to tell him everything that had happened with Caleb or pretend it had never happened.

"Me?" Jordan asked, raising an eyebrow as if the question surprised him. "I'm perfectly fine."

He didn't look perfectly fine, but Brynn didn't know what else to say. She wanted to tell him that she'd ended things with Caleb for good, but that might imply that she hadn't before, even though nothing had happened between them since she'd gotten closer to Jordan. Just thinking about Jordan's reaction made her nauseous. Besides, tonight was about Evergreen Acres, not Brynn Callaway. She would explain later, when the carnival was over and she'd had a chance to choose her words.

"Hey, you two!" Katie's voice echoed from the darkness seconds before she appeared wielding an iPhone. "Big smiles!"

"Hey, Kate," Brynn said, weakly scooting closer to Jordan. She shot a look at him, but his pensive expression had already been replaced with a camera-ready smile. Brynn swallowed and willed herself to do the same.

Katie snapped a few shots, and as she ordered them to make silly faces, Jordan's shoulder pressed against Brynn's back. His body vibrated with the same tension that was gripping hers.

"Ugh, just the cutest," Katie said, oblivious as she swiped through the shots. "Oh, I almost forgot!" Katie tapped at the screen before passing the phone to Brynn. "Check it out!"

It was a page of Instagram search results for the hashtag #christmasatevergreen. Katie practically squealed as Brynn scrolled, message after message mentioning the catch phrase. There must have been hundreds of posts. She could feel the warm damp of Jordan's breath as he read over her shoulder.

"Are these about *our* Evergreen Acres?" Jordan asked, his eyes wide.

"Yes!" Katie said. "Brynn put signs up at each booth encouraging people to use the hashtag. I guess they did!"

Brynn scrolled through a few of the profiles now following Evergreen Acres. "A bunch of these posts aren't even local." She tapped on one profile from Sydney, Australia. "See?"

"Maybe they just wish they were here," Katie said, her eyes sparkling with excitement. "Whatever the reason, we are officially trending!"

"That's amazing!" Brynn said.

"Even I know what that means," Jordan said with a chuckle.

Tyler had returned to his DJ booth, switching to a more subdued playlist while the volunteers packed up for the night. A saxophone rendition of "O, Holy Night" drifted their way and a bit of Brynn's anxiety melted away as she soaked in the excitement of these two people amazing people. Something tugged at her stomach as her eyes lingered on Jordan's crinkled eyes, and she had to force herself not to throw her arms around him in celebration.

Just then Charlie appeared as he weaved his way through the tents, still sporting his acrylic white beard though he'd changed back into his regular clothes. "What a night," he said, joining them, his eyes shining as he gazed misty eyed over the snow-flocked forest. "Figured I'd better change into something better suited for manual labor."

"Santa was the talk of the night," Brynn said. "I don't think you ever sat down."

"Not true," Charlie said. "More than one kid asked to sit on Santa's lap!" His face was flushed with so much excitement that he really did look like an off-the-clock Kris Kringle. "I didn't want to miss a minute of it. Those kids followed me everywhere." He laughed. "If I played Santa every night, my doctor would never have to get on me to exercise, that's for sure."

"Hey, gang!" Gina said, zipping her parka to her chin as she trudged up the rocky hillside to join them. "I don't know if I've sold that many trees in a whole week, let alone one night!"

"Things are looking good for Evergreen Acres," Brynn said, unable to suppress the emotion in her voice as the reality truly hit her.

"We still have two nights to go," Jordan said, with a sharp edge that hadn't been there before. "Let's not get ahead of ourselves. Something could still go wrong."

Brynn offered a tiny shrug in response to Katie widened her eyes at Brynn, but all she could do was shrug. Meanwhile, Charlie and Gina were too busy chatting about sales to notice Jordan's mood. They headed back into the shop, each looking decades younger as they recounted all the mutual friends they'd seen that night.

"I'm going to lock up," Jordan said, not meeting anyone's eyes as he disappeared into the darkness.

"Is he trapping us in here forever?" Katie asked, half-joking.

"The gate opens automatically from the inside," Brynn said, totally unaware of her words as something ugly twisted inside her. "It's just to keep people from driving in."

"Is he mad because Caleb was here?" Katie asked, looking over her shoulder to make sure he was completely out of earshot. "And what was with Gag Me? Did they talk to you?"

"I don't..." Brynn said, trailing off as she watched for Jordan to reappear in the glow of the streetlights that lined the driveway. She sighed. "Caleb was apparently here to profess his love to me," Brynn said, relishing her best friend's aghast expression. "As for Jessica?" She made a face. "I have no idea why she came. They both said it was her idea."

"That's too weird," Katie said. "So, what did Caleb say? Does Jordan know?"

Brynn bit her lip. "I promise I'll fill you in later," she said apologetically. "I should see if Jordan needs me."

Before Katie could say more, Brynn jogged down the gravel drive, trying her best not to roll her ankles on the uneven gravel. She pulled out her phone and tapped the flashlight icon, which barely illuminated the dark path. Though she had barely noticed the cold, a bone-deep chill began to creep through each layer of her clothing. She wondered how much of that was actually from the frigid temperature.

She slowed as she neared Jordan and she tried to steady her breath as she drew close.

"Hey, you," she called brightly.

He slowed, but didn't turn back as she caught up and began to walk beside him.

"What's wrong?" she asked.

"Nothing," Jordan said flatly, his gaze fixed on the gate ahead as the gravel turned to pavement.

"Are you still up for filming?" Brynn asked before biting her lip. Even she was annoyed at the chipper neediness in her words.

Jordan face remained unreadable. Had he forgotten?

"Katie can't help you?" he finally asked.

"She has a date, remember?" Brynn's heart was a kick drum. "But you're the one who asked me to do it, remember?" This wasn't coming out right. "We can just cancel if you don't—"

"I said I'll do it, so I'll be there," Jordan interrupted.

"Oh," Brynn said quietly. "Okay."

The cold way he spoke to her was new, and as Brynn swallowed the lump forming in her throat, she thought she would take his snarky anger any day over this.

"This is really a one-person job," Jordan said as they reached the gate.

Brynn searched in vain for the right thing to say. "I guess I'll go see if any of the volunteers need help." She hesitated. "Do you want to meet me at the shop?"

"Meet you at the shop," he echoed, not looking back.

Her lungs felt deflated as she pressed a hand against her thundering chest, willing him to turn back. He didn't.

Brynn entered the shop a few minutes later, her nose stinging as the heat penetrated her numb face. As she approached the counter, she found Greta and Gina counting out a cash box. "Hey, Mom."

"Hey, dear!" Greta said as Gina sat the empty box on the mismatched pile behind her. "I was just saying I can't wait to come back tomorrow."

"That would be great, Mom," Brynn said. "It means a lots to have you here."

It looked like her mother had more to say, but there was no mistaking the pride shining in her eyes as she gave Brynn a quick squeeze and beelined for the exit. Brynn turned to find a grinning Mayor Lopez holding open the door, and the two of them disappeared into the night.

Brynn shook her head, trying and failing to suppress a smile as the door swung closed.

"Never thought I'd see Mayor Lopez back in the romance game," Gina said, snickering as she entered numbers into her calculator.

"Yeah, I'm not sure what to make of that," Brynn said, chuckling along with her. "But if they're happy, then good for them." She peeled open a mini candy cane from the box on the counter and stuck it in her mouth.

"I am beat!" Gina said, swallowing a yawn. "All cash boxes are totaled and accounted for, and nearly every volunteer has officially checked out." She pushed her glasses up her nose as she dragged a finger down her list.

"I'm just missing Randy Wilder's nephew, one of the choir ladies, and that Sutkamp fellow," Gina said. "But Charlie brought in all their money, so I'm not too worried about it."

"I'll check outside, but I'm sure they just forgot," Brynn said. "Though I wouldn't be surprised if Sutkamp considers himself above such mundane tasks as signing out. I saw him throw a stack of flyers into the trash."

"You never know with that one," Gina said, her fingers moving lightning fast on the keyboard.

"At least the roads aren't bad tonight," Brynn said, resting her elbows on the counter as she gazed out into the clear darkness.

"Everything has been amazing," Gina said, smiling wearily as she entered figures into a spreadsheet. "Enough flurries to feel the holiday spirit, but not enough to make a mess. Happy people, lots of sales, the whole town pitching in." She shook her head in amazement. "Just perfect." She shot a look at Brynn. "Bravo, my dear."

"I think it says more about the people of Twin Falls than it does about me," Brynn said dismissively, though she couldn't hide her proud smile. "I'm honored to be a part of it."

"I thought you had some videos to make tonight," Gina said, pulling some papers off the printer and smoothing them into a stack.

"I do," Brynn said. "Anything you need before I go?"

"You can take some of these cookies off my hands," Gina said, shoving a plastic container in her direction. "Other than that, I'm good and Charlie's probably finished closing up the back."

"Okay," Brynn said, wrapping a few cookies in a napkin before tucking them into her coat pocket. "Thanks, Gina. See you tomorrow."

The creaking of her boots on the porch stairs was too loud as Brynn headed for the parking lot, blinking as the icy wind stung her eyes. Brynn felt a confusing swirl of emotions as she saw Jordan's empty parking spot. It was hard to believe this was the same place that had been filled with music, lights, and the cheers of a couple hundred people just an hour or so earlier. She swung open her car door, then stopped, pausing to look back over the frosted fields and hillside.

This farm had felt like home to Brynn these past few weeks. She had accomplished everything she came here to do. Evergreen Acres was safe, at least for another season. The positive publicity from her time there had done everything she'd hoped to win back the favor of her fans. She knew should be thrilled, and she was, but that feeling was mingled with guilt, trepidation, and too many other emotions to name.

Later she would play back this moment hundreds of times, turning it over and over until her frustration gave way to exhaustion. Wondering what she might have seen if she'd been less preoccupied. How everything might have been different if she'd just told Jordan to forget about filming that night. But by then, none of it mattered. Not anymore.

TWENTY-SEVEN

"Are you sure you don't want to film yours?" Brynn asked Jordan for what felt to him like the tenth time. "I never would have asked you to drive here this late just to help me."

"I'm just not in the mood," Jordan replied coolly, sliding his phone back in his pocket as Brynn reviewed playback from the footage he had just recorded for her. "Another time, maybe."

He could tell she wanted to talk. She'd been eyeing him cautiously since she'd gotten there, tried several times to get him to talk about his night, but Jordan just couldn't do it. Shouts and laughter drifted from the alley through the back door, probably college kids staggering toward the pub for reverse happy hour. Most downtown businesses had been closed since six, but another sort of commerce was just getting started. Between the café with craft beers to the historic theater showing some old black and white movie, Twin Falls had a small but bustling nightlife that continued until after midnight.

Once Brynn had packed up her stuff, Jordan followed her through the curtain, throwing on his jacket as she stopped at the register to shut down the computer. The blue glow of the security lights threw giant crooked shadows across the exposed brick walls. Jordan watched as two men with briefcases loaded into a

Lyft, their loosened ties and pink faces hinting at a meeting over half-priced pints. Jordan tugged on his gloves as two fire trucks sped past, lights swirling but sirens silenced.

As the white glow of the monitor illuminated Brynn's face, Jordan felt a sudden urge to walk out of the store without another word. He knew Brynn thought he was angry with her; he could tell by the way she tiptoed around him all night. But the truth was, he didn't know what he was feeling.

The way Caleb's eyes had roamed over every inch of Brynn had made Jordan want to scream. That look of familiarity said everything he needed to know about Brynn's history with Caleb, about how close they had been.

How close they still looked to be.

His throat tightened as he remembered how Brynn had acted all nervous and flustered the second Caleb had walked in. He felt kind of sorry for Jessica, who surely couldn't have missed the way Caleb ogled Brynn right in front of her.

But two voices fought to be heard inside his head, and Jordan didn't know which way to turn. This anger, or fear, or whatever he was feeling made everything that much easier. He could let her go. She wanted to leave Twin and he was being given every chance to step away. He should walk away before he was left behind, whether that happened when she moved or when she got back together with Caleb.

But the other voice hissed at him, promising Jordan it was too late. He felt an animalistic need for her, an absolute obsession that he couldn't shake. He wanted to rip Caleb's throat out, wanted to wrap himself around Brynn's smooth body, wanted to claim her as his own like some kind of neanderthal. A part of him wondered if he could stop himself from following her, even if it happened to be to a foreign land of sunshine, palm trees and horrible traffic.

The first fifteen minutes of his drive to Planted were filled with the memory of her sweet breath on his lips, the way she'd kissed his neck, millimeter by millimeter, until she reached his ear, almost sending him over the edge before they'd even begun.

He'd spent the second half of the drive shouting curses to the empty truck cab, promising himself he was done. He wasn't about to destroy everything good in his life for whatever this was. Feelings fade. He was better off this way, better off saving himself before he lost himself in something he couldn't survive.

The statistics don't matter when it happens to you.

His mind was an utter mess as he waited for Brynn to finish, waited to rush to his truck, drive home, and have a strong drink with no one around but his dog.

Jordan felt Brynn's eyes on him and realized too late she'd said something.

"My mind is somewhere else," he said. "What did you say to me?"

"Nothing," Brynn said quickly. Her face was drawn, and she looked every bit as exhausted as he felt. He hated to see her like this, and though he didn't think he could bear to hear what she had to say, he couldn't help but want to comfort her.

"You're so good at this stuff," Jordan said, watching her fingers fly over the keyboard as she dragged the video sequences into the right folders. "I learned a thing or two from watching you and plants are kind of my area of expertise."

"I'm glad," Brynn said, as a tight laugh escaped. "I have struggled so hard to keep this Obliqua alive."

"You didn't mention that in the video," Jordan said.

"People want me to have all the answers." She shrugged, but her shoulders were slack, as she tied her hair into messy topknot. "If I don't, they'll just go to Jessica."

"Jessica," Jordan repeated. "Wait, the Green Goddess lady isn't the same Jessica as...?"

He trailed off, but Brynn nodded and as he suddenly realized what it must mean for Brynn to see her enemy with her ex, something cracked inside him.

"That woman has nothing on you," Jordan said before he knew what he was saying. He was so delirious from the last 36 hours, he might as well have been drunk, but he couldn't take it back now. But as he watched her eyes fill with tender hope, he knew, given the chance, he would say it again.

"You really think so?" Brynn asked, a small smile on her lips as she slid off the stool and Jordan held his breath as she headed towards him.

She stopped so close that their shoes touched, her forehead a single inch from his chin. She gazed up at him, her eyes giant pools of need and longing. The air was electric, and the silence was loaded with everything that neither of them could say.

My God. He wanted to bury his face in her neck, drink her in one last time. He barely registered his phone vibrating against his thigh as everything disappeared besides the radiant emanating from her body. She tipped her face toward his and her glistening lips parted the tiniest bit. He let out a deep quivering breath, pressing his lips to her cheek as if he could swallow her. They inhaled and exhaled, neither daring to move or speak as warmth spread to every part of Jordan's body. He whispered a moan and she replied with a ragged sigh. He didn't even try to stop the smooth fingers that slid under the hem of his sweater, greedily gripping his hips as he bit her lip. He wouldn't be the one to stop this. He didn't know how.

"Maybe you should check that," Brynn whispered when his

phone started vibrating again, this time shaking both their touching thighs. Her lips grazed his as she slipped her hand deep into his jeans pocket. She searched with her fingers in a way that was anything but innocent, and he stifled a moan as she tugged the phone free. She grinned at him, mischief in her dark green eyes as she pressed the phone into his hand: She knew exactly what she was doing.

Finally, Jordan turned his face, pressing his cheek against her forehead, one arm gripping her back as he glanced at his phone.

His blood ran cold. Seven missed calls, too many missed texts to count. It must have been ringing the whole time they were filming. He unlocked his phone, barely feeling Brynn tighten her grip as he feverishly scrolled.

No.

"What is it?" Brynn whispered.

NO.

"Jordan?" Brynn asked in a shaky voice.

"Fire," he whispered, the words itself burning his lips, as time stopped, and he remembered where he was. He grabbed his keys and ran for the door.

"What do you mean 'fire'?" Brynn called, chasing after him as Jordan fled into the empty street.

"The fire trucks!" Jordan yelled over his shoulder. "Evergreen Acres is on fire!"

He tried to call Charlie as he ran for his truck, but it went straight to voicemail. He dialed again. And again.

The streets were empty as he sped through downtown, reaching ninety as he silently prayed no police officers were lying in wait. The timestamp from the first call had been more than a half hour earlier. It wasn't until Jordan reached the highway that he realized he'd left Brynn behind. His finger hovered over her name in his recent call list, but he locked the phone instead. A primal cry filled the cabin, a sound Jordan had never before heard himself make. He slammed his fists against the steering wheel in fury, willing time to slow as he sped towards home.

All this had happened while he was playing influencer. He'd turned off his ringer and disappeared into Brynn's reality, while down the road his life was literally going up in flames. A sickening shame washed over him when he recounted each time he'd almost gone home that night, each time he almost didn't go to Planted at all. If he had just listened to his head, this might never have happened. The metallic taste of panic filled his mouth as the road stretched on without end.

As he skidded around the last curve, he could just make out the farm's woven wire fence in his headlights. He squinted, willing the dark shadows in the distance to form the shape of something familiar, but all he could see were flashing lights and the jet-black winter night. He saw an orange glow further up the hillside, but a thick fog made it impossible to see more.

Not fog. Smoke.

He floored it up the driveway as gravel pelted the underside of the truck, slamming his brakes a few yards behind the fire engines. He threw open the door, not bothering to close it behind as he ran toward the people and lights. As he ran toward the heat. He vaguely noticed a car door slam behind him as he sprinted toward the line of police officers blocking the path to the store.

"Stay back!" an officer shouted, and Jordan saw a Twin Falls County Sherriff's office patch on his leather sleeve.

"This is his place!" another office yelled, and Jordan recognized the mustached older man as Tony Harris, one of Charlie's oldest friends. Jordan clutched his throat as his world began to tilt, but he refused to back down. He ran back a few feet, taking in the scene around him for the first time: five trucks, twice that many cruisers and more uniformed bodies than he could count. Everyone was here. It must be bad.

Jordan sprinted along the human barrier, spotting two officers who weren't looking his way as they chatted and looked up the hillside. He took a deep breath, ducked his head and barreled through.

"Sir, stop!" a female voice boomed after him and he heard rapid footfalls growing closer. "You need to stand down!"

Just then Charlie stumbled into his path, rounding the corner from behind the shop, and Jordan nearly plowed into him before falling into his embrace.

"They're doing everything they can, Bubba," Charlie stammered, sweat dripping from his face to Jordan's next.

The officers who had pursued him finally caught up, but they stood at a respectful distance once it became clear Jordan wasn't going to run into the flames.

"Where is it?" Jordan demanded.

"West field is the worst," Charlie said, nodding in the same direction Jordan had seen the orange glow as he drove in. "The BLM land above is burning too."

"And the animals?"

"The big guys are down by the road," Charlie said, pointing to the dark field. "Officer Tessay put the baby goats in a few crates from the K-9 unit in since they'd slip right through the fence. The rest are in carriers and crates in the farmhouse with Toby."

Jordan closed his eyes as the information refused to make any kind of sense.

"How bad?" he finally asked.

"I don't know," Charlie said, shaking his head sadly. "I'd gone home hours ago. Some long haul driver out on 515 saw the flames and called it in."

"I should have been here," Jordan said, swallowing back a white-hot fury that was boiling him from the inside.

"Don't do that," Charlie said firmly as he pulled Jordan close once more. "We don't have time for that nonsense. Not tonight."

"What can I do?!"

He felt his ribcage rip in two as her cry reached them through the inferno's roar above them. He turned as Brynn ran towards them, panting as she ignored the warnings of the nearby officers. She must have followed Jordan in her car, though he was relieved she hadn't tried to keep up with him. "What can I do?!" she repeated when she reached them, her eyes wild and desperate.

"You've done enough," Jordan spat as he turned away, ignoring the confusion and hurt on her face. He pushed past Brynn and Charlie, his eyes burning as he ran further up the hil. Before he could see the flames himself, someone grabbed his arm and twisted it behind his back.

"I can't let you go any further!" the man shouted, and Jordan recognized the voice of Tony as he struggled to release his arm. "It's not safe! They'll cuff you if they have to!" Tony wheezed, but his grip tightened. "Please—don't go any further, Jordan!"

Tony preferred nachos and beer to working out at a gym, and Jordan knew he could outrun him if he could break free. But before he could move, he heard a deafening crack high above, followed by a thunderous rumble that violently shook the ground beneath them. For a moment, everything seemed to move in slow motion. There was no point. Jordan went slack as he allowed Tony to guide him back down to safety, Brynn and Charlie arm in arm as they followed close behind.

"I'm so sorry," he heard Brynn say. Was she crying?

"We're OK," Charlie reassured her, his own voice thin and raspy. "The animals are out, and everyone is safe. That's all that matters."

Jordan pressed his lips together, his arms crossed as he watched arches of water and white foam penetrate the thick smoke that blanketed the smoldering hillside. He coughed as a cloud of acrid fumes choked his throat, but he didn't dare look away.

He heard soft footsteps, and he didn't need to turn to know it was Brynn who had cautiously sidled up to him.

"Can I get you anything?" Brynn asked, her voice wobbly and broken as she timidly placed a hand on his arm.

"Go home," he said, his hollow voice sounding very far away as he ignored the fresh tears that spilled down her cheeks.

"There's nothing to be done right now," Charlie said gently to Brynn, as he hurried over and put an arm over her shoulder. "We all need to just stay out of the way so these people can do their job."

"I guess," Brynn sniffed, but he could hear reluctance in her voice.

"I'll keep you updated," Jordan heard Charlie promise.

He didn't look back. Not until her soft footfalls had been swallowed entirely by the shouts below and the earsplitting thunder from above. And by then, she was gone.

TWENTY-EIGHT

Brynn tightened the blanket around her shoulders as the blurry lights emanating from the TV refused to make sense. She glanced at her phone, pressing the side button to illuminate the screen. Still nothing.

After reloading on the same websites and continuously flipping through local channels for hours, the news stations had finally begun to air coverage of the fire. Though the same information kept repeating over and over, she was afraid to turn it off.

She hadn't reached out to Jordan, though she'd come close to calling him at least once every five minutes. But anytime she'd scrolled to his number, she heard his brutal iciness as he'd told her to leave.

Screw it.

She swiped the screen and tapped Jordan's name before she could change her mind. She heard nothing but silence, then after a moment, an automated voice telling her to leave a message. She sighed and hung up, only then noticing the time: 6:04 a.m. Thank goodness his phone was off. Hopefully he was sleeping.

Her eyelids felt like little weighted blankets as she forced herself to focus on the news. She was sure she'd miss something if she fell asleep, sure she'd lose her opportunity to actually do something. Staying awake felt a little like penance, though she still couldn't put her finger on exactly what she'd done wrong.

She blinked as an overly caffeinated news anchor began her shift. "Firefighters and law enforcement from two counties joined forces early this morning to contain the Evergreen Acres fire," she said, "but not before hundreds of premium Christmas trees were destroyed." Brynn felt like she was going to throw up, even though she'd lost count of the number of times she'd heard this information. "A spokesperson for Evergreen Acres told KSAW that the farm's Christmas carnival is cancelled for the rest of the weekend. They would like to ask their customers to keep an eye on social media for updates."

Brynn swallowed as a fresh wave of panic gripped her chest. She picked up her phone and tapped Facebook, then Instagram, even searching TikTok and the Evergreen Acres website. Of course, there were no updates. That was Brynn's job. Or, at least, it had been.

Brynn blinked and wiped a sticky cheek, her mouth chalky as she shielded her eyes from the bright light that was shining on her face through the window, dazing Brynn as it reflected off a thin dusting of snow that must have finally stuck. She sat up, rolling her stiff shoulders as she noticed a courtroom now filled the TV screen; a hair-sprayed judge barking orders at two sheepish looking men. Her eyes widened. How long had she been asleep?

She snatched up her phone and saw a missed call from Charlie. Trepidation flooded her stomach as she checked the volume: the ringer was still on. She must have slept right through it. She tapped the voicemail repeatedly as it loaded, willing it to play as her heart tried to escape out of her chest.

"Hey, Brynn, Charlie here," she finally heard, the familiar

warmth of his voice filling her living room. "Sorry I didn't call sooner. Things were pretty hectic around here as I'm sure you can imagine." He paused and she could barely make out a hushed whisper in the background. "Listen," Charlie continued after a moment. "The fire is out, but it's probably best if you don't come in today. Everything's taped off until the police can finish their investigation." Her breath caught in her throat. "I'll call you soon. Take care, Brynn."

She swiped at her face as hot tears blurred her puffy, bloodshot eyes. But what could she do? She groaned and threw the blanket to the floor before standing and wiping her nose on the sleeve of her sweatshirt.

The last thing she wanted was to post on social media, and she obviously wasn't needed at Evergreen Acres. She would shower and get to the store—*her* store. As she turned off the TV, thinking of her little urban jungle and the customers who might come in on this desolate Saturday, she felt a tiny glimmer of anticipation.

Jordan swallowed his cold coffee as something wet pressed against his hand. He glanced down as Toby stared at him with is soulful patient eyes. Jordan sighed and scratched the dog's head, prompting Toby's tail to wiggle his entire body enthusiastically. Jordan pinched the bridge of his nose and groaned.

He slept in fits and starts once the first responders had cleared out and Charlie had taken all the smaller animals home with him for the night, all except Teddy the tortoise who was currently snoozing in the kitchen. Nightmares of pungent flames and deer with eyes rolled back in terror filled his mind every time he drifted off. He'd given up around five and had been pacing the farmhouse and downing cup after cup of coffee ever since.

Jordan and Charlie kept vigil on the porch all through the wee hours of the morning, a reluctant compromise with the officers who were tasked with safely securing the perimeter as the firefighters battled the flames. Jordan could barely remember a word they'd said to each other during that time. He couldn't believe after everything they'd done to save this place, it could all be snatched away, just like that.

He didn't turn on the news. The anchors didn't know anything he couldn't see by walking out his front door. But he felt impotent as he stomped around his house in the same path over and over again. He glanced down at Toby, who loyally followed him from room to room.

"Come on, boy," Jordan said. "We need to get out of this house."

He tugged on his cap and threw on his work coat. Untouched snow glittered as they stepped out the front door, mocking them like icing on an abandoned wedding cake. It was hard to believe the farm had been teeming with more than fifty emergency personnel just a few hours earlier. If it weren't for a stray coffee cup here and there, he might have dreamed it. If only.

He wondered if Larry Krebs had heard about the fire. He didn't live in Twin, but he lived close enough. Not that it mattered. He would have to hear the bad news, one way or another.

Jordan hiked up the hillside, his stomach wrenching as he passed the untouched abandoned booths. It seemed like years ago the carnival had brought this place to life. As he got closer, he saw that a fine layer of soot covered every table, every tent. Up here, even the snow had turned into a mucky ashen gray.

He ducked beneath the caution tape as Toby ran to keep up. He had tried to prepare himself for this moment—had tried to picture scorched earth and ruined fence posts. But try as he might, it had been too painful to picture the dead trees. But now, here they were, row after row of charred jagged pines, the few remaining branches jutting out like the paralyzed wings of a bird that would never fly.

He had to count the trees they'd lost eventually. A warped orange ribbon caught his eye, and he bent down, rubbing it clean between his fingers. It was a sold tag, one of hundreds that had marked the Krebs mall trees. Melted and illegible, it was impossible to know which stumpy skeleton it had once belonged to. Jordan sobbed, his throat burning as he kicked at the earth and hurled the mutated label, but the wind caught its pathetic curled body and it fluttered to the ground inches from his boot.

He sank to his knees, the black rock slicing into his palms as a roar vibrated the earth around him. As his tears fell into the sooty mud, he realized the sound was coming from him.

TWENTY-NINE

Brynn braced her hands on the bathroom sink, breathing slowly she tried to calm down. She met her reflection in the mirror and was relieved to see she looked better than she felt. Her eyes were no longer red and veiny, the skin beneath no longer purple. Her complexion appeared to glow beneath the thick layer of foundation, and she could almost pass as someone who actually slept. It was amazing what some heavy duty eye drops and a good concealer could do.

Schmoozing with a bunch of network execs was the last thing Brynn felt like doing, but what good would it do if she cancelled? Sure, she would have to go on her own, but that wasn't what bothered her the most. Jordan still hadn't returned her calls or her texts, and she'd finally decided to leave him alone the day after the fire. He clearly didn't want to talk to her.

Imploding her own career was the last thing she should do today. Besides, maybe one of these V.I.P.s could help Evergreen Acres, though she wasn't sure how. She had no idea how bad the damage actually was, but figured if she hadn't even heard from Charlie or Gina, it must be pretty bad.

Her heart froze as her phone lit up, but it was only a text from Katie:

Stopping by to grab memory card so I can upload Friday's tape!

Thank God for Katie.

Brynn couldn't imagine what life would look like without her. Katie was manning the store again today, and she had been more than eager to do it. Just a few months ago, Katie couldn't tell a fern from a philodendron, but now she was pruning, watering, and answering questions left and right.

Planted in Twin was suddenly flourishing, with new customers coming in every day. At first, they had mostly seen her on TV or from following Evergreen Acres, but now, more and more people had heard about it around town. In her darkest nights, Brynn had been absorbed by a secret fear that her shop just wasn't good enough to make it. Now she could finally breathe, knowing that once locals realized Planted was there, the little store spoke for itself.

Brynn pinned back one side of her hair, then the other, leaving half tumbling down her neck in loose curls. Back in her bedroom, she stepped into the conservative blue cocktail dress she'd bought the week before. She tried and failed to reach the top of the zipper, but eventually resigned herself to the fact that her hair would cover most of it. As much as she wasn't looking forward to maintaining socially appropriate small talk, she knew she needed to look good. She needed to look like a TV star.

As she slipped on her black high heels, the doorbell chimed.

"Just a sec, Kate!" she yelled down the hallway. Brynn glanced at the clock and realized she'd better start driving. She grabbed a tiny clutch she could stuff a few essentials into and hurried down the hallway, digging through her work bag for the memory card as she flung open the door.

But it wasn't Katie who was standing on her doorstep.

As she gaped at Jordan, she couldn't help but notice the snug, gray blazer he wore over a crisp, white tee. With his rugged bone structure and signature stubble, he looked like he had stepped out of a luxury car commercial.

"What are you doing here?" she finally asked, reluctantly stepping back as he stepped into the foyer. She did not have time for this today.

"I'm here for the Homestead lunch," he said flatly, spinning his truck keys around his finger.

"I mean, OK, but—"she sputtered, trying to make sense of this information. "I assumed you weren't coming, with everything that happened. We haven't even spoken in days."

Jordan shrugged. "Looks like I was right on time. Besides, there's nothing to do at home except wait." He hesitated and his stoic mask slipped for just a second. "We lost the rest of the Krebs order. Ninety percent was destroyed. There's no way we can fill it, so they're going out of state."

"Oh, Jordan," Brynn said, her heart breaking. "I am so sorry."

"Yeah, well, I figure a little free publicity can't hurt," Jordan said.

The sting of his comment cut right through Brynn, even though she'd just had the same thought moments earlier.

"Well, thank you," Brynn said tightly, not sure what else to say. "I guess we'd better get going."

Jordan's eyes stayed fixed on the road as Twin Falls shrank behind them. Brynn had offered to drive, but he had insisted, mostly because it gave him something to do. He knew he had to process the last few days at some point, but today was not that day.

Brynn plugged her phone into the dash and chose a jazzy Christmas playlist as they cruised the barren highway, the rocky cliffs in the distance appearing even more desolate than usual. They were both unusually quiet, and Jordan was grateful that Brynn mostly stared at her phone.

Occasionally, she tried to engage him in some light topic, pointing out a roadside farmers market or talking about New Year's resolutions. He generally responded with one-word answers and eventually Brynn gave up. They drove the rest of the way in silence, both pretending to focus on the lyrics to every song that played.

Jordan knew he was being unfair to her, but he was too depleted to give anything more. He was just so *mad*. He was mad at the entire world and everything in it. He was mad that bad things kept happening to him while other people seemed to skate through life. He was mad that he had lost control and careened right into utter destruction.

His headache was back, throbbing as it had been for most of the past three days, untouched by anything in his medicine cabinet. Charlie had stopped by several times, bringing bagels and reporting on the measly payout they'd been told to expect. Their insurance would only cover equipment and ready-to-go inventory, but the majority of the damage had been to trees that were still growing. Evergreen Acres had some crop insurance that Marissa's dad had secured, but neither Charlie nor Jordan had done anything except pay the premiums since she had passed. This was going to be a long road.

Jordan tried his best to summon an iota of optimism whenever

Charlie came around, but the minute he left, Jordan fell back into a suffocating, immobilizing despair. Other than compulsively walking every inch of the property from dawn until dusk, feeding Toby was the only thing he could manage to do.

He sensed Brynn beside him, her rigid body wound like a rubber band about to snap. She was tapping her bare knee, shifting the hem of her dress as she stared at her phone. He hadn't seen her wear her hair like that before, pinned back like one of those women in the old paintings. What was that artist's name— Bodicello?

It would be so easy to simply to reach over and rest one hand on her milky thigh. She might look over with that coy glint, rubbing her fingers over the sensitive spot at the nape of his neck.

Or she would slap him.

"Turn here," Brynn said after an eternity of loaded silence. He pointed the truck down a tree-lined drive with quiet ponds on either side of the road, any ducks long gone for the winter. Brynn gasped as they approached the long circular driveway. Behind a valet station was a mansion with three story columns and verandas on each floor. Jordan had never known anyone who lived in a house like this. Apparently, reality TV could be more lucrative than he'd thought.

A tuxedoed valet hurried to open the passenger door as Jordan stepped out onto the polished driveway, self-conscious as he handed over the keys to his salt-splattered truck. Brynn waited for him at the foot of a marble staircase, watching him with a Mona Lisa smile.

As they entered an opulent foyer, Jordan was careful to stay on the carpet as he wiped his wet leather oxfords. The floor was pristine granite and a glittering crystal chandelier hung at least fifteen feet above their heads. Yet another tuxedoed man took their coats, while a third extended a tray of champagne flutes. They each took one, and Jordan sipped anxiously as they stood off to one side and looked around.

"Your dress," he said, gesturing to her back. "The zipper."

"Oh, right," Brynn said quietly. "I couldn't reach."

"May I?" he asked.

She nodded, and as he zipped her dress the rest of the way, his hand grazing the soft back hairs he could barely see, tiny goosebumps pressed against his fingers.

"Thank you," she said, pulling away as a rosy flush gathered in her cheeks.

He tried to calm his breathing, taking a gulp of champagne every time he caught a hint of jasmine.

"So, this is the life of a network star?" he asked, trying to fill the silence.

"I guess so," she said. "Though they basically have a whole empire. Guest speaking, books, a houseware line in Target. People even drive to Provo just to stop by the Urban Farm gift shop."

"Didn't you say Homestead only films its shows in Los Angeles?" Jordan asked, unsure why he was suddenly irritated.

"Well, Urban Farm started in LA," Brynn said. "Katie told me that after season five, it was time to renew their contract and they convinced Homestead to move the show here."

Jordan could see the unsaid in her eyes: *maybe one day I could do the same.* The sadness that had taken up permanent residence in his stomach throbbed acutely.

"You must be Brynn Callaway!" a female voice squealed. They turned to find Georgina and Paul, camera-ready grins on both their faces. Jordan wondered if Paul was wearing makeup.

"Well, I won't pretend I don't recognize you both," Brynn said, accepting a giddy hug from Georgina. Paul extended his hand to Jordan.

"You must be the other half," he said warmly. "Jordan, right?"

"Yep. Jordan," he agreed, glad to find a way to answer without lying.

"I've been really excited to meet you guys," Brynn said, her eyes shining. "Thank you for letting us come."

"Oh, please," Paul said, waving his hand dismissively. "The pleasure is ours. We've been watching your channel for weeks now."

"You have?" Brynn asked and Jordan couldn't help but feel a swell of pride on her behalf. She had worked so hard for this.

"We're really pulling for you," Georgina added.

"Thank you," Brynn sputtered, blinking repeatedly as Jordan watched her soak it all in.

"Well, make yourselves at home," Georgina said. "Lunch is in twenty."

As the couple left to welcome another group, Jordan exchanged his champagne flute for a full one.

"Where to?" he asked.

"I'm not sure," Brynn said, her eyes darting around the room as she kept a polite smile plastered on her lips. He had never seen her this nervous, and something in him began to soften as he crooked his arm in her direction.

"I've got you," he said softly.

Her eyes met his with a look of genuine surprise, followed by one of simple gratitude. As she wrapped her arm through his, Jordan resolved to do his best to be there for her today. After all she had done to help him, he owed her.

They wandered into a living room that could have doubled as a ballroom if they pushed the couches out of the center. Enormous glass snow globes decorated round cocktail tables that had been set up throughout the enormous space. A trio of violinists played a complicated string rendition of "Deck the Halls" as Jordan led Brynn to one of the few empty tables.

"Do you know anyone here?" he whispered.

"I mean, technically?" Brynn said. "But we've only spoken on the phone."

"Well, they all know who you are, right?" Jordan asked. "I say just let them come to you."

"Yeah, you're right," Brynn said, looking up at him, her eyes glittering beneath her thick black lashes. "You have no idea what it means to have you here. I know this can't be easy for you."

"It's nothing," he said, but a honeyed warmth spread through his stomach as he allowed himself to gaze back.

"It's not *nothing*," she said, and he thought he heard relief in her laughter. "I felt like I was going to throw up back there. But with you here, well...maybe I can do this."

"You look beautiful, by the way," Jordan said, though that was putting it mildly.

"Thank you," Brynn said, playfully cocking her head. "You don't look half bad yourself."

In fact, his mouth had gone dry the moment she had flung open her door hours earlier, shock permeating every inch of him as she discovered him on her stoop. But some barrier inside had kept him from saying so, some flame of misery had still burned too strong.

"Are you okay?" Brynn asked, her eyebrows knitted in concern.

He let out an embarrassed chuckle. "I'm just glad to be here," he said, letting out a breath he didn't realize he was holding. "With you."

"You are?" she asked, looking genuinely surprised.

"I'm always happy to be with you, Brynn," he said quietly. "You must know that by now."

She swallowed and studied her lipstick-stained glass. "Sometimes I think I know how you feel, but other times I don't have a clue." She shrugged and flashed him a wry smile. "To be fair, I don't know how I feel half the time either."

"Maybe we don't need to know," he said, pressing his arm against hers as he ignored the alarms sounding in his mind. "We have maybe two weeks left until you pick up and move, right?"

"We don't know if I'll get the show," Brynn said quickly, looking around to make sure no one had overheard.

"You'll get the show," he said, locking his eyes on hers. As he grazed his fingertips along her delicate wrist, his chest felt like it was turning itself inside out.

"Ms. Callaway, Mr. Damon!"

They turned to find a sturdy man with a cocoa complexion who had to be well over six feet tall.

"So glad you could make it!" Despite his imposing stature, his jovial smile made him seem as threatening as a kitten as he stuck out one meaty hand. "Mark Barnes."

"Oh, Mr.- Mark!" Brynn said, straightening instantly. "It's so great to finally meet you." She nudged Jordan with her hip in that way that drove him wild. "Jordan, Mr. Barnes is the CEO of Homestead TV."

"Nice to meet you," Jordan said, shaking his hand.

"Thanks for making the drive," Mr. Barnes replied before turning his focus back to Brynn. "All of us are simply over the moon with your recent content," he continued, gesturing emphatically with his hands. "Between the easy-to-follow houseplant instructions and the cozy Christmas vibe of the tree farm, you've really got something for everyone."

"Brynn's pretty special," Jordan agreed, not bothering to hide the admiration that crept into his voice.

Suddenly, Brynn's face turned to stone.

"Mr. Barnes!" came a high-pitched shriek from behind Jordan.

A familiar brunette in a severe white pantsuit pressed her way into their semi-circle, and as she coquettishly threw her perfect ponytail hair over one shoulder, Jordan realized where he'd seen her before. He shot Brynn a look, but judging from her closed off expression, she hadn't expected to see her there.

And suddenly it all made sense. He'd met Jessica at Evergreen Acres, but at the time, he had no idea she was the same person who was harassing Brynn online. After all, Jessica was a popular name for thirty-somethings, so he hadn't put it together. When he thought about it, he did remember a model with a sleek black ponytail on Sutkamp's banner at the tree lighting. He'd thought Brynn had been upset because she was jealous of Jessica and Caleb. But maybe, it was something else entirely. Maybe it was just Jordan that had gotten jealous.

"Oh, hi, um...?" Mr. Barnes began, and Jordan got the impression he didn't know her. "It's nice to see you..."

"Jessica!" she finished, bending her wrist and extending it as if he might kiss it.

"Yes, right," Barnes said, politely shaking it. "*The Green Goddess* host, is that right?"

"The one and only," Jessica said, laughing, looking from Brynn to Jordan as if she expected them to join in.

"I didn't know we'd have the pleasure of seeing you today," Mr. Barnes said, glancing over Jessica's shoulder.

"Neither did I," Brynn muttered.

"Oh, Georgie is my bestie," Jessica said.

They all blinked at her.

"*Georgina*," she said, laughing airily as she waved at someone across the room and Jordan wondered if she'd had something stronger than champagne before she arrived.

"Yes, of course," Mr. Barnes said cordially. "Have you two met?" he asked, gesturing to Brynn.

"Once," Brynn said through gritted teeth and Jordan bit back a smile.

"Well, I'll see you in the dining room," Mr. Barnes said, heading toward the musicians. "Enjoy yourselves—I expect you three have plenty in common."

"*Four*," Jessica corrected and even before she beckoned him over, Jordan already knew who it would be. Caleb was smiling nervously as he stepped over to them. Jordan watched as his blue eyes hovered on the tiny belt around Brynn's waist and he willed himself not to smash Caleb's head with an empty champagne flute.

"Good to see you guys again," Caleb said, lifting his glass in greeting.

No one seemed to know what to say. Jessica was craning her head around Brynn and Jordan, probably looking for someone more important to meet. Caleb stared at his glass, nodding his head in time with the music. Brynn looked like she'd rather be anywhere else.

"I heard about your place," Caleb said to Jordan, finally breaking the silence. "So sorry, man. That's a tough break."

"Yeah, thanks," Jordan said simply.

"Testing, testing," reverberated through the sound system and Jordan was grateful for an excuse to escape the awkward conversation.

"Good afternoon, everyone!" Mark Barnes began, and everyone turned to watch him on the small stage. "Thanks for being here so close to Christmas, whether you joined us by plane, train, or automobile." He chuckled at his joke. "Okay, well, maybe no train riders today.

"I'm so glad you were able to come celebrate *the most successful* Homestead show of all time!" Mark crowed, and the audience cheered. "Our VP of Talent Development, Sofia Camp, and I would have been partners on this since the beginning, so come on up and join me, Sofia!"

A round bright-eyed woman with close cropped gray hair climbed to the stage to enthusiastic applause. So, that was the famous Sofia Camp. Brynn made a mental note to find her later and thank her in person for making all this possible.

"Georgina, Paul," Mark continued, raising his glass for a toast. "Thank you for welcoming us into your beautiful home. We are so grateful to have you as part of the Homestead family. And as our family grows..." He shot a pointed glance at Brynn, who blushed. "Next year stands to be our biggest year yet!" The applause and shouts of encouragement grew even louder. "Cheers!"

Jordan almost missed the murderous way Jessica eyed Brynn before she quickly slipped her beauty queen grin back on her face.

"Cheers!" came the lively chorus.

"Did Mark Barnes really just look at me?" Brynn whispered into Jordan's ear.

"Oh, he definitely looked at you," Jordan said, relishing the smile that spread across her sweet face. As she nuzzled into his shoulder, he pressed one cheek against her silky waves.

He knew he had no right to claim this woman, but he was so proud.

As the wait staff ushered them into the dining room, Brynn wrapped her arm around Jordan's waist. He pressed her against his side, smiling as a warm solace filled his entire body for the first time in days. As they followed the crowd through the giant archway, Jordan suddenly got the feeling he was going to be OK.

Though it hardly seemed possible, the dining room was even bigger than the room he'd just seen, with long tables crammed together in two parallel rows. Frosted glass hurricane votives sat atop white linen tablecloths and the waitstaff all posed elegantly against one wall.

Jordan found their names on little calligraphy-inscribed cards near the front of the room. They were seated near Mark, and directly across from Georgina and Paul. As Jordan pulled out a chair for Brynn, he felt a smug surge of satisfaction as Caleb and Jessica huddled together in the very back. With any luck, he could avoid those two for the rest of the afternoon.

When he glanced to Brynn, he found her watching him, a soft smile of her lips. His eyebrows rose a notch in question, but she simply leaned her head against his shoulder as if it were the most natural thing in the world. Her fragrant hair brushed against his cheek and his breath hitched in his throat. A moment later, she gently rested her hand on his thigh. He did his best not to stiffen, not to give away the heat that filled every part of him. If there hadn't been a hundred witnesses, not to mention several people Brynn wanted to impress, Jordan might have pulled her beneath the table right then and there.

Brynn couldn't believe how much coconut shrimp she'd scarfed down. Over the last few days, she'd been gripped by queasiness and had skipped more than one meal. Maybe it was the festive atmosphere, or the fancy champagne the waiters kept pouring into their glasses. But really, it was mostly because of Jordan.

It was hard to believe they'd only known each other for a month. She felt like some moon in his orbit, affected by his storms as much as his calm. And yet again she'd tried to resist his pull, but in the end, she couldn't stay away. She didn't want to.

The food kept coming as the violinists returned to the stage. It was too loud for small talk, but Brynn shot an occasional polite wave to the bigwigs seated around them as she tried to relax and enjoy the ambience. As she tried not to think about the palpable tension between her and the gorgeous man next to her.

She still couldn't believe she had reached out and caressed his thigh, the impulse leaping from her body before she could stop herself. For that, she would definitely be blaming the bubbly.

But before she could pull her hand away, Jordan had placed his hand over hers, pressing her fingers against his thigh with such need, that her heart slammed against her ribcage. Suddenly, the cacophony went mute, and everything disappeared except the places his body touched hers.

He'd released his grip when the food came, instead pressing his knee against hers the rest of the meal. Brynn felt lightheaded as she realized he was touching her where no one could see. A part of her had feared he was just showing off for Homestead, but now, she allowed herself to hope he was coming back to her.

A cranberry-topped cheesecake was placed in front of Brynn, while a waiter poured espresso into a tiny pristine cup. She dabbed at her neck with her lace napkin before downing the rest of her ice water. Coffee would be a good thing after nearly three full glasses of champagne. As the bitter liquid warmed her mouth, she decided she'd done enough thinking and interpreting for one day. She was going to enjoy this afternoon; enjoy this dynamic, thoughtful man. Whatever it meant, wherever it was going, she could figure it out later.

The guests slowly migrated back to the living room where white folding chairs had been arranged in neat rows. On each seat sat a metallic silver gift bag tied with a satin ribbon, and when Brynn peeked inside, she found a bottle of the bougie champagne they'd been served all afternoon. She laughed when Jordan elbowed her, his eyes wide at the bottle sticking out of his own bag.

As she waited for the room to settle, Brynn tugged her phone from her tiny handbag, and she saw a waiting text from Katie:

All's well @ Planted – lots of last min. shoppers! I got it covered and video uploaded. Call me later & tell me EVERYTHING.

Brynn sent off a quick reply and dropped her phone back into the clutch, just as Jordan laced his fingers through hers, resting her hand in his lap. Though heat flooded her throat, and her stomach was twisting into a pretzel, she kept her eyes at the front of the room. She could imagine how they looked to the rest of the room: a happy couple with an exciting future. It wouldn't be easy, and they would both have to compromise, but maybe—just maybe—they could make this work.

A minute later, she watched as Mark shook countless hands on his way to the stage. "Thank you for such a great celebration, everyone!" he boomed into the mic, raising his hands to silence the effusive crowd as a few stragglers hurried to their seats.

"I know I told you Homesteaders we'd be talking Christmas parade today, but..." Mark shrugged and flashed the audience a playful grin. "Work can wait 'til tomorrow, right?"

A smatter of applause and cheers greeted his words and Brynn got the feeling Mark was well-liked by his employees. She couldn't help but think that by this time next year, she might be an employee of sorts too. An actual Los Angelean. What was it Katie told her they called themselves?

Angelenos.

The word felt impossibly foreign.

"I'm thrilled to introduce a video editing team put together in honor of Urban Farm's journey," Mark continued as a projection screen automatically lowered behind him. "It's not every day a show reaches fifty episodes!"

The crowd went wild, and Georgina blew the crowd a kiss as Paul put his hands together in a sign of gratitude before wrapping his arms around his wife.

The lights dimmed and the words "Happy Holidays, from our family to yours!" filled the screen.

Brynn settled in her chair, resting her head on Jordan's shoulder as she watched a montage of photos of a younger Georgina and Paul. Her stomach fluttered a moment later when Jordan rested his own head against hers. She could hear his heartbeat, and she could smell cologne mixed with his usual soapy scent. She smiled as she pictured him saving it for special occasions.

The screen went black for a few seconds and the crowd exchanged looks of good-natured excitement. But when the screen filled once more, it wasn't with Georgina and Paul—it was with Brynn and Caleb. Every part of Brynn turned to ice as her brain processed the grainy image she was seeing.

The room began to swim as Brynn frantically scanned the audience, but it impossible to find any familiar faces in the darkened room. She couldn't breathe as she turned to find Jordan staring at the screen with dull, vacant eyes, and even in the darkness she could see his colorless face.

Suddenly, the frozen image began to move, and Brynn gasped and clutched her mouth as she realized it was a video.

What was this?

She felt Jordan's body stiffen and he jerked his hand from her grip, but she couldn't tear her eyes from the screen. As the video zoomed out to reveal a background of tagged pine trees, Brynn realized it was the night of the carnival. Her temples pounded as she tried to understand what was happening.

Suddenly, she heard her own voice emanate across the rapt crowd.

"All I care about is making money and getting famous," she watched herself say. *"I'm a fake—and fans are pathetic—and not even worth it."*

Brynn's mouth fell open in horror as the footage played on. The video was clearly pieced together, the way it jumped around in time and excluded Caleb's side of the conversation completely. Her dress clung to her clammy chest as she willed herself to stay in her seat, hiding herself in the somewhat anonymous cover of the dim lighting.

She hadn't said those words. In fact, she'd never *thought* those words. She forced her eyes back to the screen. Though her magnified lips continued to move, her words became unintelligible as tiny white sparks flashed in her periphery. She forced herself to keep her face neutral, even as her intestines swelled with dread as she felt a hundred heads swivel in her direction.

Why wasn't anyone stopping this? She could just make out Mark Barnes huddled with Sofia Camp as another man repeatedly tapped a remote. And that's when it finally hit Brynn. Someone had hijacked the presentation.

A sudden violent fury pulsed through her as she fought to keep down her coconut shrimp. Only one person was capable of something this malicious.

"The stuff online is all for show," she heard herself say, the words flowing past in impossible defiance. *"They're going to kill—the plant—anyway."* The room began to spin, and she felt like she was trapped. *"... I'm not dating Jordan. He is nothing to me. The fans love it."*

No, no, no, no.

Those words she remembered, at least some of them. She'd said them so Caleb would tell Jessica to leave Jordan alone. She'd said them to *protect* him, but it all sounded so wrong. She was terrified to look at Jordan's face.

But the video just kept going.

"You're a great guy Caleb." Brynn stared at her lap, knowing she might vomit if she looked at the screen. *"The night we had meant something,"* she heard herself impossibly say. *"I was just waiting for you, hoping you'd give me another chance."*

Oh. My. God.

Just as Brynn was about to surrender to a death of shameful humiliation, the audio stopped, and she looked up. But it still wasn't over, and this time, the video zoomed in even closer. She felt a wave of repulsion as she watched Caleb kiss her, dread slicing through her as she remembered what came next. She couldn't look away as she watched herself lean into Caleb's embrace. The footage cut to black just before she had pushed him away. She began to shake uncontrollably.

Someone turned the lights back on.

"Jordan," Brynn whispered, desperately tugging on his arm, but his eyes were hard and unreadable as he jerked away.

Before she could say another word, he fled, barreling over the knees beside them on his way to the aisle as people scrambled to move out of the way. She was vaguely aware Mark was speaking into the microphone, not that it mattered. All eyes were on her.

"Jordan!" Brynn whisper-shouted, grabbing her purse as she climbed over the back of her chair and chased after him. She could feel her career shattering into a thousand pieces with every step, but in that moment, all she cared about was him.

"Jordan, *wait!*" she yelled, no longer bothering to keep her voice down. Her toe caught on a chair leg, but she caught herself as her hands slammed onto the cold marble. "Sorry," she muttered to no one in particular, as she picked up her purse and scrambled to her feet. She could feel hundreds of eyes boring into her back as she ran.

She finally caught up to Jordan in the foyer, and the broken pain in his eyes as he took his jacket made her feel as if a grenade had detonated inside her.

"Jordan, please!" she begged, barely able to speak as she tried to catch her breath. She grabbed his arm, but before she could turn him to face her, he roughly shook her off. "I know how bad that looks," she said, tears blurring her vision. "But just let me explain, please—"

"I'm leaving," Jordan interrupted in a curt, cool voice that sent daggers through her stomach. "Ask Caleb to drive you home."

"What—no!" she protested, shoving herself in his path and forcing him to stop. "You must have seen how that video was cut together, right? All choppy, and some of it was even out of order, I swear—"

"I don't care, Brynn," Jordan said through gritted teeth, disgust dripping off every letter of her name as he pushed past her. He charged outside, ducking his head against the brittle wind as he ripped his valet ticket from his pocket.

"You know Jessica did this!" Brynn shouted, not bothering to get her own jacket as she followed right at his heels.

"All the signs were there, every red flag, and I just kept ignoring them," Jordan spat, finally turning to face her. His eyes were brimming with an electric rage that sent fear rippling down her spine. "From the beginning, I knew better. I *knew it*, any yet I kept going." He shook his head. "I'm honestly glad this happened," he said with a cold hollow sound, and as Brynn realized he was laughing, began to sob. "I got lucky this happened," he added, staring right into her blurry eyes.

"Jordan, please!" she pleaded. "If you would just give me two minutes, I—"

"Brynn, *stop*!" Jordan bellowed.

She froze, but her uncontrollable heaving sobs continued. She'd never heard him yell before.

He let out a shuddering sigh of desperation.

"I'm not mad at you," he finally said, his voice weary as a sad smile twisted the corner of his mouth. "I'm mad at myself."

She opened her mouth to speak, but closed it when he shook his head, watching as the valet handed over his key fob before Jordan passed him a folded bill.

"This is not the kind of place for me," Jordan continued, the anger in face replaced with an expression of weary defeat. "Not this plastic, photoshopped world, broadcast for the whole world to see." He pressed his lips into a line. "Thank God I saw that before I lost more of my life than I already have."

"Jordan, please," Brynn said, her words were almost a whisper.

"Don't come back to Evergreen Acres," Jordan said matter-of-factly, which somehow hurt even worse. He swung open his door, glancing back only once with those steely umber-colored eyes. "Find someone else you can use to get your dream job."

Jordan's face blurred as a fresh wave of blistering tears flooded Brynn's eyes, clumping her carefully applied mascara as they tumbled down her face. He climbed into his truck, slamming the door, and the valet jumped out of the way as he pealed out down the driveway.

"Miss?"

Brynn turned as yet another tuxedoed member of the household staff held out her leather jacket.

"Thank you," she said, taking it before wiping her nose on her bare wrist.

"Do you need some help?" the woman asked, genuine kindness in her eyes.

"No, I'll be fine," Brynn said weakly. "Thanks, though."

Once the woman followed the valet driver back inside, Brynn was alone. She took a deep, shuddering breath and watched as the vapors from her lips turned to smoke. She pressed her eyes shut and swiped at her cheeks before pulling her phone from her purse.

"Mom?" she said, in a shaky voice when she heard the line pick up. "Can you come get me?"

THIRTY

"Eat," Greta commanded, sliding a plate in front of Brynn. Brynn eyed the cheesy scrambled eggs, made the way her mother knew she liked them.

"Thanks," Brynn said, hiding her face in her folded arms.

"You have to eat something, honey," Greta said, scooting a chair beside Brynn.

"My stomach hurts," Brynn said. She finally looked up and the concern in those familiar eyes demolished the dam that had been keeping her words at bay. "I ruined everything, Mom," she continued. "Jordan hates me—"

"Oh, he doesn't hate you," Greta interrupted.

"He watched Caleb kiss me in his own front yard," Brynn said. "I would hate me too." She sniffed and grabbed a tissue from the nearly empty box. "And let's not forget, Evergreen Acres is worse off now than if I had never shown up in the first place."

"That fire had nothing to do with you," Greta said.

"Maybe not, but it's all connected," Brynn said. "He would have been home if I didn't force him to help with my stupid video, and—well, it doesn't even matter. *Nothing* matters." She groaned and stabbed at the eggs before setting her fork back down. "And now, I doubt Homestead TV will even take my calls, let alone offer me a TV show."

"Have you heard from them?" Greta asked and Brynn shook her head. "Well, don't jump to any conclusions. Like you said, the whole thing was suspicious. They're successful businesspeople. I'm sure they can smell a rat."

Brynn sighed. "Everything I've worked so hard for is gone, just like that."

"Now, you know that's not true," Greta said, rubbing Brynn's shoulder. "You have your family. You have some amazing friends, and you have your *shop*. That was also your dream, remember?" Brynn reluctantly nodded as her mom gained momentum. "Go ahead and cuss and cry and mourn. But when that's over, take a minute to remember how much you still have."

"It's just hard to see anything except destruction right now," Brynn sniffled.

"Heartbreak will do that," Greta said, rolling her eyes when Brynn shot her a warning look.

Brynn pressed her hands against her eyes. If this was heartbreak, then she'd never had her heart truly broken before.

"Listen, sweetheart," Greta said, scooting the eggs closer and stealing a bite. "I know it may not seem like it now, but you'll be OK. It's just a run of bad, dumb luck, but none of this makes you a bad person."

"Tell that to Jordan," Brynn muttered. "He already thought the odds were stacked against him and then I came along and made everything worse."

"Brynn," Greta said, squeezing her hand reassuringly. "You know who you are, and just as importantly, you know who you are *not*. It's not your job to make people see that."

Brynn glanced over Greta's shoulder as the back door flew open and a harried-looking Katie swept into the room.

"There you are!" Katie huffed, breathless as her eyes skipped from Brynn to Greta. "Hey, Mrs. C."

"Will you eat?" Greta asked as she stood, offering her chair to Katie as she headed toward the stove. "Be a shame for all this to go to waste."

"Well, I won't say no to that," Katie said, her eyes widening as she saw the platter of waffles on the counter. "Thank you."

Katie pulled off her coat and draped it over the back of the chair as she took a sip from a steaming mug that Greta set in front of her.

"I've been calling you non-stop, but it just goes straight to voicemail," Katie scolded. "I had no idea where you were."

"Sorry, I haven't charged my phone," Brynn said. "How did you know where to find me?"

"She called me looking for you," Greta said as she slid a sheet of waffles back into the oven to warm.

"Are you okay, Bee?" Katie asked, her eyes full of concern.

"Oh, I've been better," Brynn said wryly, then steeled herself and turned to face her friend. She sighed. "How bad is it?"

"Well, it's not great," Katie said, keeping her voice light.

"I figured," Brynn said. "And the network?"

"Not taking my calls," Katie said apologetically.

Brynn groaned and pressed her forehead into her hands.

"Jessica is such a snake!" Katie said, her words full of conviction. "Homestead must be able to see right through her."

"It wouldn't change things for me if they do," Brynn said, feeling numb. "There's enough truth in that video to put an end to my chances once and for all." She dabbed her nose with the tissue. "My mom was right; I can't keep pretending to be someone I'm not."

"That's not exactly what I said," Greta protested as she set a bottle of syrup on the table.

"Well, it's true, Mom," Brynn said, feeling exhausted to her bones she watched a few snowflakes lazily drift past the garden window.

"Well, it's only a few days until Christmas," Katie said, forking a bite of Brynn's eggs. "Maybe everyone is just off work." She shrugged, but her voice had lost most of its assurance. "Maybe they've already forgotten all about the lunch."

"We both know that's not true," Brynn grumbled, but she appreciated her friend's effort.

"Why don't you take the day off," Katie said, raising her hands to silence Brynn before she could argue. "The shop is doing great, and I can handle it just fine." She pressed her lips together and gave the air a pointed sniff. "Besides, you're in no shape to see customers."

"I can't ask you to do that again," Brynn protested.

"You didn't ask," Katie said. "And it's not up for negotiation."

Brynn sighed. "I don't deserve you."

"But you do," Katie said, taking her by the shoulders and putting her face close to Brynn's. "And even if you can't see that, I can."

"I just don't know where it all went wrong," Brynn said, new tears waiting their turn in line.

"Maybe one day this will be a good thing," Katie said before shoving a chunk of buttery waffle into her mouth.

Brynn shot her a look.

Yeah, right.

"Hear me out," Katie said, swallowing and wiping her mouth with a napkin. "This is a chance to get back to your roots." She smirked. "Pun intended."

Brynn groaned, but her mind was churning through everything Katie had said. She couldn't remember the last time she felt like she was in the cockpit, not strapped into coach hoping she'd gotten on the right plane. Maybe Katie was right.

Her throat felt raw as she accepted a glass of apple juice from her mother. Brynn knew the only thing that might make her feel better would be to stick her hands in some potting mix and plant something. When nothing else seemed to make sense, Brynn could always find solace in her little green world. The more she thought about it, she realized she couldn't remember the last time she'd gardened just for fun. At least not when the cameras weren't rolling.

She stopped.

The cameras.

"Kate, will you give me a ride home?" Brynn asked.

"Course," Katie said through a mouthful of waffle.

"Thanks," Brynn said, as something began to take shape in her mind. "There's something I want to do."

"Good morning!" Gina called, her voice a little too cheerful to be believable as Jordan trudged through the gray slush between that led to the shop.

He grunted a vague reply as he climbed the porch, resisting an urge to yank the wreath from Gina's hands and toss it on the woodpile. Instead, he bit his cheek and held the wreath steady as Gina wrapped a wire around a pinecone, securing it into place.

As she added a few more pinecones, Gina shot furtive glances in his direction, which Jordan pretended not to notice.

"So, how are we this morning?" Gina asked, cautiously.

"I know you saw the video," Jordan said quietly.

"I promised myself I'd let you bring it up," Gina said with a mixture of embarrassment and relief. "Didn't it seem weird to you?" she asked. "First, how it was edited together all weird, I'd like to know how it ended up online before that lunch thing even ended."

"I just don't care, Gina!" Jordan said, more sharply than he intended. He heaved an exhausted sigh. "I'm sorry. I'm just spent."

"I know," Gina said, picking a stray leaf that had landed on his shoulder. "And you know we're all here for you." She hesitated and appeared to carefully consider her next words. "I think you should watch that video one more time, maybe see if you can read between the lines."

"I appreciate what you're trying to do," Jordan said, putting the wreath back on its hook on the front door. "But I'm staying offline for now. Things were much easier when I still lived in the Stone Age."

He stomped the muck from his boots before wiping them on the mat for good measure.

"Thought I would put together the addresses for today's deliveries," Jordan said.

"It sure was nice of the mayor's boys to offer to help," Gina said brightly.

He nodded, but he didn't tell her how pointless it all felt.

"Oh, I grabbed the mail," Gina said, passing him a stack of envelopes. "Jordan, have you looked in a mirror?" she asked as he flipped through the stack, relieved when he didn't find yet another certified letter from the bank. "If you came to my door in the dark," she continued, "I'd probably hide and call 911." She chuckled. "What you need is a nap, a shave, and a good cry."

"How can you be so upbeat?" Jordan asked. "All we've got left is the death rattle."

"Folks are still coming in!" she scolded, swatting him on the shoulder. "And you know wreaths are a big last-minute seller. It ain't over 'til it's over!"

Jordan's groaned as his eyes landed on a glossy postcard with a cartoonish fire hydrant wrapped in Christmas lights: *Buy Your Tickets Now to the Christmas Eve Firefighter Ball!*

It seemed a million years ago, laughing with Brynn at the carnival, as they agreed to give the annual Christmas wish.

"Oooh, the Firefighter Ball!" Gina exclaimed, following his gaze. "If I close up in time, I'm stopping at the mall to look for something glitzy."

"I'm just not feeling it," Jordan said.

"I think anyone can understand why," Gina said kindly, "but you'll go. You're a man of your word." She patted him gently on his bicep. "Besides, we owe the fire department a lot of gratitude for what they did out here."

That was an understatement. Sure, they'd lost a lot of trees in the time it took for the fire to be called in and the various departments to arrive, but it could have been so much worse.

Jordan could picture all those volunteer firefighters, kissing their kids goodnight or just sitting down at the movie theater as their phones pinged with the emergency. He would never be able to properly thank them for what they'd saved.

"Why don't you take the morning off?" Jordan suggested. "Head to town and find something to wear."

"That's mighty kind," Gina said. "But the mall's open until nine, maybe even later with Christmas coming."

"I insist," Jordan said firmly as he managed a weak smile. "I need to get all this paperwork in order anyway." He gestured to the empty parking lot. "I think I can handle these giant crowds."

"Well, if you insist," Gina said, and a giddy joy spread across her face. "I'll call my girlfriends and see if they want to meet for lunch. Want me to grab you something snazzy while I'm out?"

"I've got a tux already," Jordan said.

"With a boring black bowtie!" Gina cackled. "I'll keep my eyes open for something a little more festive."

Gina headed into the shop and Jordan slowly followed. As he stepped into the cozy pine-scented store, he heard a whirring sound high his head and looked up. A little model train was creaking its way around the ceiling, its muffled whistle blaring every so often. He remembered that sound, echoing from some place deep in his childhood.

"Nice touch, huh?" Gina asked, coming up behind him with her coat and purse in hand. "Brynn pulled that from the back before the carnival. Was it your dad's?"

"My mom's," Jordan said quietly. "But I don't understand, the engine went missing more than a decade ago."

He could feel Gina's eyes on him, but he kept his face even.

"Brynn said she found it in a secondhand shop," she said, clucking approvingly. "That girl can be a bit of a hot mess, but she's got a heart of gold."

Jordan swallowed the knot in his throat as he headed behind the counter, knocking over a candy cane yard sign on his way.

As he clicked the mouse to wake the computer, he met Gina's eyes.

"I'm fine, Gina," he said.

"Well, then, off I go," she said with a hint of reluctance. "Call me if you need anything."

Jordan grunted a farewell. Sure, it felt good to give Gina a fun day in town. But more than that, he was glad to be alone.

THIRTY-ONE

"Merry Christmas!" Brynn said, forcing the holiday cheer as she held open the door for a customer to exit. She rubbed her hands together as she entered the cozy shop, willing her teeth to stop chattering as she flipped the sign on the door to *Closed for Lunch!* before locking the deadbolt.

"What are you doing here?" Katie asked, glancing at her watch as she came out from behind the register. She looked like a little short-haired troll doll, with her green spiky hair and her round eyes wide with concern.

"Let's make a video," Brynn said.

Katie looked thoroughly confused, but in true form, she followed Brynn to the back without a word.

Greta was right; Brynn did still have so much good in her life. But if some of it had to burn, she wasn't about to let Jessica's match do it. Those flames would only come from Brynn.

"Do you want to rehearse?" Katie asked, setting up the camera on the tripod.

"Nope," Brynn said, flipping on the filming lights, her heart thumping against her ribs. "Today, we're improvising."

"You're the boss, Bee!" Katie said, inserting a memory card and a fresh battery into the camera as Brynn pulled out her compact and applied a layer of ChapStick to her otherwise bare face.

"That's what you're wearing?" Katie asked, nodding to the faded cactus hoodie Brynn's mom had brought her back from Sedona.

"Yep," Brynn said and to her credit, Katie simply shook her head and finished setting up.

"Hey, Kate," Brynn said as she stashed her bag under the table.

"Mm hmm," Katie said distractedly as she raised the tripod.

"I love you," Brynn said, her voice breaking a little on the words.

"Well, my love language is clearly acts of service," Katie said with a grin, pointing to the camera.

Brynn laughed, but a little tear snuck down her cheek before she could swipe it away.

"Let's do this," she said. She twisted her hair into a topknot she didn't bother to check and grabbed a heart leaf philodendron, its long tendrils dragging on the ground as she carried it to the table and gently placing set it in the center.

As Katie cued up the camera and began her countdown, Brynn rubbed her thumb over the little leaves, remembering how often she'd done that in college, almost like a security blanket. This plant was even older than her friendship with Katie.

The red light blinked expectantly at Brynn. She shoved her shoulders back and took a deep breath.

"This was one of my very first plants," Brynn said into the lens, placing both hands on the ceramic pot. "I got it my freshman year when I was lonely and homesick, and for a whole year, this plant was my best friend."

"I talked to this plant a lot," Brynn continued. "And I still talk to plants the way some people talk to dogs, baby voice and all."

She could see Katie emphatically nodding from the shadows and Brynn bit back a laugh.

"This plant might be special, but it's far from rare," Brynn continued, picking up pace. "You could drive down to Publix and get one right now." She rubbed a smooth leaf between her fingertips. "It's basic, ordinary, and if you ignore it for a few weeks, you might find it's grown into a tangled mess. Pretty much like me."

She smiled at her own lame joke.

"I first started making videos to connect with like-minded folks; folks who got along as well as I did with plants. It was fun to share my garden and to see what other people were growing. But somewhere along the way, I lost sight of where I started."

She swallowed, and her heart thundered as she forgot all about the lens and the blinking red light.

"The truth is I hate wearing makeup every day," she said, "just like I hate plants that need a full-time babysitter." She reached below the counter. "So, I'm done!"

She pulled out a jumble of brown shriveled vines, the last green, Swiss-cheese filigree barely visible.

"This is my Monstera Obliqua, the one so many of you are hoping to win," she said, with frank, unapologetic honesty. "I killed it. If you want high-maintenance plants that cost a small fortune, go watch *The Green Goddess*. I'll even link you to her page in the comments."

Though she couldn't see Katie's face through the bright lights, Brynn could imagine her shocked expression. Brynn took a deep breath and continued.

"I know everyone has seen the video by now," she said before biting her lip and bursting into laughter. "I guess I should clarify *which* video, huh?"

She braced her hands on the edge of the old wooden table and stared right down the barrel as she held up a finger.

"Here's what's true: One—I did act like a compete monster at Grantway Market." She flipped a second finger, then a third. "Two—I only went Evergreen Acres because I wanted you all to like me better. Three—I pretended Jordan was by boyfriend so Homestead would give me my own TV show."

As she kept talking, the words came easier, and she felt lighter than she had in weeks.

"I'm going to keep making videos, even if none of you are here to watch them." She shrugged. "They're going to be about whatever I find interesting, not what I think you want to see. It's going to be weird and nerdy and possibly messy as hell, but you know what?" She stuck out her chin and smiled. "That's who I am."

Burn, baby, burn.

"If you're still watching, I need you to know something before you click that unsubscribe button," she said, emotion in her voice. "Everything I said about Evergreen Acres was an understatement. Those pine-scented fields are a part of history, so much more important than anything you can buy with a swipe or a click." She took a shallow breath. "If you believe in hope and faith and community, the true spirit of Christmas, then I need your help. One last time."

Jordan yawned and stretched his arms over his head, unsure when the world outside the window had darkened to black. He glanced at his watch and realized he should have locked up an hour ago. He didn't feel especially tired; it was more of a numb, vacant feeling. He stood and cracked his back, pushing the wooden chair under the counter before setting the computer to sleep.

It wasn't until he'd grabbed his coat and switched off the house lights that Jordan realized the little train set was still circling the ceiling. He tipped his head back and watched as it doggedly chugged along on its ancient track. He couldn't believe Brynn had remembered the missing engine, and his chest lurched into a throbbing ache as her pictured her delicate round face, with those exuberant green eyes.

A part of him felt pity towards Brynn, anger that someone would go to such lengths to humiliate her not only in front of the network, but the entire world.

But another part, an even bigger part was mortified. Jordan had been lying to himself. He hadn't been keeping his emotions out of it, not like he'd promised himself over and over. That woman had snuck her way into every fiber of his being, and he hadn't even realized how far gone he had been until it was all over.

He couldn't breathe just thinking about the video, as if someone kept continuously knocking the wind out of him. He could still see Caleb's arm pressing Brynn close before he pressed his mouth on hers. Jordan wanted to punch him in his stupid face, but he knew he would go through with it if he ever got the chance. Jordan may not like the guy, but he hadn't owned him a thing. When it came down to it, Brynn hadn't owed him anything either.

He couldn't remember what time he'd last eaten. Despite the fact that his last drink had been the expensive champagne at the party, Jordan felt hungover and disconnected. He braced a hand against the wall as the engine sped along above him. Before he could stop it, flashes of their night in the farmhouse suddenly seized every molecule of his mind. Brynn's wet lips drawing goosebumps down his flesh. Her smooth thigh wrapped around his bare torso. The electric shock that permeated them both when he'd lost all control and melted entirely into her body.

A low, quaking moan erupted from deep within him and as he bit his fist hard until the image faded. He pulled himself together and tugged the dangling switch, waiting for the train to stop chuffing.

The bell on the door jingled as he heard footsteps enter the shop.

Great.

"Sorry, we're closed!" Jordan called, composing himself as best as he could before stepping around the tree stand display.

He froze as everything in him turned to venom.

Caleb stood a few feet away, self-consciously gripping the strap of a messenger bag that was slung over one lean shoulder.

"What's up, man?" Caleb said, managing a small smile as his eyes darted around the empty store.

"What do you want?" Jordan asked in a flat voice.

"I want to talk to you," Caleb said.

"No, thanks," Jordan said, not bothering to hide the brittle anger that brimmed to the surface. "I need to lock up and you need to leave."

"I told Brynn to give me another chance," Caleb said, moving to block Jordan's path. "I love her, and—"

"Are you deaf?!" Jordan barked. "I don't care." He took menacing step closer to Caleb. "What the hell is wrong with you, man?"

But Caleb just stood there and gaped as if he were actually

afraid of Jordan.

Fine.

If he wouldn't leave, Jordan would. He resisted the urge to shoulder check Caleb as he beelined for the door. He could lock up later.

"She turned me down!" Caleb shouted, and Jordan's hand froze on the metal handle. "She's in love with you," he added, quieter now, a note of dejection in his voice.

Jordan swallowed and insides twisted and grinded in fury. He forced his face steady as he slowly turned back.

"I'm pretty sure we saw different videos, pal," Jordan said, completely aware of how hulking it made him look as he crossed his arms over his chest.

"I'm pretty sure we did too," Caleb said, eyeing him nervously before digging his hand into his bag.

Jordan watched with a cold fixed stare as Caleb pulled out a laptop.

"May I?" Caleb asked, gesturing toward the counter.

Jordan shrugged. "Whatever."

"Jessica filmed what I thought was a private conversation between me and Brynn," Caleb said, setting the computer on the counter beside the desktop.

"Yeah, no shit," Jordan said. "What's your point?"

"She cut it together to make Brynn look terrible," Caleb said. "She was really angry with me after she saw me with Brynn."

"Jessica sounds like a real sweetheart," Jordan said coolly.

"She was understandably jealous," Caleb said as he clicked his track pad. "But, yeah, I know. I didn't know she could be like that."

"I have to go," Jordan said, trying his best not to raise his voice. "I don't really care what you have to say. I heard what she said about me, and let's not pretend that kiss was somehow photoshopped together."

"The kiss *was* real, but I kissed her, and she pulled away and—"

"It doesn't matter!" Jordan roared and he felt a surge of satisfaction as Caleb's blue eyes went wide. "I don't know you, Caleb," Jordan said, impatience and frustration threatening to burst forth at any time. "I'm sure you're a perfectly nice guy." He gritted his teeth and pressed an angry finger against his own chest. "Me and Brynn? We both used each other. Maybe she got a better deal, or maybe we both lost, but either way, it's over."

He pressed the heel of his hand against his temple as his pulse began to drum behind his eyes. "I'm not going to stand in your way if you're looking for my blessing," Jordan said with a contemptuous chuckle. "Good luck to you, man."

"I gave Jessica an ultimatum," Caleb said, as if he hadn't heard a word. "If she handed over the full, unedited footage of our conversation with Brynn, I would make sure it stayed anonymous." He swallowed and leveled his gaze to Jordan. "And if she didn't? I'd make sure everyone of her millions of followers knew what she did."

Jordan just blinked and said nothing. Why wouldn't this guy just leave?

"Tell you what," Caleb said, running a hand through his douchey surfer highlights. He ejected a memory card from the laptop and made sure Jordan was watching as he set it on the counter before slipping his computer back into his bag. "I have another copy at home. What you do with it is up to you."

"Why do you care?" Jordan asked.

"I'm just trying to make things right," Caleb said, and Jordan hated to admit he believed him.

"Brynn's the most amazing woman I've ever met," Caleb said, turning back from the open door as a blast of frigid air rustled through the store. "I hope she finds what she's looking for." He managed a somber smile. "If that means you, well...then you're the luckiest guy on the planet."

And with that, he disappeared into the night, leaving Jordan more confused than ever.

THIRTY-TWO

"Hello? Earth to Brynn!"

Katie's snapping fingers jerked Brynn back into reality. She knew she was spiraling, but she couldn't help it. Her fantasy had flitted back and forth from imagining everyone unsubscribing to her channel, to picturing a leasing sign on her store's window as she packed as many plants as she could into the back of the Civic.

"You might as well take off now if you're just going to dwell anyway," Katie said, raising an eyebrow as she smiled at Brynn.

"I don't even know what time it is," Brynn said, sighing as she glanced at her watch. "You sure you don't want me to help with the poinsettia order?"

"For the third time, *I'm sure,*" Katie said, shaking her head as if she didn't know what do with Brynn. "Go on, get out of here!"

"Well, promise you'll call me if you get slammed," Brynn said, reluctantly scooping up her purse and jacket.

"It's Christmas Eve," Katie reminded her, shoving her towards the door. "I doubt anyone even knows we're open. I brought my clothes with me, so I'll change here and meet you at the fire station."

"OK, if you're sure," Brynn replied, aiming for nonchalant, but her voice came out a few octaves higher than usual.

Katie grabbed her and pulled her in to a bone-crushing hug.

"You got this," she said. "Trust me."

Brynn took a deep breath, in and out, before she pulled away.

"You're right," Brynn said. "Thanks, Kate."

"You sure I don't look ridiculous?" Jordan asked, catching his reflection in the glass door before he swung it open.

"It's a hunter green bowtie," Gina said, rolling her eyes. "If I had my way, it would have been the one with the light-up ornaments."

"Well, at least you gave me options," Jordan said with a laugh as Gina swatted away his hands before he could make the bow crooked. He waited as she adjusted it until it met her approval.

Megan and Charlie hurried over from the parking lot as Jordan held the door open against the biting wind.

"Who's ready to party?" Charlie asked, grinning as he held open his jacket to reveal red suspenders that bordered his ample belly.

"Men!" Gina said, throwing a beleaguered look to Megan who laughed as they hurried into the warmth of the glowing hallway.

As they joined the queue of guests, Jordan realized he'd forgotten how much the fire department decorated at Christmas. They weren't even in the cafeteria yet, but every inch of the 1970's building was decked out in glittery snowflakes hung from fishing wire and hundreds of blinking ivory lights. The hum of music ricocheted down the hallway, and Jordan remembered hearing that a local jazz band would be taking requests all night.

They wiped their feet before stepping onto the pristine red carpet, where, if Jordan's memory served correctly, they'd find a photo op with a backdrop to rival any Hollywood movie premiere.

Charlie's eyes were glittering with anticipation and Jordan felt a pang in his gut as he wondered if his dad had accepted their new reality. Maybe he was just better at ignoring it.

"So, am I finally going to meet this mystery man?" Jordan asked, nudging his sister with his elbow.

"I never said anything about a mystery man," Megan said, her eyes widening in innocence.

"I thought I was the only one in the dark," Charlie said, grinning.

Megan's face flushed bright red.

"I can't blame the woman, the way you two hassle her," Gina said, swatting Charlie with the back of her hand. "Ain't nobody's business but their own."

"Thanks, Gina," Megan said as the line slowly inched forward. "But I can handle those two."

When they reached the end of the red carpet, they indulged Gina as she ordered them to pose in front of the backdrop stamped with the department's acronym TFFD, something Brynn would call a 'step and repeat'. In one photo, Charlie stuck his gut out even further than Santa's and Megan was laughing so hard that tears streamed down her cheeks. Still, Jordan couldn't help but feel they were missing someone.

As Jordan threw open the heavy oak doors, they were engulfed by the sounds of a jazzy rendition of "Santa Claus is Coming to Town." Whoops and cheers filled the packed room, though the only people on the dance floor were lots of twisting children and one young couple managing to slow dance to the peppy rhythm.

The rest of the crowd was standing in the buffet line or circling the bar. Jordan planned to get his hands on something strong as soon as possible. As they found some empty chairs to dump their coats, Jordan willed himself not to look for Brynn.

"Merry Christmas, folks!" Mayor Lopez shouted, clapping them each into a quick handshake-hug as they exchanged greetings.

His jolly face grew somber as he gripped Charlie's hands between his own. "I'm so sorry to hear about Evergreen Acres."

"Thanks, Carl," Charlie said, nodding politely, but Jordan could see him swallowing his emotion.

"Evergreen Acres had a great run," Jordan said, taking a deep breath. "I can't believe this is how it ends."

"Personally, I'm still holding out for a Christmas miracle," the mayor said, forcing a confident smile. "But in the meantime, if there's anything I can do, please let me know."

"Thank you," Jordan said. "You've always been so good to us."

"Where's Brynn?" the mayor asked, looking behind them as if she might pop out from beneath their jackets.

"She's not here?" Jordan asked.

"I thought she'd come with you," the mayor said, and Jordan could tell from his earnest expression that he wasn't an active YouTuber. "Well, it's still early. Grab some food. The choir starts in ten minutes!"

"Will do," Jordan said, eyeing the bar.

"I've got dinner plans myself," Mayor Lopez said, throwing Jordan a wink as he walked away and offered his arm to someone. She gave a wave to Jordan, and he recognized Greta, wearing a splash of lipstick and a velvet black dress. He smiled and raised his hand, noticing Brynn was nowhere to be found.

Jordan slid his phone from his pocket, his thumb hovering

above the darkened lock screen.

"Shall we grab something with a kick?" Charlie asked, nodding toward the bar.

"Absolutely," Jordan said, putting away his phone.

If she decided to bail, he couldn't blame her. In fact, he couldn't blame her one bit if she'd already decided to move on.

THIRTY-THREE

"Hey, this is Katie Dilworth!" a voice chirped through the Civic's toasty interior.

Brynn groaned and hung up, tossing her cell onto the passenger seat.

Where was she? They were supposed to meet almost an hour ago. Brynn had found a spot in the corner of the lot where she sat idling, watching the influx of guests trickle down as hardly anyone gave her a second look.

She watched the firehouse entrance and sighed. She might already be too late. Maybe she should just head home.

But then, she pictured Jordan standing there, frozen on the stage just as he'd been at the tree lighting. She could see the hurt in his face when he realized she had misled him once again.

No.

She was going to have to put on her big girl panties and walk through those doors alone

...in ten minutes. She'd give Katie ten more minutes to show up. She glanced at her phone once more before pounding the wheel in frustration.

"Ready?" Mayor Lopez asked.

Jordan tore his gaze from the couple taking selfies in front of the Christmas tree and tried to regain his composure.

"As I'm gonna be," he replied.

"No Brynn, huh?" the mayor asked gently.

Jordan shook his head. "I guess not."

"Well, I'll buy you a drink to commiserate later," the mayor said, putting an arm around him as he guided him toward the stage. "In the meantime, it looks like you'll have to give the Christmas wish alone."

Jordan's face must have betrayed his anxiety.

"Listen, there's nothing to be nervous about," the mayor said, gripping his shoulder. "Keep it short and festive and you can't go wrong!" he lowered his voice conspiratorially. "Were you here the year we had that pro-wrestler give the wish?"

"I don't think so," Jordan said, not really paying attention.

"Her Christmas wish was, 'Stay wicked, Twin Falls.'" Mayor Lopez made a face. "That was the whole speech! You couldn't do worse than that if you tried."

"Yeah, I'm sure it will be fine," Jordan said, thinking of the generic comments he'd scribbled on the index cards in the lapel of his tux. It certainly wasn't worse than that speech, but he didn't think it was much better. It was in that moment that he admitted to himself he had truly believed Brynn would show up.

Mayor Lopez gave him one more friendly squeeze before mounting the stage. Jordan waited on the side, staring out at the crowd as he sipped his old fashioned. Everyone was dancing and eating, drinking and talking, but as soon as the mayor tapped the microphone, they all turned expectantly toward the stage, hundreds of smiling faces pointed his direction. Jordan's heart began to thunder.

"Ladies and gentlemen...Merry Christmas Eve!" Mayor Lopez boomed, and the crowd roared back with cheers and enthusiastic applause. "Thank you all for coming out tonight and for being here for one of our time-honored traditions: The Twin Falls Christmas wish!" The crowd erupted. "This blessing for the coming year precedes my time as mayor...back in the Stone Ages, I know!" His joke was met with polite laughter.

"But this year's wish comes to you from our very own Jordan Damon of Evergreen Acres Christmas tree farm!"

The crowd hooted and clapped as Jordan climbed the stage and took the microphone from the mayor.

Jordan's eyes scanned the audience and he silently scolded himself. Did he really think she'd just be standing out there on the dance floor, watching?

"Thank you, Mayor Lopez, and Merry Christmas, everyone," Jordan said as the crowd beamed up at him, and already he was doing better than he'd expected. "I'm especially honored to be here tonight after all the firefighters did to save our farm." The crowd cheered. "Evergreen Acres might not be standing if it wasn't for what you did. Let's hear it for the fire department!"

The crowd let out their loudest whoops yet as Jordan scrambled to organize his index cards.

"Wait!"

The voice thundered from the darkness behind the whispering crowd. A beautiful woman in a glittery red evening gown stepped into the light of the dance floor, her yellow hair tucked into an elegant bun. Her hunter green eyes swept up to meet his and her cherry red lips curled into a nervous smile as she readjusted the package under her arm.

"Brynn?" he said quietly, but the name cascaded into the microphone and across the crowded room where people began to stare between them with growing interest.

The air in Brynn's lungs disappeared as Jordan's eyes swept over her. She took a deep breath, trying to quell the wooziness. Fainting was the last thing she needed right now. She hitched up her skirt and hurried to the stage, stabilizing the giant box under her chin as she climbed the steps.

Her eyes met his and her heart nearly ricocheted off the stage.

"May I say something?" she asked him, amazed her voice came out at all. She tried to still her quivering fingers as they gripped the metallic wrapping paper.

His face was impassive as he gave her a stiff nod. She quickly rested the box on the floor before stepping to the microphone as Jordan stepped away.

"Hi!" Brynn said, wincing as feedback reverberated over the room. "Sorry," she muttered with an embarrassed giggle. Suddenly, she saw her mother in the front row, and Greta gave Brynn an encouraging thumbs up. Brynn made a mental note to ask her mother about the mayor, whose arm that was currently wrapped possessively around her waist.

"Friends and neighbors," Brynn began again, her pulse thundering in her ears. "This town has a legacy of community unlike any I've ever seen. Twin Falls is a place worth fighting for, and it breaks my heart to imagine ever leaving." She took a deep breath and continued. "I have a Christmas wish I'd like to share," she said, then lowered her voice to Jordan. "If it's okay with you." Her heart squeezed as he shrugged and looked everywhere but at her. She steeled herself.

"I wish for us the next year looking out for each other, caring for our neighbors." She was so nervous, she thought she might faint. "And I want to thank all of you for getting that wish started off on the right foot."

She grabbed the wrapped package and shoved it into Jordan's hands.

"Open it," she whispered.

He eyed her suspiciously, but began to tear open the paper, exposing a long white cardboard rectangle. As the bright stage lights illuminated the clumsily drawn border, Brynn felt sick.

This had all been a last-minute idea, and the closest thing the office supply store had to her vision was one of those tri-fold poster boards like she'd used for the science fair in middle school. So, she'd made the best of it, cutting off the outer two panels and carefully writing the words in black marker.

As Jordan tore off the last of the paper, he staggered backward and clutched his chest as if someone had hit him. His face blanched as his confused eyes searched hers.

"What is this?" he asked, his voice barely audible.

He held the board in front of him to take a better look, and the crowd began to cheer as they saw the front. It was a hand drawn check for $150,000.

"Well, it's not actually the real thing," Brynn said quickly, pulling a tiny envelope from her pocket before handing it him.

"But a check didn't really have the same 'wow' factor. I was hoping to come up with something more like the ones on Publishers' Clearing House, but I worked with what I had."

Jordan's mouth opened and closed again, and Brynn's own eyes began to sting as she saw his fill with tears.

"Thank you to everyone for helping me keep this secret," Brynn said as she steeled herself and leaned into the mic. "Thanks to so many of you—and some Evergreen Acres fans around the world— our Christmas wish can begin tonight."

She turned back to Jordan, who was as pale as the new fallen snow.

"Please accept this on behalf of the town that loves you so much," she said, her voice cracking. "To Evergreen Acres!"

"To Evergreen Acres!" the audience roared back as the band began to play "Aude Lang Syne".

Brynn could just make out Charlie in the crowd, furiously wiping his eyes as he blew kisses to everyone around them. Gina openly sobbed; her hands raised above her as if praising the heavens. Even Russell Sutkamp offered a cordial golf clap from his seat next to the buffet.

Brynn swiped her fingers under her eyes in a vain attempt to keep her mascara from smudging.

"I'm sorry for everything," Brynn said to Jordan, placing a hand over the mic to muffle her words. "It took some time, but now I know why I came to Evergreen Acres. I came to help you, and that's enough for me."

She ran from the stage, barely hearing Jordan's voice as it called out behind her, but she didn't stop to listen. Though the dancing had resumed, many people still watched, and a path cleared as she darted for the exit.

"Brynn, *please!*" she heard Jordan yell from somewhere close behind.

Suddenly, Dylan stepped in front of Brynn, his eyes full of concern, Madison right behind him. "Do you need help, Brynn?" he whispered, and she couldn't help but smile as he stood tall and puffed out his chest. If she had run into them on any other day, she wouldn't have been able to resist taking a photo of them in their matching red and black formalwear.

"I'm OK, Dylan," Brynn sniffed. "But thank you."

She knew it was Jordan who grabbed her arm before she even she whipped around to face him. Dylan eyed her, but took a step back.

"You never owed me an apology, Brynn," Jordan said, breathless. "But I have so much to be sorry for. I acted like a complete ass."

She didn't correct him, though she knew she wasn't without blame. She had made right choices for all the wrong reasons, chasing things she hadn't even wanted. But this was Christmas. This was a second chance.

"I can't stop thinking about you," Jordan said, hesitantly allowing his fingers to graze the back of her bare arm. "You're too good for me, but I'll do whatever it takes to earn you."

"But you didn't want me," Brynn managed, her insides churning as bit back a sob.

"I always wanted you," Jordan said, his own eyes shining with hunger as he pulled her closer. "From that first day I saw you, trying to take a selfie, I wanted you." He swallowed and stepped closer. "I'm in love with you, Brynn."

Everything slowed around her as her body wanted to stay, and her mind told her to run.

"I don't know what to say," she finally managed.

"Say you can't get that night of your head," he said, a shy smile on that ruggedly chiseled face. "Say you're going to ignore my calls for weeks to punish me for being such a dick. Say anything." He swallowed and Brynn saw a vulnerability in those chocolate eyes that nearly broker her heart. "Just please, talk to me."

"Jordan, I—"

"Brynn!" She turned to find a breathless Katie, wearing the same turtleneck and jeans she'd been wearing at the shop earlier.

"What happened?" Brynn asked, trying to hold back the hurt and accusation that rippled from her mouth.

"I'm so sorry," Katie wheezed. "But Homestead, they came—"

As she gulped more air, Mark Barnes stepped forward, Sofia Camp right at his heels, and his eyes lit up when he spotted Brynn. She shot Katie a questioning look, but she was too busy guzzling a bottle of water that Jordan's sister Megan had just handed her.

"Merry Christmas, Brynn," the Homestead CEO said as he stepped closer. "Same to you, Jordan."

"What are you doing here?" Brynn stammered.

Sofia smiled. "Brynn, we'd like to formally offer you a syndicated lifestyle show on Homestead TV, all about houseplants and gardening."

"Really?" Brynn squeaked. "After everything that happened?"

"An anonymous video was sent to the office with the entire uncut footage," Sofia said. "What was done to you was not only unfair, we believe it was also illegal." Brynn released a breath she didn't realize she was holding. "Unfortunately," Sofia continued, "we have no way of knowing where it came from."

Brynn had at least one educated guess.

"We had our suspicions from the beginning that a competitor

may have been behind this," Mark added. "However, when we called to inquire on the matter, she—or *they*—vehemently denied any knowledge of the video. However..." he shot a meaningful look in Jordan's direction. "She did offer some very insightful information about a fire that took place on your land."

"Get your hands off of me!" a haughty voice screeched over the music.

Brynn watched as two police officers quickly restrained Russell Sutkamp, his baby smooth face turning purple as he cursed under his breath.

"I don't understand," Jordan said.

"Don't stand there looking so innocent," Sutkamp shouted, his eyes locking with Jordan's. "One accident tips the scales, and you just think it's your right to destroy a man's entire empire?!"

Brynn shot Jordan a questioning look. "Did you know this would happen?" she whispered.

"Not even in the slightest," Jordan whispered back, as the officers led an apoplectic Sutkamp to the door in handcuffs.

"The tip mentioned a plan to sabotage your Christmas festival," Mark said, steepling his fingers together apologetically. "Our, well, *informant*, I suppose you'd call her, played a recorded phone call in which Sutkamp discussed a plan to interfere with your power source."

Brynn and Jordan could do nothing except gape open-mouthed.

"I'm no investigator," Sofia added, "but I think the police will find that Sutkamp accidentally started the fire, then fled the scene. His biggest mistake was keeping his mouth shut on the matter, silently hoping no one would discover his involvement."

"That bastard!" Jordan said, shaking his head.

"So, Sutkamp was working with Jessica?" Brynn stammered, before registering the uncomfortable look on Mark's face. "Er, the *informant*?"

"Seems that way," Mark said, raising his palms in a way that suggested he'd rather not get involved. "But all that aside, your channel has become a place of sincerity and warmth, two qualities we highly value at Homestead." He smiled and extended his hand. "What do you say? Will you join the Homestead family?"

Brynn froze as her mind stretched in a dozen different directions. After everything, they wanted her. Not only that, but they wanted the *real* her.

"I am so honored," Brynn managed to say. "Truly. But—" She took a deep breath. "Everything I want is here in Twin Falls. As exciting as a TV show would be, I'll find a way to make life work without one, just like everyone else." She swallowed, feeling like a giant rock was wedged in her throat. "Thank you so much for the offer, but I'm not leaving."

She swallowed before impulsively grabbing Jordan's hand. His calloused fingers immediately wrapped through hers as he pulled her body close. When she snuck a glance at him out of the corner of her eyes, she couldn't help but mirror his childlike grin.

"We had a feeling you might say that," Sofia said, shooting a knowing glance to Mark. "And we're on the same page. Twin Falls is relatable, authentic...and we want to produce the show here."

"You do?" Brynn squeaked.

"Absolutely," Mark said as Sofia excitedly slapped her hands together.

Brynn spotted Dylan off to the side, watching with a proud smile.

"I know more than one person from town who you could hire

on the show," Brynn said.

"The more local hires, the better the tax break," Mark said with a good-natured chuckle. "And if Jordan's open to it, we'd love to have him as well."

"Me?!" Jordan asked.

"We've been toying with the theme of indoor plants versus outdoor plants," Mark explained, his eyes gleaming with excitement. "Something for everyone, for every kind of home."

"I don't know what to say," Jordan managed.

"Sleep on it," Mark said. "We can talk more next week. In the meantime, we'd love to have you join us for the Christmas parade. We can fly you out tonight after the party."

Jordan looked at Brynn as if to say, *your move.*

"That's very kind," Brynn said. "But I actually have Donuts with Rudolph in the morning." She caught Greta watching misty-eyed from the crowd and smiled. "And I plan to spend Christmas with my family."

Both Mark and Sofia looked disappointed, but they never stopped smiling.

"We'll have our people call your people," Jordan said and Brynn bit back a laugh.

"Fair enough," Mark said before turning to Sofia. "Think we have time for some refreshments before we hit the road?"

As they headed toward the dessert table, Brynn and Jordan's eyes widened at the same time as their eyes settled on two women huddled very closely together. Two very familiar women to both of them.

Brynn gasped and elbowed Jordan as they watched Katie tuck a hair behind Megan's ear. "Did you know about this?!"

But Jordan didn't say a word as he dumbly watched Megan laugh at something Katie had just said.

"How do they know each other?" Brynn hissed and Jordan simply shrugged. But before she could wonder if they were just friends, Katie leaned over and planted a quick kiss right on Megan's lips. Suddenly, Brynn knew exactly who Katie's mysterious date had been.

"Great news, guys and gals!" Mayor Lopez's voice boomed through the speakers, and they turned to find the sweaty, exuberant mayor on stage. "We've already met this year's fundraising goal for the fire department!"

The crowd cheered.

"Now, grab that special someone," he continued, tipping his beer suggestively in the direction of Brynn's mother. "It's time to slow it down for a little turn under the mistletoe."

As the band began to play "I'll Be Home for Christmas", Jordan stepped back, his eyes grazing Brynn's entire body with slow, seductive appreciation, never letting go of her hand as he drank in every curve. Brynn shuddered as his eyes traveled from her lips and down her neck as she remembered his fingers tracing the exact path that night in his house.

"I don't think you could get more beautiful," Jordan said, his voice low and husky as he pulled her to the center of the dance floor, his eyes never leaving hers. She pressed her body against his, bending his head so her lips were buried against his neck.

"Do you have any idea what's going through my head right now?" Jordan whispered, his breath hot on her forehead.

"If it's anything like mine, it's absolute chaos," Brynn mumbled back, her eyes drifting closed as he buried his nose in her hair.

"Mm," he replied. "But I do know one thing. Having you, right here in my arms, is the only thing that matters tonight."

Brynn lifted her head and met his soft, devoted gaze.

"It looks like I'm staying in Twin Falls after all," she said.

"You deserve every bit of it," Jordan said softly, his eyes drifting to her lips and back again.

"So, where were we?" Brynn said, biting her lip as a grin spread across her face. "I think you were saying something about being in love with me?"

"Right," Jordan said, his neck reddening as he gripped her tighter. "I did say that."

"Well, that's pretty crazy, considering we hated each other a month ago—"

"Hate is a strong word," Jordan interrupted, his eyes never leaving hers.

"But I'm falling pretty hard too," she said, her vision clouding for the millionth time that week, but this time, it felt amazing. "Now that we have some time, I just want to learn everything about you." She took a deep breath. "Love is kind of a scary word, but it's the only word that fits."

"It doesn't scare me anymore," Jordan said, his eyes earnest as his fingers drew a lazy circle on her chest. "If you still have any room for me inside this big old heart of yours..." He dragged his lips to her ear. "Well, I'm all yours."

Brynn could only nod as goosebumps spread down her skin. Jordan pressed himself against her as his lips found hers, slowly at first, and then with a feverish, urgent need. Someone in the crowd began to catcall, but neither broke free of the other.

When at last they breathlessly pulled apart, Jordan wrapped his arms around her, engulfing her body in his warm embrace.

He rested his chin on her head as they slowly swayed in time to the music. Hot tears began to slowly trail down Brynn's cheeks, but she didn't wipe them away as they fell against Jordan's tuxedo jacket.

The song ended and the band began playing something upbeat as Jordan rolled Brynn into a playful twirl before twisting her back and dipping her. She wished she could bottle up the way he watched her, looking at her as if he was devouring her inch by inch with his eyes.

"So, what do you think?" Brynn asked, when he'd stood her back on her stilettos. "Ready to be a TV star?"

"I don't know," Jordan said, looking a bit nervous as he considered the question.

"You love talking about trees!" Brynn said. "Remember how much you enjoyed making that video?"

"They did mention outdoor gardening," Jordan said, raising an eyebrow. "I'd hate to unleash you on the peppers and tomatoes without warning them first."

"I won't argue with you on that," Brynn said, laughing. "Maybe that can be Dylan's area of expertise."

"Tell you what," Jordan said, wrapping one arm possessively around her waist as he began led her to an empty corner of the dance floor. "Like Mark suggested, I'll sleep on it." He smiled, and everything in Brynn became liquid. "Tomorrow's Christmas," he said, smoothing her hair with one hand. "I'm starting thing anything is possible."

Brynn gazed into those warm brown eyes, no longer guarded or wary. She would never forget the way he looked at her tonight. Part devotion, part hunger, and something she was beginning to recognize as love.

She gazed around the room and silently counted her tribe, old and new. Gina, playfully twisting in front of Charlie who sipped from a pint. Katie and Megan, apparently smitten, huddled alone in the corner, seemingly lost in each other's words. Madison and Dylan never once stopped dancing, not even when his dad Henry followed them around snapping photos on his phone. Even Greta and Mayor Lopez were too busy canoodling by the stage to give them a second look.

This time, Brynn was the one to press her lips to Jordan's, taking her time as their kiss softened to something patient and true. Somehow, nothing had turned out like she'd wanted—not her show, not her dreams, not her future. And yet...despite it all, everything was absolutely perfect.

ABOUT THE AUTHOR

Willa Frederic is a pseudonym for Galadriel Stineman. In addition to writing novels, Galadriel is an award-winning TV and film actor, screenwriter, and acting teacher. She lives in Los Angeles with her husband and two children.

DAP BOOKS

DI ANGELO PUBLICATIONS

Di Angelo Publications was founded in 2008 by Sequoia Schmidt—at the age of seventeen. The modernized publishing firm's creative headquarters is in Los Angeles, California, with its distribution center located in Twin Falls, Idaho. In 2020, Di Angelo Publications made a conscious decision to move all printing and production for domestic distribution of its books to the United States. The firm is comprised of ten imprints, and the featured imprint, Reverie, is inspired by the long-lasting legacy of fiction and adult literature.

REVERIE